SOMETHING MORE

SOMETHING MORE

JANET DAILEY

KENSINGTON BOOKS
www.kensingtonbooks.com

KENSINGTON BOOKS are published by

Kensington Publishing Corp.
850 Third Avenue
New York, NY 10022

Library of Congress Card Catalogue Number: 2007925428

ISBN-13: 978-0-7582-1984-8
ISBN-10: 0-7582-1984-9

First Hardcover Printing: July 2007
10 9 8 7 6 5 4 3 2 1

Printed in the United States of America

Chapter One

A steady drizzle fell from the blanketing clouds, graying the Wyoming landscape and obscuring the bigness of it. The first pale shoots of the country's famed green grass poked their heads through the wet mire underfoot. But Luke McCallister paid no attention to their promise of new life as he rode over the ground, his wide shoulders hunched against the slow-falling rain.

The yellow slicker he wore kept out the wetness, but it offered little protection against the morning's damp chill, which invaded his bones and added a new element to the dully pounding hangover that made him feel much older than his thirty-eight years.

Each stride of his horse jarred his head; each creak of saddle leather and bawl of a calf resounded in his ears with the loudness of clanging cymbals, drawing involuntary winces. But his blue-gray gaze remained fixed on the dark, shiny rumps of the Black Baldie cows, all with calves sporting fresh Ten Bar brands on their hips, directly ahead of him.

Luke McCallister would have been the first to admit it was lousy weather to be moving a herd of cattle. But with the spring branding finished, the time had come to move the herd to spring pasture.

On a ranch the size of the Ten Bar, it wasn't a job to be postponed because of a little rain coming down. Fortunately for Luke it was a mindless task, one that required little in the way of concentration.

To a stranger, there was little about Luke McCallister that would have set him apart from the half dozen riders pushing the herd. He had the tall, rangy look of an ordinary cowboy, broad shouldered and narrow hipped from a lifetime in the saddle. There was a triangular shape to his face, sun-browned skin stretched taut over hard, chiseled bone. Laugh lines cut parenthetical grooves on either side of his mouth and creased the corners of his eyes, the faded gray-blue of worn Levi's.

At the moment, he looked a bit worse for wear from a little too much Wild Turkey the night before. For those who knew him, like young Ten Bar ranch hand Tobe West, that was a typical state for Luke, too common to rate any notice.

Luke was easily the last person a passerby would have guessed to be the one who held the reins to the famed Ten Bar Ranch, one of the oldest in Wyoming. Back in the glory days of the old cattle barons, the Ten Bar had laid claim to over a million acres. But time and taxes had whittled its size to a mere 350,000. But it was all prime cattle country, rugged and vast, a land of rimrock and wide draws with native grasses growing belly deep on its tabletop buttes and sheltered basins.

Located in the sparsely populated eastern side of Wyoming, its broken terrain was part of the bridge between the towering mountains of the Rockies and the rolling sweep of the Great Plains. Cottonwood trees grew along the draws watered by the mountain snowmelts, and lodgepole pines studded the higher slopes of its boulder-strewn hills. But always there was grass, vibrantly green in the spring, tawny yellow in the summer, sun-cured brown in the fall, before the white of winter snows settled onto it.

On a clear day, it was a land of long vistas, the kind that excited the imagination and conjured up memories of the time when

Butch Cassidy and the Sundance Kid had ridden over this range en route to their Hole in the Wall hideout roughly a day's ride away.

But the shrouding drizzle evoked no such scenes to stimulate the mind. All was veiled in the gray mist that melded sky and land. The cattle plodded through it, mud squishing and sucking at their cloven hooves, as they strung out in a long, black line meandering in the general direction of the distant pasture gate, pushed by the flanking riders while Tobe West and Luke McCallister brought up the rear.

Ahead on the left, the crooked shape of a bent pine tree jutted from behind a dark boulder. Luke stared at it for a long minute before the significance of the landmark registered. It was time to swing the cattle up the draw toward the gate.

He puckered his lips to whistle a shrill signal to the lead riders. But his mouth was dry as cotton, and the sound that came out was barely more than a loud hiss, loud enough to startle Tobe's horse.

"What the heck was that?" Tobe shot him a questioning look.

"Me." Luke managed a wry grin. "I was trying to signal them to make the turn."

"That's the weakest excuse for a whistle I ever heard." The sparkle of laughter was in Tobe's eyes, bright with shared amusement.

"It was kinda pathetic," Luke agreed with a smile, and thought about giving it another try but couldn't summon the energy. "I guess you'd better do it, Tobe. And while you're at it, send Mark ahead to open the gate."

Tobe nodded and pursed his lips, emitting an ear-splitting whistle that jolted Luke all the way to his toes and drew an involuntary groan from him at the new hammering it set off in his head. When one of the lead riders pulled up, Tobe passed on Luke's orders with a combination of hand signals and a ringing shout.

Wincing anew, Luke muttered without rancor, "Has anybody

ever told you that you've got a voice with the clang of a church bell, Tobe?"

"In weather like this, that's what a man needs," Tobe retorted, then flashed him a wicked grin. "Jarred your head a bit, did it?"

"About as bad as a sledgehammer would," Luke admitted, his temples still throbbing from the effects of it.

Up ahead, Mark Cranston, the son of a neighboring rancher hired on as temporary roundup help, reined his horse away from the herd and spurred it toward the pasture gate, out of sight beyond the next fold in the hills. Meanwhile, the riders on the right flank pressed the leaders, turning them up the draw.

Luke watched as the black line of cattle curved in the right direction, briefly prodded out of their walk into a slow jog. Luke's own horse picked up its pace, crowding the stragglers at the rear.

"Not much farther now," Tobe observed.

"Can't come soon enough for me," Luke replied, conscious of the steady drip of water rolling off his hat and the spreading chill that numbed his fingers.

"Me either." Twenty-one-year-old Tobe West snatched another glance at Luke, the man who was both his boss and his idol.

From the time he had stuck his feet in his first pair of Justin boots, Tobe had wanted to be a full-fledged cowboy, even dreamed of owning his own ranch someday, something bigger than the measly eighty acres his pa rented. Growing up, he'd always had a horse to ride, and his pa had always kept a few steer on the eighty, enough for Tobe to practice his roping and play at being a cowboy.

He was only fifteen when his pa got killed in a car wreck. They had continued to rent the old Trevor place and Tobe had kept his horse, but they hadn't run any more cattle. The closest he had come to cowboying after that had been day work at local ranches, but those jobs had rarely amounted to more than a week or two a year.

Then, three years ago, his mother had died of cancer, leaving Tobe with a younger sister to raise and no money. Jobs in Glory, Wyoming, were about as scarce as rain during a drought. He'd been washing dishes at Ima Jane's Rimrock Bar & Grill when Luke McCallister had come in one night for supper and stayed for a few drinks.

At some point Luke had said something to Tobe; two seconds later, Tobe had started pouring out all his troubles to him, bemoaning the responsibility of his little sister and the cowboy life that would never be his. Right then and there, Luke had offered him a job and a place for him and his sister to live at the Ten Bar.

Truthfully, Tobe had been half afraid that Luke had been too drunk to know what he was saying. But his fears had been groundless. He had a home and a job at the Ten Bar.

Some people thought Luke drank too much. But Tobe didn't see it that way. Besides, it wasn't like Luke got mean when he drank; he got loopy and a bit irreverent. In Tobe's book that was harmless.

"Yessiree," Tobe continued, "the cab of that pickup is gonna seem warm and dry after the wet deck of this horse. I can't crawl into it soon enough to suit me." He slapped a length of wet rope against his rain-slicked chaps to hurry along a lagging cow with her calf.

"It's a cup of steaming hot coffee I want to wrap my hands around," Luke countered, thinking of the thermos waiting for him in the truck, filled with coffee laced with a liberal amount of the hair of the dog that bit him. Or in this case, *turkey.*

Tobe threw him a smiling glance, striving for a man-to-man air. "Don't drink it all. As cold and damp as I feel, I could use some of that special brew of yours."

"I'll—" Luke never got the rest of his sentence out as a calf bawled in sudden panic and the middle of the herd veered wildly away from a stand of cottonwood trees growing along the draw. A split second later, Luke spotted the culprit, as a spindly-legged man in a voluminous black coat charged out of the trees, flapping his arms like a scarecrow to scatter the black cows.

"Who the heck—" Tobe sputtered.

"Take a wild guess," Luke murmured in mild annoyance, as

the flankers worked to settle the herd back into line again and give the man on foot a wide berth. "That crazy old Saddlebags Smith is back again." His disgust gave way to amusement as he eyed the woolly-bearded man in the floppy hat. "You'd think after all these years of looking for that outlaw gold and coming up empty, he would give it up as a lost cause."

"Not him." The young cowboy threw an exasperated glare at the old man. "He'll die lookin' for it." Satisfied that the cattle weren't going to invade his little area under the cottonwoods, the geriatric treasure hunter sifted back beneath their branches to stand guard. "Do you suppose he thinks that gold is buried in those trees?" Tobe wondered, his interest momentarily piqued.

"Who knows?" Luke lifted his shoulders in a disinterested shrug, then idly ran a glance over the small cluster of cottonwoods. "It doesn't seem likely to me. Those trees are younger than he is."

Startled by the comment, Tobe examined the grove again, then hid his chagrin by scoffing, "Just about everything is younger than that old coot." A contemplative quality entered his expression. "When we didn't see hide nor hair of him during calving time, I thought he'd probably kicked the bucket this winter."

"I wouldn't have been surprised." But truthfully Luke hadn't given the old man much thought.

It wasn't that unusual for Saddlebags not to be seen. In fact, an actual sighting of him was rare. Sometimes a rider might come across an old camp or catch sight of a narrow shadow flitting among the rocks, but that was about it. Every once in a while— like now—somebody would come up on him.

"Where do you suppose he goes in the winter?" A frown puckered Tobe's forehead.

Such speculation would require more effort than Luke's fragile head wanted to exert. He settled for hearsay. "Tip Connors claims to have seen him in Cheyenne."

"But how would he get there?" Tobe persisted. "He doesn't have a truck, no means of transportation."

"He probably thumbed a ride."

"Maybe," the young cowboy conceded. "But I can't imagine anybody givin' that old codger a ride. He'd stink up a truck worse than last year's dirty underwear." He grimaced at the thought, then frowned again. "I never understood why you let him grub around this place. You should chase him off the Ten Bar."

Luke just smiled. "Saddlebags is harmless."

The moniker came from the two sacks, bulging with the whole of his worldly belongings, that the old man carried slung over his shoulder like a saddlebag. His rightful name, according to his identification papers, was Amos Aloysius Smith, formerly of Kansas City, Missouri. As suspicious as Smith sounded, the Amos Aloysius part had a definite ring of truth to it. It was hardly the kind of name someone would make up.

According to Ima Jane Evans, bar owner and local authority on everyone within a hundred miles, Saddlebags Smith had no family—or any criminal record, for that matter. He didn't smoke, drink, or swear. Rumor had it that he was a mute, but Ima Jane insisted he could talk if he was so inclined, although Luke couldn't recall ever hearing a single word pass from the old man's lips.

"Harmless, he may be," Tobe declared, "but he's still a nuisance, always poking around and digging holes. It used to be he'd fill them back in, but not anymore. Now he just leaves 'em for some cow to stumble into and break a leg."

"He's getting old." Luke knew the feeling. And each breath of the chill, damp air intensified it.

"Old!" Tobe snorted a laugh. "Ancient is more like it. Why, he must be eighty if he's a day."

"Probably. I know he's been roaming the Ten Bar since before I was born."

Over the years, Saddlebags Smith had become almost as big a legend as the story of the buried gold itself. No one knew anymore exactly how much had been stolen by the outlaws who had robbed a train all those years ago—and found themselves with more loot than their horses could carry. One source had put the figure at a quarter million; another had claimed a hundred thousand in gold bars. Given the penchant for exaggeration in such tales, Luke had always figured it was probably much lower.

According to legend, a posse had caught up with the bandits two days later, but the gold was never found. The one surviving outlaw had taken the secret of its hiding place with him to the gallows.

"When you get right down to it, it doesn't matter. It may be nothing but a wild-goose chase, but at least he has a reason to wake up in the morning." There was a hint of envy in his eyes when Luke glanced at the dark, narrow shape among the tree trunks.

For himself, the dawn of a new day was an empty thing that he usually poured whiskey in to cut the bitter taste. It was a bleak fact, one he didn't care to face without a bottle of Wild Turkey at hand.

"Let's get these cattle moving," he said with a rare show of ill temper. "We keep poking along like this, it'll take all day."

He jabbed his horse with a spur, sending the animal lunging toward the closest cow. Immediately the straggler broke into a trot and crowded the ones in front of it. The sudden insistence on haste created confusion. Separated from its momma, a calf planted its feet and bawled in protest, then took off like a shot when Luke reined his horse toward it.

Passing wide of the cottonwoods, the tail end of the herd began the gradual climb out of the draw. It was slick going, traveling over muddy ground chewed up by previous hooves. Of their own accord, the straggling cows with their calves spread out seeking firmer footing.

When one pair ducked back toward the draw, Luke automatically sent his horse after it, gritting his teeth against the jarring his head took. Finally turning the cow and calf, he herded them back toward the others. But the angle of climb was steeper, with sections of the slope eroded to expose dark banks of undercut soil.

They began the scrambling climb up the slope, hooves digging for purchase.

Suddenly Luke felt the horse falling from beneath him as a whole chunk of ground gave way under them. Instinct alone warned him that the horse was going over backward. The remnants of a hangover dulled his reflexes, making him a split-second slow to dive off the uphill side of the saddle.

A wildly flailing hoof dealt him a glancing blow an instant before he went headfirst into the muddy bank. The softness of the sodden dirt cushioned much of the impact as he more or less skidded to a halt, the horse crashing to the ground below him.

Something clunked him in the head, knocking off his hat and coming to a rest atop an outstretched arm. He lay there for a dazed second, conscious of the cold, wet mud beneath him and the misty rain on his cheek. For a moment, Luke felt too tired and sore to move. But already his horse was clambering to its feet, giving itself a head-to-tail shake that sent the empty stirrups flopping.

The slip and slide of another set of hooves signaled the arrival of Tobe West on the scene. "Luke? Are you okay?"

Lifting his throbbing head, Luke spit the dirt from his lips. "I'm fi—" He found himself staring into the mud-caked eye sockets of a human skull.

The shock of the macabre sight drove out any lingering effects from both the fall and the hangover. With an alacrity that was laughable, Luke sprang from the skull, cursing a blue streak, his face almost as pale as the partially exposed skeleton protruding from the eroded bank.

Tobe gaped in astonishment. "Would you look at that?" he murmured and swung out of the saddle. Luke stared at the remains in shaky silence, waiting for his heart to stop pounding like some Sioux war drum. Emerging from the stand of cottonwoods, Saddlebags Smith shouted to them, "Whatcha lookin' at?"

A glint of devilment flashed in Tobe's eyes. "Wouldn't you like to know?" he yelled back.

Smiling wanly, Luke muttered, "You're an ornery son of a buck, Tobe."

The cowboy chuckled. But Saddlebags Smith wasn't laughing. In a frenzy, he charged toward them, traveling as fast as his ancient body would carry him.

"It's mine!" he screamed again and again, his false teeth clattering with the vehemence of his claim. "That gold's mine! You can't have it! It's mine by rights!"

Still grinning broadly, Tobe glanced at Luke. "Shall we let him have it, or not?"

But Luke was beyond seeing the humor in stringing the old man along. Before he could call a halt to it, the sharp-eyed treasure hunter saw the skeleton's bones and came to an abrupt stop. For a furious instant, dark eyes glowered at the two of them from beneath white tufting brows. As quickly as he'd left the shelter of the trees, Saddlebags scurried back to them.

Reaching down, Luke scooped up his hat and scraped the worst of the mud off of it before pushing it onto his head. The misty rain fell a little harder as he stepped closer to examine the skeleton, feeling more sober than he had in years.

"I wonder who it is," he wondered idly.

"An Indian probably," Tobe guessed indifferently.

Luke doubted that. "Most of them didn't bury their dead in the ground." Another chunk of soil crumbled loose, exposing a bony hand and a glint of metal. Crouching down, Luke brushed off some more, then straightened. "Indians didn't wear class rings, either."

"A class ring?" The cowboy frowned in surprise.

"That's what it looks like to me." Luke gestured at the gold ring, glistening now in the soft rain. He sighed, knowing he was in for a long and wet day. "Come on. Let's get those cattle headed for the gate before they scatter all over the place."

He headed down the slope to catch his idly grazing horse. Tobe glanced uncertainly at the skeleton. "What about him?"

"What about him?" Reins in hand, Luke walked the horse a few steps, watching for any sign of injury and seeing none.

"You aren't going to just leave him here, are you?" While not clear what should be done next, Tobe was sure that wasn't it.

"Why not?" Luke countered with a mocking smile and stepped a foot in the stirrup to swing into the saddle. "I don't think he's going anywhere."

"That's not what I mean, and you know it," Tobe declared in frustration. "There's a dead body here."

"Your powers of observation are astonishing, Tobe," he mocked dryly.

"But . . . we have to do something. Call somebody," Tobe insisted earnestly.

Taking pity on him, Luke nodded. "As soon as we get back to the ranch, I'll call John Beauchamp and let him know about our very dead friend here. After that, it's his business, not mine. Are you coming?" He stopped his horse next to Tobe. "Or are you going to stay here and hold services?"

"I'm coming." Tobe climbed back on his horse and followed Luke up the slope after the cattle.

At the top, he threw one last glance over his shoulder. He saw a glimpse of pale bone against the darker soil; then his eye was caught by a furtive movement in the draw. It was Saddlebags Smith, hurrying to cross the open ground, a big sack bouncing on his back.

"Saddlebags is lightin' out," he said to Luke.

"He probably figures it's going to get too crowded around here when the sheriff shows up." But Luke didn't bother to look back. Right now, he was more interested in a good long swig of one-hundred proof.

Chapter Two

A stock trailer loaded with saddled horses clattered behind the pickup as it bounced along the muddy track through the winter pasture. Luke sat hunched against the cab's passenger door, carefully balancing the last cup of coffee from the thermos, his hat pitched forward, shadowing his eyes.

Tobe was behind the wheel. For once his mind wasn't wandering all over the place, the way it usually did, daydreaming about all the things he was going to do and have someday.

Working on the Ten Bar was only part of his dream, though it was a big part of it. As far as he was concerned, there wasn't a better outfit in the whole state of Wyoming. Sure there were bigger ones, even richer ones, but none that were better.

On the Ten Bar, work was still done, more or less, the same way it had been done a hundred years ago. Come roundup time, no noisy helicopters swooped into canyons, beating the brush to chase out cattle; men on horseback did that. There were no calving sheds; the cows gave birth on the open range. On the Ten Bar, calves were still roped and dragged to branding fires, instead of being herded into squeeze chutes.

Even the hay for winter feed was cut, windrowed, and stacked using horse-drawn machinery. It took longer with horses, but, like Luke said, he didn't have a bunch of money tied up in tractors, mowers, and mechanical balers—machinery that was both expensive to purchase and maintain, and tended to break down at inopportune moments.

At today's prices, cattle ranching offered a marginal profit at best. It behooved a man, Luke said, to cut operational costs where he could. On the Ten Bar, just about everything was done the tried-and-true cowboy way.

And Tobe ate up every minute of it, determined he would have a ranch of his own someday and run it the same way. He was convinced beyond a doubt that he couldn't have a better teacher than Luke McCallister.

Admittedly, the wages were skimpy even with room and board factored into them. And the vagaries of Wyoming weather made working conditions far from ideal most of the time—winter's blizzards and freezing temperatures, spring's rain and mud, summer's heat and sudden thunderstorms, and autumn's mix of all three.

In some ways, the life hadn't turned out to be as romantic as he had pictured it. At times it was downright monotonous and never ending.

Tobe had said as much to Luke one time. Luke had just grinned and clamped a companionable hand on his back. "You're right, Tobe," he'd said. "Weeks like this one should have more Saturday nights in it."

Not that Saturday nights were all that exciting, considering there wasn't much in the way of entertainment in Glory except for Ima Jane's Rimrock Bar & Grill. In fact, life in this part of Wyoming tended to be pretty boring.

At least it had been until this morning when Luke had discovered that body. It had to be the most exciting thing that had happened in the area in a hundred years. A body. An honest-to-God body. Not the half-gnawed bones of some animal. A body.

Tobe stole another glance at Luke. It wasn't like him to be this quiet. He decided it must have been the shock of finding himself eyeball to eye socket with that skull.

"It must have been kinda grisly looking," Tobe blurted.

"What?" Luke's side glance held only blankness.

"The skull," he replied as his imagination took off on a new track. "Was there still"—he searched for the right word—"meat on it?"

"Nope." Casual as could be, Luke lifted the thermos cup to his mouth.

"How long do you suppose it takes for flesh to rot off the bones once a corpse has been buried?" Tobe wondered thoughtfully.

"The experts at the state crime lab could probably tell you," Luke ventured.

"More than likely," Tobe agreed. "And if they know that, then they can probably give a rough idea of when he got put in the ground, too." He cocked his head to one side and frowned. "Who do you think it could be, Luke?"

"Some guy wearing a 1938 class ring." Luke shrugged and took another quick sip of lukewarm coffee between jolts of the bouncing pickup.

"How do you know for sure it was a guy?" Tobe challenged that assumption, warming to the thought of solving a mystery.

"It seems a safe bet," Luke replied. "The ring was man sized."

"But a girl wears a guy's class ring when she's going steady with him." But Tobe wasn't sure girls did that way back in 1938. "How did he die?"

"I didn't think to ask him," Luke answered, grinning crookedly. "And as I recall, he wasn't doing much talking."

"Very funny," Tobe muttered, unamused. "I meant—was there a bullet hole in the skull? Or had it been bashed in?" he questioned, wishing he'd taken a closer look at it. "You know, if he was murdered—"

"I think you'd better rein in that imagination of yours, Tobe,"

Luke suggested dryly. "For all we know, the man could have died of natural causes."

The thought was clearly deflating. Tobe frowned over it for a minute. "But if he did, then how did he get buried out there?"

Nodding, Luke released a puzzled sigh. "That's the sixty-four-thousand-dollar question, isn't it? To my knowledge, there was never anyone buried on the Ten Bar in the last eighty years or so."

"See, that's just it," Tobe declared, warming again to his mystery. "It isn't logical for him to be buried out in the middle of the Ten Bar unless"—he paused for effect—"some kind of foul play was involved. Otherwise he'd be buried in a cemetery like everybody else."

The wipers slashed back and forth across the windshield, smearing the falling mist across the glass. Their rhythmic thwack-thwack temporarily filled the silence that followed Tobe's remark.

On the other side of the rise lay the headquarters of the Ten Bar Ranch, tucked back in a fold of the rocky hills. A creek made a wide swing around it before wandering off across the valley. The steady drizzle threw a gray veil over the collection of corrals and buildings. Only the century-old barn stood out, the rain darkening its heavy timbers, giving it solidness and bulk.

No other structure vied with it for prominence. A double row of pine trees, planted years ago as a windbreak, marked the former location of the ranch house. Now they were silent sentinels, protecting the blackened rubble and charred ruins that remained.

Never once did Luke's glance stray to the old house site. Home for him was now a single-wide trailer parked on the other side of it. In the falling rain, the nondescript beige of the trailer's metal siding merged into the surrounding landscape.

The only spot of bright color in the scene came from the yellow school bus as it rolled away from the ranch yard, heading down the lane that would take it to the main road five miles distant. Luke's glance paused on it.

"It looks like Dulcie's home from school already," he remarked idly. "I hadn't realized it was so late."

But he didn't wonder where the time had gone. His thoughts were on the fast-approaching nighttime hours to be faced—and somehow filled. But he knew he'd fill them the same way he always had—with the help of a bottle. It was a fact that no longer troubled him, if it ever had.

Tobe, on the other hand, couldn't have cared less that his kid sister was home from school. It was something to be expected, therefore unimportant. The hour of the day, though; that raised other questions.

"Do you think Beauchamp will come out yet today to collect the body?" He had visions of the skeleton being disinterred as night fell, with lights strategically placed around the sight, blackness swirling around the edges of the scene.

"It's hard to say," Luke replied with indifference. "As long as the body's been in the ground already, I don't know what the rush would be to dig him up. It probably would be easiest just to wait until morning."

"Yeah." Tobe sighed his disappointment and slowed the truck as they approached the pasture gate.

When the pickup rolled to a stop, Luke climbed out of the cab and went to open the gate, taking the thermos cup of laced coffee with him. One-handed, he dragged the gate through the mud and waited for both pickups with trailers in tow to drive through, then drained the last fortifying swallow of the tepid liquid. As soon as the gate was closed and latched, Luke trotted to the waiting pickup and climbed back into the dry cab.

"Do you want me to drop you off at the trailer?" Tobe lifted his voice to make himself heard above the rumble of the pickup over the wood-planked bridge that spanned the creek.

Luke thought about the question for a full minute. "Might as well," he agreed finally. The phone call had to be made. Postponing it accomplished nothing. "Let the boys know I've got their checks ready and waiting for them."

"Will do." Tobe stopped the pickup thirty feet from the trailer.

Head down, Luke crossed the sloppy ground to the metal steps, conscious of the smell of wood smoke the rain resurrected from the fire-charred rubble. He paused long enough to scrape the worst of the mud from his boots, then mounted the steps.

The aroma of freshly baked chocolate chip cookies greeted him when he walked inside. Turning, he shrugged out of his slicker and hung it on a hook by the door.

"Aren't the others coming?" The voice belonged to eight-year-old Dulcie West, a slender waif of a girl with long blond hair the pale color of moonlight.

"They'll be along directly," Luke told her, his mouth curving in an automatic smile.

"Fargo baked a batch of cookies for them," she said, as if it were news.

"I noticed." Rubbing his cold hands together, he headed toward the kitchen, the sound of his footsteps accompanied by the muted clink of his mud-caked spurs. "I hope he's got hot coffee to go with them," he murmured, though he knew at the Ten Bar there was always coffee in the pot.

"Did you fall down or something?" Dulcie stared pointedly at his wet and muddy clothes.

"I had to bail off when my horse took a tumble." Luke continued into the kitchen, trailed by the big-eyed girl.

Over by the stove, Fargo Young took the last sheet of cookies from the oven and pushed the door closed with the stub of his left arm, the result of a car accident thirty years ago that had severed his arm below the elbow. But it wasn't the loss of an arm that had turned him from cowboying to cooking and keeping house; crippling arthritis had forced him out of the saddle. On a good day, he could still ride and rope with the best of them. The good days were a rarity now.

Over the years Fargo Young had become something of a permanent fixture at the Ten Bar Ranch. Truthfully, Luke couldn't remember a time when Fargo hadn't been around. It had long been one of Fargo's boasts that he had been there to pick Luke up when he'd been bucked off his first horse. For all Luke knew, that was true.

He had no idea how old the guy was. His sun-leathered face had more lines in it than a weather map. But the outdoors had a way of aging a man's skin that had nothing to do with the accumulation of years. There was more gray than brown in the stubble of a beard that shadowed his cheeks. Fargo rarely bothered to shave but never let his whiskers grow long enough to qualify as a genuine beard.

When asked, Fargo always claimed to be fifty-something—the "something" always varied with his whim of the moment. The same held true for his place of birth. To one person, he would say he was from Texas, to another, Montana. Even if the state stayed the same, the town changed. It had gotten to the point where local folks had quit asking. Luke had stopped years ago, certain the man's past was no big mystery. Fargo was simply the type who enjoyed spreading misinformation.

Fargo set the cookie sheet atop the range and ran a critical eye over Luke. "From the looks of you, you landed in a mud hole when you bailed off."

Wryness brought a gleam to Luke's eyes. "The bank was almost as wet as one." He walked straight to the coffeepot. "I'm soaked to the skin and chilled to the bone."

"In that case, you'll be needing some of this in your coffee." Fargo retrieved a bottle of Wild Turkey from the cupboard and set it on the counter next to him.

"You got that right." He twisted off the cap and poured a hefty shot of it into the coffee. After taking a hasty blowing sip of it, he crossed to the telephone, dragged out the slender directory, and flipped it open to the listing of emergency numbers.

"Who're you calling?" Fargo arched a bushy eyebrow. After all the years he'd spent on the Ten Bar, he figured he had earned the right to be nosy.

"The sheriff." Luke dialed the number.

"The sheriff? What for?" His curiosity piqued, Fargo motioned for the girl to take over the task of removing the cookies from the sheet.

Ignoring his questions, Luke spoke into the receiver's mouthpiece. "This is Luke McCallister at the Ten Bar Ranch south of Glory. I'd like to speak to Beauchamp if he's in."

"Dang it, Luke—" Fargo began in cranky protest.

He held up a silencing hand as a familiar voice came on the line. "Hello, Luke. It's been a while since I've heard from you. How have you been?"

"Fine. Just fine," Luke lied with the ease of long practice. "I was calling to report that we came across some human remains while we were moving cattle today."

Fargo's mouth gaped at the announcement. "You found a body?!" he croaked in disbelief.

Big eyed, Dulcie swung away from the stove, a chocolate chip cookie flying off the spatula with the suddenness of her turn. "A body?" she breathed the words.

Similar questions came from the sheriff. Sticking to simple, hard facts, Luke explained about the accidental unearthing of the skeleton; the discovery of the class ring; and concluded with, "Once I saw the ring, I didn't look any further. I figured you would want to check things out for yourself."

"Besides the ring, there wasn't any other identification?"

"Like I said, I didn't look. I figured that was your job."

"You're right, of course," Beauchamp agreed on an absent note. "It's better if the area remains undisturbed until our people get there."

"Will you be coming out yet today?"

There was the smallest hesitation. On a suddenly cynical note, Luke guessed that the veteran politician was trying to determine the level of priority he should give the discovery.

"We'll be there within the hour," Beauchamp replied, clearly having decided that if he was going to err, it would be on the side of caution.

With the receiver returned to its cradle, Luke turned and found himself looking into Dulcie's soulful blue eyes. "The Ten Bar isn't a cemetery." Her voice sounded small and uncertain. "How come somebody got buried on it, Luke?"

As an orphan, Dulcie had firsthand knowledge of such things as death, burials, and cemeteries. It was a knowledge that had turned her into a quiet, withdrawn child, slow to smile and slower still to laugh.

Luke had learned the usefulness of both smiling and laughing. He flashed her a smile of unconcern. "That's what the sheriff is going to find out."

It was a nonanswer, given to shield her from further unpleasantness. Luke knew that bodies didn't bury themselves, which meant there was only one likely reason for that body being buried on the Ten Bar: somebody had believed it wouldn't be found.

"Whom do you suppose it could be?" A frown dug furrows into Fargo's brow as he pondered the question.

"It doesn't matter. It isn't our problem." Luke took a drink of coffee, wanting to believe that.

Chapter Three

Word of the skeleton unearthed on Ten Bar land spread through the area with the speed of a wildfire. Speculation followed hot on its heels. Every time two people got together, the subject invariably crept into the conversation, replete with the latest rumor—whether fact or fiction.

Some claimed strands of brown hair had been unearthed with the skeleton; others insisted the hair was black. A few swore that bits of a plaid fabric, pearl snaps from a cowboy shirt, rivets, a zipper, and a metal button stamped with the Levi name had been discovered. But the majority scoffed at that, claiming that not a single scrap of clothing had been found with the body, clearly indicating the body had been naked as a baby when it was dumped in its grave.

On only two things everyone agreed. In addition to the class ring that had been found with the body, the skeleton had also had a full set of false teeth.

They were important clues, to be sure. But after six weeks of speculation and debate, no one in or around Glory, Wyoming, had been able to figure out the identity of the remains found on the Ten Bar Ranch. Every name suggested, someone else knew where they were either living or buried. But instead of slowing down the talk, it fueled it.

As always, the Rimrock served as the central clearinghouse for any and all information about the case. Ima Jane Evans had long been the collector and dispenser of all the latest happenings in the area. The locals had realized years ago that if there was anything going on, Ima Jane would know about it—sooner rather than later. Every Saturday night, they crowded into the Rimrock to catch up on the news, confident of coming away with a juicy tidbit of gossip or two. Ima Jane rarely disappointed them.

No one had any doubt that the Rimrock was better than a newspaper. A lot of things went on that a newspaper just wouldn't print. But Ima Jane didn't believe in censorship. If something was said, she repeated it. No newspaper would do that.

Of course, the locals regarded it as irrelevant that Glory, Wyoming, wasn't big enough to have a newspaper. Strictly speaking, Glory wasn't even considered a town anymore. Fifty years ago, when the population dropped to fifty-one, it lost its post office. Most maps of the state didn't bother to include Glory. There wasn't even a sign on the state highway identifying the collection of buildings grouped along its right-of-way. A snowplow had knocked it over three years ago, and the state hadn't gotten around to erecting a new one.

Strangers to the area rarely glanced twice at the little roadside community unless they were hungry or in need of gas. When they did, they invariably noticed the tall, red block letters spelling out the word *RIMROCK* painted across the bar's second-story front and assumed it to be the town's name. Few were ever curious enough to inquire about the accuracy of their assumption.

Once, a freestanding sign close to the road had proclaimed the structure to be the RIMROCK BAR & GRILL, setting occasional travelers straight—or, at least, prompting them to ask the town's name. But rotting wood and a strong wind had turned the sign into one of the area's distant memories, something to be recalled with the same absent fondness as the Glory Post Office.

Ima Jane and Griff Evans had opted to pocket the insurance money rather than spend it on replacing the sign, reasoning that such advertising was wasted on the locals. As for the infrequent stranger, there was a neon COORS sign in one front window, and a second that read EATS in the other window. A person would have to be literally blind not to figure out there was food and drink inside.

Both signs were aglow when Luke swung his pickup into the parking lot. It was half past six on a Saturday night, the sun still lingering in the western sky, but the lot was already crowded with its usual collection of pickups and utility vehicles, along with a sedan or two.

Luke parked his truck in one of the few empty slots remaining and switched off the engine. After slipping off his sunglasses, he hooked them on the visor and opened the cab door, pocketing the keys. As he stepped out, an old blue pickup pulled into the lot. Tobe West was behind the wheel, a towheaded Dulcie barely visible beside him and Fargo Young propped against the passenger door. Luke waited while they parked not far from his location.

When they joined him, Fargo rubbed his growling stomach and complained, "I'm so hungry I could eat the hair off a hog. I wonder what Griff fixed for a special tonight." He sniffed the air, searching for an aroma that might tell him.

Tobe didn't have food on his mind. "Do you think Ima Jane has heard anything new about our skeleton, Luke?"

Neither subject held any interest for Luke, something neither man would have understood if he told them. Knowing that, Luke replied, "Why don't we go find out?"

When he headed toward the door, Tobe and Fargo fell in step with him. Dulcie trailed behind her brother, a pale and silent shadow.

The Rimrock was the kind of small cowboy bar that could be found in every town, large or small, throughout the West. Its decor ran to wood paneling on the walls with local brands burned into it at intervals. Mixed in with a scattering of mounted antlers and horns were framed photographs of area heroes caught in action at the local rodeo, riding rank bulls or broncs, bulldogging a steer, or snaring a calf.

The minute they set foot inside the bar, Fargo chuckled with glee. "Hot dang, if he didn't fix ribs tonight," he declared. "How did Griff know I had me a taste for a man-sized slab of 'em?"

All but drooling in anticipation, Fargo made straight for an empty booth along the wall, its cushioned seats covered in patched and faded vinyl. Tobe followed him, with Dulcie bringing up the rear. Luke branched off, wending his way around the tables to a vacant stool at the bar. Ima Jane had his glass of Wild Turkey and water waiting for him when he slid onto the stool.

"Hi, handsome." Her smile offered its usual warm welcome. In Ima Jane's case, it was genuine. "You'd better let Fargo know that Griff fixed his fall-off-the-bone-tender ribs tonight."

Luke grinned. "His nose told him that when he walked in the door."

Ima Jane laughed. "If he wants some, he needs to get his order in quick. They're flying out of that kitchen like they had wings."

"Don't they always," Luke replied, watching over the rim of his drink while she tilted a frosty mug under the beer tap and pulled a draw.

"You've got that right." She worked as she talked, never missing a beat and always smiling. "And why not? Griff is the best cook in a hundred miles. The first time I tasted his cooking, I knew he was the man for me."

At forty-nine, Ima Jane Evans was a slender and attractive woman, with short, curly hair, its color a rich, gleaming brown. Clairol brown, Ima Jane called it with a laugh. By nature, she was a people lover who loved to listen as much as she loved to talk. An inveterate gossip she might be, but everyone agreed there wasn't a malicious bone in her body.

A waitress sailed past the bar, calling, "Two Cokes, one Bud, a Bourbon and branch."

"Coming right up," Ima Jane acknowledged, then slid another glance at Luke, her dark eyes all bright and knowing. "Have you heard from Beauchamp in the last day or two?"

"Nope," Luke drawled in disinterest and downed another swallow of diluted whiskey.

But the mention of Beauchamp caught the ear of Doug Chalmers, a cowboy at the Cross Timbers Ranch, west of Glory. "Sam Hunt told me that Beauchamp finally got the report from the crime lab. They said the body was that of a white male in his mid- to late twenties," he said, quick to volunteer the information and eager to learn more. "The way I heard it, they couldn't determine a cause of death."

"Mid- to late twenties, you say?" Another cowboy poked his head around to peer along the bar at Doug.

"That's what I heard." Doug glanced uncertainly at Ima Jane, seeking to verify his facts. He relaxed a little when it became clear no correction was forthcoming. "Why do you ask?"

The other man frowned. "It just struck me as kinda young for a man to lose all his teeth."

"I wouldn't go saying that around Johnny Fayne if I were you," Luke advised, his mouth twisting wryly. "He might take exception to that."

His observation drew a round of laughter from the others gathered at the bar and brought a sheepish look to the cowboy's face. Between bulls, broncs, and a penchant for brawling, Johnny Fayne had lost all his teeth before he reached the ripe old age of nineteen. He was forever handing his dentures to someone for safekeeping before he climbed on a rank one or jumped into a brawl.

"With Johnny, those choppers spend more time out of his mouth than they do in it, that's for sure," Doug remarked.

For a moment, Luke thought the talk might get sidetracked into a discussion of Johnny Fayne. That hope proved to be short-lived.

"If that fella was in his middle twenties, then he must have been in the ground sixty-seventy years or more."

"How do you figure that, Joe?" Doug turned to the rancher who had offered the thought.

"I was going by the date on that class ring he was wearing," the man explained, then fixed his gaze on the woman behind the bar. "Did they ever find out what school that was from, Ima Jane?"

Seconds ticked without an answer, a sure sign to everyone that she knew something. Her smile widened as she took note of her suddenly rapt audience.

"They did more than that." She paused again, deliberately allowing the suspense to build while she set the drinks on the tray for the waitress. Finished, she wiped her hands on a towel. "They've identified the body."

There was an instant of silence before she was bombarded with questions from a dozen different directions.

"Who is it?" asked one.

"How did you find that out?" another asked.

"When did you hear that?"

"Are you sure?"

"As sure as I'm standing here," she confirmed.

"How come you never said anything before now?" Joe Gibbs demanded, a bit huffy.

She gave him a big-eyed look of innocence, a betraying twinkle of laughter in her expression. "You never asked, Joe."

"Well, I'm asking now!" he exploded in exasperation. "Who is it?"

Ima Jane sighed in exaggerated regret. "I don't know."

"You don't know?! But you just said—" the rancher sputtered.

She held up a calming hand. "I said . . . they had identified the body. Unfortunately, Beauchamp won't release the name until the next of kin have been notified." She glanced again at Luke.

"Don't look at me." He drew back, shaking his head, denying he had any knowledge. "I haven't heard a word from Beauchamp in weeks."

"You must have some idea who this guy was, Ima Jane," Doug insisted.

Disappointed in Luke's answer, Ima Jane shrugged. "All I know for sure is that the man was from out of state."

"I knew all along it had to be a stranger," Joe declared. "Didn't I tell you that, Hank? It just makes sense. No one from around here has come up missing."

"Yeah, but . . . who was this guy?" Doug argued. "What was he doing here? And how did he end up getting buried on the Ten Bar?"

Ima Jane lifted her hands, palms up, an infectious smile spreading across her face. "As they used to say on the old radio serials, 'Stay tuned for the next installment.' "

Her comment drew a round of laughter from the men at the bar, the honest, belly-laugh kind. But it satisfied them that she had no more information to relate. With feigned casualness, one by one they drifted away, taking their drinks with them, to spread the news.

All except Luke. He remained at the bar, nursing his drink. He smiled into it as the idle hum of voices behind him grew to an excited buzz.

Temporarily without a drink order to fill, Ima Jane poured herself a cup of coffee and wandered to Luke's end of the bar. Her glance traveled over the room, ending its arcing sweep when it reached Luke.

"I was certain Beauchamp would have talked to you about his findings." The probing search of her bright eyes told Luke that she wasn't convinced he hadn't spoken to the sheriff.

"Why do you think he would?" he countered, amused rather than annoyed by her persistence.

"The body was found on the Ten Bar." Her tone made it clear that she regarded the answer as obvious. "It's only logical that once Beauchamp discovered the man's identity, he would check to see if the name meant anything to you."

"Why should it?" A slow smile softened the scoffing response. "If Joe Gibbs is right in his figuring, that body was in the ground long before I was ever born. It isn't likely the name would mean anything to me, especially if he wasn't from around here. I'm sure Beauchamp knew that." He downed another swallow of his drink, welcoming the whiskey burn in his throat.

"Just the same, I'm surprised he didn't check. His name might be somewhere in the ranch records, indicating he'd worked at the Ten Bar in the past or—"

"Does anybody have records that go that far back?" Luke mocked lightly. "And my father never talked much about cowboys who had worked for him in the past. In fact, I can't recall that he ever did."

"Are you sure?" Her eyes sharpened on him in skepticism.

He released a laughing breath. "Ima Jane, you can pump all you want, but I can't give you information that I don't have."

"I know. But it's all so frustrating," she said in sudden disgust. "I don't understand why Beauchamp is making such a secret of the name. He's known the man's identity for a week."

"Really?" Luke arched an eyebrow in surprise.

Ima Jane was quick to read his thoughts. "Yes, really. Unfortunately I didn't find out until this afternoon when a state trooper stopped in for pie and coffee."

"And you managed to pry the information out of him," Luke guessed.

"It wasn't hard." A small smile of self-congratulation showed briefly, then faded with the onset of another memory. "I would have gotten the name, too, but he couldn't remember it," she said, then added, "He seemed surprised that Beauchamp hadn't released it."

"You know how Beauchamp is," Luke said, with a dismissing movement of his shoulders. "He believes in going strictly by the book. I don't imagine it's all that easy tracking down someone's next of kin after a half century has passed."

"That's just it." Irritation flickered in her expression. "According to the trooper, he's already done it. Supposedly he talked to a relative Monday or Tuesday of this week."

Luke frowned. "Then what's the holdup in releasing the name? Did the trooper know?"

Ima Jane sighed. "He thought he was probably waiting for some records to arrive verifying the man's identity. Someone has clearly never heard of faxes or Federal Express."

"Irritating, isn't it?" he teased.

"In a word, yes." But she smiled when she said it, then went to take a drink order from the waitress coming up to the bar.

Absently Luke studied the girl, his glance skimming her face, noting its pale and frazzled look. He waited until Ima Jane had filled her drink order, then asked curiously, "When did Liz Frazer start working here?"

"This is her first night." She paused and lowered her voice to a confidential level. "She and Ken need the extra money."

"Why? The last I heard, Ken was working for the Box M. He didn't quit, did he?"

"No. They need money for the baby. Liz is expecting, and his insurance won't cover it."

"So, Ken's going to be a papa." He tried to be happy for him, but all he felt was his own pain. He downed the rest of his drink, then pushed the empty glass toward Ima Jane. "I need a refill."

Taking the glass, she gave him a look of motherly reproval. "Do you plan on drinking your supper tonight, or should I put in an order to the kitchen for you?"

Luke knew it usually took two drinks before the numbness set in. Tonight it might require three. "After I finish that drink you're pouring now, you can tell Griff to throw a steak on the grill for me."

"It isn't good to drink on an empty stomach, Luke." She poured a hefty shot of Wild Turkey into the glass, then added some more cubes and a splash of water.

"It is for me."

But Ima Jane wasn't fooled by the sexy smile he flashed her.

Everyone knew his smiles only went skin deep. Inside he was still raw and hurting. She set the drink before him and watched as his strong hand closed around it and lifted it to his mouth.

"What do you find in there, Luke?" she asked after he'd taken a sip.

There came that smile again, intent on deflecting the question. "I'll let you know when I find it, Ima Jane," he said and winked.

A sigh of regret slipped from her. "This grieving has gone on too long, Luke."

"Is that what people are saying?" His smile remained in place, but there was a coolness in his eyes.

"That's what *I'm* saying."

"Everyone's entitled to their opinion. Here's to yours." He lifted his glass in a toasting salute, then tossed down a swallow.

Her mouth thinned at the gesture. "You haven't been to church in ages, Luke. Why don't you come tomorrow?"

"Are you worried about my soul?" Luke jested.

"Among other things."

"Such as?" he asked in an amused voice dry with challenge.

Always free with her opinion, Ima Jane wasted no time offering it. "It's high time you started dating again. A strong, handsome man like you, you ought to have your arm around a woman instead of sitting here by yourself hugging that drink."

"Turning matchmaker, are you?" He grinned, then turned sideways on the stool, casting a jaundiced eye over the customers in the bar. "Take a look and see if you can find any likely candidates. And don't suggest Babs Townsend. She's been married and divorced three times. A track record like that only spells trouble. More trouble I don't need." His glance paused briefly on a fresh-faced blonde with a scattering of freckles on her nose. "Sally Crane is single, but she's barely nineteen. That's like robbing the cradle." Swiveling back, he directed a smug glance at Ima Jane. "You'll have to admit, the choice goes from slim to none."

"How about the one who just walked in?" she murmured, the light of the insatiably curious leaping into her eyes.

With a turn of his head, Luke glanced toward the entrance. There was no missing the woman who paused inside the door. She had on an oversized cotton sweater the color of antique gold that failed to hide the ripeness of her figure. A pair of wheat-tan slacks accented the long length of her slender legs. A pair of sunglasses sat atop auburn hair that was a mass of long, unruly curls, curls that gleamed like silk in the muted bar light.

"Who is she?" Luke knew he had never seen her around before. Drunk or sober, he wouldn't have forgotten a woman who looked like this one.

"Never saw her before," Ima Jane admitted, then threw him a sly glance. "She's a looker, though."

Ignoring that, Luke centered his attention on the woman, studying the hesitation in her manner as she made a visual search of the bar's interior. She fastened her glance on a point at the rear, tugged the strap to her purse a notch higher on her shoulder, then struck out in the direction of the restrooms, an easy grace to her striding walk. Luke tracked her until she disappeared from view.

"Did you see that?" Ima Jane chuckled.

"What?" He took a sip of his drink.

"Every man in the bar sat up straighter when she walked in. And a few got kicked under the table."

"I'm not surprised."

"I wonder what she's doing here?" Ima Jane murmured, curiosity surfacing again in her voice.

"Probably just passing through." He felt a trace of regret at the thought, which amused him.

Without really intending to, he found himself watching for her return. She was back within minutes, the sunglasses no longer roosting atop her head. This time she walked directly to the bar, giving Luke a full frontal view of her face. Beautiful was too strong a word to describe her, a decision he based mainly on the refreshing honesty of her features. Her eyes were big and brown, and direct in their regard. He was almost sorry that Ima Jane was the object of her interest. She slid onto a stool two seats from him and flipped open her purse.

"What would you like?" Ima Jane inquired, studying her customer with curious eyes.

"Coffee, please, and"—she pulled a road map out and laid it on the bar top—"some directions."

"I had a feeling you were lost." Smiling, Ima Jane filled a thick white mug with coffee and set it before the woman, adding a spoon, a pitcher of cream, and a glass canister of sugar.

"I don't think I'm lost, exactly." The curve of her lips held a touch of self-deprecating humor. "I'm just not sure where I am." She added two spoonfuls of sugar to the mug and stirred her coffee. "I was told if I stayed on this highway, I would come to a town called Glory. I was hoping you could tell me how much farther it is."

Startled, Ima Jane blinked in surprise. "You're looking for Glory?" What had previously been simple curiosity now took an avid turn.

"Yes." She hesitated, suddenly uncertain. "Have I taken a wrong turn somewhere?"

"It isn't that," Ima Jane hastened to assure her, suppressed laughter bubbling in her voice. "It's just . . . strangers coming to Glory are about as rare around here as palm trees."

"I can believe that." The woman smiled, and it was like a light had suddenly been turned on, illuminating her entire face. "The town isn't even listed on the map. Is it very far from here?"

"This is it," Ima Jane informed her.

"This is what?" Confusion showed in the woman's expressive brown eyes.

"Glory. You're here."

"You're kidding." Disbelief riddled her voice. She half turned, glancing behind her toward the entrance. "I could swear there wasn't a sign—"

"A snowplow knocked it down a few winters back." Luke joined the conversation.

When she turned her dark brown eyes on him, he had the urge to lift her off that stool, slide his fingers into those rich auburn curls, and feel the softness of a woman's body in his arms once again. It was an urge that told him the liquor was working its magic, blocking the unwanted memories and unlocking the old wants and desires of the flesh.

It was an impulse he wouldn't have entertained if she had been local. But this woman was safe. Strangers might come to Glory, but they never stayed. There were no job opportunities here, no future. The town was dying, slowly but surely, like so many other small rural communities.

"It's a relief to know that," she said on a sighing note. "I couldn't imagine how I had missed the sign when I was watching so closely for one."

"Let me be the first to welcome you to Glory, Wyoming. My name's Ima Jane Evans. My husband, Griff, and I own this place."

"It's a pleasure to meet you, Mrs. Evans."

Ima Jane laughed at such formality. "Nobody ever calls me that. I'm just Ima Jane to everyone. We pretty much stick to first names around here."

"It's the same way at home, for the most part." The coffee mug was halfway to her mouth before she thought to add, "My name is Angie Sommers, by the way."

"Glad to meet you, Angie Sommers," Ima Jane replied then indicated Luke with a wave of her hand. "This is Luke McCallister. He owns the Ten Bar Ranch outside of town."

Putting a foot on the floor, he straightened from the stool and extended a hand to her. "Hello, Angie."

After switching the mug to the other hand, she reached out to take his. "Hello, Luke."

It had been a long time since he'd held a woman's hand. It felt small and smooth and warm, with a gently firm grip. Luke held it a few seconds longer than was necessary, betraying his rising interest in her. A recognition of it registered in her expression, along with an answering flicker of cautious interest. That told him right then and there that she wasn't the kind of woman who was free and easy with men. Part of him was disappointed.

Observing the exchange, Ima Jane inserted a sly, "In case you're wondering, Angie, Luke is single."

A hint of color rose in her cheeks. Luke covered the awkward moment with a chuckle, resuming his seat. "Don't mind Ima Jane. Along with all the other things she does on the side, she's been thinking about trying her hand at matchmaking."

"And what's wrong with that?" Ima Jane challenged in mock indignation. "Here I have two attractive people sitting at my bar— alone on a Saturday night. What's wrong with trying to bring them together if I can? Surely there's no harm in that, is there?"

"No, there's no harm in it," Angie agreed, her smile pointedly polite, offering no encouragement to either of them.

"You've made your pitch, Ima Jane. Now it's time to back off," Luke told her, amused by the ploy.

"If you say so." Ima Jane lifted her shoulders in an expressive shrug and shifted over to the bar sink, then caught up a towel to wipe the glasses on the drainboard. "Where is home for you, Angie?" she asked, changing the subject, but Luke knew better than to think she was giving up.

"Southern Iowa." Holding the mug in both hands, Angie sipped at its sweetened contents, then lowered it, murmuring appreciatively, "Mmm, the coffee tastes good."

"What brings you to Glory?" Ima Jane was too nosy not to ask.

"Some family business."

Startled by the answer, Ima Jane halted in midswipe. "You have family here?"

Luke could practically see Ima Jean sifting through her memory banks trying to recall which of the local residents had relatives in Iowa.

"In a manner of speaking, I—wait a minute." Angie abruptly lowered the coffee mug and turned wide, questioning eyes on Luke. "What was the name of your ranch again?"

"The Ten Bar," he replied, with a slightly puzzled frown.

"The Ten Bar." She tested the sound of it, then dived into her purse, digging until she came up with a small, spiral notebook. She flipped through the first few pages; skimmed the handwritten notations on them; then planted the pad of her finger on a page and released a low, exultant laugh. "The Ten Bar. I knew that sounded familiar." Her dark eyes were sparkling when she looked at Luke. "That's where my grandfather's body was found."

The announcement stunned both Luke and Ima Jane. But Ima Jane was quicker to recover her speech.

"That was your grandfather?" she repeated on an incredulous note, then darted a quick glance at Luke. "We had heard the body had been identified, but they hadn't released any name."

"They're probably waiting until they get the records I brought with me before they make it official." Angie returned the notebook to her purse. "But there really isn't any doubt it's him."

"What was your grandfather's name?" As always, Ima Jane went straight for the facts.

Angie hesitated ever so slightly before answering. "Henry James Wilson." Then she added, with a smile of fond remembrance, "But my grandma always called him Hank."

Luke fired a glance at Ima Jane, but the significance of the name clearly hadn't registered. Smiling to himself, he took a leisurely sip of his drink and wondered how long it would take before the name sunk in.

Chapter Four

"**A**nd now you've come all the way to Glory to claim the body. That's nice." Ima Jane nodded in approval. "Will you be taking him back to Iowa for burial?"

"That's what I'd like to do," Angie admitted, then switched her attention to Luke, the shine of barely suppressed excitement in her eyes. "Meeting you practically the minute I arrived—it almost seems fated. You see, I planned on getting directions to your ranch so I could visit the place where his body was found. I know Grandma would have wanted me to do that. Would you mind showing it to me? Sometime when it's convenient for you, of course."

"Luke would be happy to show you," Ima Jane volunteered when he hesitated.

A dry smile slanted his mouth. "In case you haven't noticed, Angie, Ima Jane always sticks her nose into everybody's business."

"Luke McCallister, that is an awful thing to say," Ima Jane protested, both hands coming to rest on her hips in a combative pose.

"It's also the truth," he retorted, then glanced sideways at Angie Sommers. "Have you eaten tonight?"

"No." But she seemed to hesitate as if she had a fair idea of what was coming next and was still trying to decide on her answer.

"Neither have I. Let's grab ourselves a table and over dinner we can settle on a time for you to come out to the Ten Bar." He swung off the stool and picked up his drink to drain it, then added the warning, "Believe me, as long as you keep sitting here, Ima Jane will ply you with questions until she's learned your whole life story. And she'll do it so slickly you won't even realize it until it's over."

Ima Jane was quick to object. "I resent that, Luke."

"But you can't deny it." A smile crinkled his eyes, taking any sting from his words.

"You're right. I can't." She grinned and waved the towel in her hand, shooing them away from the bar. "You two go have your dinner. I'll have my chance another time."

This time Angie didn't hesitate, pausing only long enough to gather up the map, her purse, and her coffee cup before sliding off the stool. All the way from Iowa, she had driven with her fingers mentally crossed, hoping she would have the opportunity to talk at length with the owner or foreman of the ranch where her grandfather's body had been found. She certainly hadn't expected it to come so quickly—or that he would be so young. At least, young in the sense that she had expected him to be much older.

She cast another glance at Luke McCallister as he guided her toward a vacant table. She had never been very good at guessing people's ages, but she suspected he had to be somewhere in his middle to late thirties. Strictly speaking, he wasn't handsome, but there was no denying his rugged good looks were attractive in a rough, masculine sort of way. And she would have been less than honest if she didn't admit to a tingling awareness of him as a man. That was part of the reason she had hesitated about having dinner with him. That, and the possibility that a lot of time might be wasted fending off passes.

"Ima Jane meant what she said," Luke remarked when he

pulled out a chair for her. "She's confident that she'll get another crack at you."

"Why's that?" Angie placed her coffee mug on the table, then sat down in the chair, laying her purse across her lap.

"She figures you'll need a place to stay tonight, and the closest motel is sixty miles away." Luke sat across the table from her. "They have rooms upstairs that they rent out . . . usually to stranded motorists."

"I'm afraid she'll be disappointed. I already have a place to stay tonight." Angie saw the flicker of surprise in his blue-gray eyes and smiled. "I borrowed my uncle's pickup camper to make the trip. It's a gas hog, but I have a bed, a kitchen, and a teeny bathroom."

He chuckled, and the low rumble of it was decidedly appealing. "I can hardly wait to see Ima Jane's face when she finds that out."

"She seems nice." Angie glanced back to the bar.

"She is nice. Just nosy." He raised a hand, signaling to one of the waitresses. "Griff offers a very limited menu," he informed her. "You can have your choice of steak, fried chicken, or today's special—which happens to be barbeque ribs. All the dinners come with salad, french fries, or baked potato. For sandwiches, there're hamburgers or hot dogs."

She laughed softly. "When you said limited, you meant it."

"It keeps the waste and spoilage down, and the inventory fresh. Operating a business in a small community solely dependent on the local trade, you have to keep it lean to survive."

In the background, a jukebox blared a country tune, competing with the steady chatter of voices, occasionally punctuated with laughter. Angie ran an idle glance over the crowded tavern.

"It looks busy tonight," she remarked.

"On Saturdays it always is. Some say they come for the food and stay for the gossip. The rest claim it's the other way around. I guess it's a toss-up which is the bigger draw."

Angie noticed a waitress approaching their table. "Is there anything in particular you'd recommend?" She took a sip of coffee, watching Luke over the rim. He was much too easy on the eyes.

"Take your pick. It's all good," he said, with an idle shrug, then sat back in his chair, turning to the waitress. "Hi, Liz. How's it going?"

"Don't ask," the sun-streaked blonde replied, looking flustered and rushed as she flipped through her order pad, searching for a blank page.

"I understand congratulations are in order." Something gentle and warm entered his expression, softening all the hard, sharp angles in his face.

"Ima Jane told you, did she?" A sudden small and shy smile appeared in the girl's face, bringing a glow to her eyes.

"Naturally," Luke replied, then explained to Angie, "Liz is expecting."

"How wonderful." Angie was quick to express her joy for the girl.

"It *is* wonderful." The waitress nodded. "Scary but wonderful." Someone called to her from another table. "Coming," she promised, the harried look returning to her face when she directed her attention back to them. "What can I get you?"

"Steak." Angie said the first thing that popped into her mind, then went with her choice. "Medium, with french fries and Italian dressing on the salad."

"How about you, Luke?"

"The usual steak. Griff knows what I want. And another drink."

She scribbled down the order, then flipped the pad shut, glancing at the mug in Angie's hand. "Do you need a refill on that coffee?"

"Please."

"I'll be right back with the pot—and your drink, Luke." She started to move away from the table, then stopped and lightly touched Angie's shoulder. "We're all sorry about your grandpa."

Too stunned by the expression of sympathy from a total stranger, Angie wasn't able to voice a response before the waitress moved away from the table. She was still struggling with the surprise of it when she glanced at Luke and saw the twinkle of laughter in his eyes.

"I did tell you that gossip was served right along with food and drink," he reminded her. "By now, everyone in the place knows who you are and why you're here—and are busy speculating on everything else."

The breath Angie had unconsciously been holding came out with an explosive little rush of astonishment. "You told me, but I never expected it would spread that quickly." Coming from a small town herself, she probably should have.

"If there are any secrets around here, I can guarantee they won't be secret for long."

"I believe you," Angie murmured, suddenly conscious of the number of looks being directed her way.

The waitress sailed back to their table with Luke's drink and a full pot of coffee. She poured some in Angie's mug; dropped off two sets of silverware wrapped in a napkin; and moved off to make the rounds of the other tables, refilling cups.

"What do you do back in Iowa?" Luke asked after she had gone.

"I teach." Angie took a tasting sip of the coffee, then reached for the sugar canister on the table to sweeten it some more.

"Which grade?" Luke had an instant image of her surrounded by a group of kindergartners with their faces lifted in rapt attention while she read to them from a storybook, bringing the words to life with animated expressions.

"Actually *grades* would be more accurate," Angie corrected. "I teach American history and government at the local high school."

He frowned in surprise. "To teenagers?!"

Amused by his reaction, Angie smiled. "At times it's a real challenge, but I enjoy it." However, the last thing she wanted to talk about was herself. "Have you always lived around here?"

"All my life."

"And, all of it on the Ten Bar Ranch?"

"All of it," he confirmed.

"I guess the ranch has been in your family for a while, then."

"A while."

Frustrated by his failure to elaborate, Angie sighed and shook her head in mock disapproval. "You must have gotten low marks in class participation when you were in school. A 'yes' or 'no' answer doesn't tell a teacher how much you know."

He had the good humor to smile. "I don't suppose it does. If you spend much time around Ima Jane, it becomes a kind of self-defense to keep too many answers from being pried out of you."

"You clearly value your privacy."

"Doesn't everyone?" he countered, again avoiding a direct response.

"To a degree, yes." But with Luke McCallister, Angie had the feeling it bordered on an obsession. She couldn't help wondering why.

For a tick of seconds, neither spoke. Then Luke filled the void. "Anybody around here can tell you that a McCallister has owned the Ten Bar since it came into existence back in the eighteen-eighties. At one time it was one of the largest spreads in the state. But over the years, sections of it have been sold off to cover financial losses or taxes. Now, there's roughly three hundred fifty thousand acres within its boundary fences."

"That's still a lot of land by Iowa standards. Back home, a farm is considered big if it has more than four hundred acres."

"Different area, different agriculture. In rough country like this, it takes about two hundred fifty acres just to support one cow and her calf."

"You raise cattle, then."

He nodded. "Most years we carry about five hundred head through the winter."

* * *

Over in a booth along the wall, Fargo Young shoved the platter back from the edge of the tabletop. All that remained of the large slab of ribs were the bones, slicked clean of meat and sauce. Pushing his full stomach out, he gave it a satisfied pat and sighed his contentment.

"That Griff knows how to fix ribs," he declared and dug in his shirt pocket for a toothpick. "I think I got me enough room left for a big wedge of apple pie. How about you? Are you gonna have anything for dessert?" He looked across the table at Tobe.

Dulcie sat quietly beside him, nibbling indifferently at her hamburger and swinging her legs back and forth, imitating the rhythm of a cantering horse.

Tobe shook his head. "I'll just have another beer." He drained the brown glass bottle in front of him, then shot another look at Luke's table. "What do you suppose Luke is talking to that girl about?"

Idly picking at the scraps of meat caught between his yellowing teeth, Fargo briefly studied the pair. "Looks to me like Luke's doing more listenin' than talkin'." But the sight of them prompted another thought. "What was the name of that girl's grandpa again?"

"Wilson," Tobe replied. "I think Liz said his first name was Henry."

"Wilson, Wilson, Wilson," Fargo repeated, with a troubled scowl. "That name rings a bell somewhere, but I'll be danged if I can think why."

"I know," Dulcie inserted.

"I know something, too," Tobe flashed in irritation. "I know you'd better quit dawdling around and get that hamburger eaten. I never saw anybody as slow as you are."

Guiltily she ducked her head and took another bite, chewing at it desultorily. Fargo took pity on her. "You just hush up there, Tobe, and let her talk."

"She doesn't know anybody named Wilson," Tobe scoffed.

"Don't pay any attention to your brother, Dulcie," Fargo told her. "You just say whatever it is you were gonna say."

She glanced out of the side of her eyes at Tobe, then made a project of swallowing the food in her mouth. Her response, when it came, was small and uncertain.

"I was just going to say that was the outlaw's name, too."

"What outlaw?" Tobe's challenge was full of pure scorn.

Fargo yanked the toothpick from his mouth, his entire face brightening. "Wilson. Ike Wilson. That was the name of one of those train robbers. You don't suppose—" But he didn't finish the thought, breaking off the sentence as he scooted from the booth. "I gotta find out. If Liz comes back, order me some pie," he said, then gave Dulcie a pat on the head. "Good thinkin', girl."

When the steaks were delivered, Angie wasted no time slicing into hers. Luke went through the motions of taking a last sip of his drink while he studied her bent head with its mass of gleaming auburn curls, conscious of the contradictions she presented. The casual disarray of her hairstyle suggested a personality that was carefree and breezy, someone quick to embrace life. The readiness and ease of her smile echoed that.

All of which was, no doubt, true about her. But beneath it all she was also intelligent, with a keen, analytical mind. He'd only had glimpses of it, but enough to know that all her innocent-sounding questions were leading somewhere. There was more she wanted from him. And he had yet to decide if he wanted to give it.

"You're right. The steak is delicious." She sliced off another bite. "I didn't realize how hungry I was until I started eating."

"Traveling has a way of whetting the appetite." He picked up his own knife.

"How true." She popped the bite of steak in her mouth.

"I have to admit I'm a little surprised you came all this way to claim the body of someone you never knew, relative or not." He watched her reaction, catching only the slightest hint of unease.

"My grandmother would have wanted me to."

"I take it she's no longer living?" he guessed.

"No. She passed away ... almost eleven years ago." Her thoughts turned inward, a shadow of grief passing over her expression, an emotion that Luke was quick to recognize. Then she was all bright-eyed warmth again, alive to the moment. "We were always very close. You could say she raised me. She moved in with us after my father died and my mom took over running the farm. So Grandma was the one waiting for me when I got off the school bus. She was the one who made sure I had my homework finished, listened to all my woes, and kissed away my hurts, real or imagined. Mom was always in the fields, or up to her elbows in grease, repairing some piece of equipment."

His glance skimmed her in reassessment, but the conclusion didn't change. "I never would have guessed you were raised on a farm," he admitted. "You look more like a town girl."

"You won't think so after I've been in the sun a few hours and the freckles start popping out," Angie replied, with a definite twinkle. "Grandma called them sun kisses and said they were evidence of how much God loved me. When I was younger, I used to wish He didn't love me so much. And with this hair"—her fingers flicked the ends of a darkly red curl—"I never tan no matter how long I'm in the sun. The freckles just run together, giving me the look of one."

He smiled at her little joke while he turned over the information she had given. "What about your mother? Is she still living?"

She nodded. "And still farming. No matter what I say, I can't seem to convince her that she's getting too old to be bouncing around on a tractor from dawn 'til dusk. But she won't consider selling the place—or leasing the fields to any of our neighbors."

"It's odd that she didn't come with you. After all, it was her father's remains that were found."

44

"This is the wrong time of the year for a farmer to be taking long trips, so I came in her place." She picked up a crispy french fry and trailed it through the ketchup she had squirted onto her plate. "That's one of the main advantages of being a teacher—you have the summers off."

Angie deliberately didn't mention that her mother considered the entire trip more than just unnecessary and impractical. In her opinion, it was sheer foolishness. And she hadn't minced words about it when she learned of Angie's intentions.

Angie's argument had been simple: if she didn't go, she would always wish that she had. And she didn't want to live the rest of her life with that regret.

Mentally shaking off the thought, Angie popped the ketchup-tipped french fry into her mouth and crunched it while directing a considering glance at her table companion. "I imagine this is a busy time of year for you, too."

"Some days more than others," he acknowledged.

After the smallest hesitation, she charged forward with her plan. "How does tomorrow afternoon stack up for you?" Angie didn't give him a chance to answer. "I was hoping, since it's Sunday, that I could stop out and you could—"

"Scuse me, miss." A cowboy with a short and grizzled excuse for a beard and his left shirtsleeve pinned back to conceal the stub of his forearm dragged out an empty chair from their table, angled it to face Angie, and promptly lowered his aging bones into it. "I heard it was your granddad's bones that were found."

Pulling her glance from the shirtsleeve, Angie stared at his leathery face, all seamed with wrinkles, and managed to keep the startled stammer out of her answer. "That's right." She darted a quick look at Luke, not sure what to make of the interruption—or the one-armed cowboy.

But his attention was on the cowboy, amusement gleaming in his eyes. "Why don't you pull up a chair and sit down, Fargo?"

The remark sailed right over the old cowboy's head as he

turned a puzzled glare on Luke. "Have you gone blind or some-thin', Luke? I'm already sittin' down."

"I know," Luke responded dryly, then switched his attention back to Angie while using his knife to gesture at the cowboy. "This ill-mannered old coot is Fargo Young. I'm sad to say, he works for me. I sorta inherited him from my father along with the ranch."

"And a lucky day it was for you," the one-armed cowboy fired right back.

Luke just grinned and finished the introductions. "Angie Sommers from Iowa."

After hurriedly brushing the french fry salt from her fingers, Angie extended a hand in greeting. "It's a pleasure to meet you, Mr. Young."

He started to reach for her hand, then stopped. "Sommers. Your name's Sommers?" A surprised frown deepened the furrows in his face. "I thought it was Wilson."

"Wilson was my grandfather's name," she explained.

He nodded, understanding registering in his expression. "I hadn't thought of that. For a minute there, I'd about decided Liz had got the name wrong." Belatedly he took her hand and gave it a vigorous pump, then released it to squint one eye at her as he sharply probed, "Your granddad—he wouldn't happen to be any kin to that train robber Ike Wilson, would he?"

The robbery had happened so many years ago that Angie hadn't expected anyone would make the connection—at least not so soon. Suddenly tense and self-conscious, she opened her mouth to an-swer, but it was a full second before she could force it out.

"As a matter of fact, he was Ike Wilson's grandson." Even to her own ears, the delivery sounded much too casual and falsely offhand.

But Luke McCallister seemed to be the only one who noticed it as Fargo Young slapped his thigh. "I knew it! I knew it was gonna be somethin' like that." Turning and craning his withered neck, he raked his gaze over the crowd until he located the object of his search. Pursing lips and teeth, he emitted a short, shrill whistle, then yelled, "Hey, Joe! Joe Gibbs, c'mere a minute!"

Several heads turned at the shouted call, but it was a short, heavyset man at the bar whom Fargo motioned to with a summoning gesture. Like every other male in the place, Joe Gibbs wore a cowboy hat, boots, and jeans. At the throat of his western-cut white shirt, he wore a bolo tie ornamented with the silver head of a longhorn. Snug-fitting Levi's swooped low, as if straining to hold up the underside of his rounded belly. As he straightened from the bar and ambled toward them, there was something about the way he carried himself that marked him as a rancher rather than an ordinary hand.

Drink in hand, he stopped at their table, his glance flicking to Angie with undisguised interest even as he addressed his words to the one-armed cowboy. "What do you need, Fargo?"

"I want to test your memory a minute, see if you recall that story folks used to tell about a kin to one of those outlaws coming here to look for the gold they buried." Fargo studied him with sly, watchful eyes.

"I remember something of the sort. Why?" His glance remained on Angie.

"This young lady here is Angie Sommers. It was her granddaddy's bones we found out at the Ten Bar," Fargo announced.

"Yes, I heard." Turning to Angie, the rancher nodded gravely. "You have my condolences, Miss Sommers."

"That's very kind. Thank you," she murmured, conscious that more than one set of ears was listening to this conversation.

"It turns out, Joe"—Fargo leaned back in his chair, smugly pleased with himself—"he was the grandson of the outlaw Ike Wilson."

"You don't say." The rancher showed his surprise, then grunted, "I guess no one has to wonder anymore whether he found it."

"Wait a minute," an old woman at the next table spoke up. "I remember my dad telling me about him. He let him stay in that old line cabin out in Booker's Canyon, the one they built back when all of that land was Ten Bar range. That guy packed up and left. My dad said so."

"He sure didn't go very far," someone else said, drawing a round of subdued laughter.

The woman took exception to the comment, turning huffy. "It's true. I remember my dad telling me how this guy showed up at the ranch one day after being there five or six months. My dad said he'd never seen anybody look so downcast and dejected. He told my dad that he was giving up and going home."

"That was always the story I heard." Fargo nodded in emphatic agreement.

"I'll tell you one thing for a fact," the woman threw out in challenge. "My dad went out to the line cabin a couple weeks later. He said he never saw that old shack look so clean. There wasn't a thing out of place—and nothing had been left behind."

"I see what you're getting at, Marge," another customer inserted thoughtfully. "If he packed all his stuff, where is it now? They dug all around where the body was found and didn't find a thing. Not even so much as a comb or a razor."

Suddenly comments began coming from all directions as everyone joined in the discussion.

"Wasn't he supposed to have a map that would take him right to the gold?" someone asked, then added quickly, "That was always the story I heard."

"If he had a map, my dad never saw it," Marge replied. "But he did say that the guy was real confident about finding the gold when he first arrived. Dad was always sure he knew something nobody else did."

"You're right, Marge," the rancher Joe Gibbs agreed. "I remember now there was talk of how he would go around describing certain landmarks and asking people if they remembered anything like that around here."

"Yeah, wasn't there something about a tall rock that looked like a pillar?" someone else recalled.

"I always heard it was a rock shaped like an eagle's head," someone in the back offered.

Angie could feel the excitement spreading and growing, touching everyone. Except Luke McCallister. If anything, it aroused only amusement in him.

Chapter Five

Fargo scooted his chair closer to Angie, the wooden legs scraping across the planked floor. Resting his stubby forearm on the table, he leaned toward her, his gaze fastening on her with burrowing intensity.

"What do you know about all this talk of a map?" he challenged. "Did your granddad really have one?"

"If he did, it's news to me." Which was the truth—as far as it went. "Certainly no one in my family has ever said anything about a map."

Her response failed to satisfy Fargo. "If your granddad didn't have a map, how come he seemed so sure he knew where the stolen gold was hidden? And why'd he go around describin' landmarks to folks and askin' if they'd seen anything like that around here?"

"I really couldn't say," Angie hedged the truth, nervously aware of her audience. Her hand was halfway to the purse lying on her lap before she managed to check the movement and reach instead for her knife. Desperate to divert more questions, she asked, "Are there any landmarks like the pillar of rock someone mentioned?"

Old and half crippled with arthritis Fargo might be, but there was nothing wrong with his vision or his hearing. His eyes had observed that abortive gesture of her hand toward her purse, and his ears had picked up the nervous edge to her voice. Suspicion and curiosity merged in his mind, leaving him convinced that she was hiding something, and wondering what it was.

Her question drew an amused snort from him. He was smart enough to recognize a diversionary tactic when he saw one. She might fool others with her innocent act, but she hadn't fooled him.

"There's probably a half dozen such rocks like that around here. With a little imagination, you could call 'em pillars," he replied, being deliberately as uninformative with his answers as she was.

Disappointment took the brightness from her eyes. As if realizing that, she averted her glance to the food remaining on her plate.

His reply drew a quick comment from the crowd. "It's true, there are a lot of pillar-like rock formations, Fargo. But most of them aren't tall enough to cast a long shadow."

"What has that got to do with anything?" someone else scoffed.

Uncomfortable with all the amused glances aimed at him, the first speaker turned slightly defensive. "The way I always heard the story about the pillar, at a certain hour of the day, its shadow was supposed to point to the place where the gold was buried."

"You watch too many old movies, Pete," a voice mocked.

The comment drew a round of laughter and more gibes.

"What time of day was it, Pete? High noon?"

"Probably ten at night."

"Are you sure it didn't have to be a certain day of the year, too, Pete?"

After initially reddening at the razzing from his friends, the man called Pete finally managed to smile. "I never said it was true; only that it was the way I heard the story told."

Through it all, Angie carefully concentrated on the food before her. But somewhere along the line, she had lost her appetite, and the steak that had been so tasty before now had about as much flavor to her as cardboard. All the while she struggled to appear only mildly interested in the run of conversation around her even as she strained to catch every scrap of information, useless or not.

"How much did they steal anyway?"

"Two hundred thousand, wasn't it?"

"I thought it was a million or more."

"Boy, are you dreaming? Back in those days, nobody probably ever saw a million dollars all in one place—unless it was Fort Knox."

"It may not have been a million, but I bet it's worth that now if a fella could find it."

"Hey, Ima Jane," Joe Gibbs called to the woman behind the bar. "Whatever happened to those old newspaper accounts of the train robbery and the shootout with the outlaws south of here? You know, the ones you used to have hanging on the wall?"

"On a shelf in the back room somewhere," she answered, then volunteered, "I'll see if I can find them."

Leaving the bar, she pushed through the double swinging doors into the kitchen. Griff was at the grill, testing the doneness of the T-bone steak on it. A slender-built man with a gray crewcut and long, sour face, he tossed a brief, identifying glance in her direction, then switched his attention back to the steak.

On her way through the kitchen, Ima Jane checked to see how many orders he had yet to fill. Only one was clipped above the grill.

"As soon as you have that order dished up, cover the bar for me, will you?" she said and headed for the back storeroom.

"Where are you going?" His frown sent an eyebrow arching into the terrycloth band he wore around his forehead to keep the sweat from dripping onto the food.

Ima Jane stopped, a hand poised on the doorknob. "You'll never guess who that body turned out to be," she said to him, excitement over the news bubbling up again. She knew better than to wait for her husband to ask. If he never found out, it wouldn't bother him a bit. "It was a man named Henry Wilson. But here's the good part,

Griff," she rushed, seeing boredom set in. "He was the grandson of one of those outlaws who robbed the train. He came here years ago to look for the gold they stole."

"How do you know that?"

She grew impatient that he should question the veracity of her information. "Good heavens, Griff, everybody has heard the story about the grandson turning up here years ago to search for the gold."

"I'm not talking about that." He brushed off her answer with a dismissing wave of the tongs in his hand. "I meant—how do you know that's who he was?"

"Because his granddaughter is out front." The smile she sent him went from ear to ear.

"She's here," he repeated in surprise. "Why?"

"She came to claim the body, of course," Ima Jane replied, mildly exasperated that he hadn't figured the reason out for himself.

"But that's my point," Griff argued. "Why would she come to Glory when the body's not here?"

Ima Jane shrugged off the question as unimportant. The woman was here; that was what mattered. "She said something to Luke McCallister about wanting to see where the body was found. Don't forget to watch the bar for me." Turning the knob, Ima Jane gave the storeroom door an inward push. "I've got to find those old newspaper accounts of the robbery that we used to have hanging out front. You don't happen to remember where I put them?"

"Third shelf, back by the napkin boxes." The old adage "A place for everything and everything in its place," Griff regarded as a law. The kitchen and storeroom were his bailiwick, and woe to the person who didn't put something in its designated place.

"What about you, miss?" Joe Gibbs addressed the question to Angie. "Were you ever told how much was stolen?"

"No." Unable to eat another bite of the now tasteless food, Angie laid her fork down and reached for her coffee, needing to keep her hands occupied with something. "I do know the amount varied with each newspaper. But I have no idea which one was accurate." She tried again to be the one doing the questioning and glean more information without being obtrusive about it. "You mentioned something about a shoot-out?"

"Yeah. That happened when the posse caught up with them," Joe Gibbs explained. "The robbers started shooting as soon as they saw them. When the gun battle was finally over, two of the gang were shot up pretty bad. Both of 'em ended up dying from their wounds. Ike Wilson—your ancestor—was the only one of the bunch to survive and stand trial. And they hung him."

"Does anybody know where this shoot-out supposedly took place? You said something about it being south of Glory." Angie lifted her coffee cup with studied casualness.

"It was on Ten Bar land." On that, the rancher was definite. Then he tilted his head to one side, frowning in uncertainty. "I always had the impression it took place only a few miles from the ranch house. Have I got that right, Luke?"

"That's the way I always heard it." Idly swirling the few cubes in his drink glass, Luke sat all lazy and loose in his chair, most of his weight tilted against a wooden armrest. His glance strayed briefly to the rancher when he answered, then came back to Angie, vaguely watchful and amused. "The story goes that, supposedly, old King McCallister—the founder of the Ten Bar—heard the shooting, got some of his boys, and rode out to join the fray."

"According to my dad," Marge spoke up, "when King McCallister and his riders arrived on the scene, the tide of the battle turned in favor of the posse. But the railroad detective heading up the posse never gave him or his men any credit for it. He didn't even mention King by name in any of his reports. Some of the folks around here were pretty upset about it, but King just shrugged it off."

At least now, Angie understood why she couldn't recall the name McCallister being mentioned in any of the various accounts she'd read. "You didn't tell me that any of your family was involved in the capture of the outlaws," she said to Luke, her smile gently chiding.

"The fight was pretty well over when they got there."

Angie came back to her original question, still unanswered.

"Where did the shoot-out take place? I don't think you ever said whether you knew its location or not."

"I guess I didn't, did I?" His mouth slanted in a smile of half mockery. "Now that I think about it, it isn't very far from where your grandfather's body was found. Ironic, isn't it?"

The coincidence seemed somehow eerie. Rather than comment on it, she asked, "How far is 'not very far'?" She smiled quickly, making a joke out of the question. "Something tells me the definition of 'not very far' in Wyoming isn't the same as it would be back in Iowa."

An answering smile crinkled Luke's eyes, lethal in its attraction. "Probably not," he agreed. "As the crow flies, it's probably less than a mile."

"I knew it would be different," she declared. "In Iowa, we'd measure it in yards."

"Here it is." Ima Jane came out of the kitchen, carrying the framed newspaper accounts. On her way to Luke and Angie's table, she snatched a bar towel off the counter and wiped the dust from the frame's glass front.

Before she could show it to Angie, the heavyset rancher intercepted it and ran a verifying glance over the trio of age-yellowed clippings, then nodded in confirmation. "This is what I was talking about." Joe Gibbs offered it to Angie. "All the facts are right here in these newspaper stories. The conductor got killed during the robbery. Shot him in cold blood, they did."

Obligingly, Angie took it and skimmed the century-old articles mounted beneath the glass, then handed it back to Ima Jane. "Actually I have copies of these."

"You do?" Ima Jane said in startled response.

Angie laughed at her look of astonishment. "It's really not so surprising. There aren't many family trees that contain a genuine outlaw. I grew up hearing bits and pieces about him. And like any kid, I became fascinated by the story and always wanted to know more." She paused to choose her next words. "Obtaining copies of articles from newspaper archives isn't all that difficult. I have a family scrapbook filled with mementos and stories about various members, including ones that have been written over the years about the robbery."

"Well, isn't that smart," Ima Jane declared. "More people should make the effort to document their family history. I've been after Griff for years to do that for his. According to his grandmother, one of his ancestors served under Custer and died at the Battle of Little Big Horn. But do you think I can talk him into finding out if it's true? Why, the way he digs in his heels in absolute refusal, you'd think I was asking him to open a can of spaghetti sauce and pass it off as homemade."

Her analogy elicited a round of good-natured laughter and glances of approval directed at the sour-faced man behind the bar. It confirmed what Griff Evans had long proclaimed: every dish out of his kitchen was made from scratch or it wasn't served. He not only butchered his own meat, but he also personally rendered the lard that was used to make his incredibly tender and flaky pie crusts.

Drawn by all the talk about the robbery and buried gold, Tobe West left the booth and joined the small group that had gathered around the attractive redhead. His sister, Dulcie, was right on his heels, as constant as a shadow.

"Can I see that?" He reached for the framed clippings Ima Jane held.

Without a moment's hesitation, she passed it into his hands, then frowned absently as she searched the walls for an empty space among the numerous photos and memorabilia. "I need to find someplace to hang that up again."

Rising onto her toes, Dulcie tried to get a peek at the yellowed articles her brother studied with such interest, then gave up the effort as futile and snuck a glance at the woman seated at the table across from Luke. Used to being ignored by adults, she was suddenly flustered to see the stranger looking straight at her.

"Hi, there. What's your name?" A wonderfully warm smile curved the woman's mouth.

Embarrassed by the sudden attention, Dulcie edged closer to her brother, trying to disappear behind him. Tobe glanced down at her, then appeared to realize the question had been addressed to her.

"That's my sister, Dulcie," he tossed out the answer and turned his curiosity toward the good-looking redhead. "I'm Tobe West. I work at the Ten Bar for Luke." He bobbed his head in the direction of his employer.

"Angie Sommers," she volunteered her own name, then switched her attention back to Dulcie. "Dulcie is a very pretty name."

A thousand times Dulcie had wished for a more ordinary name. Never once had she considered her own to be pretty. The unexpected compliment had her blushing to the roots of her white-blond hair. But the corners of her mouth tilted upward in a tentative smile of pleasure that this woman should think it was.

At her failure to reply, Ima Jane stated the obvious: "Our little Dulcie is a bit shy, I'm afraid." She then leaned closer to explain sotto voce, "Both her parents are gone. The poor dear's an orphan. Such a tragedy for one so young." She made a show out of noticing their plates and inquired in a louder voice, "Are you two finished here?" When Angie nodded that she was, Ima Jane signaled to one of the waitresses, indicating that the dirty dishes needed to be cleared away. "I hope you left room for some homemade pie," she told Angie. "No one bakes a tastier one than my Griff."

Angie pulled in a quick breath and exhaled it with a shake of her head. "No, thanks. I couldn't eat another bite," she said in utter sincerity.

"Would you like more coffee?" the waitress asked as she stacked their plates on her serving tray.

"I've had plenty, thanks." Angie placed a hand over her cup, then glanced toward the front windows, noting the night-darkened world beyond them. "It's getting late, and I've had a long day. If you could just bring me the check?"

"Don't bother doing that, Liz," Luke cut in. "Just put her dinner on my tab."

"That's generous of you, but if anybody is going to be owed favors around here, it's not going to be you," Angie informed him, then opened her purse and removed her wallet. "I'm paying for both meals, Liz."

With a flick of his fingers, Luke motioned for the waitress to do as she was instructed. "Give the lady the check, Liz. I'm not going to wrestle her over it."

While Liz retrieved the meal tab from her apron pocket, Ima Jane took advantage of the opening provided. "You'll be needing a place to sleep tonight. Griff and I have a—"

"You're out of luck this time, Ima Jane," Luke interrupted. "Miss Sommers brought her bed with her. She has a camper parked outside."

"Yes," Angie confirmed, then asked, "Is it all right if I park overnight in your lot?"

"Of course, it's all right." Ima Jane was quick to agree, relieved that Angie wasn't going to slip entirely away from her. "I only hope it won't be too noisy for you when everyone starts leaving."

"As tired as I am after driving all day, I probably won't hear a thing once my head hits the pillow." With the fatigue of the long trip pulling at her, Angie suspected that statement was more true than she realized. She counted out the money to pay the check, added a gratuity for the waitress and laid it on the table with the check, then looked pointedly at Luke. "Would it be convenient for me to come out to your ranch tomorrow afternoon?"

"Collecting on that favor already, are you?" Amusement tugged at one corner of his mouth.

"Why not?" she countered, with a grin.

"Why not, indeed," he murmured. "How does one o'clock sound?"

"That's fine." She snapped her purse shut. "How do I get there?"

"Ima Jane can give directions in the morning," he said.

To which, the woman quickly agreed. "I'll be happy to do that."

"Thanks." Rising from her chair, Angie slipped the long purse strap over her shoulder and sent a last glance at Luke. "I'll see you tomorrow at one."

"I'll be there." He nodded and watched as she turned and made her way to the door.

With her departure, Luke's table was no longer the center of the room's attention. Ima Jane returned to the bar, and Joe Gibbs drifted off to hustle a game of pool. Still poring over the newspaper clippings, Tobe sat down in the recently vacated chair across from Luke. Dulcie crowded close to his arm and tried to see what was so interesting about the old newspaper stories.

Fargo frowned curiously at Luke. "Why's she coming out to the ranch tomorrow?"

"She says she wants to see where her grandfather's body was found." There was a vague movement of his shoulders that said Luke didn't completely buy into the reason she'd given.

Fargo grunted a response and stared at the door, his thick brows puckering together in a perplexed frown. "It still don't make sense."

"What doesn't?" Tobe glanced up, almost glad of an excuse to quit reading.

"Her granddad coming all the way out here to look for the gold." Fargo flung a hand in the direction Angie had gone.

Unable to follow Fargo's thinking, Tobe asked, "Why wouldn't he come look for it? If I thought I knew where it was, I'd sure be there looking."

Fargo pounced on that answer. "That's it exactly. Why did he think he knew where it was buried? According to her, there wasn't any map pinpointing the location."

"Just because she didn't know about it, that doesn't mean he didn't have one," Tobe reasoned.

"You're probably right on that." Fargo nodded after giving it some thought. "He must have had a map, else he wouldn't have gone around askin' people about mysterious landmarks."

"He didn't need to have a map to do that," Tobe countered. "He could have been asking about places that were described in the letter."

"What letter?" Fargo drew his head back in startled challenge.

"The letter they talk about in this article." Tobe tapped a finger on the glass directly over the newspaper clipping about the outlaw's execution.

"What are you talkin' about?" Fargo demanded. "I don't remember anything about a letter."

"That's not my fault," Tobe retorted a bit testily. "It says right here, 'As a final request, the condemned outlaw asked to be allowed to write a farewell letter to his wife and family. The request was granted.' "—

"That's it." The one-armed cowboy slapped a hand on the table and chortled with glee. "He told 'em in the letter where the money was buried. He didn't draw a map. He wrote one."

Chapter Six

A sharp pound-pound-pounding finally penetrated the layers of sleep. At almost precisely the same instant, Angie had a vague awareness of light against her eyelids. Quick to blame the source of brightness on a vehicle's high beams, she rolled over onto her side and dragged the covers over her head to block the glare.

But no roar of an accelerating engine followed it, no crunch of tires rolling over gravel.

Instead, there came the probing query: "Angie, are you up yet?" The words registered, along with their implication it was morning, but Angie couldn't place the woman's voice. Somewhere a bird sang, its cheery trill providing another indication that day had dawned.

Not wanting to believe it, Angie pulled the covers off her head and opened one eye a crack. All the windows in the camper were closed, but they couldn't hold out the invasion of daylight, only dim its intensity.

It can't be morning yet, she thought with a protesting groan.

A second rap-rap came from the camper door, this time tentative in its lightness. The voice echoed it.

"Miss Sommers?"

With a brief flash of recognition, Angie realized the voice belonged to Ima Jane Evans. Part of her wondered what on earth the woman was doing knocking on her door so early in the morning. As much as she longed to go back to sleep, she couldn't bring herself to ignore the summons.

"Just a minute," she called in a sleep-slurred voice.

Fumbling with the covers, she slid to the edge of the bed, tucked up high in the camper's cab-over section. Careful to avoid the low ceiling, Angie swung her legs out of the bunk and, more or less, lowered her feet onto the cushioned bench, one of a pair that flanked the camper's built-in table. From there, she stepped to the floor and gave the hem of her T-shirt nightie a tug to make sure she was decently covered.

Still groggy with sleep, she pushed the tangle of her curly auburn mane away from her face and half staggered to the door, located at the rear of the camper. She opened it a crack and instantly recoiled from the blast of bright sunlight, throwing up a hand to shield her eyes from its harsh glare.

"Oh, dear, I did wake you, didn't I?" Ima Jane guessed at once. "I'm so sorry."

"That's all right." Angie continued to use her hand as a sun visor, blinking as she peered through finger slits at the woman on the ground. Belatedly she wondered, "What time is it, anyway?"

"A little after nine o'clock."

"Nine?!" Her mouth remained open in shock. By nature, she was an early riser, usually up with the sun. The last time she'd stayed in bed this late had been back in her college days after she'd been up most of the previous night cramming for finals. "I never sleep this late," she finally murmured, a remnant of disbelief in her voice.

"Obviously you were very tired," Ima Jane concluded.

"Obviously." But Angie thought it was more likely a form of letdown after all the tension and excitement of getting here. "What was it you wanted?"

A big smile lit the woman's face. "I came to invite you to have breakfast with us."

Breakfast. She hadn't even had that vital first cup of coffee yet. "That's kind of you."

"Good. Griff said to tell you he'll have it on the table in twenty minutes. The front door's open and the coffee's hot. Just walk right in as soon as you're ready." With a farewell wave, Ima Jane headed back to the bar and grill, leaving Angie staring blankly after her, trying to recall why she had accepted the invitation.

The promise of hot coffee ultimately galvanized Angie into action. Foregoing a shower to conserve the supply of fresh water in the camper's holding tank, she washed the sleep from her face, brushed her teeth, and threw on a pair of jeans and a soft yellow T-shirt. After combing the snarls from her hair, she pulled it back and secured it at the nape of her neck with a yellow scrunchie to match her top. Make-up she kept to a bare minimum, a touch of mascara and a hint of lipstick. In record time, even for her, Angie swung out of the camper and crossed the empty parking lot to the bar and grill.

Silence greeted her when she walked in. After the noise and hubbub of last night's crowd, it seemed unnatural, not a soul in sight. Feeling like an intruder, she hesitated.

"Hello? I'm here," she called.

One of the doors to the kitchen swung open and Ima Jane poked her head out. "There you are. I thought I heard someone," she replied, then said over her shoulder, "Don't worry about keeping anything warm. Angie's here. You can dish up whenever you want." She pushed through the door and headed straight for the bar area. "How about some coffee?" She lifted a coffeepot off its burner plate on the back bar.

"Please." Angie crossed the empty room and quickly claimed the coffee mug Ima Jane set on the bar counter.

The woman's dark eyes twinkled when she saw Angie wrap both hands around the mug. "I see you're like me. I don't function all that well until I've had my first cup."

"Sad but true," Angie admitted, savoring that initial jolt of caffeine.

Ima Jane poured a cup for herself, then motioned toward a nearby table with place settings for three. "Have a seat," she said as she emerged from behind the bar. "We always have our meals down here even though we have a little apartment upstairs. It doesn't seem to matter what Griff is preparing; there's always something he needs from the kitchen down here. Personally, I think he just likes cooking in the big kitchen best."

"We all tend to be creatures of habit," Angie offered, by way of a response, and sat down at the table, more interested in drinking her coffee than making conversation.

To Ima Jane, silence was clearly something to be avoided at all times. "Isn't that true," she agreed and hopped to a different subject. "After we closed last night, I rearranged the pictures and found a place to hang the old newspaper stories about your outlaw ancestor." She motioned toward the wall behind Angie. "It looks good there, don't you think?"

Obligingly Angie glanced over her shoulder to note the location of the framed articles. As she turned back, a man came out of the kitchen deftly balancing a large serving tray.

"It's a perfect location," Angie remarked, then caught the aroma of spicy sausage and a faint whiff of vanilla mixed with cinnamon. Hunger suddenly gnawed at her empty stomach.

"If you're talking about those old newspaper articles, they'd better look good hangin' there 'cause I ain't movin' any more pictures around. Last night was enough," Griff stated in a grumbling voice and lowered the serving tray onto the table next to theirs. "She messed around here for two hours makin' me switch things around, movin' this one here and that one there, then changed it all around again."

His complaints failed to make a dent in Ima Jane's warm smile. If anything they seemed to amuse her. "Don't pay any attention to my husband," she said to Angie. "He isn't happy unless he has something to gripe about."

He responded with a loud harrumph, then nodded curtly to Angie when Ima Jane made the introductions. Before Angie had a chance to acknowledge him, Griff turned away and lifted two individual platters of food off the serving tray. He set one before Angie.

"We're having French toast and sausage this morning." The announcement had the ring of a challenge.

"It's one of my breakfast favorites." Angie unwrapped the silverware and laid the napkin across her lap.

"Then you'll love Griff's version," Ima Jane informed her, as she dipped her knife into the mound of whipped butter on her plate. "He makes his own cinnamon-raisin bread, which is delicious all by itself, but the recipe for the egg dip is one of his most closely guarded secrets. The one for his sausage is probably second. He made it, too. In fact, everything he serves is made from scratch, including the butter."

"You churn your own?" Angie asked in amazement.

"Always," Ima Jane inserted when her husband only nodded. "We have this wonderful Guernsey cow named Molly that gives us the richest milk. Griff used to milk her himself every morning and night, but it got to be too much. Now we have Andy Fry do it. He lives here in town with his folks. Next year he'll be getting his driver's license and he's trying to earn enough money to buy a used pickup."

Angie started to ask if the syrup for the French toast was homemade, but one taste and the flavor of it reminded her of the brown sugar syrup her grandmother used to fix.

For a moment there was silence at the table while they ate their first few bites of breakfast. But it didn't last. To no one's surprise, Ima Jane was the one who ended it.

"The tongues really started wagging after you left last night, Angie," she remarked, fastening bright eyes on her.

"Did they?" Angie murmured, for something to say.

"Did they ever!" the woman declared in exaggerated emphasis. "The place was absolutely buzzing. No one could stop talking about the letter, and speculating about what might have been in it."

The fork with a bite of sausage on its tines froze in midair, halfway to her mouth. "The letter?" Angie tried for ignorance.

"Yes, the letter Ike Wilson wrote to his wife. You know, the one mentioned in the article about the hanging." With her knife, Ima Jane gestured toward the framed newspaper clippings on the wall behind Angie.

"Oh, that one." She breathed a silent sigh of relief. Until that moment, Angie had forgotten there had been any reference to it in the newspaper stories of the day.

"Everyone is dying to know if your family still has it. It's terrible the way people tend to throw old letters away, without a thought of the interest the next generation might have in such correspondence." Ima Jane didn't come right out and ask whether it was still in existence, but the inference was clear.

Nodding, Angie stalled while she tried to decide how much she wanted to tell about it. "History scholars are always bemoaning the loss of old letters and journals that are thrown away by people who don't understand their value as doors to the past."

"I can imagine," Ima Jane murmured in empathy, then waited several beats until it became obvious Angie wasn't going to answer voluntarily. "So, does your family still have the letter Ike Wilson wrote before he was hanged?"

"Fortunately we do." Deliberately Angie stuffed a forkful of food into her mouth, making it impossible to talk and chew at the same time.

"You do!" Losing all interest in the food before her, Ima Jane lowered her fork and focused her attention on Angie with undisguised avidity. "What did it say?"

"The kind of things you would expect a man to write his wife and son when he knows he's about to die," she replied, attempting a shrug of indifference.

Ima Jane wasn't about to be put off by that uninformative answer. "Such as?" She leaned closer, inviting Angie to confide.

She shrugged again and kept her eyes on the plate of food. "How sorry he was. That sort of thing."

Frowning, Ima Jane said with insistence, "Surely he told her about the gold that was stolen?"

"I suppose you could say he did indirectly when he referred to being convicted of robbing a train."

Ima Jane sank back in her chair, crestfallen at the news. "You mean, he didn't tell her where the money was hidden?"

Her wits sharpened after a night's sleep, Angie smoothly dodged a direct answer. "Did you really think he would? Don't you know the authorities were anxious to recover that money? They were bound to read the letter before they sent it on. I'm sure Ike Wilson knew that."

"I hadn't considered that," Ima Jane admitted and sighed in regret. "Everybody's going to be so disappointed, though. They were certain he'd told his wife where the money could be found. After all, your grandfather was convinced he knew where it was when he came here. It seemed logical to believe the letter had indicated where to look. Now . . ." She let the thought trail off, unfinished, her expression turning glum.

Silence reigned for several seconds, broken only by the muted clink and scrape of silverware on plates. Then, Griff picked up the subject with a thought of his own.

"Just because he didn't spell out the location of the stolen loot in so many words, that doesn't mean he didn't leave some clues to its whereabouts," he suggested a bit gruffly. "Something, maybe, that would only mean something to his wife."

"Of course. That has to be the answer," Ima Jane declared, all enthused again. "Why didn't I think of that?"

A grunt of amusement came from Griff. "Knowing you, you would have come up with it sooner or later."

"Probably." The airy agreement was barely out of her mouth before she once again directed her attention at Angie. "You didn't, by any chance, bring that letter with you, did you?"

Never in her whole life had Angie been able to lie convincingly.

Knowing that, she chose her words carefully. "I did bring the family scrapbook with me. I remember my grandma always kept the letter in it."

Both statements were facts that led to a fallacy. The letter wasn't in the scrapbook; Angie had tucked it into a zippered pocket inside her purse.

"I would love to read it," Ima Jane admitted with unabashed candor. "After breakfast, why don't we go through the scrapbook and see if it's there?"

Having anticipated the request, Angie had already decided it would be harmless. "I'll be happy to show it to you," she agreed and stabbed a bite of syrup-drenched bread with her fork. "Don't let me forget, though, to get directions to Luke McCallister's ranch. I promised I'd be there by one o'clock."

"You won't have any trouble finding the Ten Bar. It can't be much more than forty-five minutes from here," Ima Jane told her. "Even if you left a little after twelve, you'd still arrive with time to spare—" The telephone on the back bar rang, interrupting her and startling Angie with its harshness. Ima Jane sighed in mild disgust and arched a knowing glance at her husband. "What do you want to bet that's Joanie Michels calling to say she'll be late?"

"It wouldn't be the first time," Griff replied with marked indifference.

"Isn't that the truth?" Ima Jane agreed, but there was a good-natured smile on her lips when she pushed back from the table and went to answer the phone.

It rang once more, loud and long, assaulting Angie's ears again. Thankfully Ima Jane picked up the receiver before it could ring a third time. After an initial exchange of hellos, she sent a little "I told you so" look at her husband and said into the phone, "Yes, Joanie. What can I do for you?"

Griff didn't acknowledge the glance and made no attempt to keep a conversation going now that his wife was absent from the table. Which left Angie free to concentrate on the rest of her breakfast while Ima Jane chattered away in the background. She was still on the phone when Angie cleaned up the last of her French toast.

Sighing in contentment, she sat back from the table. "That was a fabulous meal, Mr. Evans. I've been in five-star restaurants where the food didn't taste half as good as this."

"Thanks." Despite the compliment, his expression never lost its sour quality.

It pushed Angie to convince him of her sincerity. "I'm serious. If you were in a large city, people would be standing in line to eat here."

His glance ran over the tavern's rustic interior with its planked floor, scarred tables, and mismatched chairs. Something wistful crept into his eyes. "I used to think about movin' to Cheyenne— or maybe Denver—and openin' up a restaurant there. A steak house, maybe, with a limited menu, but everything on it fresh and the best quality—like here."

"I'm surprised you haven't."

"How could I?" The vinegar of defeat was in the look he sent her. "In order to get the money to start somewhere else, I'd have to sell this place—and who'd buy it? No one in his right mind, that's for sure."

As much as she wanted to encourage him, Angie recognized the truth of his statement. She asked instead, "Have you tried to sell it?"

He answered with a slow nod. "I've got a FOR SALE sign I stick outside every now and then. It's gotten plenty of laughs but no buyers. When the real estate agents find out it's in Glory, they don't even want to talk to me. I can't say I blame them either." Rising to his feet, he gathered up their dirty plates and silverware, stacking them atop each other. "Want more coffee?"

After a second's hesitation, she nodded. "I would, thanks."

"Be right back with the pot." He loaded the dishes on the serving tray and headed for the kitchen with it.

Talking about the restaurant had resurrected all of Griff's old feelings, both the sweet yearning and the utter futility of it. He was trapped in this place, as surely as if it were a prison with bars at the windows and shackles around his legs. Resentment boiled up in him, rising like a black and bitter gall in his throat. There was no hope that he'd ever be free of this place. No hope at all, short of winning a lottery.

Or finding that outlaw gold.

The thought brought him up short. For a moment Griff almost laughed at the sheer improbability of it. Then he started wondering. Wondering about things—like the tales of the rock pillar that was supposed to point to it. That girl's grandfather had been so sure he could find the cache of stolen money. And there was that letter Angie Sommers had—the one written by the outlaw Ike Wilson.

Wouldn't it be something if that letter really held clues? He pushed through the swinging doors to the kitchen. And wouldn't it be something if he could find it?

The door whooshed shut behind him, and his face cracked with a smile of silent laughter. He stood for a full minute inside the kitchen, fantasizing over the possibility.

The muffled sound of Ima Jane's voice pierced through his reverie. Two things registered at once: the weight of the dish-laden serving tray in his hands, and his promise to get coffee. Not bothering to unload the tray, he shoved it onto the sink counter. With a kind of eagerness he hadn't felt in years, Griff exited the kitchen to fetch the coffeepot.

As he finished refilling Angie's mug, Ima Jane rejoined them. "We were right," she announced, taking her chair. "Joanie's going to be late."

A harrumph of nonsurprise came from Griff. "What's her excuse this time?" He poured more coffee into his cup.

"The car won't start, and Bud is out with the pickup checking cattle." She took a tentative sip of her coffee, then pulled back, making a face of distaste. "This is cold. Would you get me a fresh cup?"

"Sure." He took the cold coffee from her and headed back to the bar with both the cup and the coffeepot.

Lifting her voice, Ima Jane said to him, "Joanie said she'd be here as soon as Bud got back, but would we please start setting things up."

"Don't we always," he grumbled and dumped the cold coffee in the bar sink.

Ima Jane tasted a bite of the French toast remaining on her plate, but it, too, had grown cold while she was on the phone. With a sigh, she laid her silverware on the plate and pushed it back as Griff returned to the table with her coffee.

"Want me to warm that up in the microwave?" He gestured to her plate.

She hesitated, then shook her head. "No. My hips really don't need the calories." She gathered the cup to her. "I'll just drink my coffee, then give you a hand with the pulpit."

Doubting her hearing, Angie asked, "Did you say 'pulpit'?"

A smile stretched Ima Jane's mouth. "I did, indeed. We hold church services here every Sunday."

"You're kidding," Angie blurted in amazed delight.

"I'm not, I promise," she replied. Then she explained, "You see, nine years ago, heavy snows caved in the roof of the town's only church, collapsing one of the sidewalls in the process. Unfortunately, the loss wasn't covered by insurance and, so far, we haven't been able to raise enough money to build a new one. In the meantime, since the Rimrock is the only place in town big enough to hold everyone, we have church here on Sunday." Pausing, she ran a self-conscious glance over the interior. "I know it isn't exactly an appropriate place of worship—"

"Oh, but it is," Angie insisted. "Back in the days of the Old West, a saloon often doubled as the town church."

"Really? I didn't know that." Ima Jane lowered her cup to stare in surprise.

"It's true. Saloons were invariably the first substantial structures built in a town. I guess," Angie allowed a smile to show, "the first settlers in a town had a greater thirst for whiskey than they did for the Word. And, just like here, saloons were the only places large enough to accommodate a crowd, which made them the logical choice."

"Isn't that something, Griff?" She gave her husband's arm a pat of amazement. "And here I thought our situation was unique."

"I'm afraid not." Always fascinated by the history of the Old West herself, Angie couldn't resist the chance to share interesting tidbits of it. "Most saloon keepers looked at church services as being good for business. Probably because, back in those days, most of the preachers were the hellfire-and-brimstone kind—true Bible-thumpers determined to put the fear of God in their listeners. And after a heavy dose of Godly fear, some listeners felt a desperate need for a drink. Of course, some saloons didn't shut down at all, and people continued to drink and gamble during the sermon. And in some places, the saloon owners insisted that services be held on Saturday because they did more business on Sunday."

"How do you know all that?" Ima Jane marveled.

"I teach American history." Angie smiled. "A long time ago I found out that students pay more attention when you include bits of background trivia along with major historical events," she explained. "It keeps history from seeming so dry and boring, little more than a bunch of dates to be memorized and later forgotten."

"I hadn't thought of it that way. Still," she studied Angie with bright, speculating eyes, "to know so much about saloons and churches seems unusual."

"Probably, but I did my college thesis on the role religion played in settling the West. The Old West has always been a special love of mine. It probably comes from watching all those Western movies with John Wayne and Randolph Scott when I was growing up." That, and all the whispered family stories about her outlaw ancestor.

Ima Jane looked at her askance. "You're too young to remember Randolph Scott."

"In theory, yes." Angie smiled at the comment. "But he was my grandmother's favorite actor. Every time one of his old movies ran on television, we watched it. It didn't matter how many times she might have seen a particular one before; we watched it again." Her expression grew thoughtful. "I think she liked him so much because he reminded her of my grandfather. She showed me a picture once, and there was a definite similarity around the nose and eyes."

Remembering that, especially the half-wistful and half-painful look in her grandmother's eyes, Angie felt again the sadness of her grandmother's passing.

Seeing that sadness in Angie's face, Ima Jane remarked, "You still miss your grandmother, don't you?"

Without a trace of self-consciousness, Angie nodded. "I expect I always will."

"Did she ever remarry?" Ima Jane wondered.

"No. She used to say she was the kind of woman who could love only one man, and that man was my grandfather. 'My blue boy,' she used to call him," Angie recalled.

"Blue boy?" Ima Jane repeated, her curiosity aroused.

"Yes. He had a birthmark the color of lapis right here." Angie touched a spot high on her left temple near the hairline. "A blue nevus is the proper name for it. It's very similar in size to a large mole, only it's blue. The shades can range from light to dark."

"Interesting," Ima Jane murmured.

Griff leaned forward, resting both elbows on the table while he held his cup near his mouth. "Did she ever hear from him while he was here looking for the gold?"

"Only two letters. One he wrote shortly after he arrived in the area when all the enthusiasm and excitement for the search were still fresh. In the second and last one, he talked about giving up and coming home. There was a sense of despair in it, not so much in the words, but between the lines."

"Sounds like you still have those letters, too," Griff surmised.

"Yes." Smiling absently, Angie recalled, "Grandma always

kept them in the drawer of her bed stand. Nearly every night before she went to sleep, she'd take them out and read them. The writing is so faded from all the times she ran her fingers over the lines that you can barely read them now. There are even a couple places where the ink has been blurred by tear stains."

Griff didn't care about all that sentimental nonsense. "Did he mention whether he found any of the places he'd been askin' people 'bout?"

"No. In fact, he only made one reference to his search." She paused to recall the exact wording. Like her grandmother, she had long ago committed the letters to memory. " 'It's all confusing, Hannah. Nothing I've found makes sense.' " Angie pulled her gaze from its sightless stare into space and glanced at her tablemates. "That's what I meant about the note of despair in his last letter."

"Sounds like he was searching in the wrong area," Griff murmured thoughtfully.

"Who knows?" Angie lifted her shoulders in a shrug of ignorance.

"And it isn't likely we'll ever know either." Ima Jane released a heavy sigh and lowered her cup, glancing at her watch. "Heavens, look at the time, Griff. It's already after ten. People will start arriving in another twenty minutes. We'd better get moving." She was on her feet, snatching the cup from his hand and grabbing the water glasses before the last sentence was out of her mouth.

"Would you like some help?" Angie offered, rising to her feet.

A look of gratitude flashed across the woman's face. "Are you sure you wouldn't mind—"

"Mind?!" Angie laughed at the idea. "I'd love it. This will be like stepping back in time."

"Except Reverend Firsten is far from being your old-time Bible-thumper," Ima Jane declared, eyes twinkling. "A more soft-spoken minister you couldn't find anywhere. Isn't that right, Griff?"

He grunted his lack of interest in the subject.

"What would you like me to do first?" Angie asked when Ima Jane started toward the kitchen.

"You can begin by dragging the tables over against the front wall while Griff and I get the pulpit from the back room. A couple of the tables will have to be stacked on top of each other, but we'll give you a hand with those."

"Sounds good." Angie grabbed the edge of an empty table and started pulling it across the floor, smiling at the thought of the look on her mother's face when she'd learn that in Wyoming people attended church in a bar. It would be a severe shock to her Methodist-strict soul. Angie regarded it as an experience not to be missed.

" 'Where sin abounds, grace does much more abound,' " she murmured to herself and laughed softly.

Chapter Seven

Ima Jane was lighting the altar candles when the first congregation members arrived. Only seconds earlier, Angie had set the last folding chair in place, one of a dozen that supplemented the bar chairs, arranged now in orderly rows to serve as pews.

She stood back and studied the transformation of a bar into a place of worship. A long black curtain hung from hooks fastened to the ceiling encircled the long bar, completely hiding it from view. Along the end wall, a cloth of wine-colored velvet embroidered with a gold cross was draped over one of the bar tables that now saw duty as an altar. Above it, there was a portrait of Jesus against a stained glass background. The neon beer lights in the front windows were silent and dark, hidden behind tightly drawn curtains. To the left of the altar, a speaker's podium served as the pulpit, its new use confirmed by the wooden cross tacked on its tall front.

There were few visible reminders identifying the place as a bar. Even the tables lined up along the wall were covered in white sheets. Yet, mixed in with the scent of burning candle wax, Angie detected telltale traces of stale tobacco smoke and spilt beer. She liked the combination.

A quick glance at her watch warned Angie that she had scant ten minutes before the services were scheduled to start. As she took a step toward the door, Ima Jane intercepted her.

"You *are* going to stay for the services, aren't you?" Her expression held the beginnings of dismay.

"I was on my way out to the camper to change." Angie pulled at the front of her yellow T-shirt, drawing attention to her inappropriate attire.

Ima Jane dismissed her concern with an expansive wave of her hand. "Good heavens, you don't need to bother doing that. Church here is pretty much a come-as-you-are thing."

"Maybe, but just the same I think I should change to a blouse."

Before Ima Jane had a chance to pooh-pooh her plan, Angie slipped out the door, crossing paths with Joanie Michels, who was on her way in, the bottom half of a cardboard box clutched in her arms.

Startled, Joanie did a double-take, then stared after Angie while continuing to walk forward, one hand outstretched to catch the door. Not looking where she was going, she walked right into Ima Jane.

"Excuse me." She bounced off, identified the obstacle in her path, and apologized in an embarrassed rush. "I'm sorry, Ima Jane. I didn't see you standing there." Instantly she turned curious eyes after Angie. "That woman—is she the granddaughter Tiffany Banks was telling me about? I forget her name."

"Angie Sommers," Ima Jane supplied it, then studied the ash blonde with a questioning look. "When did you talk to Tiffany?"

"She called me this morning to fill me in on everything we missed last night." Joanie paused in the doorway, watching until Angie strode out of sight, then stepped inside and breathed a frustrated sigh. "That's part of the reason I'm late this morning. That, and the car. I swear if Bud doesn't get that thing fixed or else trade it for something more dependable, I'm going to wring his neck. Now, what's left to—" She looked around in amazement. "You've got everything set up."

"Angie gave us a hand."

"She did?" With a thoughtful look, she glanced toward the curtained windows and the parking lot beyond them. Another sigh slipped from her when she turned back. This one held regret. "Wouldn't you know the one Saturday night we don't come in, that's when all the excitement happens? We had Warren and Peggy over for dinner last night," she explained in an aside. "I wanted us all to meet here and have a night out, but Bud insisted that we eat at our place and play cards afterward. After Tiffany told me what we missed, then the car not starting—believe me, he got an earful this morning."

"Poor Bud," Ima Jane murmured in amused sympathy.

"Poor Bud?" Joanie scoffed in indignation. "Poor me, you mean. You know as well as I do how picky Peggy is about her food. Sometimes I think she is impossible to please. It makes me wonder what they eat at home. I swear, she hates everything. So, tell me—" She paused to pull in a quick breath, but never got any further with her request.

"Do you have the programs, Joanie?" The inquiring voice came from the front row of chairs where an elderly couple sat.

Her head jerked toward the pair, her mouth curving in an automatic and perfunctory smile. "I've got them right here, the programs and copies of the hymns Reverend Firsten picked out for this morning's service." She held up the box, then said in an undertone to Ima Jane, "You might know the Hoopers would be here already." She laid a hand on Ima Jane's shoulder as if to excuse herself and murmured a hasty, "There isn't time now, but after church you need to fill me in on everything that happened last night. You know how Tiffany is. She never gets anything right."

Off she went to deliver a set of the church programs and selected hymns to the Hoopers. Ima Jane turned away, suppressing a sigh of annoyance. Sometimes Joanie Michels irritated her. She was the only woman Ima Jane knew who could outtalk her. Joanie absolutely thrived on dirt and loathed it when it was passed on to her with some detail missing. The woman was a gossip, pure and simple.

As much as Ima Jane wanted to complain to Griff about Joanie Michels, she held her tongue. She knew he would remind her that she was too quick to see the splinter in someone else's eye while ignoring the timber in her own. He didn't understand the difference between a gossip and a purveyor of news about the community and its inhabitants. In her opinion, Ima Jane performed a service of sorts, one that attracted customers to their establishment, which was very good for business. On that point, Griff never argued.

The door opened, admitting more churchgoers. Ima Jane went forward to welcome them, taking on the self-appointed task of meeting and greeting, a role that came naturally to her.

Tobe West was among the last to arrive, pushing his younger sister, Dulcie, ahead of him. Like every other male who had preceded him, he automatically took off his hat the minute he stepped inside, something that wouldn't have crossed his mind to do last night when the place had been a bar. He held it awkwardly in front of him, hating that naked feeling he always got when he was hatless.

"Good morning, Tobe. Dulcie." Ima Jane nodded to both, then smiled at the girl, clad in an ill-fitting jumper dress missing one button. "My, you look nice this morning, Dulcie."

Ducking her head, the girl mumbled a good morning and plucked at the threads that once held the missing button. Her white-blond hair was skinned back from her face to hang in a limp ponytail secured by a garish pair of red glass beads strung with elastic.

"Mornin', Ima Jane." Tobe scanned the rows of parishioners already seated. "I don't see that Angie woman here," he remarked in a hushed voice. Talking softly always seemed mandatory to him when he was inside a church. "I kinda thought she might be here this morning."

"She's coming," Ima Jane assured him. "She wanted to change first."

"You've talked to her this morning?" The sentence had the lilt of a question, but one that anticipated an affirmative answer.

"She had breakfast with us."

He hesitated, then gathered his courage and made a weak attempt to appear indifferently curious. "You didn't happen to find out whether she still has that letter the outlaw wrote?" he asked. Then, succumbing to an attack of nerves, he hastily explained, "Fargo and me, we were talking about it this morning, thinkin' it was likely that her grandfather had it with him. If he did, then we figured somebody either took it or it got buried with him. If it did, then all those years in the ground, it probably rotted away with the rest of him." He stopped, noticing the smug little smile Ima Jane wore.

"She still has it."

"She does?" Tobe was half afraid to believe her as excitement rolled through his stomach.

"She even brought it with her."

He stared at her, big eyed with hope and doubt. "You know that for a fact?" he whispered. "You saw it yourself?"

"No," Ima Jane admitted. "But she said she had it, and I believe her."

Someone arrived, claiming her attention. Tobe stood there, his feet rooted to the floor while he absorbed the incredible news: not only was the letter still in existence, but this Angie person had it with her!

Man, what I wouldn't give to see the letter! The mere thought was almost enough to draw a groan of longing from him.

He'd laid awake half the night thinking about that letter, certain that if he could get his hands on it, he'd find the hiding place for that outlaw gold. Maybe he didn't know the Ten Bar as well as Luke or Fargo, but he'd ridden over it plenty of times.

Last night his fantasies had taken him all over the ranch, finding the gold one time in this place, the next time in a different area. In his mind, he had even played the role of prospective buyer, looking over various properties to locate the ranch of his dreams. He even imagined himself giving orders to ranch hands instead of being the one to take them.

Tobe West, rancher. He liked the ring of that.

Suddenly it didn't seem such a far-off thing. Why, all he had to do—

Dulcie gave his shirtsleeve a tentative tug, interrupting his daydreams. "Can we sit down, Tobe?" she whispered anxiously, worried that any minute people would turn around in their seats and see them standing back there. It would mortify her.

Irritated for no good reason, Tobe nodded curtly and started to shove his hat on, then remembered in time where he was and waved his sister toward a row of empty folding chairs in the rear. She took a step toward them, then looked back to make sure he was coming. Stifling a sigh of impatience, Tobe gripped her shoulder and steered her to the chairs.

Dulcie moved halfway down the row before she sank onto a seat directly behind the rancher Joe Gibbs, confident his bulk would hide her. Papers crackled beneath her. Reddening, she slid off the chair and the papers slid off with her, seesawing through the air before settling to the floor. She scurried to gather them up, then climbed back onto her seat. Head bowed, she worked studiously to smooth away the creases in the program and music sheets, painfully conscious of the exasperation in Tobe's face.

As the hour drew near for the worship service to begin, a hush spread through the small congregation. In the gathering stillness, the click of a turning latch sounded loud. Sunlight flooded through the now-opened door, and heads turned to take note of the latecomer.

Even Dulcie looked, pity welling in her heart for the recipient of all the curious stares. It was the lady from last night, the one called Angie. And she didn't appear to be the least bit bothered by all the attention, smiling an easy apology for her tardiness to the group before she made her way to the nearest chair.

She paused when she saw Tobe's hat on the seat. "Is this taken?" she whispered.

"No." Tobe almost fell all over himself in his haste to remove his hat from the chair. When she sat down next to him, he juggled with his hat, the program, and hymn music to get a hand free and shove it toward her. "I'm Tobe West, Miss Sommers," he whispered, earnest and anxious. "You probably don't remember, but we met last night. I work at the Ten Bar for Luke McCallister."

"I remember." She shook his hand, then leaned forward, flashing a smile at Dulcie and waggling her fingers. "Hi, Dulcie."

Self-conscious yet secretly pleased that Angie had remembered her name, Dulcie responded with a barely audible, "Hi." But the tiniest of smiles edged the corners of her mouth.

From the altar area came the strum of a guitar, sounding the opening chord of the first hymn. The minister's gentle voice sounded almost as musical to Dulcie when he requested, "All rise."

Feet shifted, clothing rustled, papers shuffled, and throats cleared as everyone stood up. Dulcie stared at the unfamiliar words on her sheet. She tried to sing along, albeit very softly, but she didn't know the tune. Something told her nobody else did either.

Beside her Tobe mumbled the words and pretended often to lose his place. But Dulcie noticed that Angie's head was lifted in song. Rarely did she glance at the words on the paper. Her voice, while not particularly strong, had a pleasing sound and seemed to follow some sort of melody. Dulcie decided to copy her. She ended up coming in about half a note behind.

On the "Amen" part, the congregation was of one voice, singing it with relish. Dulcie held her note a little too long, breaking it off abruptly when she realized her voice was the only one still singing. She felt hot all over and blushed when Angie glanced her way with a wink of understanding before bowing her head when the minister began his prayer. Dulcie did the same, then snuck a peek to see if Angie closed her eyes when she prayed. She did, so Dulcie squeezed hers shut, too.

All through the service, Dulcie made furtive checks of the stranger in their midst, the woman everyone was talking about because of the outlaw gold.

Too soon, it seemed, the service was over, and the standing and milling began. This was the part Dulcie hated. She wished they could walk out the door and go home, but Tobe always hung around and talked.

When he stood up, Dulcie rose to her feet with reluctance, resigned to the misery of waiting. "Ma'am?" Reaching out, Tobe caught Angie's arm when she would have walked away, then jerked his hand back and nervously fingered his hat when she turned around. "Uh, Luke said something about you comin' out to the ranch this afternoon."

"That's right. Around one o'clock." She seemed mildly puzzled by the conversation.

"Yeah, well, I was thinking, uh . . ." He looked down at his hat and shifted his weight to the other foot.

"Yes?" Angie peered at him, now curious.

He pulled in a deep breath, hesitated, then met her gaze and hurriedly moistened his dry lips. "Well, Dulcie and me are headed back there now. I thought maybe . . . you'd like to ride along with us?"

"That's very kind of you, but—"

"It's no trouble," Tobe jumped in. "And that camper you're driving—well, the ranch lane is pretty rough. You could bottom out in some of the ruts."

"Oh." The single sound held both understanding and the beginnings of concern.

"That's why I thought it might be better if you rode with us." Then he rushed, "And don't worry about gettin' back. I can easily run you back when you're through at the ranch. Then Dulcie and me can grab a sandwich and save Fargo from having to fix supper."

"If you're sure I'm not putting you out," she began.

"Oh, I'm sure." His grin was big and broad.

She smiled in return. "In that case, I'll accept your offer of a ride."

"Great." Still smiling, Tobe shoved his hat on and gave it a tap. "Dulcie and me are ready to leave whenever you are."

Dulcie couldn't believe her ears. Was Tobe really going to leave right now—without hanging around to talk? She took another look at the lady. Tobe's announcement seemed to catch her unaware as well.

"You mean, right now?" she said, with a surprised jerk of her head, then glanced at her watch. "But Luke isn't expecting me until one."

Tobe shrugged off that concern. "Luke's not gonna mind you being thirty or forty minutes early. He's not doin' anything today anyway."

"In that case," her smile of acceptance was quick and warm, "just give me a minute to stop by the camper and grab a hat, and I'll be ready to go."

"Great!" Excitement thudded in his veins. Scared that she might change her mind between here and there, Tobe said, "We'll walk along with you. My truck's parked near your camper anyway."

Taking her agreement for granted, he motioned for her to precede him, then noticed the jam of people at the door waiting to shake hands with the minister. With no side exit available, they had no choice but to crowd in and hurry people along.

For a moment it looked like his rudeness would be rewarded when the Roushes gave up their place in line. Then Ima Jane waylaid them just as they reached Reverend Firsten, and Tobe almost groaned aloud.

"There you are, Angie. I've been looking for you." Ima Jane reached for Angie's arm, with every intention of drawing her off somewhere.

But Angie quickly clutched her outstretched hand. "It's a good thing you caught me. I would have left without thinking to tell you."

"Left?" Ima Jane repeated, thrown off balance by the statement. "I don't understand. . . ."

"Tobe's giving me a ride out to the Ten Bar. I'll probably see you when I come back." After a kind of farewell squeeze and pat of Ima Jane's hand, she turned to the minister. "It was a lovely service, Reverend."

A smile and a handshake, and she was gliding out the door into the bright sunlight, leaving Tobe standing there dumbfounded. If he hadn't seen it for himself, he would never have believed anybody could extricate herself that smoothly from Ima Jane's clutches. He had already braced himself for a lengthy discussion, going over all the what-fors, whys, and what-ifs of her decision to ride with him.

Ima Jane was the first to recover her speech. "I don't understand. How—"

Realizing he was about to be trapped in that dreaded discussion, Tobe broke in, "She'll explain it all when she gets back." He pushed his sister out the door and tipped his hat to the minister. "Good day, Reverend Firsten. Nice sermon."

Once outside the bar, instead of slowing down and savoring his victory, he lengthened his stride to catch up with Angie. Dulcie trotted at his heels.

Moments later, Angie emerged from the camper, sporting a Yankee baseball cap, her purse slung over a shoulder. She followed Tobe to his pickup and climbed in the passenger side.

Griff was inside the Rimrock, drawing open the curtains at the front window, when he saw her swinging into the cab. He frowned, eyes narrowing to verify her identity. But there was no mistaking the fiery red lights in her dark hair. Not even the baseball cap could hide all of them.

Moving away from the window, he went in search of his wife. As expected, he found her chattering away with Joanie Michels and pulled her aside.

"Was that the Sommers gal I just saw leaving with Tobe West?" he demanded with a scowl.

"Probably. She said he was giving her a ride out to the Ten Bar."

"I thought she wasn't supposed to be there until one."

Ima Jane lifted her shoulders in a high shrug. "Obviously there's been a change in plans."

"I guessed that much myself," he snapped, his temper surfacing in sarcasm.

"Then why did you ask me?"

"Because—" He checked the angry bitterness that came out and tried again: "She said she was going to show us that letter—the one the outlaw wrote—after breakfast and never did it."

"I'm sure she'll let us see it when she gets back."

But Griff couldn't shake the fear that maybe she would change her mind about it. She might have slipped off to avoid that very thing.

"How long will she be out to the Ten Bar? Did she say?" His glance strayed to the front window. Outside a dust cloud hung in the air, raised by vehicles exiting the graveled lot.

"She didn't say," Ima Jane admitted. "But she told Luke that she wanted to see where her grandfather's body was found. How long could that possibly take? An hour or two, at the very most, I would think."

The scowl began to recede with the coming of a new thought. "I wonder if she remembered to lock her camper before she left."

Ima Jane expelled a short, chiding breath of amusement. "Honestly, Griff, you worry about the darnedest things. Even if she forgot to lock it, nobody around here is going to take anything out of it."

"Just the same, when she comes back, you need to warn her she should keep it locked." He walked off and busied himself with the task of closing and stacking all the folding chairs.

Chapter Eight

The wind blowing through the pickup's open windows had an invigorating freshness to it. Turning, Angie let it play over her face. It was nothing at all like the country air back in Iowa. Rather, there was something mysterious and wild about it, sharp with a faint, barely detectable trace of pine, something that echoed the rugged and empty terrain before her eyes.

On either side of the highway, the land flexed its mighty muscles in undulating swells that rolled back to a tangle of canyons, rock-strewn hills, and flat-topped mesas. Beyond it towering mountains thrust jagged snow-capped peaks into the sky.

It was an awesome sight, one she'd had little opportunity to appreciate on her way into Glory. She'd been too busy watching for signs along the highway that would direct her to her destination. Now she was free to gaze about and absorb the impact of it all.

"Ever been to Wyoming before?" Tobe had to practically shout the question to make himself heard above the roar of the motor and tunneling wind.

Angie dragged her glance back inside the cab, and skipped it over the little girl seated between them to look at Tobe. "First time," she admitted. "It's beautiful."

Tobe nodded, then struggled to keep the conversation going, scared that they'd get all the way to the Ten Bar without him finding out anything. "Thought maybe you might have been here before. On vacation, or something."

"What?!" She tapped her ears, indicating she couldn't hear him.

Frustrated by the noise, Tobe impatiently cranked his window up. It cut down some of the roar. "I said I thought you might have come here on vacation."

"Oh." Her head lifted in understanding. "No. It was always in the back of my mind to come someday, but I never got around to it until now."

He searched for a response to that, something that would take the conversation where he wanted it to go. "I thought maybe you had because of your grandfather. Him disappearing out here, I mean."

"My family always thought he'd left this area."

"Oh." He saw the miles sliding away, and his chances with them. Desperate, Tobe threw subtlety out the window. "Do you still have that letter Ike Wilson wrote?"

According to Ima Jane, she did, but Tobe was reluctant to name his source.

"Yes." She pushed back a strand of hair the wind had whipped across her face.

"I'm surprised you still have it."

Tipping her head, she looked at him with wide, curious eyes. "Why would you be surprised?"

"Because." To him it was so obvious, he didn't know exactly how to word it. "I figured your grandfather would have brought it with him when he came to look for the gold." When she said nothing, Tobe felt obligated to explain his reasoning for it. "There have to be clues to the gold's place in that letter. Otherwise, your grandpa wouldn't have been so sure he could find it."

"That's true," she acknowledged. "But you have to understand that, in many ways, my grandfather was a very cautious man. If he had taken the letter with him and it had been accidentally destroyed or lost, then it would have been gone forever."

"I hadn't thought of that." His shoulders slumped.

"Like I said, he was a cautious man."

"What did he do? Memorize it?" Tobe couldn't imagine trusting anything so valuable to memory alone.

He remembered back in school the agony of trying to memorize the Gettysburg Address—and the miserable job he'd done of it. To this day he wasn't sure what came after "Four score and seven years ago our fathers."

Her quick laugh at his suggestion was thankfully free of any ridicule. "No, he didn't memorize it. He copied it off, stroke by stroke and word by word."

That made sense. Tobe was a bit chagrined that he hadn't thought of it. "I guess you've read the letter yourself." He stole a glance at her, encouraged by the openness of her answers.

"Many times."

The ranch gate was another mile up the road. Time was shortening. "Were there clues in it?"

"My grandfather always thought there were."

Tobe wanted to throw his hand in the air in exasperation at her nonanswer. "Did you see them when you read it?"

"I don't know."

"What do you mean, you don't know?" That worried him.

"I mean, there are any number of things in the letter that if you want to believe they're clues you can read them that way. Or, they could be exactly what they appear to be—an attempt to express his thoughts and feelings."

"How can you say that?" Tobe protested in a kind of borderline despair.

There was a lengthy pause before she answered. "I suppose, because the letter is typical of its time in many ways. Back in those days, letters written by someone of education tended to read like prose." She saw Tobe's puzzled look and explained: "For example, if someone was writing a letter today, he might say something as simple as, 'It rained this morning.' Years ago, his ancestor would have been much more descriptive, writing something like, 'Morning brought a blessed shower of rain to drench the parched earth.' And he might have gone on to write, 'No sight matches the beauty of the arcing rainbow that I now view out my window.' "

"It sounds pretty fanciful." And silly, Tobe thought, but he didn't say that out loud.

Her low laugh was soft and warm with understanding. "Back then, such style of writing was normal and expected. And our way would have seemed cold and abrupt."

"If you say so," he said on a sigh. "But I sure would feel funny if I had to write like that." He pushed on the brake pedal, slowing the truck as they approached the ranch turnoff. "You're tellin' me that's the way the outlaw's letter reads?"

"Exactly." A pair of tall creosote posts flanked a metal gate that marked the ranch entrance. A single-lane dirt road curved away from the gate to twist through the rolling terrain. On the gate itself, there was a board sign with the words TEN BAR RANCH lettered in black against a dusty white background.

Tobe pulled off the highway and stopped the truck in front of the closed gate, throwing the gearshift into PARK. He reached for the driver's side door handle. Anticipating his action, Angie was quicker. She had her door open before he could pull the handle.

"I'll get the gate." She hopped to the ground, tossing her purse on the seat.

"You don't—" He broke off the protest, realizing it was too late. Instead, he called, "You'll have to close it again after I pull through."

"Don't worry." There was amusement in the smile she sent to him. "I know all about chasing cows off a highway after a gate has been left open. I was raised on a farm."

At an easy trot, she went around the front of the vehicle to the gate. There was no fumbling with the latch, no weak-muscled straining and tugging to push the gate open. Watching her, Tobe revised his opinion about her. She might look like a town girl, but she had definitely handled that gate with the practiced ease of a country one.

After swinging the gate wide, she waved him through. He pulled the truck ahead, checked the rearview mirror to make sure the pickup had cleared the gate; then waited, with the engine idling, while she closed it. Again Tobe was obliged to give her high marks when she gave the gate a tug, verifying it was securely latched.

She trotted back to the pickup and hauled herself into the cab next to Dulcie, all smiles and only a little bit breathless from the exertion. "All set."

Nodding, he sent the truck forward onto the rough and rutted track. "It was a good thing you double-checked that gate," he told her. "The wind torque off the semis has been known to shake it open if it isn't latched tight."

"It's the same at home." She bent the bill of her cap back, pointing it up. "How long have you worked at the Ten Bar?"

"About three years. Ever since our mom died."

"I'm sorry." Her glance was quick and full of compassion. "What happened?"

Before he knew what he was doing, Tobe found himself pouring out his entire life story, everything from his father's death and his mother's battle with cancer to Luke's offer of a job and place for both he and Dulcie to live, including his dream to have his own ranch.

"It'll take me a while, but I'll have my own place someday." His words had a determined ring as the old confidence in his dream resurfaced. With it came the memory of that outlaw gold, a potential shortcut to the fulfillment of his dream. It prompted Tobe to consider the letter again, and the possible significance of its contents. "Ima Jane mentioned that you brought the outlaw's letter with you."

That information had been relayed over breakfast, Angie recalled. Luke McCallister had warned her that Ima Jane was a gossip, but Angie hadn't guessed the woman would be so quick to broadcast what she had learned—and right before church, too. Not that it mattered if people knew. The letter's existence was far from a secret.

"I brought a photocopy of it," she confirmed. "The original is back home."

"You're cautious like your grandfather, aren't you?" Tobe observed with a quick grin.

"The letter has a historical value, like any other correspondence of its time. It needs to be preserved and kept safe for that reason alone." Angie kept one hand braced against the door's window frame as the pickup bounced over the road's numerous bumps and ruts.

"I hadn't looked at it that way." His forehead puckered in a thoughtful frown. "But I guess you're right. Just about anything old is worth money to someone these days."

In her opinion, its value was historical rather than monetary, but she didn't attempt to explain the difference between the two to Tobe.

"I've been thinkin' about something," he began, then stopped as if suddenly unsure of himself. He was nervous and it showed in the twitching lift of his chin and the uneasy shifting of his weight.

Angie took pity on him and asked, "About what?"

"I've been thinkin'," he began again, carefully avoiding her eyes. "I'll bet if I read that letter I'll recognize whether there are any clues in it."

He sounded so naively positive that Angie had to fight back a smile. But some of it crept into her voice. "Do you think so?"

"I know so." In his eagerness to convince her of the fact, he took his eyes off the road and inadvertently increased the pressure on the accelerator pedal, sending the pickup shooting forward—straight at a deep chuckhole.

Angie saw it and yelled, "Look out!"

Tobe slammed on the brake and wrenched at the steering

wheel. Simultaneously Angie jammed a hand against the cab roof and stretched an arm across Dulcie to keep her from being thrown into the dash. Despite his attempt to swerve around the chuck-hole, one front wheel dropped into it. The hard bounce lifted all three of them off the seat, slamming them sideways.

"Sorry," he mumbled after they all managed to right themselves, then threw a quick, embarrassed glance toward Dulcie and Angie. "Are you okay?"

"I think so," Angie murmured uncertainly and checked with Dulcie, who nodded affirmation. She laughed shakily in relief. "You weren't kidding when you said the road was rough."

"The spring rains really tore it up, and Luke hasn't gotten around to having it bladed yet," Tobe explained while making a point of keeping his attention on the dirt track ahead of them. A sudden smile split his face. "Now, if you want to go for a really wild ride over this, just climb in with Luke when he's been drinking."

"He drinks a lot, doesn't he," Angie remarked, thinking back to last night and the way his glass had never stayed empty for long.

"I didn't mean to give you the wrong idea, Miss Sommers," Tobe rushed, anxious to make sure she didn't think ill of the man who was his idol. "Luke drinks, but he's no drunk."

"Of course not." But she was saddened by the thought that he might be on the road to becoming one, then shook it off as no concern of hers and focused her eyes on the rolling land around them. The distinctive shape of a barn's hip roof jutted into view. "Is that the ranch up ahead?"

"Yup. It's just around that hill."

Angie glanced at the girl seated in the middle. "You've been very quiet, Dulcie. I don't think you've said a single word this whole trip."

In response, she dipped her chin lower and squirmed ever so slightly.

"Dulcie never talks much," Tobe inserted. "She's a little shy."

Angie leaned sideways, at a confiding angle. "Don't tell any-one, but I was, too, when I was your age." Dulcie slanted her a look loaded with skepticism. "It's true. Cross my heart," she in-sisted, making a quick crisscrossing gesture with her fingers. "Es-pecially around people I didn't know. I was always afraid I would say something silly and they'd think I was stupid. So I wouldn't say anything, just listen and try to be invisible."

"You're not shy now." Hidden within the observation was a question that Dulcie wasn't quite bold enough to ask.

"Nope. I'm not," Angie agreed, with a bright twinkle in her eyes. "That's because the more I listened, the more I realized that everybody says something silly sooner or later. Others sometimes laughed, but they didn't think worse of the person. So I decided I might as well open my mouth and laugh, too." She tipped her head closer to whisper, "You need to try it sometime. It's a lot more fun."

To Dulcie's relief, Angie, straightening to sit erect once more and looking around with interest when they pulled into the ranch yard, didn't seem to expect a reply. Tobe drove straight to the trailer and laid on the horn. As the tires crunched to a stop near the steps, he hit it once more, then switched off the engine. The dust plume that had trailed them from the highway now swept forward to encircle the pickup in a billowing tan cloud.

Luke stepped out of the trailer in white-stockinged feet, his hair uncombed, his shirt unbuttoned and hanging loose over his jeans. He glowered at Tobe. "Will you lay off that—" He broke off the ill-tempered growl when he saw Angie climbing out of the passenger side.

"There's no need to get upset with Tobe," Angie said, her voice all warm and breezy. "He was only trying to warn you that he was bringing company."

Dulcie could have told her that Luke wasn't upset. Not really. It was simply that his head always hurt in the mornings, and loud noises made it hurt worse. Luke had explained it all to her a long time ago. He'd said that he didn't want her to think he was mad if he happened to snap at her; it was only the pounding in his head that made him do it.

"I thought you weren't coming until one." Luke's eyes narrowed on her, a vague confusion clouding them, thanks to the dullness in his head.

"It was my idea," Tobe spoke up, as he swung down from the pickup. "As rough as that lane is, I was afraid she might damage her camper, so I suggested she ride with me."

She cocked her head to one side, a suggestion of amusement around the corners of her mouth. "Do you have a problem with my being early?"

He looked at her for a long second. She stood at the base of the steps, her hands casually perched on her hips, the bill of her baseball cap flipped up, and her long hair pulled through the hole at the back of it to hang in fiery dark waves. All sunny and fresh faced, she looked exactly what she claimed to be—a farm girl.

It was an easy step to imagine her sprawled on a bed of hay all kissable and willing. Too easy.

"No, it's no problem," he lied. "Fargo's about to put dinner on the table. You're welcome to join us. Knowing the way he cooks, there's always enough food for two or three more people."

"I'll pass on the dinner, thanks. I'm still full from the huge breakfast Ima Jane fed me." Her glance paused on the cup in his hand. "But I'll drink some coffee if you have it."

"We always have a full pot at the Ten Bar." He pushed the screen door open wider, inviting her inside.

"Something told me you would." She came trotting up the steps.

When he shifted to the side to let her precede him into the trailer, Luke caught the sparkle of amusement in her eyes. The sight of it aroused his suspicions and prompted him to ask, "What do you mean by that?"

There was something teasing in the sidelong look she gave him. "You look like you still need a couple more cups."

"Why?" He frowned, then realized how grouchy he sounded.

"Your eyes." She discreetly pointed to them with the tip of a finger. "They're still a little bloodshot, a sure sign you're still struggling with a hangover."

He stiffened, but the expected denial didn't come. Instead, his mouth stretched in a faintly sheepish grin that was potently attractive. "Guilty as charged, ma'am," he admitted, with a little mock bow.

His response made her laugh and broke the tension that had so briefly begun to flutter in her stomach. She continued past him, sweeping into the mobile home. The trailer's layout was typical, with the living room opening directly into a large kitchen and dining area. Standing by the table, a one-armed Fargo glanced around when she approached.

"Saw you comin'," he said. "I already got a place set for you at the table."

"You can put it away again," Luke spoke from behind her. "The lady only wants coffee."

"Might have known I went to all that trouble for nothin'," he grumbled and scooped up the silverware, dumped it on the plate, and carried them back to the kitchen counter.

"Have a seat." Luke waved her toward a chair.

Angie smiled her thanks, noticing that somewhere between the front door and the kitchen he had managed to tuck his shirt in and button three of the buttons. He was working on a fourth.

"How do you take your coffee?" Fargo asked as he poured some in a cup.

"With sugar," Luke answered for her, then smiled at her slightly startled glance. "I wasn't *that* drunk last night."

"It was early, though, wasn't it?" she jested in fun. But it both pleased and unsettled her that Luke had remembered the way she liked her coffee. Most people didn't notice such details about others.

"The sugar bowl's on the table. Help yourself." Fargo placed the cup in front of her, then sat down in his usual chair, the one closest to the kitchen. He shot an impatient glance at Tobe and Dulcie. "The food's gettin' cold. You'd better hurry up."

The pair took their seats, leaving the chair at the head of the table for Luke. By the time he sat down, he had his shirt buttoned and his hair showed the tracks of a quick finger combing that had smoothed much of its previous sleep-tousled look. Tobe nodded to Dulcie. "It's your turn to give the blessing," he said matter-of-factly.

She darted a self-conscious glance at Angie, then bowed her head and clasped her hands in a prayerful pose. "Dear Lord, bless this food and those who eat it. Amen." Her voice was small and anxious.

"Now, that's what I like," Fargo announced, smiling across the table in approval. "A grace that's quick and to the point."

The tiniest glow of gratitude lit Dulcie's eyes. Luke killed it with a cynically dry, "If we've got that over with, how about passing the roast beef down here?"

Angie had a good mind to hit him. Instead she tried to undo the damage his thoughtlessness had done. "Fargo was right, Dulcie. That was very well done. Simple prayers are often the best kind."

Mollified a bit by Angie's warm praise, Dulcie managed a faint smile. Then the business of passing food dishes and filling plates occupied her attention, and that of everyone seated at the table except Angie.

For a time, the conversation was centered around it, with requests for butter, salt and pepper, or gravy. Once they actually settled to the task of eating, the talk quickly turned to the subject of the lost outlaw gold, with Tobe volunteering the information that Angie had brought with her a copy of the letter Ike Wilson had written. Fargo was quick with his questions about it, asking many of the same ones that Tobe had. Tobe supplied most of the answers, repeating what Angie had told him. Luke listened, but he didn't show much interest in the discussion except for an occasional wry smile.

It was Tobe who finally dragged him into the conversation. "If you saw that letter, Luke, don't you think you'd recognize if it had clues to the hiding place?"

"Why ask *him?*" Fargo took umbrage with that. "I was on the Ten Bar long before he was even a gleam in his father's eye."

"I know that, but—" Tobe looked to Luke for help.

It came, but not in the form he expected. "Letters. Clues," Luke mocked in sardonic humor. "You both talk as if the gold's still there."

Startled, Tobe lowered his forkful of green beans. "It has to be."

"Why?" Luke fired the question, amusement glinting in his eyes.

"Because . . ." Suddenly uncertain, Tobe glanced first at Angie, then at Fargo before finally turning a worried look on Luke. "Nobody's found it."

"And how do you know that?" Luke countered.

This time Angie spoke up, confident and calm. "I think it's safe to say that if it had been found, we would have heard about it long before now."

He made a sound in his throat, one coated with suppressed laughter. "You're assuming an honest person found it."

"What do you mean?" she asked even as her mind raced to consider this new possibility.

"There's only one way the discovery of the gold would have become common knowledge: the person who found it also turned it in to collect the reward."

"And only an honest person would do that," she said, following his logic.

"Why settle for just the reward when you could keep the whole thing with no one the wiser?" Luke reasoned. "And if you kept it, you certainly wouldn't broadcast the fact that you'd found it. More likely, you'd take off and live the high life somewhere far from here."

"And you think that's what happened," Tobe concluded glumly.

Luke nodded. "Probably within months or even days after the outlaws were caught. You can bet there were plenty of people scouring their back trail looking for it when the gold wasn't found with them."

A heavy sigh spilled from Fargo. "I guess it would have been easy enough for someone skilled at readin' signs to backtrack them and find the spot where they buried it."

"No," Angie stated without hesitation. "There were heavy rains in the area when Ike was captured. It would have washed away their tracks."

The certainty in her voice brought looks of surprise and doubt. "Was that in the letter?" Fargo frowned.

"No. One of the newspapers mentioned it in conjunction with an article about the damage done by the rains. A road or a bridge or something like that was washed out. I don't remember exactly now."

Unimpressed, Luke stated, "Just the same, the gold was probably found years ago." To back up his belief, he added, "Most experts will tell you that the majority of these so-called lost or buried treasures in the West were actually found within the same era. Only their legends lived on."

A long silence followed his statement, one weighted with thought. Then Fargo conceded grimly, "You might be right, Luke. That gold might be long gone. But there's only one way we'll ever know for sure, and that's to find where it was hidden and see if it's still there."

Angie sipped her coffee and said nothing. There really wasn't anything to say. Fargo had said it all.

Chapter Nine

Luke pulled on his hat and followed Angie out the door into the bright sunlight. Catching the screen door, he eased it shut then turned to find Angie waiting for him.

"I meant to ask," he said, "can you ride?"

"You mean . . . horses? Yes." She cocked her head. "Why?"

He looked off to the west. "It's about two miles to the spot where your grandfather's remains were found. If we take the pickup, we can get close, but we'll have to walk the last hundred yards or so. Or, I can saddle up a couple horses and we can ride straight to it."

"Let's ride then." She didn't have to think about her decision. "I'd like to get the feel of this country from horseback."

"That can be done."

As they went down the steps with Angie in the lead, her glance was drawn to the fire-blackened ruins that she had seen when she first entered the ranch yard with Tobe. "Is that where the ranch house once stood?"

"Yep." He never so much as glanced in the direction of the charred rubble.

Unconsciously she slowed her steps, knowing that fire often destroyed more than wood walls and furnishings. It consumed family mementos, irreplaceable photographs, and items of purely sentimental value.

"Were you able to save anything?" Angie wondered.

"By the time I arrived, it was in full flame." He was ahead of her now, on a course to the barn and adjacent corral.

Tarrying a little, she noticed the tall weeds growing right up to the edges of the gray-black square where the house had stood. Their presence indicated the fire hadn't been a recent one.

"When was the fire? This past winter?" she guessed.

"Four years ago."

"What?" Angie came to a complete stop. "If it's been that long, why haven't you cleaned the mess up?"

He swung back to face her. "I don't think that's any of your business." He said it with an easy smile, but there was an underlying determination that made it clear he didn't intend to discuss his reasons with her.

She started to argue the point, then clamped her mouth shut and smiled ruefully. "Sorry. I didn't mean to meddle in your affairs. It just . . . came out."

His wide shoulders lifted, indicating he took no offense. "It happens, especially if you spend much time around Ima Jane."

"Maybe." But Angie suspected her curiosity was a bit more personal. She came abreast of him and together they walked toward the massive barn. "All the same, Ima Jane seems like a good-hearted woman."

"A good-hearted woman with a very long nose," he added dryly.

She smiled in spite of herself. "I wouldn't say that."

"You haven't known her as long as I have," Luke countered, then gestured to her purse. "Were you planning on taking that along with you?"

Angie touched the shoulder strap as if suddenly realizing it was there. "I'm so used to carrying it, I guess I forgot I had it. Is there someplace I can stash it in the barn?"

"There's a cupboard in the tack room. You can leave it there," he suggested.

"That will work fine."

From the trailer's kitchen window, Fargo watched the pair making their way toward the barn, their faces turned in conversation, giving him a view of their profiles. One-handed, he held another plate under the water gushing from the sink faucet, rinsing it off before setting it aside to be loaded in the dishwasher.

The whole time he replayed in his mind the discussion at the dinner table regarding the hidden cache of stolen money and the outlaw's letter. Yet, no matter how many times he mulled over the long list of unknowns, he always came to the same conclusion: that letter was bound to hold answers for most of them.

"I sure would like to get my hands on that letter," Fargo gave voice to the wish without realizing it.

"Me, too," Tobe chimed in as he tore off a long strip of cellophane wrap and stretched it over the bowl of leftover potatoes. "Regardless of what she said about it maybe not meanin' anything, I still think there's something in that letter that will lead you right to the gold." He cleared a section of shelf in the refrigerator and pushed the bowl onto it. "You think that way the same as me, don't you?"

"It's got to be that way." Fargo stepped to one side, giving Dulcie room to empty the water glasses from the table into the sink. "Nothin' anybody could say will convince me that her granddad came all the way out here on a possible-maybe."

"Yeah, but he didn't find it." Bending, Tobe took a plastic storage container from a lower cupboard shelf and set it on the kitchen counter next to the serving bowl with a portion of green beans in it.

"How do we know that?" Fargo challenged, inwardly studying over it.

"How do we know?" Tobe's eyes widened in an incredulous stare. "The man's dead."

"Yup, he's dead," Fargo agreed, sliding the last dirty plate under the faucet. "But not of natural causes, I'd wager."

"Are you saying he was killed?" Tobe forgot all about putting the beans away and walked blindly to the sink, bumping into Dulcie on her way back from the table with another pair of glasses.

"That's exactly what I'm sayin'." Through the window, he saw Luke swinging a saddle onto the back of a flea-bitten gray gelding, a calm and quiet mount, not known for being excitable or contrary.

"But," Tobe began in a dazed voice, "if somebody killed him to get the gold, then—"

"The gold or the letter," Fargo inserted, as he turned off the tap, shutting off the flow of water from the faucet. "It could have been either one."

"What difference does it make?" He stared at Fargo with eyes bereft of hope. "The letter would have led him to the gold. Either way it's gone."

"Maybe. Then again, maybe not. It might still be there, waiting to be found," he reasoned, then sighed heavily. "It's the not knowin' for sure that gnaws at you. On one hand, a man would be a champion fool to look for something that isn't there. But on the other, what if it is, and he just sits on his duff? It strikes me that fella is dumber than the first."

"Yeah," Tobe murmured absently, mulling over the problem.

"Which brings us right back where we were," Fargo stated. "There's only one answer to this."

Tobe came to the same conclusion. "The letter."

"Yup." There was the scrape of plate against plate as Fargo took the top one off the stack and set it in the dishwasher.

"I wish I could see it. Read it." The longing was like an ache inside Tobe. Frustration knotted his hands into fists. "If there are any places on the Ten Bar described in it, I know I'd recognize them. I hinted as much to her on the way here."

Fargo turned with a jerk, his sharpened gaze pinning Tobe. "What did she say?"

His shoulders hunched in a shrug. "Nothin'. Somehow or other, the subject got changed and I didn't have a chance to bring it up again."

"Figures," he snorted in disgust. "My guess is she changed the subject deliberately. You could probably talk 'til your hair turns blue and she wouldn't show it to you."

"You're probably right," Tobe agreed reluctantly. Then he mused to himself, "I wonder where she keeps it."

The same thought had crossed Fargo's mind more than once since he'd learned of the letter's existence.

Outside, Luke snubbed the bay tight, pulling its nose back toward the saddle before he stepped aboard. As always, the stockinged bay put up a token fight, crow hopping a dozen feet across the yard before flattening the hump in its back and dropping into a trot.

"Fargo"—Dulcie paused in the act of carefully turning the water glasses upside down in the top rack of the dishwasher—"if you found that gold, would you be rich?"

"Whoo-eee," he barked the laugh. "I hope to shout I'd be rich."

She tipped her head back, her eyes all round and serious. "What would you buy with it?"

"Buy?" He hadn't given that much thought. "I don't know. I guess I'd get me a new pickup—I've never had me a brand-spanking new one—then probably some nice clothes." He looked down at the stub of his left arm, then unconsciously massaged the atrophied muscles leading to it. "I might even look into getting one of those mechanical limbs. Not like the one I got, but one that looks like a real arm and hand."

"Would there be enough to buy a house?" she wondered.

"Sure, with money left over."

But the possessions that could be acquired meant little to him. He had never cared about such things. He hungered for something else entirely. Security.

He had already passed the sixty-year mark. Every time that fact slipped his mind, the ache in his bones reminded him of it. Arthritis, the doctors said. Sometimes he was so stoved up with it he could hardly get out of a chair. With only one arm, he didn't know how many useful years he had left.

He'd cowboyed his whole life and didn't have a dollar in the bank to show for it. He had no home and no family, save for Luke. And he couldn't know for sure how much longer Luke would keep him on. The pittance he'd get from Social Security wouldn't amount to enough to support himself. The thought of being stuck in some nursing home, a government charity case, galled his pride.

Old, broke, and crippled, he stood smack-dab on the doorstep of his so-called golden years, and it scared the hell out of him.

But if he could find that outlaw gold. . . . Need gripped his heart and squeezed hard.

That letter. If only he could get a look at that letter.

The barn and corrals were left behind as Angie rode alongside Luke, their horses traveling at a slow rocking canter. Overhead a puffy white cloud drifted across a high blue sky, and the sun was a big, yellow blaze of light right in the middle of it.

Away from all evidence of civilization, she was again struck by the wildness of this country, a wildness that excited the imagination of a girl raised on Hollywood Westerns. Massive boulders and the occasional tree-studded land that climbed and dipped and tumbled and curled. There were no stunning vistas, no majestic peaks to awe her, just rough, rugged terrain, the kind that laughed at a plow. The urge was there to explore it, to ride and ride and ride until she reached the barrier of those distant peaks. An impossible wish, but one to savor all the same.

Luke reined his horse down to a fast walk and turned it onto a narrow cow path that circled below a tall outcropping of rocks. Angie swung the gray behind him and listened to the companionable creak of saddle leather and the intermittent click of horseshoe striking stone, sounds that seemed to suit the landscape.

The cow trail angled across the side of a hill, making a gradual and leisurely descent to the bottom of it. There it disappeared in a grassy fold of the hills that gradually widened into a kind of valley. A slender creek wound through it, its course marked by a stand of cottonwood trees.

"The body was found over there." Luke pointed across the creek to a steep hill. Near the base of it a huge chunk had been gouged from its side, exposing bare earth.

The sight sobered her. It was like looking at an opened grave. "I see it," she said quietly.

Cutting across the valley's narrow floor, they splashed through the stream and rode directly to the spot. When they reached it, Angie immediately dismounted. Holding on to one rein, she walked to the edge of the grave site. Luke came up and silently took the gray's rein from her, then led both horses to a section of grass and left them there to graze.

Her gaze traveled over the length of exposed ground, absently noting the new shoots that had sprung up, evidence that nature had already begun its work to cover the scar. She couldn't have explained why, but she crouched down and scooped up a handful of dirt. It was dry and crumbly between her fingers, without the loamy texture of Iowa's rich soil. She let it slide from her hand, then brushed off the grains that clung to her skin as she straightened to stand erect.

Somewhere a bird sang. Its song wasn't one Angie recognized, but its music was sweet and clear. Surrounded by stillness, she became acutely aware of the horses' loud chomping, the jingle of bridle chains, and the soft rustle of a breeze through the grass stems.

Turning, she located Luke standing a few feet away. With his cowboy hat pulled low, his face was in shadow. But she sensed he was watching her.

"It's very peaceful here," she remarked.

"Yes." He wandered closer, seeming to recognize her need to talk now.

She looked back at the spot that had been her grandfather's grave site for so many years. "I never knew him. But my grandmother talked about him so much that it feels like I did. I guess she made him come alive in my mind. At the same time, I suppose talking about him kept him alive for her."

"Probably."

"She said he was a good man, solid and dependable," Angie recalled, "someone you would want at your side if you were in trouble."

His sideways glance was dry and skeptical. "That seems a strange thing for her to say, considering the way he left her to come out here and chase a dream."

"It looks that way now," she admitted. "But you have to remember that back then, this country was in the middle of the Great Depression. He had no home, no money, no work—and a baby on the way. It was sheer desperation that prompted him to look for that gold."

"And you, of course, are here strictly out of a sense of family duty." His mouth twisted in a smile, droll with mocking doubt.

"I—" Angie began, then broke it off when a rock clicked and clattered, the striking bounce of it sharp in the afternoon's stillness. She glanced around in time to see a dark-clad figure in a floppy hat scuttling out of sight behind a boulder on the opposite hill. She saw Luke was staring in the same direction. "Who was that?"

"Your rival," Luke replied, amusement glinting in his blue-gray eyes.

"Rival? What do you mean?" she said, in genuine confusion.

He held her gaze. "You're here to look for the gold, aren't you?" It wasn't so much a question as a challenge.

"I—" Angie faltered, then tried again, hedging, "I never said that."

"No, you didn't say it. I did. But it's true, isn't it?"

She searched his face, but his expression indicated he was amused rather than contemptuous. She pulled in a long breath and expelled it in a rush, nodding. "It's not the only reason, but it is the main reason."

"I thought so."

"I know you think it's silly." Angie wasn't sure why his opinion mattered to her, but it did. "But you have to understand, I've dreamed about looking for the treasure ever since I was a kid in pigtails. Later, when I was older, I did some research; verified facts; and, basically, only toyed with the idea of looking. It was never really a goal until . . ."

"Until you were notified about the body being found," Luke guessed, still vaguely amused and aloof.

"Yes." The admission brought the return of a previous question. "What did you mean about that man in the rocks being a rival?"

Luke shifted his attention to the granite outcropping across the way. "That man was Amos Aloysius Smith, better known around here as Saddlebags Smith." He wasn't sure, but he thought he could see the rounded crown of a hat peeking from behind a boulder. "He's spent the better part of the last sixty years looking for that gold. He hasn't found it yet."

"Really." She studied the same area before turning curious eyes on Luke. "Where does he live?"

"Wherever his search takes him."

"But what about in the winter?" Angie protested. "Surely he doesn't camp out then."

"No. He usually disappears sometime in late fall and shows up again come spring. It's rumored that he goes to the homeless shelters in Cheyenne or Laramie."

Her brow furrowing, she redirected her glance to the empty grave. "You said Mr. Smith has been in the area for over sixty years?"

"About that. Why?" He cocked his head, studying the clean, sculpted lines of her profile.

"Don't you think it's strange that not a single remnant of clothing was recovered with my grandfather's body? Not a button from his shirt or a rivet from his jeans. Nothing. Not even a moldy leather wallet. Just the class ring and his false teeth." She treated him to a direct look, her eyes strong and clear. "According to my grandmother, when he left, he took three changes of clothes—two work shirts and one white one, two pair of jeans and khaki work pants, underwear, and a heavy wool jacket—his shaving kit, toothbrush, and mirror; a Swiss Army knife and a gold pocket watch and fob that had belonged to his father; and his wallet with two dollars in it. And, of course, the class ring, which served as his wedding band when they married because he couldn't afford to buy two." She paused, glancing again at the dry and crumbly dirt. "It isn't so odd that his extra clothes and shaving things weren't found with him. But what about his watch and knife and wallet? What about the clothes he was wearing?" Her expression darkened with a kind of anger. "It's as if he was robbed and stripped, his body dumped and covered with dirt. You'll certainly never convince me he was running around stark naked, keeled over and died, and a bunch of dirt conveniently slid down to cover him."

Luke didn't argue. "I think it's likely that his death was the result of foul play." It was an easy leap from that to the reason behind her previous question. "You're wondering if Saddlebags had something to do with it."

"You said he's been here for better than sixty years, trying to find the gold. Isn't it possible that he might have killed my grandfather to get his hands on the copy of the letter he had? Why else would he persist so long in his search?" she reasoned.

"I admit it all sounds very logical. But somewhere in the back of my mind, I seem to recall that Saddlebags didn't show up around here until after your grandfather's time. I wouldn't swear to that. You might ask Ima Jane when you get back. She'd probably know."

"I'll do that." There was a determined set to her features.

Luke found himself grudgingly admiring her for it. "You do

realize that even if Saddlebags is responsible, it's doubtful you'd ever be able to prove it after all this time—unless you can persuade him to confess."

"You're probably right. Even if he still had some of my grandfather's things in his possession, he could say he'd found them somewhere. Who knows?" Angie shrugged. "Maybe he did. Maybe my grandfather hid the letter somewhere in his things and the killer couldn't find it."

"It's hard to say," Luke agreed.

"Last night you mentioned that it wasn't far from here to the place where Ike Wilson was captured."

"A couple miles, give or take," he replied. "Do you want to ride over and see it?"

"I would, thanks." She started toward the grazing horses. "Maybe we can talk some business on the way there."

A knowing smile pulled at the corners of his mouth. *Here it comes,* he thought and gathered up the bay's trailing reins.

Chapter Ten

L uke held the gray's bridle while Angie mounted, then made the expected response. "What kind of business is that?"

There was a richly humorous quality to the low laugh that greeted his question. The gleam of it stayed in her eyes as she collected the reins and lightly chided, "As if you hadn't already guessed."

Reins in hand, he gripped the saddlehorn, smiling crookedly. "But I'm hoping I'm wrong." He stepped aboard the bay and reined it around, pointing its nose in a southwesterly direction. "It's over this way."

He led out, spurring his horse up the steep part of the hill. Angie followed on the gray. The lunging climb made conversation too difficult. She waited until they had crested the hill before she attempted to resume the subject.

"You're not wrong," she began.

"I was afraid of that." The arid tone was intended to put her off, but Angie wouldn't be defeated so easily, not after she'd come this far.

"Look, I know you don't believe the gold's still there—"

"But you want me to help you look for it anyway," he inserted, his side glance dry and taunting. "What were you thinking about paying me for this help? Were you going to suggest going *half-sies?*" The use of the childish term was deliberate, a reflection of his attitude toward the entire matter.

Determined to convince him otherwise, Angie continued, "I know you think it would be a total waste of time, and you could be right—"

"I am."

She ignored that. "Believe it or not, normally I'm quite practical and sensible. I'm honestly not the type who takes off at the drop of a hat to go chasing after mythical pots of gold. Like you, I'd probably shake my head in pity for the person who did. But this is different."

"Naturally." His rejoinder was loaded with dry mockery.

Instead of getting angry or upset with him, Angie laughed. "I asked for that, didn't I?" she said, purely rhetorically.

This wasn't the reaction Luke had expected. A quick glance detected no hint that she was either offended or frustrated. Judging from the gleam in her eyes, her enthusiasm for the project hadn't been the least bit affected by his remarks.

"Let me explain what I meant by different," she went on. "Like you, I'm not convinced the gold is still there. If it is, great. If it's not, that's okay, too." She paused a beat. "This probably doesn't make sense, but . . . it's the looking for it that's important to me. Not the finding of it. Whatever the outcome, I just know I need to look."

"No one's stopping you," Luke replied, his gaze fixed on the pasture gate ahead of them. "You certainly have my permission to follow after Saddlebags and search to your heart's content."

"Thank you. Your permission is appreciated, but it's your knowledge of this land that I really need. I haven't seen very much of it, but in what I have seen, twice I've noticed rock formations that, with a little stretch of the imagination, could be described as pillars."

The remark caught his attention. "Then, rumor was right—the letter mentions a pillar."

Angie nodded. "Among other things. But the pillar alone wouldn't be significant unless its location happens to be in proximity to . . . those other things," she concluded, deliberately vague.

"I see," Luke murmured, intrigued against his better judgment.

"I am prepared to pay you for your time, whether we find the gold or not," she told him. "I don't have a lot of money, but I have saved some."

They reached the pasture gate. Without dismounting, Luke maneuvered the bay horse in position to unhook it, then swung it wide to let Angie ride through, then reversed the procedure to close it.

When they were once again on their way to the canyon mouth, Luke asked, "Why me? Why not Tobe or Fargo—or any number of other people I could name who are familiar with the area? They would undoubtedly jump at the chance."

"That's the problem," she replied easily.

Luke frowned, not following her line of reasoning. "What's the problem?"

"I don't know about the other people you could name, but Tobe and Fargo both, at least, *want* to believe the gold's still there, if they don't actually believe it already."

"And that's bad, I take it," he guessed, amused by the twisted logic of that.

A wide smile showed him the even line of her white teeth. "It isn't that it's bad; it's just not good. Or to be more specific, it isn't what I need."

"Why not?"

"Because, in their eagerness to believe, they can become blinded, see only what they want to see. I want someone who will look at the letter and all the information I've gathered with a critical eye. Someone who will tear things apart and poke holes in my theories. In short, I need someone to play the role of devil's advocate." Her sideways glance was warm and teasing. "And I have the feeling you would be a natural at it."

Her glance barely registered with him. He was too busy digesting the news that she was willing to show him the letter—and whatever other information it was that she had.

"What makes you think I can be trusted?" Luke countered. "How can you be sure I won't use that information to find the gold myself and cut you out of it completely? After all, it's finders keepers."

"You could do that." Her gaze briefly made a scrutinizing study of him, but the curve of her lips showed an utter unconcern. "But I don't think you will."

"Why not?"

"Because something tells me you can be trusted."

Luke all but laughed aloud at that. "You'd be putting a lot of faith in someone you don't know at all."

"I know more about you than you might think."

"I suppose Ima Jane was the source of all this knowledge of yours." That thought didn't sit well.

"From the standpoint that she said almost nothing at all about you, you could call her a source."

His eyes narrowed in question. "How does that make her a source?"

"Because it's a kind of endorsement by omission. If you had a whole long list of faults, she would have raced to tell me."

"And you're basing your opinion on that?" Luke countered in amused derision.

"Not hardly. Ima Jane was only one factor."

"And what were the others?" he asked, interested to discover how her mind worked.

"My own observations about you." The gray gelding snorted and swung its nose at a deerfly perched on its left wither.

"And what were they?" Luke wondered.

"You mean, other than your hangover this morning?" The teasing light was back in her eyes.

But her comment touched a sore spot, hardening the muscles in his jawline. "You definitely have a way of avoiding questions you don't want to answer. I noticed that about you last night."

"I don't mind answering them. Some things are just difficult to explain. Take Fargo and Tobe, for instance."

"What about them?" He had the uneasy feeling he shouldn't have asked that.

"How many ranchers do you know who have a one-armed old man and a wannabe cowboy on their payroll?"

"Fargo came to work at the Ten Bar years before my father took over the ranch. Even with only one arm, he could ride and rope as well as your average cowhand in his day," Luke retorted, stiff in the old man's defense.

"But his day has passed, and he's still with you," Angie pointed out.

"So? He cooks and cleans instead of cowboying now. As for Tobe, after his mother died, he needed a job and a place for him and his sister to live. No one was standing in line to offer him either. There were two bedrooms in the trailer going unused. Tobe's a hard worker and eager to learn. And before you go thinking that's generous and noble, the cattle market's down, and both Tobe and Fargo work cheap."

"I'm sure they do." Angie smiled and focused on the country before them. "Is it much farther to the canyon?"

"It's just over that rise." He touched a spur to the bay, lifting it into a canter.

Following him, Angie urged her mount into a lope. When they topped the hillock, Luke reined in. The restive bay sidestepped and chomped on the bit, eager to stretch its legs some more.

"This is where I was always told the posse caught up with them." He nodded toward a tangle of brush and fallen boulders that flanked the canyon's entrance. "The way I heard the story, the posse had lost the trail and was doubling back to pick it up. When they came over this rise, there were the outlaws riding straight toward them."

"One of the outlaws opened fire first," Angie said, remembering the accounts she had read about the gun battle. "That's when the shooting started."

"Supposedly the three robbers tried to reach the cover of those rocks." He pointed to the boulders that were the farthest from them.

In her mind, Angie could picture the scene: The posse charging down the hill, guns blazing; the outlaws spurring their weary mounts and firing desperate shots at their pursuers; the thunder of pounding hooves; the reverberations of gunfire; the acrid smell of powder smoke.

A horse stumbling and falling, pitching its rider; an outlaw pulling up to give cover to his downed compatriot, who was frantically scrambling to reach him; under the posse's withering fusillade, the outlaw giving cover being shot from the saddle; the downed compatriot grabbing the horse's reins and trying to mount, but before swinging into the saddle being riddled with bullets.

Ike Wilson the only one making it to the rocks, and upon seeing the fate of his friends, stepping from behind the boulders with his hands raised in surrender.

The quick and violent gun battle with the train robbers lasting scarcely minutes.

"Do you want to ride down there?" Luke's question brought her back to the present.

After a second's pause, Angie shook her head. "There's no need." Even as she spoke, she was busy studying the terrain, trying to implant the image of its layout in her mind. Then, another idea occurred to her. "If I showed you a detailed map of this area, could you pinpoint this location on it?"

"Probably." His glance ran over her face, but he didn't ask the expected question. He chose another instead: "Is there anything else you'd like to see?"

Her smile was quick and full of humor. "A lot, actually, but that can wait for another time." Neck-reining the gray, she turned it from the canyon. "We can head back to the ranch now."

"Whatever you say." Luke swung the bay in a half circle and pointed it toward home. Both horses broke into an easy trot. For several yards neither rider spoke. Then Angie could take the wondering no longer. "What about my offer?"

"I'm not interested."

She was frustrated by the absolute indifference in his voice and expression, but she refused to give up. "Why?"

"Summers are short in Wyoming. There's a lot of work that needs to get done while the weather's good. I don't have time to waste it gallivanting around looking for buried treasure."

"If the situation were reversed, I might feel the same way you do," Angie conceded. "But I'd like you to give my offer a little more thought before you make a final decision. After all, what have you got to lose? I've already said I'll pay you for your time. And if, by some wild chance, we happen to find the gold, there'll be a sizeable bonus for you." She checked to see his reaction, but his features revealed little of what he was thinking. "Personally I've never known a farmer yet who couldn't use some extra cash. I can't imagine it's any different for a rancher."

The corners of his mouth lifted in a lazy curve. "Like I said before, a lot of people around here would snap at that kind of deal. But I'm not interested in dream chasing."

It was said with the conviction of a man who had given up on such things. Angie stole a quick glance at him, wondering what had caused him to stop hoping. Then she corrected herself—something told her he hadn't stopped hoping; he had turned his back on it.

Why? she wondered. The urge was there to ask and probe. Wisely she recognized that he wouldn't welcome her meddling in his personal life. In fact, it was probably the quickest way to guarantee she'd never get any help from him.

Yet his comment demanded a response. "Look at my offer this way," Angie suggested. "It will give you the perfect chance to say 'I told you so.' "

He laughed, a low and throaty sound accompanied by humor

lines fanning from the corners of his eyes. "It would do that, wouldn't it?"

"There's only one way to find out," she told him and let the subtle challenge be the last word as she kicked the gray horse into a lope.

No longer winded from his scramble over the rocks, Saddlebags knew it was time to move. He had a hefty hike ahead of him to reach his camp. But he stayed where he was, surrendering to the weariness of his tired, aching body.

He'd sit here a little while longer, he decided, letting his head loll back to rest against the boulder supporting his back. He was in full sun, his dark clothing absorbing the heat of its rays. The warmth felt good. His circulation wasn't what it used to be, and the temperature didn't have to fall much anymore for him to get chilled.

He closed his eyes and basked in the sun. His body was still, but his mind wasn't. As always, he puzzled over the impulses that kept pushing him back to the site where the skeleton was uncovered. Even during those first few days after it was found, when the place was crawling with people digging and sifting through the dirt, he had crept back to watch, wasting valuable time that could have been better spent in his search.

Again he found himself wondering whether they'd been able to identify the remains. Was that what kept gnawing at him? Had he gotten a glimpse into his own future?

It was certain that one of these days, this ancient body of his was going to give out. The way he felt, that time wasn't far off, either. Truth to tell, he hadn't figured he would make it through this past winter. But he had.

"I don't know if I'm glad or sorry about that." Talking to himself had become a habit over the years, a way to satisfy that inner need to have a human voice touch his ears. "Yup, me and death are gettin' closer and closer. One of these times, I'll just keel over—with no one ever bein' the wiser."

Was that what he feared? Dying alone? Without a proper marker on his grave like that body on the hillside?

"No marker?" He snorted a laugh. "There wouldn't even be a burial. This tough ole flesh of mine would be food for the carrion eaters, my bones dragged from here t' kingdom come."

A grimness gripped him; then he shook it off with a sigh, his eyes opening to mere slits. "They gotta eat somethin'. Might as well be me. It's for sure I'll be past carin'. An' I don't imagine there's anybody still livin' who would shed a tear over my passin' anyways. I expect they wrote me off for dead years ago."

He stared at the sky and watched the parade of faces in his mind, their images as sharp and fresh as if he'd seen them only yesterday. Age had withered his body and grayed his hair, but not the people Saddlebags remembered. The intervening years had left no mark on them. It was one of his mind's cruelties, to fool him into believing he was still young, too.

"Sure'd be nice to die clutchin' that gold in my hands," he murmured wistfully.

The unlikelihood of that settled over him with all the crushing heaviness of the granite boulder at his back. In those long ago years of his youth, he had been convinced that his search would ultimately end in success. Now he was only convinced of the futility of it.

But he refused to quit looking. Giving up now meant admitting that his entire life had been wasted on the search. No, the time for quitting had run out decades ago.

A tear slipped down his cheek when Saddlebags considered all the things that might have been. He left it to dry on his skin, not wanting to expend the energy it would take to wipe it away.

"It's a shame I ain't as crazy as everybody thinks I am," he murmured, then cackled at the thought.

But there was no getting around the truth: his mind was just as sharp as ever. So was his hearing; his ears picked up the steady drum of hoofbeats, the sound gradually increasing in volume as the horses neared him.

"Must be that McCallister boy and that other person."

Inactivity had stiffened him. Saddlebags had to make two attempts before he finally made it to his feet and peeked around the boulder to verify his guess. Years of staying out of sight to keep others from knowing his search areas had become too deeply ingrained. Even now, when there was no need to be secretive, he remained behind the boulder.

His keen eyes recognized McCallister the instant the two riders cantered into view. He switched his focus to the second one.

"Wonder who the redhead is?" he murmured, untroubled that he didn't recognize her. Unless she lived at one of the neighboring ranches, he wouldn't know her from Solomon's pet donkey. "She seems kinda pleased about something," he observed and shifted his gaze to McCallister. "Takin' her out for a Sunday ride to show her around the place, are you?"

The pair slowed their horses to descend the slope. This time they didn't stop at the former grave site, although they both glanced in its direction as they rode by.

"Kind of a morbid thing to show a girl when you're courtin' her anyway," Saddlebags stated, then grinned. "Course, it could always spook her an' give a fella a chance t' put his arms around her." He chortled at the thought, his false teeth clicking together.

Another possibility struck him with all the suddenness of a lightning strike.

"She could have known the guy that was buried there." The instant the words were out of his mouth, Saddlebags remembered the soberness of her expression, the tinge of sadness when she had scooped a handful of the soil and held it. And he remembered, too, the way McCallister had stood back and watched, not joining her until she said something to him.

"They identified the guy." A tightness seized his chest. Immediately he argued with himself, "You don't know that, you crazy fool." He thought about that, then answered, "No, I don't know it for a fact, but there's one person who would." Pushing away from the boulder, he turned. "Stay out of it, you old coot. It's got nothin' to do with you." He nodded and picked his way among the rocks with care. "Maybe. Maybe."

The canter blew away some of the cobwebs, leaving Angie feeling refreshed and vaguely exhilarated, her resolve strengthened. Her face glowed with it when they pulled up at the ranch's massive barn. Shifting her weight to the left stirrup, she started to swing out of the saddle and felt the warning twinge from her thigh muscles. She turned the instinctive groan into a laugh.

"Something tells me I'm going to be stiff and sore in the morning." Hanging on to the saddlehorn, she lowered herself to the ground, stretching muscles that didn't want to be stretched. "I'd forgotten how long it's been since I was in the saddle. That's what I get for giving you such a hard time about your hangover."

"That ought to teach you." Luke led his horse to the corral fence and looped the reins in a half hitch around the top rail.

"It should." Angie copied his movements, then hooked the stirrup on the saddlehorn and went to work loosening the cinch. "Holding your head isn't nearly as embarrassing as holding your backside."

Something moved in the deep shadows just inside the open barn door, catching Angie's eye. Dulcie sidled into view, dressed in a pair of cutoffs and a faded red T-shirt, her sockless feet shoved into dirty, frayed sneakers.

"Hi, Dulcie." Angie smiled at the girl. "What are you up to?"

"Nothing," she mumbled and toed at the ground, both hands clasped behind her back.

"Is Tobe in there?" Luke nodded, indicating the barn. "Tell him to come out and give a hand with these horses."

"He's gone."

"Gone. Gone where?" He stopped with the saddle pulled halfway off the horse's back. Snorting, the bay gelding swung its body out from under it.

Dulcie shook her head, indicating she didn't know, then offered, "He said he wouldn't be gone long." She darted an apologetic glance at Angie. "He didn't think you'd get back so soon."

"Obviously," Luke muttered dryly and carried the saddle and its heavy pad over to the corral, then hefted it onto the top rail. He walked back to his mount, his glance running to search the area around the trailer. "Are you here by yourself? I don't see Fargo's truck."

"He was out of tobacco. After we got through with the dishes, he went into town to get some."

Luke stepped to the gray when Angie started to drag the saddle from its back. "I'll get that for you."

"I can manage," she refused, with a smile. "I may be out of shape but I'm not weak."

He watched as she toted it to the corral and lifted it onto the fence. Turning, he reached for the saddle blanket and started wiping the sweat from the bay's back, then glanced curiously at Dulcie, suspicion forming in his mind.

"What were you doing in the barn, Dulcie?"

She ducked her head and chewed at her lower lip, trying to avoid answering his question.

"Dulcie," Luke repeated with a note of warning.

"Playing."

"You were playing with those wild kittens again, weren't you?" he guessed, then noticed the tight way her arms were pressed behind her. "One of them finally scratched you this time, I'll bet."

Nodding, she dropped her chin even lower. "Just a little scratch."

Angie darted a look of concern at Luke, then moved toward the girl. "You'd better let me take a look at your arm, Dulcie. Even a little scratch can become a bad one if it becomes infected."

With great reluctance, Dulcie drew both arms from behind her back and presented the injured one to Angie for inspection. Blood seeped and smeared from the scoring marks left by tiny, razor-sharp claws, making it difficult to judge the depth of the cuts.

"I'll bet it hurts, doesn't it?" Angie ventured and received a small nod from Dulcie. Placing a hand on the girl's shoulder, she gently turned her toward the mobile home. "Come on. We'll go to the trailer and get you cleaned up."

"There's a first-aid kit on the pantry shelf in the kitchen," Luke told her. "Dulcie can show you. I'll see to the horses."

"Would you bring my purse when you come?"

"Sure."

Dulcie stood on a chair pulled up to the kitchen sink while Angie gently washed her arm with soap and water. The first-aid kit lay open on the counter next to the sink, a can of antiseptic spray sitting beside it.

"It stings, doesn't it?" Angie guessed when Dulcie sucked in a hissing breath.

"A little," she admitted.

"That should do it." Angie turned on the faucet, letting the water run and adjusting the temperature of it. "If there are any germs left, the spray should take care of it."

Once the soap was rinsed from Dulcie's arm, Angie tore off a couple sheets of paper towels and dried it, carefully blotting the scratched area.

"How big are the kittens?"

"Not very big." There was a long pause before Dulcie offered an unsolicited explanation. "The yellow one doesn't mind if I pet her. But she got scared when I picked her up. That's when she scratched me."

"She was probably afraid you were going to take her away from her momma and her brothers and sisters." Angie sprayed a generous coating of antiseptic over the scratches. Several of the deeper ones continued to ooze blood.

"I would *never* have taken her away from her momma." Dulcie looked stricken at the suggestion.

"I know you wouldn't. But the kitten didn't know that."

"I guess not."

Angie dabbed at the gathering droplets of blood. "We'll need to put a Band-Aid on a couple of these so you don't get blood on your clothes."

"Okay." Dulcie watched while Angie rummaged through the first-aid kit for some medium-sized Band-Aids. Her eye was drawn to the rich russet red of Angie's long wavy hair. "I wish my hair was the color of yours."

There was a rueful twist to the smile Angie briefly directed Dulcie's way. "When I was your age, I absolutely hated it."

"But it's beautiful," Dulcie protested, aghast.

"You don't know how the other kids used to tease me—and call me things like Carrot-top and Cherry Head. The worst of all was Red Rooster, because they'd flap their arms like a chicken and crow." She peeled off the protective strips on one bandage, exposing the adhesive side.

"I'll bet it was mostly boys who did that."

"Mostly."

"Sometimes they call me Whitey," Dulcie admitted when Angie placed the Band-Aid over a scratch and smoothed the adhesive ends firmly onto her skin.

Their heads close, Angie glanced at Dulcie, her eyes atwinkle. "That's as bad as Carrot-top." The wideness of her grin invited laughter, and Dulcie giggled, finding humor in a situation where before there had been only hurt. "Believe me," Angie said with a wink, "there are women who would pay lots of money to have pale blond hair the color of yours."

Unconvinced, Dulcie made a face. "It's ugly."

"It's beautiful. The color of moonbeams."

"Moonbeams." The description caught her interest.

"Moonbeams," Angie repeated with emphasis and smoothed

the last bandage in place. "And just think—God made your hair that color on purpose. He wants everyone to know how very special you are to Him."

The desire to believe that was in her eyes, but doubt held her back. "How do you know that?"

"My grandmother told me," Angie replied as Luke entered through the trailer's rear door.

He paused at the sight of the two heads bent close together, one pale and fair, the other dark and vivid. There was something sweetly innocent and intimate about the scene that made him catch hold of the door, stopping it from swinging shut and revealing his presence.

"And when I got older I learned she was absolutely right," Angie continued. "The color of your hair is beautiful; the color of my hair is beautiful. But they're different, and that's good."

A perplexed frown knitted Dulcie's forehead. "But what did you do to make the kids stop calling you names?"

A smile deepened the corners of Angie's mouth. "You mean, instead of socking them in the nose?" Dulcie clamped a hand over her mouth, smothering a giggle at Angie's response. "My mom suggested that I make a point of finding something nice to say about their hair every time they called me a name. It took a while—quite a while, in fact—but eventually they did stop teasing me. I think it becomes hard to be mean to someone who's nice to you."

Dulcie thought about that for all of two seconds, then released an exaggerated sigh and declared, "That wouldn't work with Tommy Foster. He's mean to *everybody*."

"That might indicate he needs it the most."

"Tommy?!" she said with wide incredulity, showing more animation than Luke had ever seen before.

Angie laughed at Dulcie's reaction, then challenged lightly, "Why not?"

"Because—" Dulcie groped for an explanation, then settled for the single word she had already spoken. "Besides, his hair is always dirty and yucky."

"Then tell him how nice it looks when it's clean."

"Maybe." Tired of talking about Tommy Foster, Dulcie sought to change the subject by grabbing a chunk of hair from her ponytail and drawing it forward to studiously examine its long, pale strands. "The color *is* kinda like moonbeams," she concluded, then lifted her gaze to Angie's hair, a wistful quality entering her expression. "But I still wish it was curly like yours."

Angie threw her head back and laughed, a sound that was spontaneous and warm. A glimmer of hurt feelings appeared to dull Dulcie's eyes. Before she could retreat into her shell of silence, Angie explained, laughter still in her voice, "You aren't going to believe this, Dulcie, but when I was younger, I used to iron my hair so it would be straight like yours."

Dulcie's eyes popped wide with astonishment. "Why would you want it to be straight?"

"Because that was the popular style. But, after burning myself with the iron a couple of times, I realized that not only was it too much work, but it was also too dangerous trying to make my hair be something it was never meant to be. So, I decided to accept that it was red and curly—that it wasn't going to change and that I might as well enjoy it just the way it is. I'm a lot happier now."

Dulcie studied her own hair again. "Maybe I could do that."

"I'll bet you can," Angie told her. "I'll bet you can do anything you set your mind to do."

There wasn't an ounce of shyness or self-doubt in the smile Dulcie beamed at Angie. "I could, couldn't I? I mean, I did get that yellow kitten to finally let me pet her." Without a pause, she made the jump to her next subject. "I thought I might call her Sunshine, 'cause she's yellow like sunshine. Don't you think that would be a good name for her?"

"It sounds like a perfect name. But I'd wait a while before I'd try to pick her up again if I were you." Angie tapped an admonishing finger on the tip of Dulcie's nose, a gesture that was full of affection and one that, like this scene, resurrected old memories for Luke. The painful kind.

He released the door, letting it swing shut with a little bang that slammed the one in his mind. Both Angie and Dulcie turned to face him with a start of surprise. Dulcie's smile vanished at the sight of him, a look of dejection stealing through her expression.

Stung by her reaction to him, Luke narrowed his eyes to make a sharp sweep of her arms. "Got the scratches all cleaned up, I see."

"That's right." Angie stood up and returned the first-aid kit to its proper place on the pantry shelf.

He looked pointedly at Dulcie. "Maybe next time you'll remember those kittens are wild."

Head bowed, she mumbled, "Yes, sir."

But he knew she wouldn't. She'd already given the kitten a name. Sunshine. But he couldn't remind her of that without revealing how long he'd been standing inside the door listening to them—something he was reluctant to do.

"Since Tobe hasn't shown up yet, I'll give you a ride back to town whenever you're ready to go," he said to Angie, in an abrupt change of subject.

"I'm ready now."

"Good." He took a step toward the door.

"You'd better run and put on a clean top before we go, Dulcie," Angie told her. "You have blood on that one."

Dulcie's eyes widened in surprise. "Am I going with you?"

Startled by the question, Angie shot a confused glance at Luke, then answered, "Of course you are. You can't stay here on the ranch by yourself. Now, scoot."

Dulcie glanced uncertainly at Luke as if expecting him to object. In that instant, she looked young and vulnerable, much too young to be left alone even if Tobe should return five minutes after they left.

"You heard her—scoot," Luke said, his reply echoing Angie's, and Dulcie took off for her room like a cannon shot. Luke watched her a moment, then cast a bemused sideways glance at Angie. "What kind of a spell have you cast over her?"

"Spell?" She looked genuinely confused. "What do you mean?"

He wanted to comment on Dulcie's new animation and liveliness, but that sounded vague—and a little silly. Discarding that explanation, he chose another. "I overheard some of your conversation earlier," he admitted. "I've never heard Dulcie talk so much before."

Angie held his gaze for a long, silent second. Then her lips curved in a faint smile. "Maybe she doesn't do much talking because nobody takes the time to listen." She used a gently suggestive tone rather than a judgmental one. But it still hit its target.

"Ouch," Luke reacted, with a mock wince.

She laughed, and the sound had the same enveloping warmth and spontaneity that he'd heard in it before with Dulcie, the kind that was meant to be shared. He felt the pull of it—and of her. He wanted to catch her up in his arms and spin her around, pull off that ridiculous ball cap, and bury his hands in that mass of long red hair and find out if those lips were as kissable as they looked.

But he put a brake on such thoughts, fully aware it wouldn't stop with just a kiss.

"I'd better leave a note for Tobe so he doesn't wonder where Dulcie is when he comes back." When he crossed to the counter to tear off a sheet from the scratch pad by the telephone, Dulcie dashed breathlessly into the kitchen, the yellow top exchanged for a clean but slightly wrinkled blue one.

"I'm ready," she announced.

"That was quick." Angie smiled in approval.

"We'll go just as soon as I finish this note to your brother." Luke glanced up from his hastily scribbled message and noticed the hairbrush in her hand. "What's that for?"

"I've got straw in my hair," Dulcie explained, self-consciously touching her ponytail. "I thought I'd brush it out in the truck so you wouldn't have to wait for me."

"Good idea." Luke nodded absently and signed the note, then carried it to the table and placed it in plain sight. "We're all set. Let's go."

As the two filed ahead of him toward the door, the entire scenario seemed too much like a family outing for Luke to be comfortable with it.

Chapter Eleven

The first few miles were covered in silence, with Luke keeping all of his attention on the road. Beside him in the seat, Dulcie had freed her hair from its elastic band and dragged it all in front of her. Stroke after methodical stroke, she ran the brush through her hair. The last wisp of straw had long since been removed, yet she continued to comb the bristles through it, all the while studying the way it had begun to glisten.

Glancing at Angie, she whispered with barely suppressed excitement, "It kinda shimmers like moonbeams, doesn't it?"

"Definitely." Angie's smile of agreement was quick and warm, reaching all the way to her eyes. "Here." She reached for the brush, the ponytail twister wrapped around the handle of it. "Let me put it in a ponytail for you."

Dulcie passed her the brush, then turned sideways in the seat, as much as the seat belt would allow, and presented her back to Angie. With practiced ease, Angie gathered up the long, straight hair and began smoothing it into place with the brush.

"Do you really know where that gold is buried, Angie?" Dulcie asked unexpectedly. "Tobe says you do."

"I'm afraid your brother is wrong this time." Angie softened her words with a smile. "I wish I could walk right to the spot and pick it up, but I can't."

Dulcie, lost in a daydream, gazed at the pickup's worn seat cushion. "I wish I could find that gold." The fervency in her voice was moving.

"What would you do with it if you found it?" Angie wondered curiously.

In answer, Dulcie asked, "Do you think there would be enough gold to get a ranch for Tobe and a house for me?"

"Probably. Is that what you want? A house?" With the twist tie she made the first wrap to secure Dulcie's ponytail.

Dulcie nodded. "A home that's just ours. Nobody else's. That's not wrong, is it?" she asked, suddenly uncertain.

"Of course it isn't," Angie assured her. "Everybody likes to feel they belong somewhere."

"Gold." A sardonic humor curled through Luke's voice and glittered in the glance that ricocheted off Angie. "Now, you've got *her* dreaming about finding it."

"There's nothing wrong with dreaming." She pulled Dulcie's hair through the last wrap and arranged the long tail to hang smooth and straight.

"There are dreams, and then there are pipe dreams." Luke reduced the pickup's speed as they approached the collection of buildings that comprised the town of Glory. "That gold is a pipe dream."

But his negative attitude had no effect on her. Smiling easily, Angie murmured a confident-sounding, "We'll see."

"You certainly will," Luke countered, his amused tone as dry as the roadside dust. As he braked to make the turn into the parking lot of the Rimrock Bar & Grill, his glance flicked to the two pickups already there. "Now we know where Tobe and Fargo are."

The tavern door opened, and out piled Ima Jane with Tobe, Fargo, and Griff crowding close behind her, all of them clearly in a hurry.

"I wonder where the fire is?" Luke cocked a puzzled glance at the group.

"You don't suppose there is one?" Angie's glance raced over the building's roofline, searching for smoke.

Their attention focused elsewhere, the group led by Ima Jane was halfway to the parking lot before they saw Luke's truck pull in.

As one, they instantly changed directions and converged on it, forcing Luke to stop in the middle of the lot.

Luke stuck his head out of the window. "What's the problem?"

Ignoring him, Ima Jane went straight to the passenger side, her expression a study of concern. "I'm so glad you're back, Angie," she declared. "Tobe saw somebody messing around your camper."

"My camper?" Angie repeated in disbelief.

"When?" Luke fired the question at Tobe.

"Just now—when I was driving in."

"Who was it?"

"I don't know," Tobe admitted. "I only got a glimpse of him out of the corner of my eye when I pulled in."

"Tobe thinks the guy was trying to break into your camper. We were on our way to investigate and make sure everything was okay." Ima Jane inserted. "You'd better come with us, Angie," she urged.

In a slight daze, Angie reached for the door handle. "But why would anybody want to break into my camper?" she argued in confusion. "There's nothing in it but my clothes and some snacks."

"After all this talk about the gold and Wilson's letter, you have to ask why?" Luke mocked in amazement and switched off the engine while simultaneously reaching for the driver-side door.

An agitated Ima Jane waited for Angie as she climbed out of the truck. She paused to hold the door for Dulcie as she scrambled out of the passenger side, all agog over this frantic flurry of activity and its cause.

"You did lock your camper when you left, didn't you?" Ima

Jane hurried after the men already bound for Angie's pickup camper.

"I'm sure I did. It's almost automatic." Walking swiftly to keep pace with the woman, Angie dug the key to the camper from her purse.

By the time she reached the camper, the others were already there. Before she could insert the key, Luke tried the knob. It turned under his hand, the latch clicking.

"You can forget the key," Luke told her, pulling the door open.

"I could have sworn I locked it," Angie frowned in bewilderment, then glanced at Tobe. "You saw me, didn't you?"

"I don't know if you locked it or not." He shrugged his lack of knowledge. "I wasn't paying any attention."

Luke inspected the dead-bolt lock. "Were these scratches here before?"

Bending closer, Angie studied the small metal scars around the keyhole. "I'm not sure." She regretted that she hadn't taken the time to notice such details when she borrowed the camper.

"Hadn't you better check and see if anything's been stolen?" Fargo suggested.

"I guess I should," Angie agreed, conscious of the uneasy flutterings in her stomach.

When Luke swung the door open for her, she took a step forward. Griff shouldered his way in front of her. "I'll go first and make sure nobody's hidin' in there."

That possibility hadn't even occurred to her. She stopped in her tracks, offering no protest when Griff hauled himself into the camper.

"I'll come with you." Hitching up her skirts, Ima Jane climbed in after her husband.

"Me, too." Tobe crammed in behind her.

Smiling grimly, Luke opened the door wider and waved Fargo toward its high steps. "You might as well go in, too, and give Beauchamp another set of fingerprints to sort through."

"No, thanks." Fargo remained where he was, his mouth quirked in a wry smile, and held up the metal pincer hook that served as his left hand. "Besides, this claw of mine doesn't leave fingerprints."

The camper shell rocked and groaned with the shifting movements of its occupants. From inside came the sounds of bathroom and closet doors opening and closing, curtain hoops scraping across rods, and the odd thump without an identifiable cause. Somehow Griff managed to squeeze past the others and appear in the doorway.

"If there was anybody in there, they're gone now." He swung to the ground and turned back to give Ima Jane a hand out of the camper.

"I'm not sure, but I think someone has definitely been in there," she told Angie. "But you're the only one who can tell for sure."

Angie waited until Tobe emerged, then climbed into the camper. Her eye went first to the blanket and sheets hanging loose from the mattress in the cab-over bunk. All had been neatly tucked under when she had returned to the camper before church and lingered long enough to make up the bed.

Then she noticed the family scrapbook lying on the table of the recessed dining nook. It had been stowed in the overhead cupboard along with her area maps. The folder with those same maps now lay on a seat cushion. Angie was certain, beyond a shadow of a doubt, that she hadn't left them there.

Last night she'd been too tired to do more than undress and crawl into bed. This morning, there hadn't been time.

Knowing that someone had been in the camper gave her an eerie feeling, one Angie found difficult to describe. Something told her she wouldn't sleep as soundly tonight as she usually did.

A check verified that her clothes were still in the closet and the few items of jewelry she'd brought with her were still in the drawstring bag tucked in her cosmetic case. Other than those things, she had left nothing of value in the camper.

All eyes were fastened on her when Angie returned to the doorway. "Well? Was I right?" Ima Jane prodded her with the question.

"Yes. Someone's been in here," Angie replied, still distracted by the discovery. And disquieted by it, too. "But nothing seems to be missing."

Griff's eyes narrowed on her. "Are you sure?"

"Yes." She stepped down from the camper.

"What about Wilson's letter?" Fargo wondered. "Are you positive that wasn't taken?"

"Gracious!" Ima Jane pressed a hand to her heart in a gesture of shock. "I hadn't even thought of that."

"Don't worry. I still have it." Angie patted her shoulder bag. "It's right here in my purse."

"That's a good thing," Ima Jane declared in relief. "I know it's only a copy of the original, but I'm glad it wasn't stolen just the same."

Was that what they were after? Angie wondered, then decided she didn't want to know the answer to that. Inadvertently she glanced at Luke, and the grimness of his expression seemed to confirm her own unvoiced suspicions.

"It's time we called Beauchamp and reported this," he announced.

"Nothing was taken," Angie said, as a kind of protest. There was a part of her that didn't want to treat any of this too seriously. And involving the police would do exactly that.

"Breaking and entering is still a felony," Luke reminded her.

Still reluctant, Angie shook her head. "Just the same, there's no sense in bothering the sheriff on a Sunday. I have to meet with him tomorrow anyway. I'll tell him about it then."

"Have it your way." But there was a definite edge to his voice.

"Imagine someone breaking into your camper. And in broad daylight, too." Ima Jane all but tsked in disapproval, then gasped loudly, struck by a sudden thought. "Were any blankets or food missing, Angie? Did you notice?"

"No, I . . . I never even checked—"

Luke interrupted her answer. "If you're thinking it might have been Saddlebags, you're wrong," he told Ima Jane. "We saw him this afternoon at the Ten Bar. And unless he can sprout wings, he couldn't have made it into town ahead of us—not on foot."

"It was a thought." Ima Jane looked a little disappointed that it had turned out to be a wrong one. But she was quick to shake it off and send a bright-eyed glance around the group. "Now that the excitement's over, why don't we all go back inside and have some coffee." Compassion warmed the look she gave Angie. "You look like you could use some."

Angie smiled back. "You're right. I could."

"Count me out," Luke said. "I need to get back to the ranch." He half turned to leave, then noticed Dulcie. "Are you riding with me or coming back with your brother?"

"With Tobe." Her upward glance never quite made it to his face.

When the others started toward the tavern, Angie lingered. Ima Jane paused. "Aren't you coming?"

"In a minute," she promised. "I need to talk to Luke about something first."

"What do you need?" he asked when the others moved away. But he didn't turn to face her, his expression oddly aloof, without its usual hint of amusement.

After a brief hesitation, Angie made her request. "You indicated earlier that you could locate the site of the shoot-out with the posse on the map I have. I wonder if you could take a few minutes and do it now."

Luke didn't hesitate at all. "Maybe another time. I've got evening chores waiting for me back at the ranch."

"You're upset about something." She was certain of that. "What?"

He regarded her in wry amazement, his mouth twisting in a lazy smile. "Why do you think someone broke into your camper?"

"I'm not sure." When she remembered the maps and the family scrapbook, honesty made her add, "They might have been looking for the letter."

"Give the teacher an A," he mocked in a droll voice.

"But they didn't get it," Angie reminded him, touching her purse again. "I have it right here."

"And who knows that?"

"You, Ima Jane, T—"

"Enough said." He swung toward his truck, then pivoted back. "Do yourself a favor, and don't leave that letter in your purse. And wherever you end up putting it, make sure you're the only one who knows it. Either that or post the damn thing on a wall inside the Rimrock. Which would be the safest thing to do."

He turned on his heel and walked off, little puffs of dust rising with each strike of his boots on the graveled lot. Her gaze followed him, lingering on his long and lanky frame, a rider's narrow hips tapering out to wide shoulders. Angie smiled to herself, secretly pleased by the discovery that his irritation was rooted in a concern for her safety. Something told her he didn't want to care, which further irritated him that he did.

That was something Angie understood. Being attracted to the owner of the Ten Bar Ranch had never been part of her plans for this trip. But that fact was becoming more and more difficult to ignore.

When Luke's pickup accelerated onto the highway, Angie closed the door to the camper and automatically locked it, well aware that a locked door was no deterrent to a bold thief.

As she returned the key to her purse, her fingers brushed the photocopy of the letter tucked inside it. The contact reminded Angie of Luke's advice. She smiled again. There was a third option that probably hadn't occurred to Luke.

Upon entering the Rimrock, Angie saw no trace of its earlier church disguise. The floor was once again crowded with bar tables and chairs, scarred with use. Liquor bottles and drink glasses stood in full view on the shelves of the mirrored back bar. No fragrant candle burned to mask the scent of stale tobacco smoke and sour beer.

Clustered around one of the tables near the long bar sat Ima Jane; her husband, Griff; Tobe; and Fargo. Only Dulcie remained apart from them, perched quietly on a chair at a nearby table, her hand lightly stroking the ponytail drawn over one shoulder.

"There you are, Angie. Come join us," Ima Jane invited and immediately began issuing orders. "Tobe, pull one of those chairs over here for her. Griff, get Angie some coffee." When Griff rose, she added, "and bring a spoon, too, for the sugar."

"Might as well bring the pot back with you," Fargo told him. "I could use a refill."

The instant Angie arrived at the table, Ima Jane urged her into the chair Tobe held. "How are you feeling?" she asked, resuming her seat to study Angie with concern.

"Fine," she insisted and leaned back to give Griff room to set the spoon and coffee cup in front of her.

"Are you sure?" Ima Jane pressed, then murmured, "It has to be an unnerving experience for you to have someone break into your camper like that."

"It is," Angie admitted and poured two spoons of sugar into her coffee. "I still don't understand why anyone would bother. There certainly isn't anything of any value in there—although Luke thinks they were after Ike Wilson's letter."

"Don't you?" Griff frowned.

"I honestly don't know what to think." She took off her ball cap and shook her hair to let it fall in thick, loose waves about her shoulders.

"If you ask me, it's a good thing you had it with you," Tobe declared as he swung a leg over the seat of his own chair, straddling it. "Otherwise it would be in someone else's pocket now."

"You might be right." Angie swallowed a sip of coffee, feeling the sweet, strong burn of it travel down her throat and bring a jolt of caffeine to her system, banishing the last remnant of shaky nerves. Lowering the cup, she released a troubled sigh. "But even if the thief had taken the letter, I'm not sure he would have had anything."

"Are you kiddin'?" Fargo scoffed. "It could point him straight to the gold."

"It might," she conceded, using a tone that stressed doubt. "I know my grandfather was convinced that it could. But I must have read it a thousand times and—" Breaking off the sentence, Angie set her cup down and flipped open the purse in her lap. She reached inside and pulled out the folded photocopy of Ike Wilson's letter. Opening it, she smoothed the creases left by the folds, then pushed it across the table to where Fargo and Griff were seated.

"You read it for yourselves," Angie told them, "and see if you can find anything more than a few vague references."

With surprising swiftness, Fargo reached out and pulled the letter to him while Griff crowded against his shoulder to read it with him. Still straddling his chair, Tobe half walked and half dragged it closer to peer across Fargo's arm at the letter.

"What does it say?" Ima Jane got up and went around behind the two men, then leaned over them to get her own look at it.

"That handwriting is sure hard to read." Tobe directed his complaint at Angie.

"A different style of penmanship was taught in those days," she explained.

"It's a pity the schools today don't put more emphasis on it," Ima Jane commented absently, as she gave up trying to read over her husband's shoulder, and returned to her seat.

"With the advent of computers, it's on the verge of becoming a lost art." Angie sipped at her sweetened coffee, eyeing the two men over the cup's rim as they pored over the letter.

Without effort, she visualized it in her mind: the masculine scroll of the handwriting, the partially underlined date in the upper-right-hand corner, the affectionate salutation, and the body of the letter itself.

12 *July*, 1887

My dearest Caroline,

It grieves my soul to write this to you, my love. Gold is a curse. I regret that my crime cannot remain forever hidden from you. Tomorrow I die on the gallows. Outside the church bell rings the hour. All that awaits me is a deep, dark hole, a fitting end for murdering thieves. What has happened to the pillar of righteousness you married? The question will haunt me constantly all evening. Temptation dragged me to the bottom. Evil lured me into its shadow. Did not my father's teachings warn me that greed for wealth points only to destruction?

I alone survived to ride out of that canyon. My sinners in crime met their death there at its very entrance. By God's grace I lived. I cannot say if that is right or wrong. God has forgiven me. My heart soars like an eagle in flight. Jesus once again is my salvation and my steadfast rock, as I know He is yours. He will not let this bury you. Cry your tears, my love, but do not be dragged under by this. Nor let it put you high upon an empty shelf. For your sake as well as our son's, happiness is a reward you both deserve, not the pain I have caused you. Live for tomorrow and place it in God's hands. Mighty will be your return.

Your repentant husband,
Isaac Alfred Wilson

P.S. <u>Remember. Always remember God's way is not man's way.</u>

After a quick scan of the entire contents, Griff went back to study it word by word, while Fargo was content to read it through one time slowly and thoroughly. Angie waited until Fargo straightened away from it, his bushy brows pursed together in a thoughtful frown.

"Do you see what I mean?" she said. "He does mention a pillar, and something about an eagle, but if those are supposed to be clues, they don't tell me anything. Do they you?"

"Nope." The corners of Fargo's mouth turned grudgingly downward.

Griff was slower to let go of it. He held up the letter, waggling it back and forth. "Is this all there is?"

"That's it." Angie nodded.

"What about the original letter itself? Were there any marks on it? Anything like a drawing or a map?"

"That photocopy shows you every mark that was on the original," Angie assured him.

He shook his head. "No, I'm not talkin' about marks that are necessarily visible. A copier would pick those up."

"Then what are you gettin' at?" Fargo drew back, his eyes narrowing in confusion.

"Invisible ink, you mean," Tobe guessed, all bright eyed with certainty.

Ima Jane was skeptical. "Was that even invented when this letter was written?"

"I don't know," Angie admitted. "But even if it was, I don't think Ike Wilson would have been able to get it, considering he was locked in a cell when he wrote this."

"No, no, no," Griff inserted impatiently. "I'm not talkin' about invisible ink. I'm talkin' about the kind of indentations you make on a paper when you write heavily on another sheet that's on top of it."

"Hey, that's an idea." Tobe jumped on it. "I used to do that when I was a kid. It would look like there was nothing on the paper. Then you'd go over it with the flat of a pencil and you'd see words." He slapped Fargo on the shoulder. "I'll bet he drew a map on the paper, then wrote the letter over it."

Smiling, Angie shook her head in denial. "I'm sorry I don't have the original here to show you, but—I promise—Ike didn't do that. I thought of that, too, and checked a long time ago."

Griff harrumphed, glanced over the letter again, then gave it a little toss onto the table.

"Let me see it." Tobe reached for it. "I'll bet I can figure it out."

"You do that," Fargo taunted as Dulcie at last succumbed to her curiosity and slid silently off her chair. She sidled close to her brother and peered at the copy of the famous letter.

"More coffee?" Ima Jane suggested when Fargo drained his cup.

He shoved it away in vague disgust. "Naw, I've had all the coffee I can take. I think it's time for a beer."

When Ima Jane started to rise, Griff waved her back in the chair. "I'll get it."

"I'll drink it there." Fargo pushed out of his chair and followed Griff to the bar area. Lifting the metal prosthesis, he laid it on the bar top, wincing a little. "I should have taken this dang thing off and left it in the truck. After a while, it gets to feelin' like it weighs a ton, and the straps get to chafin'. If I wear it too long, I end up with more galls than a horse with a loose saddle."

Griff offered no sympathy, just shoved a mug of cold beer to him. Fargo downed a third of it in a couple of long gulps, but it didn't wash away the heavy dejection that had his shoulders sagging. Bits of froth clung to the tips of his stubby mustache. Turning his head, he wiped it off on the shoulder of his shirt.

"I was sure there'd be something in that letter," he muttered, then glanced at Griff. "Weren't you?"

"Who's to say there isn't?" His eyes held the sly, hard gleam of something more than mere suspicion.

"You read it," Fargo protested.

"Who's to say that's a copy of the real letter?" Griff flicked a glance at the table. "We've only got her word for that."

"That's true, but she said—"

Griff cut him off. "I know what she said. But, answer me this: if you had the letter, would you show it to anybody?"

"No."

"Neither would I. So why did she?" he demanded, throwing another look in her direction. "She doesn't seem stupid to me."

"So . . . you think that letter isn't the real one," Fargo concluded. "It's just something she made up herself."

"Can you think of a better way to throw people off track? To convince them that there aren't any clues in it?"

Needing to give this whole new idea some thought, Fargo studied the beer's dwindling suds, then took another drink and lowered the mug with a small, disbelieving shake of his head. "I don't know, Griff. The way it was written, it sounded authentic."

"She teaches history," Griff reminded him. "That's something she could have read up on—and probably did. For all we know, she might have copied parts of the original just to make it look more convincing."

The more Griff said, the more sense it made to Fargo. He leaned on the countertop and propped a foot on the black-tarnished brass rail. Looking over his shoulder, he stared toward the letter Tobe held. With each passing second, his doubt of its authenticity grew.

"If that letter's phony, where's the real one?" he murmured, voicing the thought that crossed his mind.

"She's got it with her, you can bet on that." Succumbing to his obsession for cleanliness, Griff got out a spray bottle of bleach solution and began wiping down the under-the-counter area around the bar sink.

"Probably in her purse," Fargo decided, watching as Tobe heaved a huge sigh and pushed the letter back to the Sommers woman. "She never lets that bag out of her sight. If she ain't holdin' it, it's in her lap, like now," he observed, then recalled, "She even had it with her when Luke took her out to show her where the skeleton was found. And they went on horseback."

"It's not in the camper." He spritzed some solution over the ice cooler's metal lid.

Fargo shot him a narrowed look. "You sound awful sure about that."

"You were there," Griff countered. "Did she look the least bit worried about anything being missing to you?"

He thought back, trying to remember. "She looked kinda dazed, upset, in a way."

"But there sure wasn't anything frantic about the way she looked to see what was taken. I know because I watched. I'd bet money she didn't hide it in the camper." Griff nodded with emphatic certainty.

"You're probably right about that. I know if I were her, I'd keep it in sight all the time," Fargo declared, then clammed up when Tobe walked up to the bar and hitched a hip onto the stool next to him.

"Draw me a beer, Griff." He slumped against the counter, his expression all glum and downcast. "You know, she said that her grandfather complained about being confused by the things in that letter. I can sure see why. You could study on that thing for a week and not know any more than you did when you started. Man, I was so sure I could figure out where that gold was if I ever got my hands on that letter Wilson wrote. Now . . ."

Fargo snorted an amused breath. "Kid, you are not only green, you're gullible," he declared and downed another swig of beer.

"Gullible." Tobe's head came up, quick to take umbrage.

"That's what I said." Fargo exchanged a faint, smug smile with Griff.

"What makes you think I'm gullible?" Tobe challenged, getting angry.

Fargo grinned. "What makes you think that's the real letter?"

Tobe's mouth came open as the full inference of the question hit him. A split second later, a spark of hope lit his eyes. Before he regained the power of speech, chair legs scraped and bounced across the floor, drawing the attention of all three men to the table. Griff and Fargo took special note of the way the Sommers woman gripped her purse while sliding its long strap onto her shoulder as she stood.

"I'll see you in a bit," she told Ima Jane and started toward the front door.

"No hurry." Ima Jane smiled with assurance and busied herself with gathering the dirty coffee cups off the table.

"Where's she goin'?" Griff asked when Ima Jane deposited the cups in the dish cart.

"Who? Oh, you mean Angie." She glanced at the door now closing behind the redhead. "She's just going to her camper. She wanted to shower and change before supper, and I convinced her to use the bathroom upstairs." Ima Jane paused, the line of her mouth tightening in faint disapproval. "I tried to talk her into sleeping in our spare bedroom tonight, but she insists on staying in the camper. Maybe if *you* said something to her, Griff. I just don't think it's safe for her to be alone in that camper, not after the break-in."

"She's not goin' to listen to me," Griff replied.

"She might. We have to try," she insisted.

"I'll try, but she's goin' to be just as safe one place as another."

Ima Jane stared at him in disbelief. "How can you say that after what happened this afternoon?"

"Look," he leveled his gaze at her, forcing Ima Jane to meet it, "nobody is goin' to bother breakin' into that camper again—not once the word gets out that there's nothin' in Wilson's letter but the ramblings of a condemned man."

"But I thought—" Tobe began, thoroughly confused.

"I suggest you do some more thinkin' and less talkin'," Fargo told him, with a warning glance.

Tobe still didn't understand, but he fell silent just the same and took a drink of the beer Griff set in front of him, irritated at the way people always treated him like a dumb kid.

Chapter Twelve

The setting sun's golden rays fanned over the western sky, tinting the edges of the scattered clouds. Black smoke poured from the semi's diesel stack as it roared along the highway, chased by its own giant shadow.

When the town of Glory hove into view, the trucker geared down and glanced at the old geezer slouched against the passenger door. He'd picked the guy up about ten miles back, hoping for some conversation, but beyond stating his destination, the old man hadn't said two words, just sat there staring out the window, clicking his false teeth together.

"That's Glory up ahead," the trucker said loudly, just in case the guy was deaf. He received a nod for an answer and tried again. "Want me to drop you off at the Rimrock?"

"Nope. Let me out on the other side a town." His mouth barely opened when he talked. As loose as those dentures sounded, the trucker figured they'd fall out if the old man opened his mouth any wider. Maybe in his shoes he wouldn't be so talkative either, he decided.

The highway went straight through the center of town. The

mostly abandoned buildings in the block-and-a-half-long business district blanketed the thoroughfare in shadow. The semi rumbled through it at a slower speed than usual, then rolled to a jerky stop at the corner of the last cross street, brakes squealing and grabbing.

"Here you are." The cab vibrated with the suppressed power of the idling engine.

Without so much as a "thanks for the ride," the old man climbed down from the truck, exhibiting surprising spryness for his advanced years. Curious as to his destination, the trucker watched the reflection in the side mirror. But the old man disappeared from sight almost instantly.

Air brakes whooshed and hissed an accompaniment to the grinding of gears as Saddlebags ducked into an alleyway nearly overgrown with weeds. He scurried down it, keeping to the deep shadows. "Fool's errand, that's what this is," he grumbled to himself. "It's a long walk back if'n you can't bum a ride off someone. An' what for? Nothing, that's what for."

The aroma of fried chicken drifted to him before he reached the rear of the Rimrock. He grinned when he saw the back door to the kitchen standing open. He stole close to it, ignoring the flies that swarmed against its screen door, tormented by all the food on the other side of the wire mesh.

Inside the kitchen, an aproned Griff stepped to the charcoal grill and Saddlebags heard the hiss and sizzle of a steak being turned. He tried to remember the last time he'd chewed a piece of meat, but his memory wasn't that good, and the day was too long ago to recall.

Heat wafted through the screen door, stirred by the oscillating fan whirring at high speed near the grill. Shifting to scan every corner of the kitchen, Saddlebags saw that Griff was its only occupant. He settled back to wait, confident that his vigil would be rewarded.

Sure enough, not five minutes later, Ima Jane pushed through the swinging door and entered the kitchen. Immediately Saddlebags stepped closer to the screen door and tapped on its wooden frame.

Startled, Ima Jane turned and stared in openmouthed surprise when she recognized him. Recovering, she said quickly, "Griff, it's Saddlebags."

She hurried to the screen door and pushed it open, her smile bright with a welcome that failed to disguise her curiosity.

"I didn't expect to see you. Come on in. I'll bet you're hungry." Then she called over her shoulder, "Griff, fix Saddlebags a plate of your beef and noodles."

His hesitation was slight. It was information Saddlebags wanted, not food, but he wasn't fool enough to pass up a free meal. He followed her inside and let himself be led to the break table in the corner. By the time he sat down, Griff arrived with a plate mounded with homemade egg noodles in a rich brown gravy dotted with small chunks of tender beef.

Ima Jane produced a set of silverware and a glass of milk, then sank into the chair on his left. "When did you get into town?"

"Just now." He shoveled some noodles into his mouth. They almost dissolved on contact. "Who was that redhead with McCallister today?"

He felt, rather than saw, her eyes sharpen on him. "That was Angie Sommers. Luke mentioned they had seen you."

"Sommers." He rolled the name through his mind and came up empty. "Never heard it."

"I don't imagine you have. She only arrived yesterday from Iowa."

"Iowa." He shoveled in another mouthful of food, confident that the single-word response would be enough to prime Ima Jane's pump. Whatever information she had about the redhead, Saddlebags knew she would spill it.

"Yes, it turns out that it was her grandfather's body they found on the Ten Bar. His name was Henry Wilson. I'm sure you've heard of him. He was the grandson of Ike Wilson, the outlaw— the one who came here years ago to search for the gold."

"Heard of him." Saddlebags tore off a chunk of bread and sopped it in the noodle gravy. "Before my time, though."

"We've been trying to remember if you came one year later or two."

"Can't recall." He dismissed the subject with a lift of his bony shoulders and never looked up from his plate. "Been too long."

Disappointed that she hadn't succeeded in eliciting a more precise answer, Ima Jane sighed. "I suppose it has."

"Came t' claim the body, did she?" Gravy dripped on his matted beard when he jammed the sodden bread chunk in his mouth. But he didn't bother to wipe at it. Whatever table manners he'd learned, he had abandoned them long ago.

Ima Jane nodded. "She's thinking about taking his remains back to Iowa so he can be buried next to his wife."

"No point." His stomach was full, but he continued to stuff the food in his mouth. It was a common practice of primitive man to gorge when there was plenty. It improved the chances of survival during times of want. "They're dead. They ain't gonna know it."

"I swear you men have no romance in your souls," she declared, with an amused but despairing shake of her head. "I grant you it's more symbolic than anything else, but it seems fitting that they would be reunited again after all these years."

He grunted a response and washed down the mouthful of noodles with a swallow of milk, some of it dribbling from his mouth corners.

"I'm glad Luke saw you at the ranch this afternoon." The statement seemed to come from out of the blue.

But it was the tone of her voice that caught Saddlebags's ear. It was one that signaled the pump needed a bit more priming for the well to keep flowing.

"Why?" He pushed the word through the fast-dissolving noodles in his mouth.

"Because somebody broke into Angie's camper while she was at the ranch. Fortunately nothing was taken." Her gaze was fastened on him in avid anticipation of his reaction. "But we're all convinced that whoever broke into it was looking for the letter."

"Letter?" Before he could stop himself, he shot her a quick look.

Her smile was smug with satisfaction. "Yes. The one Ike Wilson wrote to his wife before he was hung. The one everyone thinks might have clues to the gold's location."

"She brought it with her?" He scooped up more noodles, using a piece of bread to push them onto the spoon, while he pondered the many implications of that.

"A copy of it. She left the original at home. She says it has historical value completely apart from the missing gold," Ima Jane explained, much too casually. "Which is just as well because it's worthless otherwise."

"You've read it?"

"She showed it to all of us earlier. And believe me, there's nothing in it that indicates where the gold is."

"Why you tellin' me that? Think I'm gonna knock her over the head and steal it?" He threw her a cold and ugly look.

She recoiled instinctively. "I never said that."

He cackled at her reaction. "Scared ya, huh?"

"Of course not," she denied, still a little flustered.

"Not to worry. That letter can't tell me nothin' I don't already know." He talked through the food in his mouth, his loose dentures clicking and clacking.

He briefly wished he had taken out his teeth before he'd started eating. As soft as these noodles were, he could have easily gummed them.

"How can you be so positive of that when you haven't seen the letter yourself?" Ima Jane wondered with a mixture of curiosity and vague suspicion.

"Stands t' reason." He tipped the milk glass to his mouth and flushed the food into his stomach.

"How?"

"'Cause folks claim her grandfather had a copy o' that letter, an' he never found the gold."

"I wonder what happened to his copy," Ima Jane murmured. "It wasn't among the things they recovered with the body."

"That a fact?" There wasn't much more than two large bites of food left on the plate. As much as he hated to leave it, Saddlebags had the feeling that if he tried to force it down, his stomach would bust open. He pushed the food back and laid a hand across his miserably full belly.

Rising from her chair, Ima Jane reached for his plate. "How about a slice of Griff's apple pie with some homemade ice cream?"

He shook his head in refusal just as Griff shouted from the grill area, "Your order's up."

"Be right there," she called back, then glanced at Saddlebags. "You sit here and rest. As soon as I get this order delivered, I'll pack you up some food to take with you."

He waited until Ima Jane had backed through the swinging door, balancing the serving tray with its food order on one arm. Then he went to work hauling out the kitchen trash. Nobody was ever going to say he took charity. He worked for anything he got.

Griff watched him but never said a word. As soon as he plated up the last food order, Griff went to work up a bag of nonperishable items: dried beans; potatoes; flour; coffee; powdered milk; and an assortment of canned meat, vegetables, and fruit. As always, once it was all packed, he set it outside the back door.

Saddlebags had disappeared after emptying the trash, but Griff knew he'd be back to sweep up after they closed for the night. That was the usual routine.

The white cue ball struck the point of the triangular formation with explosive force, sending the first ball crashing into the rest, scattering them over the felt-covered slate. Two balls spiraled into the pockets, landing with a thud.

Flushed with the success of his break shot, Tobe swaggered over to the corner of the pool table and rubbed the chalk over the tip of his cue stick. He grinned at the onlooking Fargo. "I told you this was gonna be my game."

"We'll see." With eyebrows beetling in concentration, Fargo studied the ball layout.

With the last order from the kitchen delivered to its table, Ima Jane made a swing by the billiard area. "Do either of you need another beer?"

"I've gotta win some of my money back from this one-armed hustler first," Tobe told her when Fargo shook his head in refusal.

"Good luck." Leaving them, Ima Jane made her way to Angie's table. "Do you need a refill on that iced tea?"

"I don't think so, thanks," Angie refused, then turned to the young girl sitting with her. "How about you, Dulcie? Would you like another Coke?"

Dulcie answered with a mute shake of her head, then popped another ice cube into her mouth and crunched noisily on it.

"In that case, I'll join you two." Ima Jane pulled out a chair and sat down at their table, taking advantage of the fact that business, as usual, was slow on a Sunday night. Not counting Angie, Fargo, Tobe, and Dulcie, there hadn't been more than a half dozen customers in. Saddlebags made seven, but Ima Jane didn't consider him a customer. "You'll never guess who showed up at the back door a while ago. Saddlebags," she volunteered the answer. "Luke told you all about him, didn't he?"

Angie nodded. "He's the old man who's been looking for the gold."

"That's him," Ima Jane confirmed. "And he was very curious about you—and what you were doing out there. Of course, I explained who you were and your reason for coming. Then something interesting happened."

"What?" she asked, her curiosity aroused.

"When I mentioned that you had shown us the letter and indicated that it contained no useful information about the gold's hiding place, he acted as if he had known that all along. Which tells me that somehow, someway, he got his hands on the copy your grandfather brought with him."

"It's possible," Angie agreed. "Almost none of my grandfather's things were recovered with the body."

"I'll bet you anything that Saddlebags found them and kept them for himself. Can't you just imagine how excited he must have been when he discovered that letter among his things? And how disappointed he was afterward?"

"Luke mentioned that he's been searching for years," Angie recalled idly.

"He's grown old searching for it. If that doesn't prove how futile looking is, nothing will," Ima Jane declared.

"You're probably right." But Angie was convinced she had discovered a vital key.

"I know I am," Ima Jane insisted, then glanced at the front door, distracted by another thought. "I wonder where Luke is tonight."

"He said he had chores to do at the ranch."

"Just the same, he's usually here on Sunday nights unless they're in the middle of calving, haying, or roundup. It's not like him to stay at the ranch alone." Her statement had the ring of knowledge.

Angie had learned just enough about Luke to want to know more. "Why?"

"Why what?" Ima Jane turned, her expression blank of understanding.

"Why wouldn't it be like him to stay alone at the ranch?"

"Because—" She paused to make a quick, assessing study of Angie. "I imagine you noticed the ruins of the ranch house while you were there."

"Yes. Luke told me it had been destroyed in a fire a few years back."

Ima Jane's expression took on a wise and knowing look. "I don't imagine that he also told you his wife and two-year-old son were killed in that fire."

"No." Angie was stunned by the news. "No, he didn't."

"It was such an awful tragedy," Ima Jane recalled, with a sigh. "A fire is devastating enough, but losing your wife and child, too. . . . Luke has never fully recovered from that."

"I don't know if anyone ever recovers from a loss like that. You just learn to go on with your life."

"So far, Luke has only managed to go on living," Ima Jane said, with regret. Then she went on to explain, "The spring following the fire, a bunch of us went out there—in all, there were probably thirty of us, friends and neighbors—to help haul away all the rubble and clean up the site. We planned on pitching in to build a new ranch house, like the old-fashioned barn raisings. But Luke chased us off. He wanted it all left just the way it was—a kind of memorial, I guess. As if he needed a reminder."

"I'm sorry." For what, Angie couldn't have said exactly. A whole host of emotions welled up inside her, sympathy and regret among them.

"We all are." Ima Jane's mouth curved in a sad smile of understanding. "Most of all, I think we're sorry about what it's done to him. In some ways, he isn't the same man at all."

"That's to be expected, though," Angie stated. "We're all changed by the things we go through in life."

"That's true, I know, but—" A troubled frown altered her expression as Ima Jane searched for the words to explain her concern. "I suppose it's his drinking that bothers me most. Maybe it isn't a problem now, but in time, it will be."

On that, Angie had to agree.

Grease popped and spattered around the fat patty of ground chuck in the iron skillet. Luke lifted a corner of it with a metal spatula to see if it was ready to turn. Almost, he concluded and left it to brown a little more, then used a fork to test the potatoes boiling in another pan on the stove. The centers were still on the hard side of firm. He put the lid back on the pan and laid the fork on the spoon rest along with the spatula, then reached for the drink glass sitting on the counter.

Barely a quarter inch of amber-colored whiskey remained in the bottom of it. All the rest was ice. When he tipped the glass to his mouth, he got a noseful of cubes along with the swallow of liquor.

The fifth of Wild Turkey by the sink held less than a shot. Unconcerned, Luke emptied it into the glass, tossed the bottle into the trash, and opened the cupboard door above it. Another fifth of whiskey sat on the shelf, its seal unbroken.

As his hand touched the bottle, the lid to the potatoes rattled a noisy accompaniment to the sound of rapidly boiling water. It bubbled over the sides of the pan and fell onto the red-hot burner, erupting in a hiss of steam. Cursing under his breath, Luke swung to rescue the potatoes and accidentally bumped the whiskey bottle. It somersaulted off the shelf, struck the edge of the countertop, and cracked open like an egg, spraying liquor and chips of thick glass everywhere.

For a split second, Luke froze, torn between the shattered bottle with its pooling whiskey on the floor and the pan boiling over on the stove. But the wildly rattling lid and the smell of scorched potato water demanded immediate attention.

Swearing in earnest now, Luke jerked the pan from the burner and turned off the heat to it, then went to work picking up the chunks and bits of glass from the broken whiskey bottle. Once they were all gathered, he dumped them in the trash and stalked to the utility room for a mop and a bucket.

When he reentered the kitchen, he was greeted by the stench of two new aromas mingling with the reek of whiskey: scorched green beans and charred beef. One look confirmed what his nose had told him; his supper, dull as it had been, was ruined.

In disgust, he switched off the burners, left the pans to set, and turned to the puddle of liquor on the floor, his temper simmering with the knowledge he couldn't even console himself with a drink. He made a couple of swipes with the mop to absorb the bulk of the liquid, then jammed the mop in the bucket.

"The hell with it." He snatched up his hat and truck keys before heading for the door and Ima Jane's.

Angie waited by the cash register while Ima Jane rang up her bill. At the pool table, Tobe and Fargo were playing off the night's second rubber match. Dulcie sat alone at the table, quietly drawing on a blank sheet of paper Ima Jane had provided along with a cup of crayons. Something told Angie this wasn't the first time Dulcie had entertained herself in such a manner while waiting for Tobe.

Studying Dulcie's head, bent in concentration over her drawing, Angie was struck by the fact she had met all these people for the first time just a little over twenty-four hours ago. Yet, despite the short time she'd spent with them, she had the feeling she'd known them most of her life. The thought brought a small, bemused smile to her lips.

"Are you sure you won't reconsider and sleep upstairs tonight?" Ima Jane counted out her change.

"Thanks, but I'll be fine in the camper." Angie slipped the change in her wallet and returned it to her purse.

"If you're sure." But her expectant glance invited Angie to change her mind.

"I'm sure."

"Okay, but if you should hear any strange noises in the night, you just holler."

"I will," Angie promised, then wished her a good night and waved to Dulcie.

Watching her leave, Ima Jane half hoped someone would come prowling around the camper and instantly felt guilty for wishing such a thing. It was just that there had been so much talk, so much excitement swirling about, generated first by the discovery of the skeleton, then by Angie's arrival and the existence of the letter with its possible clues to the missing gold.

Ima Jane wished that Angie had never shown them the letter. Speculating about its contents had been infinitely more stimulating than reading them. The aura of mystery was gone, and life threatened to return to its mundane patterns. It would seem terribly dull and uninteresting after this.

"She isn't callin' it a night already, is she?" Griff's question pulled her around.

"No, she said she was going to do some reading and relax a little before turning in." Her voice sounded as flat as she felt. Ima Jane couldn't even summon up enough curiosity to wonder why Griff had asked.

He grunted a response of sorts, then swept a narrowed glance over the nearly empty tables. "Doesn't look like we'll have any more customers tonight. I'm gonna start cleanin' up the kitchen."

"Might as well," she agreed, but Griff hadn't bothered to wait for her approval. He was already heading toward the kitchen.

"Dulcie," Fargo called and propped his pool stick against the wall. "You watch this brother of yours and make sure he doesn't cheat while I'm in the john."

"Ha!" Tobe countered. "If there's any cheatin' goin' on around here, you're the one doin' it."

Fargo snorted at that and started down the back hall. "You were the one movin' the cue ball, not me," he taunted over his shoulder.

"That was an accident," Tobe protested to Fargo's back, then swung to Ima Jane, desperate to convince someone of that. "I swear it was."

"Of course." Her murmured response showed the measure of her distraction.

The first evening stars glittered against the sky's purpling backdrop. Angie paused on the Rimrock's steps to drink in the magic of the Wyoming night, breathing in air that was fresh and pure. A quietness enveloped the landscape, magnifying the stillness and the simple sounds of nature.

Cocking her head, she listened to the sigh of a lazy breeze in the nearby trees, the fluttering of wings, and a scurrying in the tall grasses near the roadside. She made a slow descent of the steps, dawdling on each tread, deliberately delaying her walk to the camper.

This was the kind of night meant for sitting on a porch swing idly contemplating the horned moon up above. A night for humming half-forgotten melodies of old songs and watching the dance of fireflies. Back in Iowa, it would be the kind of night for sitting and listening to the corn grow. She was curious to discover what it would be like in Wyoming.

The haunting call of an owl echoed from the trees, plaintive in its cry of "Whooo. Whooo. Whooo."

"Only me," Angie replied and smiled at the foolishness of talking to a bird.

The quarter moon's pale light silvered the graveled lot where the encroaching shadows failed to claim it. On the far end of the lot, the camper's white sides gleamed softly. Angie strolled toward it, regretting that it didn't come equipped with a porch and a swing. She wasn't eager to shut herself inside it, knowing how hot and stuffy it would be after being closed up all day. At the same time, she wanted to kick back and replay the day's events in her mind.

So much had happened; yet so little had happened, too. So much more was still before her.

The camper, at least, would afford her privacy, Angie reminded herself. And if she cranked out all the windows, hooked the door open, and closed only the screen portion of it, it wouldn't take long for the camper to cool down.

As concerned as Ima Jane was for her safety she would have a fit if she knew Angie wasn't locking herself in the camper. Imagining the woman's reaction if she found out, Angie couldn't help but smile.

Still smiling at the mental picture, Angie wandered past the other pickup trucks parked in the lot, invading the blackness of their elongated shadows. From far down the highway came the low drone of an approaching vehicle. Glancing around, she spotted the twin beams of its headlights in the distance, glowing like small beady eyes.

With the muffling crunch of her shoes on the gravel, she almost didn't hear the whisper of sound behind her, a sound like the rushing of air. As she started to look back, pain exploded in her head as something hard struck the side of it with a glancing blow.

She reeled backward, then staggered forward, fighting an inner blackness that threatened to swallow her. Struggling to stay on her feet, Angie stumbled against the tailgate of a parked truck and grabbed hold of it. Something jerked at her arm, pulling her off balance.

Chapter Thirteen

The drive from the ranch had done little to improve the foulness of Luke's mood. Brakes and tires both squealed when he whipped the steering wheel around, making the turn into the parking lot at a speed faster than wisdom dictated.

The swooping arc of the truck's headlights raked the building and the vehicles parked outside it, then washed over a figure struggling to rise from the ground, fully illuminating the vivid red lights in her dark hair. Intent on Angie, Luke almost missed the second figure the truck beams captured. A glimpse was all he got of the man momentarily frozen by the glare. Then he was gone, merging with the darkness of the building's shadows.

In that same flash of an instant, Luke slammed on the brakes, and the pickup fishtailed to a skidding stop. Leaving the truck running with the headlights pointed at Angie, he piled out of the cab and ran to her side. By the time he reached her, she was on her knees, sitting back on her heels. She looked dazed and a little groggy, her face unnaturally white in the beams' bright glare.

He crouched beside her, laying a hand on her shoulder while his gaze examined her. "What happened? Did you fall?" His own expression was a mixture of concern and lingering irritation.

"Yes— No—I'm not sure." She reached up and gingerly touched an area behind her ear, then winced immediately. "I think . . . someone hit me. I kind of remember hearing footsteps afterward."

"Let me look." He shifted slightly to avoid blocking the light from the pickup and carefully parted her hair. "You've got the beginnings of a bump, but the skin isn't broken. Did you lose consciousness? Even for a few seconds?"

"No," she said after some thought, then managed a weak grin. "Although for a split second, I swear I saw stars."

A part of him admired her ability to find humor in this incident, but another part of him wanted to shake her for not treating it more seriously. For the time being, Luke chose to ignore her comment.

"Can you stand?" he asked.

"Sure," she replied with easy confidence.

Just the same, Luke maintained a steadying hold on her as she rose to her feet, exhibiting a little awkwardness. Once she was upright, Angie gently cupped a hand over the bump on her head.

"Are you feeling woozy? Sick to your stomach?" He watched her closely.

"No, but my head's throbbing like it's been whacked good."

"Come on. Let's get you inside." He circled a bracing arm around her and turned her toward the entrance to the Rimrock.

"No." She stiffened in resistance. "Ima Jane will fuss all over me. Let's go to the camper instead. I'll get my—" She reached for her purse, but it wasn't there. "My purse." The pounding of her head was momentarily pushed from her mind as she began scanning the graveled area near her feet. "I must have dropped it."

But it was nowhere in sight, which didn't surprise Luke in the least. "It's not here. The guy who hit you over the head probably took it."

"But my keys are in it. And my wallet with my money and all my credit cards. And—Oh my gosh." Stricken by the realization of another now-missing item, she pressed a hand to her mouth.

"The letter, I suppose," Luke concluded in disgust. "You didn't take my advice and put it somewhere else."

"It isn't that. The letter's here in my pocket." She absently touched the side pocket of her slacks. "It's all of the pictures in my wallet. Most of them are old family snapshots that can't be replaced."

For an instant, Luke recalled all the family pictures that had been destroyed in the fire that had claimed the lives of his wife and son. Just as abruptly, he banished it from his mind.

"Come on." He took her by the elbow and turned her again toward the door. "We're calling the sheriff."

Angie hung back. "But—"

"Your purse was stolen. You were robbed, Angie." Impatience made him curt with her. "This has to be reported."

The half-formed protest died on her lips. Without another word, she let him guide her to the door.

When he reached ahead to open it for her, she murmured in amazement, "Can you believe it? I traveled all the way to Wyoming just to get mugged."

She laughed, only the sound wasn't really a laugh. There was more confusion than amusement in it.

"Yeah, the irony of it is hilarious," Luke muttered grimly and steered her through the doorway.

Ima Jane was behind the bar, putting away glasses, when Angie walked in. "Angie. Did you change your mind about—" The instant she saw Luke behind Angie, she shouted over her shoulder to the kitchen, "You'd better turn the grill back on, Griff! Luke just walked in." All smiles, she directed her next words to him. "I had just about decided you weren't coming in tonight." Ima Jane reached for the bottle of Wild Turkey. "You'll want the usual, I imagine."

"Forget the drink for now," he said, and Ima Jane froze in surprise. "You need to call the sheriff. Angie's been robbed."

"Robbed?!" The shock of his announcement didn't last. A pulse beat later, Ima Jane was hurrying out from behind the counter, throwing a brief glance at Griff when he pushed through the swinging door from the kitchen. "Did you hear that, Griff? Angie's been robbed. Quick, call the sheriff."

Fargo came strolling out of the back hall, idly drying his right hand on his shirtfront, just in time to hear Ima Jane's order. "What happened?" he demanded, suddenly alert.

Big eyed with surprise, Tobe jumped in. "Did someone break into your camper again?"

"No," Luke answered for her and led Angie to a table near the door. "They hit her over the head and stole her purse." He pulled out a chair and all but pushed her onto it. "Sit down."

"How bad are you hurt?" Ima Jane was immediately all over her. "Should we send for an ambulance?"

"No, I'm fine," Angie insisted and again gingerly touched the extremely tender knot on her head. "I just have a bump up here. That's all."

By now, the others had gathered around her chair, but Luke remained in charge. "We'd better get an ice pack on that to keep the swelling down. Dulcie, get some ice from behind the bar and a clean towel to wrap it in."

When Dulcie sprinted for the bar, Griff joined them. "There's a car on the way. It should be here in thirty or forty minutes."

"Who hit you?" Fargo questioned.

Tobe immediately added, "Did you see him?"

"No, I didn't see anything," Angie admitted, resisting the impulse to shake her head, "except a bunch of stars."

"Have you got a penlight around here, Ima Jane? We'd better check her eyes and make sure she isn't concussed." Luke dragged another chair away from the table and sat down facing her.

"I'll get it." She hurried off, passing Dulcie as she ran back to the table, dropping ice cubes out of the towel she carried. She managed to arrive with most of them and rather proudly presented the bundle to Luke.

"Maybe we should go outside and look around, see if anybody's still out there," Tobe suggested while Luke expertly tied the bar towel together.

"No point," Griff grunted.

Fargo agreed with his summation. "Whoever ran off with her

purse is long gone by now. Besides, the sheriff wouldn't like us messin' up any tracks the guy might have left."

"How's he gonna leave any tracks?" Tobe wanted to know. "That parking lot's all gravel."

"So maybe he didn't leave any tracks," Fargo agreed irritably. "But he could've dropped something. It's better if they find it instead of one of us."

No one bothered to ask Luke if he had seen anyone, and he didn't volunteer the fact, preferring to keep that information to himself for the time being.

"Here." He handed Angie the makeshift ice bag. "Hold that on the bump."

"This really isn't necessary." But she applied it against the area behind her ear and sucked in a hissing breath at the fresh pounding it ignited.

Ima Jane returned with the penlight and a cup of coffee. "Here you go." She passed the light to Luke and set the cup on the table, then heaped sugar into it. "I brought you some coffee, too, Angie. With plenty of sugar in it. There's nothing better to ward off shock."

"Thanks." But the way her head was hurting, Angie wished all of them would just go away and leave her alone.

"Look at me." Luke hooked a finger under her chin and lifted it, turning her head to face him.

"What are you? A paramedic?" Angie asked, half in jest.

"He's a fireman," Dulcie inserted.

"A volunteer." Luke qualified her answer, flicking the bright penlight off and on to check the dilation of her pupils. "Advanced first-aid courses are part of the training since fire units are often the first to arrive."

"I didn't know," she murmured, suitably chastised.

"Now you do." Finished, he turned off the light.

"What's the verdict, doc?" she asked, forcing a smile.

He smiled back, and the lazy gentleness of it warmed her. "I don't think you're suffering from anything worse than a hard knock on the head, but it wouldn't hurt to have a doctor check you."

Angie made a slight face at that advice. "No thanks. He'd probably tell me to take two aspirins and go to bed. I can do that on my own."

Luke didn't argue, but he didn't agree either. "We'll see how you're feeling later on."

"What do you wanta bet that guy was after the letter?" Tobe issued the challenge to no one in particular. "When he didn't find it in her camper this afternoon, he probably figured she was carryin' it in her purse."

"If he did, he figured wrong," Angie informed him tiredly and received a sharp, admonishing kick from Luke. Her glance flew indignantly to his face and observed the small, barely perceptible shake of his head that urged silence.

"You mean, you still have it!" Tobe's eyes were wide with surprise.

"I still have it," she admitted, then added in a rush, "If the guy had just asked to see it instead of hitting me over the head, I would gladly have shown it to him."

"I left my truck running, Tobe," Luke said. "Go park it for me."

"Sure." But he went reluctantly, worried that he might miss something important.

A curious frown carved deep lines in Fargo's forehead. "You know I could have sworn I saw you put that letter back in your purse."

"Obviously she didn't if she still has it," Luke stated. "Let's all give it a rest for now. The police will have enough questions for all of us to answer once they get here."

Less than thirty-five minutes after Griff had placed the call, a patrol car from the sheriff's office pulled into the lot. Five minutes later an officer of the state police arrived, and Angie found herself repeating the same story over again, sketchy as it was. Once she had answered all the questions to their satisfaction, she and Luke accompanied the two men outside.

After she had shown the location of the attack and again described it, the officers turned to Luke. "Where was Miss Sommers when you first saw her?"

"On the ground, here by the truck, just starting to get up."

"Did you see anything else?" The question came at last.

Luke chose his words carefully. "I'm not sure, but I may have seen someone in the shadows over in that general area." Ignoring Angie's surprised look, he pointed to the spot. "He was caught in my headlight beams for no more than a split second; then he was gone."

"What did this person look like? Can you give us a description?"

"Not really. Like I said, the glimpse I had was brief."

"Male? Female?"

"I had the impression it was a man."

"Was he tall? Short?" The questions came at him rapid fire.

"I couldn't say."

"How was he dressed?"

"I don't know. I only had a glimpse of his face. The rest was all shadow."

"Probably had on dark clothes," the deputy murmured to the state patrolman.

The officer nodded, more in an acknowledgment of the comment than an agreement with it. "Which way did he go?"

"It's just a guess, but since he didn't cut across the parking lot, he probably ducked into the alley behind the Rimrock."

"Would you show us approximately where the man was when you saw him?"

"I can try, but I doubt I'll be able to narrow the area down very much. It all happened too quickly. He was there, and then he wasn't. For all I know, I might have only imagined that I saw someone."

"It's possible, but not likely."

Luke walked them to the shadowed side of the lot and indicated a ten-foot-long strip that might have been where the man was standing.

When they had finished, the state patrolman advised, "You two might as well go back inside. We'll look around out here, check the alley, see what we find. Then we'll be in to take your written statements."

"How's your head?" Luke asked as they walked back to the entrance.

"Until you asked, I had almost forgotten it was still hurting," Angie admitted, aware that her thoughts had already turned to the new problems she faced now that she was hundreds of miles from home with no money, no credit cards, and no driver's license. Distracted by the myriad of details she would have to handle, it was becoming difficult to focus on the actual mugging itself. "You never said anything about seeing someone."

"I didn't?"

"No, you didn't."

"Just because I saw someone, that doesn't mean he was the one who attacked you," Luke reasoned.

"But if he wasn't, what was he doing out here?"

"Maybe he was taking a walk."

"Maybe," Angie conceded, thinking about her own leisurely stroll across the parking lot and her initial enjoyment of the evening. "It was a lovely night for one."

He caught her use of the past tense and smiled. "But not anymore."

Her smile held the same trace of dryness that had been in his. "It doesn't seem as peaceful as it did before."

"I don't imagine it does."

As they climbed the steps to the Rimrock's door, her flitting thoughts jumped back to the man Luke had seen. "That man in the shadows might have seen the person who knocked me down and took my purse."

"It's possible." Luke paused with his hand on the doorknob. "I wouldn't say anything to the others just yet about the man I saw."

"Why?" She frowned at his odd request.

There was a mocking lift of one eyebrow, accenting the gleam in his eye. "With Ima Jane inside, you have to ask? She'll have people pointing fingers in every direction as it is. I think it's best if we keep this little piece of information strictly between ourselves and the police."

His reasoning sounded both sensible and wise. "That's probably a good idea."

Ima Jane rose from her chair the minute they walked through the door. "Where's the patrolman and Deputy Sparks?" she asked, glancing behind them. "They haven't left, have they?"

That possibility seemed to worry her. "They're outside looking around," Luke explained, then wondered at her barely suppressed agitation. "Why?"

"Well," she glanced uncertainly at her husband, "Griff just reminded me of something that we probably should have told them."

"What's that?" But Luke had already put two and two together and come up with the answer.

"Saddlebags was here tonight," Ima Jane announced as if the news were momentous.

"Really." Luke knew his lack of any real interest wasn't what Ima Jane expected. "When was that?"

"I never noticed the time," she admitted, half disgusted with herself. "But it must have been somewhere around eight. Wouldn't you say, Griff?"

"Sounds about right," he agreed.

"It probably wouldn't hurt to mention he was around tonight." Luke sensed Angie's questioning glance. He avoided it and pulled out a chair at the table for her.

"There's more, Luke," Ima Jane said, exhibiting an unusual tension. "I didn't think too much about him showing up at the back door earlier. I assumed he was here to get a hot meal, so I had Griff fix him a plate of beef and noodles." She paused, her glance darting to Angie. "This might be all my fault, Angie."

"How could this be your fault?" Angie countered, ready to brush off the whole idea as ridiculous.

"Because . . . right from the minute Saddlebags sat down to eat, he started asking me about you. I told you that," she reminded Angie.

"I remember." The pounding in her head seemed to get worse, making it difficult to think. "You mentioned something else, too— something about suspecting he already had a copy of the letter. You thought he might have found the one my grandfather had with him."

"That's what I thought then. But, what if he only pretended not to be interested in the letter so he could divert suspicion from himself?"

"So you're saying," Luke began, a crooked smile slanting the line of his mouth, "that you think that old man waited outside for Angie, snuck up behind her, hit her over the head, and took her purse."

"Why not?" Griff reasoned. "For an old man, he gets around pretty good."

"And you know how obsessed he is with finding that gold, Luke," Ima Jane reminded him. "He's devoted his entire life to it."

"I know." As damning as it all sounded, Luke still had trouble believing Saddlebags was responsible. "In all these years he's been here, he's never given anyone a single reason to question his honesty. He doesn't even take a can of beans off a shelf without paying for it in some way."

"But think how desperate he must be feeling," Griff argued, "knowin' he might die any day without ever layin' his hands on that gold. Desperate people can do desperate things."

"It's got to be Saddlebags." Tobe pitched himself into the conversation. "Who else would do it?"

That was a question no one wanted to answer. If the finger of suspicion wasn't pointed at Saddlebags, a recluse who was virtually a stranger, then it would have to search out someone they knew—and knew well.

Luke closed the discussion. "You wouldn't happen to have any of those beef and noodles left, would you, Griff? I haven't had supper yet, and my stomach is beginning to complain."

"I could use some coffee, too." Fargo pushed his empty beer bottle aside.

"I'll get it." Ima Jane plucked the bottle off the table and glanced at Angie. "How about you? Would you like another cup?"

"No, but I could use a couple of aspirins if you have any." She rubbed her fingers over her throbbing temple. "I had a bottle in my purse, but . . ."

"Say no more." Ima Jane laid a consoling hand on her shoulder. "We always have aspirins on hand around here."

Griff was halfway to the kitchen when the swinging door rocked open and the uniformed patrolman came striding into the bar area. A handbag swung by the strap hooked over the ballpoint pen in his hand.

"That's my purse!" Angie said incredulously. "You found it!"

"It was in the alley." With a faintly triumphant expression, he dumped the contents onto a table and used the pen to separate the various items. "It looks like everything's here. Driver's license, credit cards, cash." He flipped the wallet open to show her.

"And my pictures, too," she said happily and started to reach for them.

The patrolman stopped her before she could touch them. "We'll have to dust for fingerprints, but I wanted to make certain nothing was missing first."

"Of course." Angie pulled her hand back and made a visual inventory of the items. "It's all there." She was dazzled by the discovery. "I was so sure I'd seen the last of all this."

"You were lucky," the officer told her.

"Very lucky," she agreed, thinking of all the phone calls and money transfers she wouldn't have to make—and all the time that would have been lost doing it.

But the recovery of her purse made it obvious that the thief hadn't been after money. The cash was still there in the fold of her wallet. If any of it was missing, it couldn't be more than a few dollars. Which left the question: Why take the purse at all?

Again, it seemed to come back to the letter. The realization sobered Angie.

"It appears we may have also found the object your attacker used to hit you over the head," the patrolman informed her.

Her head came up, the movement igniting twinges of fresh pain. "What was it?"

"A dead tree limb. See these strands of red hair caught in the bark?" he replied. "As branches go, this one is pretty lightweight. It's not surprising it didn't do much damage to your head. I think it's safe to say your attacker wasn't out to hurt you. He just wanted to stun you enough to get the purse."

"Maybe." Fargo's voice held a wealth of skepticism. "And maybe it was the only thing at hand to do the job."

"I wouldn't be so sure." The patrolman's chest puffed up with a slow indrawn breath. "There were definitely heavier objects scattered between the parking lot and the alley. Ones that could have been much more deadly—like a rusted fence post, a two-by-four, and part of a broken bat, to name a few. If he had used any one of those, you'd be in an ambulance on your way to the hospital right now."

"If she was still alive." When Ima Jane glanced at Angie, guilt and remorse haunted her expression. Head down, Ima Jane turned away. "I'll get your aspirins."

"Wait a minute." Griff reached out to detain her. "We haven't told the patrolman what we remembered."

"You tell him," she said. "I've already talked too much."

Those were words Ima Jane thought she would never utter. But no matter how fast she walked, she couldn't escape the truth in them.

The kitchen's swinging door slapped back and forth behind her in an ever-diminishing arc until it stopped altogether. Near the grill, the oscillating fan continued its noisy whir, alternately blowing warm air on her, then away.

Moths and mosquitoes had joined the flies beating at the screen door. In her mind, Ima Jane again saw Saddlebags's face beyond the mesh. She stared sightlessly at the spot, trapped in the memory of that moment.

A white spear of light stabbed the blanket of darkness beyond the wire mesh. Distracted and puzzled by it, Ima Jane watched as it moved slowly about, first lengthening, then shortening. She was halfway to the door before she remembered the sheriff's deputy was still outside. It had to be his flashlight she was seeing.

"What on earth did you think it was?" she scolded herself, then gasped in alarm when Saddlebags stepped from the small wedge of space between the wall and the propped-open back door.

His hard, keen eyes pinned her to the spot as he held up a silencing finger, then threw a quick look outside. Ima Jane looked, too, but there was no sign of the deputy's flashlight.

"The redhead." His voice was pitched too low to carry beyond the kitchen. "How bad was she hurt?"

"She has a nasty knot on her head, but that's all." She hesitated, then threw caution aside, driven by the need to know the degree of her guilt. "Did you do it, Saddlebags?"

But he was already ducking out the screen door. He disappeared instantly, merging with the shadows.

"Did you?" Ima Jane repeated to an empty room.

Chapter Fourteen

Hunkered against the building's raised foundation, Saddlebags scanned the alleyway, searching for the uniformed deputy still somewhere outside. As long as he remained motionless, he knew it was unlikely he would be spotted. Even if Ima Jane alerted the patrolman, chances were he would never check the area so close to the tavern's back entrance. He'd be looking beyond it, expecting Saddlebags to be running away. And at night, it was movement that caught the human eye.

Farther down the alley, the beam of a flashlight washed the rear of an old shed, giving Saddlebags the deputy's location. Saddlebags waited a few more seconds to make sure Ima Jane didn't sic the patrolman on him, then crept along the side of the building, quietly working his way to the corner nearest the parking lot.

Crouching low, far below a human's normal line of vision, he peered around the corner. An old pickup went by on the highway, its broken tailpipe striking sparks off the pavement. Saddlebags waited until the noise of its engine had faded into nothing. He used the time to identify the vehicles in the lot and choose a route that offered the best concealment.

When all was quiet once more, he broke from the corner of the building and scurried across the intervening space at a crouching trot. His heart was slamming against his ribs like a jackhammer when he finally reached Luke's old Ford pickup. But this was no time to rest.

It took two attempts before he succeeded in hauling himself over the side of the truck bed. On his hands and knees, Saddle-bags crawled to the cab area, wincing in worry at the scuffling noises he made. But there was no one about to hear them.

He felt around with his hands. At last his fingers encountered the familiar feel of stiff cloth. He cackled silently. Good ole Luke still kept that old canvas tarp in the back of his pickup.

Working swiftly, he maneuvered his body underneath, taking pains not to disturb a single fold or buckle in the canvas and using its heavy weight to verify every inch of him was covered. Wrapped in blackness, he breathed in the musty smells of dust, old grain, and a hint of mildew.

It was stuffy under the thick canvas, but the warmth of it felt good to his old bones. Making a pillow of his arm, Saddlebags settled down to wait. This wasn't the first time he'd hitched a ride to the Ten Bar without Luke being the wiser.

Confident his hiding place wouldn't be discovered, he dozed some, which was about all he did anymore. It had been years since he had slept soundly. At the first click of a latch and creak of a door hinge, he was wide awake.

There were footsteps and voices, followed by the metallic sound of car doors opening and closing. The little gathering was breaking up and, just as Saddlebags expected, the patrol cars were the first to pull out of the lot.

A few minutes later, Tobe and Fargo came out of the Rimrock and climbed into their separate vehicles. Luke was the last to emerge, but the sound of a second voice warned Saddlebags that he wasn't alone. The redhead was with him. Saddlebags was quick to detect the underlying note of weariness in her voice, discernible despite a gallant effort to disguise it.

"Look, it's very generous of you to offer," she was saying, "but there's no need at all for you to give up your bed—"

Luke's drawling voice broke in, lazy with humor, "Is that some sort of proposition?"

"It's nothing of the sort and you know it." The redhead sounded more amused than offended. "I meant that it's unnecessary for me to stay at your place. You're all overreacting. I'll be perfectly safe in the camper tonight. Believe it or not, I am capable of taking care of myself. I don't need someone to protect me."

"You're absolutely right. What you really need is a keeper."

"Don't be ridiculous." There was a smile in her voice despite the scoffing tone of her words.

"If anyone around here is being ridiculous, it isn't me," Luke told her. "In less than twelve hours, your camper has been broken into and you've been hit over the head. Someone is very determined to get their hands on that letter, in case you haven't noticed."

"It does look that way." A thread of uneasiness entered her voice.

"It is that way," Luke stated. "You know, most people after they've been hit over the head get some sense knocked into them. Your skull must be a lot thicker."

"I'm not dense, if that's what you're implying. It's just that . . ." She let the sentence hang there unfinished.

"It's just that you don't want to believe anyone here actually set out to harm you," Luke guessed at the rest of it.

"Do you?" she challenged.

"No. But greed does funny things to people—even the best of them."

"I suppose." There was a trace of sadness in her words that said she didn't want to believe it.

"Why did you ever admit you had the letter?"

"Why should I lie about it?" She sounded surprised by the suggestion.

"Why, indeed," Luke murmured dryly. "There are times, Angie, when honesty isn't always the best policy."

"Really? You don't seem to pull your punches," she chided lightly.

"We're not talking about me."

"My mistake."

"I'm curious about something else—why did you show them the letter? It's one thing to admit you have it, and another to produce it."

"I did it because—" She stopped, hesitated, then sighed. "I don't know. Maybe because I'm a teacher. I enjoy sharing information, especially something as fascinating as that letter." Saddlebags could hear the excitement building in her voice, tired as she was. "The code he used is so simple, yet so cleverly done, too. In a way, I think I wanted to see if they would catch it."

Up to that point, Saddlebags had listened with only token interest. Now he was alert to every word that was said.

"You're crazy," Luke declared.

"Probably," she agreed. "I know there was a part of me that was sorry when none of them discovered the code."

"I'm surprised you didn't point it out to them."

"The teacher in me wanted to, especially when they were so convinced the letter contained absolutely no clues at all. Or, at least, none that made sense."

"They aren't going to be convinced for long, are they?"

"What do you mean?"

"I mean that sooner or later everyone is going to find out that one of your primary reasons for coming here is to look for the gold," Luke replied.

Saddlebags stiffened under the tarp, alarm shooting through him.

"I hadn't thought of that," she murmured.

"You'd better start thinking about it," Luke advised. "Whoever wanted the letter before—without being sure it contained anything—that person will be doubly determined to get his hands on it. You're not as safe as you think you are, Angie."

She attempted a shaky laugh. "Are you trying to scare me into staying at your place tonight?"

"Have I succeeded?"

"No." But she didn't sound as definite about it as she had earlier.

"Let's compromise," Luke said.

"Compromise? How?"

"You'll be coming to the Ten Bar to look for the gold anyway, so why not make the move tonight?"

"Let me make sure I understand you. You're suggesting that I take the camper and drive out to the ranch tonight?"

"You'll be safer there, even in the camper. In town like this, right on the highway, the parking lot here is too accessible."

"That's true," she admitted.

"Good. Then I'll follow you, or you can follow me."

"All right. But it will take me a couple minutes to get everything packed away and make sure all the cupboards and doors are latched tight."

"Do you need help?"

"No, I can manage."

Saddlebags could hear the crunch of her footsteps as she walked away. After a span of several seconds, the pickup door was pulled open and the bed of the truck dipped slightly when Luke stepped into the cab. The engine turned over once, then rumbled to life, and the truck vibrated beneath him. Saddlebags shifted a little, seeking a more comfortable position for the bumpy ride that was to come.

The hour was late when both vehicles pulled into the Ten Bar ranch yard. At Luke's direction, Angie parked the pickup camper on a level stretch of ground beneath the yard's tall security light.

He looked on while Angie plugged the camper's electrical cord into the pole's outlet.

"Is there anything else you need?" Luke asked after she had closed the camper panel.

"No, I'm all set." She brushed imaginary dust from her hands.

As one, they strolled toward the camper's rear door. "How's your head?"

"Much better. The aspirin helped a lot." Pausing in the yard light's bright pool, Angie rummaged through her purse for the key to the camper door.

Luke braced a hand on the side of the camper and watched the search. "Are you still going to the sheriff's office tomorrow?"

"First thing in the morning." Keys jangled from the metal ring she pulled out of the purse.

"Then what?" Luke was thinking in terms of the procedure to be followed in claiming her grandfather's body for burial.

"Then I look for the gold. Hopefully with your help." Her smile was brief and faintly chiding. "You surely didn't think that this knock on the head was going to change my mind about that, did you?"

"Something tells me it would take more than a knock on the head to do that." And that didn't exactly cheer him.

"You'd be right." When she moved to insert the key in the lock, something fell with a thud, startling both of them. Scuffling noises came from the rubble of the old ranch house. "What's that?" Tension held Angie motionless.

Pushing away from the camper, Luke took a step toward the rubble. At almost the same instant, a cat bounded out of the tall weeds and streaked toward the barn. Luke saw it and relaxed.

"It's only a cat," he told her. "Probably doing some hunting and knocked something over."

She released a sigh of relief that was part nervous laughter. "I guess I'm a little jumpier than I thought."

"Under the circumstances, that's understandable."

Her gaze was drawn to the area of the ruins, hidden from view by thick shadows. Unbidden came the sobering memory of Ima Jane's words.

"Ima Jane told me that you lost your wife and son in the fire." The instant she mentioned his family, Angie could almost see the shutters closing, locking all emotion from his face. "How did it happen?"

"You mean Ima Jane didn't tell you?" he countered, with a smile that didn't ring true.

"I didn't ask," Angie replied quietly and waited, conscious of the lengthening silence.

Just when she decided Luke wasn't going to talk about it, he said, "They think it was started by a faulty coffeemaker. By the time I got here, the whole house was in flames."

"You weren't at home when it started," she said, noticing that he was staring straight at her, but his eyes were unfocused.

"No. I'd gone to Sheridan to buy a new bull. Fargo went with me. Bill Skinner's boy Jake was working for me then but still living with his folks. By the time Fargo and I got to the Crossbow Ranch outside of Sheridan, picked out a bull, and got him loaded in the stock trailer, it was already the middle of the afternoon. On the way home, the truck broke down. Busted fan belt. We were able to get it fixed, but—I called Mary from the garage to tell her we'd be late and not to wait up for me. I knew she was alone at the ranch, and I didn't want her sitting up worrying about where I was."

Guilt and irony twisted through his words. It was easy to read between the lines and know that Luke had never been able to stop wondering whether the outcome might have been different if he hadn't called. If she had stayed up to wait for him, she might have discovered the fire in time to save herself and their young son.

"It was after midnight when we finally turned onto the ranch lane," Luke continued. "I remember Fargo made some comment about the dark storm clouds boiling up to the south. Not long after that, we saw the glow of the fire and realized it was smoke, not clouds we'd seen. By the time we arrived, the entire house was engulfed. The heat was so intense you couldn't get within ten feet of it." He dragged in a long breath, his gaze finally focusing on Angie before sliding away. "They found Mary's body in Jason's room, just inside the door. She never made it to his bed."

"I'm sorry." Angie knew how inadequate those words were, yet they were the only ones that expressed her feelings. She paused a moment then remarked, "I'm surprised you haven't cleared all this away and rebuilt. It can't be easy seeing this all the time."

One eyebrow lifted, cool and mocking. "You don't really think that by clearing away the rubble, I'll ever forget the way they died, do you?" The pain and bitterness in his voice was almost palpable.

"Of course not." Angie hesitated, then plunged on. "But it might help you remember the way they lived—instead of being so caught up in the way they died." Angie turned, unlocked the camper door, and pulled it open. "Good night."

Without waiting for a response, she stepped inside the camper and closed the door. Luke stood outside for several more seconds, his mind unwillingly dwelling on the things she had said.

Among the rubble of the ruins, Saddlebags hugged close to the scrap of cover he'd found, a cheek pressed tight to the disintegrating charcoal beneath it, bony fingers cupped over the knee he'd banged into a charred and rutted stud he'd failed to see in the dark. But lately his sharp eyes were always failing him at night.

Straining to catch every whisper of sound, he listened to the soft footfalls Luke's boots made when he walked away from the camper. Relief sagged through him as the sound receded, moving toward the house trailer.

Even after the trailer door opened and closed, Saddlebags remained in his hiding place, listening to the occasional creaks and thumps coming from the camper. His mind drifted back, recalling the words that that Angie girl had spoken—words that stirred awake tender feelings that had been long dormant—and hardened his resolve to get rid of her while there was still time.

Chapter Fifteen

〜

With the day nearly three hours old, the morning sun at last drove the night's chill from the air. Perched high atop the corral fence, Dulcie soaked in the warmth of its direct rays and gazed about with idle interest.

Suzie, the Guernsey cow, ambled across the pasture, her large udder no longer swollen with milk. Her passing went unnoticed by the trio of draft horses busy grazing on the rich pasture grass, now and then swishing their tails at bothersome flies. Only Joe, the junior member of the draft team, lingered in the corral, nosing around the feed trough for the odd morsel of grain the others might have missed. Over by the barn, the momma cat sat in the sunshine washing her face while a spotted black-and-white kitten played with a straw just inside the open barn.

Sighing, Dulcie wished the yellow kitten would venture outside. She wished it almost as fervently as she wished that Angie would come out of the camper. She was awake; Dulcie was positive of that. She'd heard water running and sounds of someone moving about earlier. She had wanted to knock on the camper door, but Tobe had said she shouldn't bother Angie.

Later, Dulcie promised herself as the ranch pickup rumbled and clattered across the yard with Tobe at the wheel and the empty stock trailer in tow. She watched as he made a sweeping turn, then put the truck in reverse and backed the trailer up to the stock pen. After considerable jockeying, he managed to get the rear of the trailer lined up with the loading chute. When he climbed out of the cab and came around to the side of the trailer, Dulcie jumped off the fence and joined him.

"What're you doing?" she asked, watching while he crawled over the side of the chute and unhooked the trailer gate.

"Gettin' ready to load those bulls." He nodded his head in the general direction of the two big Angus bulls standing near the far corner of the livestock pen, who were eyeing the activity around the chute with suspicion. The morning sun glistened on their sleek black hides, muscles rippling as they shifted uneasily.

"Where are you taking them?" Dulcie wondered.

"Out to the herd." After some struggling, Tobe got the gate open.

"Why?"

"So we can turn 'em loose with the cows." The instant the words were out of his mouth, he shot her a look of near panic, the tips of his ears reddening. "And don't ask why. Okay?"

"Okay. Can I come with you?" she asked when he climbed back over the chute and dropped to the ground.

"Not this time." He gave her ponytail a playful tug to soften his refusal. "You'd only be in the way. It'll be better if you stay here with Fargo and play with your doll or somethin'."

Head down, Dulcie glumly dug the toe of her shoe into the dirt. She hadn't played with her doll since its arm had fallen off. But Tobe had forgotten about that, just as he'd forgotten to fix it.

A door banged shut, the metallic sound of it echoing across the yard. Dulcie jerked her head around, her glance flying to the camper. Her heart gave a little leap of gladness when she saw Angie, dressed in a long broom skirt and a matching green and blue flowered top. That gladness quickly gave way to dismay when Angie walked straight to the tall yard-light pole and unplugged the camper's electrical cord, then set about stowing it in a side panel of the camper.

Dulcie turned to her brother. "I thought you said Angie was going to stay here." There was a faint tremor of accusation in her voice.

"That's what Luke said last night," he said, sending his own curious glance at the camper.

"But . . . it looks like she's leaving."

"And she could be plannin' on comin' back, too."

A "could be" wasn't definite enough. Dulcie had to find out for sure whether she was coming back or not. Breaking into a run, she raced across the ranch yard to the pickup camper, arriving a little worry eyed and out of breath. Seeing her, Angie paused next to the pickup's driver side, ignition key in hand.

"Good morning, Dulcie."

"Morning." Hurriedly gathering her courage, Dulcie blurted the vital question. "Are you leaving?"

"For a little while. I'll be back later." Her smile was bright with assurance.

Emboldened by that, Dulcie questioned her further: "Where are you going?"

"To see the sheriff."

Understanding flashed, erasing her previous anxiety. She nodded importantly. "I guess you need to talk to him about that guy who hit you on the head."

"That and . . . other things."

"Is your head still sore?" Dulcie frowned in belated concern.

"Only a little."

"I'll bet it hurt when you brushed your hair this morning."

Angie released a throaty laugh that warmed Dulcie all the way to her toes. "It certainly did," she agreed, then reached for the door handle. "I'd better be going. I'll see you this afternoon sometime," she told Dulcie, then glanced toward the barn area and waved to Luke as he led an iron-gray gelding into the yard.

He briefly raised a hand in acknowledgment, then looped the

reins over the gelding's neck and moved to the horse's side to recheck the cinch. While he tugged it another notch tighter, his gaze followed the camper's progress as it exited the ranch yard and headed down the lane.

A thin cloud of dust swept back from the camper and swirled around Dulcie. A hand came up to shield her eyes from the stinging particles. At last she turned away and started toward the trailer with a toe-scuffing walk.

Something in the droop of her shoulders and the downcast angle of her head triggered a half-forgotten memory in Luke's mind, a memory that went all the way back to a long-ago afternoon a week before the fire. A memory of Jason looking as lonely and dejected as Dulcie. Mary had been at his side, thoughtfully studying their son.

He remembered the determined ring of her voice, and the frosty vapor her breath made when she spoke. "Jason needs a playmate, Luke. Someone to romp in the snow with him, play ball, go fishing and all the other things kids do."

"I suppose we could get him a puppy," he had replied in all seriousness and absently draped an arm around her shoulders. "The Garveys' blue heeler had a litter about a month ago. I don't think he has sold them all yet."

"Actually . . ." Pausing, Mary had tipped her face toward him. He could still see the warm and intimate light that had danced in her eyes. "I was thinking along the lines of a little brother or sister."

In the afternoon sunlight, the snow's crystalline surface had sparkled like a blanket of diamonds, blinding in its dazzling brightness. But he hadn't been able to see anything but the look in Mary's eyes.

Luke smiled at the memory, feeling again that same, swift rush of emotion he had experienced that day, an emotion as strong and pure as anything he'd ever known.

But it didn't last as his glance strayed to the blackened timbers visible above the weeds. He saw again the flames that had turned his home into an inferno, an image that destroyed all the fine feelings of a moment ago.

Conscious of that old pain and anger returning, he fired another glance at Dulcie, irritated at her for reminding him of the other, and at Angie for making him aware of the difference between dwelling on how his wife lived and how she died.

Completing the final wrap to secure the cinch, he unhooked the stirrup from the horn and swung onto the saddle. With a twist of the reins, Luke turned the gray toward the stock pen.

"Open the gate and let's get those bulls loaded," he said to Tobe.

The chain rattled briefly, and the gate swung open. Luke walked the cat-footed gray horse into the pen. The bulls snorted and hooked imaginary horns at the horse and rider, but the routine was not a new one for either pair. After a few halfhearted attempts to avoid the chute, they clattered up its planked floor one after the other. Tobe waited to prod them into the trailer.

With the gelding's work done for the morning, Luke stripped off the saddle and turned the horse into the corral, then climbed in the pickup's passenger side, joining Tobe. As they pulled away from the loading chute, Luke's glance again traveled to Dulcie, watching them from the barn's maw with that same lost and forlorn look.

"You need to get Dulcie a puppy," he informed Tobe.

"A puppy? What for?" Tobe turned a stunned look on him.

"A ranch can be a lonely place for a young girl. A dog would be company for her."

"I suppose." He spotted his sister at the barn's entrance and the small black-and-white kitten, its back arched as it hissed. "It might keep her from gettin' scratched to death by those cats."

Angie pushed out the door of the brick courthouse, trailed by the sheriff. Pausing at the top of the concrete steps, he hooked his thumbs over his belt from long habit and surveyed the smattering of traffic on the street. At first glance, he looked the image of a western sheriff, tall and on the lean side with a neatly trimmed gray mustache, his white hat raked to one side of his head, and his badge shining in the midday sun. But the protruding paunch of his belly shattered the illusion.

"Thank you for your time, Sheriff." Angie extended a hand in farewell.

"My pleasure." He gripped it briefly. "I only wish I could've been more helpful. But it isn't likely we're ever gonna know why or how your grandfather died. The coroner sure couldn't tell us. And there's no more than a dozen folks still alive who were around when your grandfather came. Their memories of the time are pretty faulty."

"I understand." She'd had few expectations that he would be able to provide answers to any of her questions.

"Naturally we'll keep our ears open," he assured her. "And, like I said, we should be getting the results back from the DNA comparisons any day now. Once we've got that in our hands, we can release his remains to you. You know how the government is these days. You gotta have all the paperwork in order, all the i's dotted and t's crossed or it's not legal. As soon as all the red tape's done, making it official, I'll get word to you."

"I appreciate that. You know where to reach me."

He nodded. "At the Ten Bar." He leveled a glance at her, his chin dipping as if he were peering over a pair of glasses. "And if you remember anything at all about your attacker, you let us know right away."

"I will," Angie promised.

"It's unfortunate we weren't able to lift any clear prints, other than yours, from the purse. And that branch—well, it was just too rough to retain anything useable. I'm afraid we really don't have anything to go on."

"I'm just glad my purse was found." Angie touched the shoulder bag. "And that nothing was taken. All in all, the scare was worse than the knock on the head."

It was easier for Angie to believe that the mugging was an isolated incident, not likely to be repeated, than to view it as a kind of pattern that had begun with the break-in of her camper.

"I wouldn't take it too lightly," the sheriff warned. "Things like that don't usually happen around here. But I've seen too much in my time not to know that the wisest course is always to be cautious, even in places that are supposed to be safe."

"How true." It was good advice, but it was the kind difficult to translate into action. Seeking to bring an end to the meeting a second time, Angie smiled. "Thanks again for everything, Sheriff."

"No problem. I'll be in touch." He sketched her a one-fingered salute. As she moved down the steps, he called after her, "Give my regards to Luke when you see him."

"I will," she promised, with a brief wave.

The afternoon stretched before her, waiting to be filled. Time was something Angie couldn't afford to waste in idleness, not if she intended to accomplish her goal. She climbed behind the wheel of the pickup camper, determined to take those initial steps to put it all in motion.

With Luke's help, if possible. Alone, if necessary.

The first would undoubtedly put her on the right trail faster. But either way produced a mixture of eagerness and excitement for the hunt.

Boredom drove Griff out the front door of the Rimrock Bar & Grill. Boredom tinged with a deep malcontent. It was the noon hour, and the parking lot was as empty as the tables inside, typical of a Monday.

Broom in hand, he attacked the accumulation of dust on the front steps and narrow porch floor. A lazy wind played with the dust he raised, scattering some of it over the thick planks and blowing the rest of it onto the graveled lot.

From the highway came the distinctive, droning vibrations of an engine traveling at a reduced speed. Griff automatically glanced up from his sweeping. All his senses went on high alert the instant he recognized the pickup camper and the redhead behind the wheel.

But Angie didn't turn into the lot or even slow down. She simply honked and waved and continued south out of town. Frustration rose in his throat, thick and tight. For a long second, he stared after her, willing her to turn around and come back.

Forced to face the futility of such a hope, Griff whirled from the sight of her rapidly receding vehicle and stalked into the tavern, the layer of dust on the steps completely forgotten.

"That didn't take long," Ima Jane observed when he walked in, then resumed her dusting of the chair rungs, one of many cleaning tasks she reserved for Mondays.

"The Sommers girl just went by."

"Is that who honked?" she guessed. "I wondered."

"Headed back to the Ten Bar it looked like. Probably already been to see Beauchamp." He frowned thoughtfully. "I wonder what she found out."

"Nothing," Ima Jane replied with a certainty that immediately seized his attention.

"How do you know?" he challenged, knowing that she couldn't have gotten the information from the handful of customers they'd had that morning.

"Because I talked with Betty at the sheriff's office around ten." Finished with one chair, she moved on to the next.

His frown deepened. "I never heard the phone ring."

"That's because *I* called *her*," Ima Jane explained indifferently. "I thought they might have learned something from the fingerprints they took off her purse. But the partial prints they lifted weren't enough to be identifiable."

"Too bad."

"I know." Ima Jane paused, a troubled look on her face. "I hate to think that anyone we know would have done that."

"I still say Saddlebags was the culprit."

"We don't know that, Griff," she protested, but without conviction.

"Why? Because you didn't see him do it?" he scoffed. "You know as well as I do that it had to be him. That old geezer probably couldn't lift anything heavier than that dead branch. And he disappeared quick enough right afterward, didn't he?"

That wasn't exactly true and Ima Jane knew it. But how could she admit to Griff at this late date that she had discovered Saddlebags hiding in their kitchen—especially when she hadn't said a word about it to the police?

"I still don't want to believe he did it," she murmured, which was the reason behind her continued silence.

"Whether you want to believe it or not, it had to be Saddlebags," Griff stated, then threw a look toward the door. "And what does Luke do? Convinces the Sommers girl she'll be safer at the Ten Bar. Talk about convenient. That ranch is the old guy's stomping grounds."

"He wouldn't hurt her." Ima Jane clung to the memory of Saddlebags asking about the severity of Angie's injury.

"We'll see." Griff started for the kitchen, then stopped. "If she was smart, she'd ship her grandfather's remains back to Iowa and hightail it there herself."

"She can't."

"Why?"

"All the paperwork isn't done yet," she explained. "It'll be another couple days before they can release the remains to her."

Another couple days. Griff absorbed this new piece of information. That wasn't much time. Not much time at all.

All was quiet when Angie arrived at the Ten Bar. She noticed the empty stock trailer standing next to the barn, a block of wood propping up its tongue. But there was no sign of Luke, or his ranch pickup. She parked the camper next to the light pole and plugged back into the outlet, then changed into a pair of jeans and a cotton top and searched out the topography map of the area.

With it in hand, she set out for the house trailer. She was

halfway across the ranch yard when Dulcie scampered out of the trailer to meet her.

"I didn't know you were back. Have you been home long?" She looked stricken by the possibility.

"Not long at all," Angie assured her and glanced toward the trailer. "Is Luke here?"

"No. He left right after lunch. Tobe, too. Have you eaten? I'll bet Fargo'll fix you something if you haven't."

"Thanks, but I grabbed a sandwich in town. Is Fargo inside?"

"Yeah. You wanta see him?"

"I would, yes." Angie smiled at Dulcie's eager expression.

"He's in the kitchen. Come on. I'll take you."

With Dulcie leading the way at a skipping walk, they went into the trailer and straight to the kitchen. Angie hesitated when she saw that Fargo was on the phone.

Noting her presence, he said into the mouthpiece, "Just a minute. I got company." He lowered the receiver and held it against his chest. "If you're looking for Luke, he's out fixin' fence this afternoon. Probably won't be back 'til chore time."

Angie had suspected something of the sort. "Do you think he'd mind if I borrowed one of his horses and went riding this afternoon?"

"That would most likely depend on whether you'd sue if you got bucked off." There was nothing in his expression to indicate whether he was joking or not.

She smiled anyway. "I won't."

"Won't what? Get bucked off or sue?"

"I won't do either one."

"Remember she said that, Dulcie, in case you have to be a witness," he told the girl, his mouth curving with the barest hint of a smile. Then his gaze was once again directed at Angie. "You can take that flea-bitten gray you rode yesterday with Luke. Jackpot isn't likely to give you any problems. He's out in the home pasture with the other horses. Dulcie can show you where to find him.

Take along a bucket of grain from the barn and you shouldn't have any trouble catchin' him."

"Thanks." She started to turn away.

"Where you goin' anyway?" he challenged, his eyes narrowing in a sharp study. "If you don't turn up come sundown, it'd be good to know where to start lookin'."

"I thought I'd ride out to the canyon where the outlaws were captured."

Fargo eyed her with suspicion. "I thought Luke took you there yesterday."

"He did, but I'd like to go back and look around some more," she answered truthfully.

"What's that you got there?" He nodded at the folded map in her hand.

"A map of the terrain showing all the major features. I'm pretty sure I can find my way to the canyon, but I thought I'd take the map along with me, as well as a compass, just in case I get turned around."

"Good thinking," he grunted in approval.

After listening quietly through the whole exchange, Dulcie spoke up: "Can I come?"

When Angie hesitated, Fargo volunteered, "You can ride along as far as I'm concerned. I might finally get something done around here with you out of my hair. Course"—he paused, shooting Angie a glance—"it's up to her whether she wants to take you along or not."

"Can I?" Dulcie's soulfully pleading look made it impossible to refuse.

"Of course you can," Angie agreed. "I'll be glad for the company."

"I gotta get my hat." Beside herself with excitement, Dulcie flew out of the kitchen.

"You best know, we don't have a mount gentle enough for a kid," Fargo advised. "But Jackpot won't mind ridin' double if you don't."

"I don't mind," Angie assured him. "And I'm certain Dulcie won't."

"Are you kidding? She'd be tickled to death," he declared, with a grin, then added a bit more soberly, "It'll be good for her to spend some time with a woman, too." Turning to the side, he raised the phone to his ear, signaling an end to their conversation. "Sorry I kept you waitin' so long," he said into the receiver. "Now, what was that you were sayin'?"

Chapter Sixteen

A pair of skinny, kitten-scratched arms tightened their wrap around Angie's waist as the flea-bitten gray gelding negotiated the sloping trail down to the canyon's mouth. The air was still, almost eerily so, and the sun was hot and strong in the sky.

At the bottom of the slope, the ground leveled out, and the gray horse automatically broke into a jogging trot, jostling Dulcie. With a slight check on the reins, Angie slowed the horse to a walk.

"This is the place, Dulcie." She cast a sideways glance over her shoulder at the girl. "What do you say we get down and walk around a bit?"

"Okay."

Kicking free of the stirrups, Angie swung a leg over the saddlehorn and slid to the ground, then reached back and lifted Dulcie off the horse. She gathered up the loose reins and let her glance travel over the empty scene, then come to a stop on the girl, noting the vague disappointment in her expression.

"Have you ever been here before, Dulcie?" she asked, suspecting this was her first visit.

"No." And she didn't appear to find anything particularly special about it.

Seeking to stimulate Dulcie's imagination, Angie attempted to set the scene for her. "According to the story Luke told me, the posse came charging off that hill we just came down and surprised the outlaws."

"That hill?" Dulcie turned rounded eyes on the sloping trail that had seemed so steep and scary to her.

"That hill," Angie confirmed. "There were about a dozen riders in the posse, racing down it, yelling and shooting. Can't you just hear the thunder of all the pounding hooves?"

"It must have been loud, huh?"

"Very loud. Now, the outlaws tried to reach the safety of those rocks over there." She pointed to the tumble of boulders at the canyon's entrance. "But Ike Wilson was the only one who made it."

"Is that where he hid the gold?" Dulcie wondered, all big eyed with hope.

"I'm afraid not." Angie smiled at the girl's bubble-burst reaction. "If he had, the posse would have found it right away. No, they had already hidden the gold somewhere else before they got here."

"Oh." Dulcie immediately lost interest in the entire subject and aimed a finger at a patch of wildflowers growing inside the canyon mouth. "Can I go pick some flowers?"

"Sure. Go ahead." The instant the permission was granted, Dulcie scampered off. Angie called after her, cautioning, "Just pay attention and watch for snakes."

"I will." But she slowed her pace only slightly.

Angie watched her for a moment, then pulled the topo map from her pocket and unfolded it. The ranch site was easy to find, but the canyon entrance proved to be more difficult.

Starting from the ranch, she tried plotting out all the jigs and jogs the terrain had forced her to make to reach this place. The unfolded map was too unwieldy to hold with one hand and trace out the course with the other.

When she started to spread it out on the ground, Angie noticed a fallen boulder lying on its side, offering her a natural tabletop. She checked on Dulcie to make sure she hadn't wandered out of sight and spotted the pale-haired girl crouched among the wildflowers.

"I'll be over here, Dulcie," Angie called to the girl and set out for the fallen boulder, leading the horse.

Hurriedly Dulcie broke off two more stems and added them to the small bouquet clutched in her other hand, then raced to join Angie. As she laid the map on the boulder, Angie smoothed out its many creases.

"What's that you got?" Rising on tiptoes, Dulcie strained to peer over her arm.

"A map. Here's—"

A shadow suddenly fell across the rock. Dulcie gasped in alarm. At the same instant, the flea-bitten gray snorted and pulled back on the reins. Angie barely managed to catch a glimpse of an old man in a floppy-brimmed hat and baggy clothes before she was diverted by the shying horse, her own pulse accelerating at a mad rate.

"What're you doin' here?" the old man growled when she turned to check the startled horse.

The sound of a human voice, as much as her own efforts, worked to settle the horse. Yet it remained alert, ears pricked at the stranger. Reassured that her mount wasn't going to bolt for home, Angie squared around to face the old man looming before her.

His hat was pulled low, completely shading his features. The effect added to the menace of his cold stare and accented the gaunt hollows of his cheeks, partially hidden by a dirty and woolly beard. There was nothing remotely friendly about him, and the crooked set of his nose did little to alter that impression. Clearly it had been badly broken at one time and improperly reset.

Her first instinct was to back away from him, but she forced

herself to stand her ground. "You startled us. I had no idea anyone was around." Angie flashed him a nervous smile and guessed
his identity at once. "You must be Amos Aloysius Smith. Luke
told me about you. I'm Angie Sommers—"

"I know who you are. Now, git out!" He flung a bony hand,
gesturing for her to leave. Dulcie squeaked in alarm and ducked
behind Angie.

For Dulcie's sake alone, Angie refused to be intimidated by the
old man's rudeness. "We will in a while." She reached back and
laid a reassuring hand on the girl's arm, then once again straightened out the map. "First I want to locate this canyon on the map.
Maybe you can help me—"

"That map won't do you no good. You ain't never gonna find
that gold. Never. You hear?" His false teeth clicked loose on that
challenging note.

"I hear," Angie replied evenly. "But it's the canyon I'm trying
to find right now. If—"

"I said t' git!" He hobbled a step closer. "Go back where you
come from. You don't belong here."

Dulcie tugged at her hand, pulling her toward the horse. "Let's
go home, Angie." Her voice trembled on a whisper.

"He isn't going to hurt us, honey." She sounded more confident
than she felt.

"I'm warnin' ya for the last time. Don't go lookin' for that
gold, or you'll live t' regret it. I promise you that."

Sweaty and tired from an afternoon of mending fence, Luke
dismounted at the corral and slipped the water jug off the saddlehorn. He gave it a testing shake, but there wasn't enough in the bottom to make a sloshing sound, let alone to wet his parched mouth.

He passed the buckskin's reins to Tobe. "As soon as you get the
horses turned out, start on the chores."

"Are you headed for the trailer?" Tobe guessed when Luke
moved away.

"Yeah. Why?"

"Bring me back some water when you come, will ya? I drank all of mine." Tobe tossed Luke his empty jug.

"Sure." He struck out for the trailer, carrying both water jugs by their straps.

A half dozen steps from the corral, his glance strayed to the pickup camper parked next to the yard light. Its door was hooked open, leaving the inner screen to keep out the ever-present flies. A shadowy figure moved beyond the mesh, drawing Luke's attention.

It was a full second before Luke realized the shape was too tall and too stout to belong to Angie. The instant that fact registered, he changed course to investigate, his stride lengthening.

He jerked open the screen door, and Fargo whirled around, looking equally startled to see Luke. "What are you doing in there?" Luke demanded, eyes narrowing to dart past the one-armed man. "Where's Angie?"

"Don't be sneakin' up on a man like that, Luke. You dang near scared me to death," Fargo grumbled and made his way along the narrow passage to the door, his bulk blocking Luke's view of the interior.

"Where's Angie?" Luke repeated, certain she wasn't inside or she would have said something.

"Out ridin'. She took Dulcie with her. They should be comin' back any time now."

"Then what're you doing in her camper?" Luke didn't like what he was thinking.

"I thought I saw Saddlebags prowlin' around it. By the time I got from the trailer to here, there was no sign of him. The minute I saw she went off and left the door open, I decided I'd better check and see if he'd ransacked the place again." He paused and shrugged, his brow furrowing thoughtfully. "I can't be sure, of course, but it don't look like anything's been disturbed."

"Saddlebags, huh?" Luke scanned the area beyond the ruins, not sure whether he believed the old cowhand. "What makes you so sure it was him?"

Fargo drew his head back in surprise, one eyebrow shooting up in question. "Who else could it be?" he reasoned. "I'm not so sure you did the right thing bringin' her out here, Luke. She's right in that crazy old man's backyard now."

"And she's in mine, too." He caught the rhythmic beat of cantering hooves and turned to see Angie riding into the ranch yard. He waved, motioning for her to come directly to the camper. She swung the horse toward them and said something to the girl riding behind her.

"What's wrong?" she asked, her glance running to Luke in concern when he stepped up to lift Dulcie down.

Without elaboration, Luke related the story Fargo had told him. Angie listened in confusion.

"It couldn't have been Saddlebags." She swung out of the saddle. "Nobody can be in two places at once, and we just saw him at the canyon."

"Are you sure it was him?" Fargo challenged.

"I'm positive. We talked to him," Angie stated, then told them about the encounter.

"He scared me," Dulcie inserted in a small voice when Angie finished.

"He didn't mean us any harm," Angie said, as much to assure Luke and Fargo as Dulcie.

Fargo harrumphed in disbelief. "Not this time, maybe, but it sure sounds like he's got plans for you in the future." He turned and spat a stream of yellow tobacco juice off to the side.

"I know that's the way it sounded," Angie admitted, but other than an initial feeling of alarm when this dirty and scrawny old man had popped up out of nowhere, she hadn't been the least bit frightened of Saddlebags. Perhaps she should have been but she was oddly glad that she hadn't. "As soon as he issued his warning, he turned and scrambled back among the boulders and disappeared."

"Warning," Fargo scoffed at the word. "Is that what you call it? Sounded more like a threat to me."

"You don't plan on taking Saddlebags's advice, do you?" Accusation rifled through the coolness of Luke's voice.

"And leave, you mean? How can I?" Angie dodged the question. "I can't finalize the arrangements for my grandfather's burial until all the paperwork is finished, and the sheriff told me this morning that it wouldn't be ready for a couple more days."

"Did you mention that to Saddlebags?" Amusement etched dry lines around Luke's mouth.

"He didn't give me a chance." The gray horse nosed her shoulder. Absently Angie reached back and stroked the gelding's velvet-soft muzzle while turning a puzzled glance on Fargo. "If it wasn't Saddlebags you saw prowling around my camper, who could it have been?"

Momentarily caught at a loss for an answer, Fargo scratched his head and fumbled around for a reply. "Maybe nobody was prowlin' around your camper. Maybe I was just seein' things. I don't know. It's for sure nothin' looks disturbed inside." He waved a hand toward the camper. "Course you need to check that yourself."

"Of course," she agreed but made no move toward the door.

"Well," Fargo dragged in a long breath and bounced a glance off Luke's face, "don't look like there's no point in hangin' around here any longer. I'd best get back to the house and check on supper."

"Good idea. Take these." Luke tossed him the empty water jugs. "I'll be up directly."

"Luke, can Angie eat supper with us?" Dulcie lifted her face to him, eager and hopeful, as Fargo ambled toward the trailer house.

"I was just about to invite her."

That was all Dulcie needed to hear. She turned beseeching eyes on Angie. "You will come, won't you?"

The girl's earnest plea would have been impossible to refuse even if Angie had been so inclined. "I'd love to."

For Luke, the sight of her smile both soothed and stirred. Seeking to break the effect of it, he took the reins from Angie's hand and held them out to Dulcie. "Here. Take Jackpot to the barn and tell your brother to take care of him."

A shocked Dulcie stared first at the reins, then at the mammoth-looking horse, then at Luke. "Me?"

Her expression brought home the fact that she'd had little actual contact with the ranch stock despite the years she'd spent around them, something that would never have happened with a more assertive child. But Dulcie was too reticent to make demands, or even complain.

"Why not? There's nothing to it," he assured her, his manner deliberately offhand. "Just start walking to the barn and Jackpot will follow."

Encouraged by his answer, she took the reins from him and backed up until the reins were pulled taut and the horse's nose was stretched toward her. She stopped and sent a half-fearful glance at Luke. He clicked his tongue to the gelding and the gray stepped forward. The instant the reins went slack, a look of panic flashed in her eyes. She hurriedly backed up another step, but the horse kept coming toward her.

"That's good." Luke nodded in approval. "Now, just turn around and head for the barn. He'll follow."

Although clearly not certain she liked the idea of turning her back to the big horse, she did as Luke suggested, then snuck a worried glance over her shoulder. Her eyes rounded in amazement when she saw the gelding plodding quietly behind her. She threw a quick smile at Luke, her whole face lighting up with delight at her accomplishment.

After watching her, Luke became aware of Angie's gaze on him. His glance flicked briefly to her. "It seems Dulcie's education has been a bit neglected."

"Fargo mentioned that none of your horses were kid broke."

"Jackpot comes the closest." Something told him Tobe wouldn't be overjoyed at the idea of using some of his hard-earned savings to buy a horse for his sister. "With careful supervision, he might work. But we're getting off the subject."

"What subject is that?"

"You and all the trouble you've stirred up with your talk about buried treasure." Moving her out to the ranch hadn't turned out to be the solution he thought it would. Her encounter with Saddlebags was proof of that. No matter how many times he told himself that her welfare wasn't his responsibility, he hadn't been able to convince his conscience. Each incident seemed to push him deeper and deeper into a corner, and Luke didn't like it.

"You've decided to help me, haven't you?" she guessed, her dark eyes glowing in anticipation of answer.

He deliberately avoided giving one. "The way I look at it, I have three choices. One, I can help you search for the gold. Two, I can let you wander all over the Ten Bar looking for it by yourself. Or three, I can order you off my property and put an end to this, once and for all. Believe me, the third option is very tempting."

"But you're going to help just the same."

Her smiling certainty irked him. "We'll discuss that after supper tonight. I'm not committing to more than that." It was his turn to smile. "With any luck, I'll blow so many holes in your so-called information about where it's buried that you'll give up the idea of looking for it."

The light in her eyes began to sparkle and dance. "But you do agree to look at everything I've got—the maps, the letter, and the instructions encoded in it—and base your decision on their merits."

"Or their lack thereof. Yes."

"You have a deal." She thrust out her hand to seal the bargain.

Luke hesitated. "Why do I have the uncomfortable feeling that I've just been trapped in a corner?"

She laughed, quick and light. "Maybe because you have."

The sound was infectious, drawing a smile from him. He took her hand and murmured, "We'll see."

"You will, indeed," Angie countered.

Before he found himself liking the feel of her hand too much, he released it. "In the meantime, you'd better go through your camper and make sure no one other than Fargo was in it." He paused a beat. "Looking for this gold may be nothing more than a lark to you, but someone out there is very serious about finding it first."

Her smile faded with the soberness of his statement. "You're thinking about Saddlebags, aren't you?"

"Everything points to him being the most likely candidate, except your camper being broken into Sunday afternoon. I'm not convinced he could have made it to town in time."

Angie thought about that a moment, then shrugged it all off. "Dwelling on who may or may not have done it won't accomplish a single thing." Her smile was back, but this time the brightness of it was forced. "What time is supper?"

"We still have chores to do. About an hour to an hour and a half."

"Good. That gives me time to clean up and change. Thanks to Jackpot, I smell like a horse." Angie sniffed at her top and wrinkled her nose. "So do my clothes." She opened the camper's screen door, then paused. "Would you mind if I used your shower? The camper's fresh water tank—"

Luke waved off her explanation. "You're more than welcome to use the shower at the trailer."

"Thanks."

"No problem. I'll let Fargo know you'll be up to use it." Stepping away, he struck out for the trailer.

Amid nips and squeals, flattened ears, and flying hooves, the horses argued over the grain in the feed trough. Ignoring the equine squabbling, Luke pulled the last saddle and damp blanket off the corral fence and carried them into the timbered barn.

A side door stood open, letting in the flaming light of a slowly setting sun. Tobe slapped the milk cow's bony hip, hurrying her outside, then closed the door and chased the barn cats away from the pail of fresh milk.

"Is that the last of 'em?" He nodded to the saddle Luke carried.

"All done."

"In that case I'm heading to the house."

"I'll be right behind you." Toting the saddle on his shoulder, Luke ducked into the tack room, swung the saddle onto its wooden tree, and draped the blanket over it to finish drying.

Before leaving the barn, he stopped and dragged its massive double doors shut, then headed for the trailer. He made a detour by the camper, but Angie wasn't there.

There was no sign of her inside the trailer either, only Tobe at the sink straining the evening's milk and Fargo at the stove stirring something simmering in a pot.

"Where's Angie?"

"Dulcie decided Angie needed to see her bedroom. Like the woman had never seen one before." Fargo placed the lid back on the pan and turned off the burner under it. "Everything's done. Just got to dish it up."

"Hold supper off a couple minutes," Luke told him. "I'm gonna take a shower first."

"Me, too," Tobe chimed in as he emptied the last of the milk from the pail.

Fargo shook his head in disgust. "Happens every time you put a woman in a house. Nobody's ready to eat when the food is," he grumbled.

But Luke was halfway down the long hall to the master bedroom, located at the opposite end of the trailer from Dulcie's. By the time he walked into the room, he had his shirt unbuttoned and tugged loose from his jeans. Crossing the room, he went straight to the adjoining bath and came to a dead stop the instant he set foot inside the door.

It had been years since he'd shared a bathroom with a woman. He had forgotten the traces of the presence a woman could leave behind. Traces more subtle than the beading moisture of leftover steam on the mirror or the damp towel hanging on the rack. It was the mingling scents in the air, scents of cream-laden soap; strawberry shampoo; and another fragrance more elusive, more evocatively feminine.

Luke had no idea how long he stood there, with the suggestion of her presence encircling him, before he finally reached in the stall and turned on the spray.

Chapter Seventeen

Angie and Luke were halfway down the trailer steps when Dulcie poked her head out the door. "Angie, I forgot to thank you for fixing my hair," she called and touched a wondering hand to her flaxen hair, hair that Angie had French braided into a single long plait.

Pausing on the steps, Angie responded with an immediate smile. "You're very welcome."

"I love it," Dulcie declared with a fervency in her voice. "It makes me feel special."

"I'm glad, because you *are* special."

"So are you," Dulcie ventured shyly.

Before Angie could reply, Tobe yelled from inside the trailer, "Hey, Dulcie, where are you goin'? You're supposed to help load the dishwasher."

After a playfully guilty grimace, Dulcie wagged a hand in good-bye, then ducked back inside the trailer. With a lingering smile, Angie continued down the steps.

"You've made quite an impression on her," Luke observed, matching her stride to stroll toward the camper.

"It's mutual."

There was no mistaking the warm note of affection in her voice.

It was not an idle response perfunctorily given. It was part of the basic honesty about her, a trait that Luke hadn't encountered all that often. It drew his glance to her.

Like Dulcie, Angie wore her hair in a French braid. At the dinner table, when it had still been damp from the shower, it had been smooth and sleek. Now, as it dried, wisps had sprung free to curl about her face and neck, softening the style and giving it a touchable look. The discovery didn't exactly please him.

Since his wife's death, he had been physically attracted to other women, but Angie Sommers attracted him on a different level, a stronger level, the kind that involved emotions. It raised his guard.

"I guess, one way or another, you've made an impression on everyone you've met," he remarked grimly.

"Something tells me that wasn't intended as a compliment." Her sidelong glance was full of teasing humor.

"You're right; it wasn't." His mouth twisted in a dry smile. "In case you've forgotten, your being here has provoked someone into violence."

With a brief shake of her head, Angie disputed that. "It wasn't me, per se, but my knowledge of the gold's location that provoked it."

"True," he conceded the point. "But like the Bible says, 'money—or gold—is the root of all evil.'"

"Actually it says '*love* of money is the root of all evil.' In and of itself, there is nothing evil about money."

"In this day and age, I can't think of many people who wouldn't *love* to get their hands on a big chunk of it." His glance cut to her, wry with accusation. "Including you, or you wouldn't be so determined to find that outlaw gold."

"I know it probably looks that way, but it really isn't," Angie replied. "For as long as I can remember, I've had this desire to look for the gold. It's splitting hairs, I know, but I'm honestly more interested in finding it than possessing it."

"Next you'll be trying to convince me that you plan on giving it away to some charity—assuming, of course, that you find it."

"Let's just say that I have plans for it." Her lips curved in a smugly secretive smile. It intensified the disappointment he felt at her answer. He had expected something better from her. "But first, we have to find it," she added.

"*We?*" Luke challenged the choice of pronouns. "I don't believe that's been decided yet."

"Not yet," she admitted, but her voice had a confident lilt to it.

With twilight's shadows lengthening and darkening, the yard light flickered on, then grew steadily stronger and brighter, casting a pool of light around the camper. Automatically Luke scanned the darkness beyond it as they neared the vehicle.

When they rounded the side of the camper, his glance swept to the door she had left hooked open. "You really should keep it locked when you're gone," he told her.

"Locking it didn't do much good the last time someone broke in," Angie reminded him, then shrugged. "Besides, it gets too stuffy inside when it's all closed up."

After opening the screened door, she climbed into the back of the camper and advanced toward the sink area and the built-in boothlike table and bench seats directly opposite it. Luke followed her, instinctively removing his hat.

"Would you like me to put on some coffee?" She reached for the glass carafe to the drip-style coffeemaker, wedged into a narrow stretch of counter next to the sink.

The camper's close confines made Luke acutely aware of everything about her. She stood only inches from him, near enough that he could separate the scents of strawberry shampoo and soap and the tantalizing fragrance of her perfume.

"You don't have to make it for me." As far as he was concerned, there was more than enough stimulation without the addition of caffeine. Turning, he tossed his hat on a bench cushion and took note of the folded map lying on the table. "This discussion about whether I'll help with your search probably won't take very long anyway."

"I wouldn't count on that so I'll just go ahead and fix some coffee anyway." She held the carafe under the faucet and turned on the tap. A pump kicked in, and water pulsed from the spigot.

There was something homey about watching Angie go through all the steps to brew a pot of coffee. Too homey. Abruptly Luke looked away and decided what he really needed was a good, strong drink. With a shock he realized it had been two days since he'd had one.

"Have a seat." She nodded toward the cushioned bench seats as she finished filling the coffeemaker with water.

"Thanks." He slid onto the bench next to his hat. Needing a distraction, he reached for the map. "What's this?"

"A topography map of this area." Turning from the sink, Angie absently brushed her hands over her jeans, wiping off the water splatters. When Luke unfolded the map, she leaned across the table, using her elbows as props. "I took it with me when Dulcie and I rode out to the canyon today. I was hoping I'd be able to identify the location of the canyon on the map, but I couldn't tell from the terrain if it was here, or here." She pointed to her two choices.

After studying the map and orienting himself to known landmarks, Luke tapped the first choice. "It's this one."

"I was hoping it would be. It lines up almost perfectly." Pushing off the table, Angie straightened and reached up to open an overhead storage area.

"Lines up with what?" Luke frowned.

"With the route I think the outlaws used." She took down a folder containing more topo maps and riffled through them until she found the one she wanted. After laying the folder aside, she opened the map and spread it before Luke. "According to the robbery reports, the train was held up approximately right here." She placed her finger on a spot, then began to trace an imaginary line. "Initially, the outlaws fled south—probably in hopes of misleading the posse into thinking that's where they were going. Then they swung back north and crossed the tracks about here."

"Are you guessing, or do you know that for a fact?" he challenged in dry skepticism.

She flashed him a quick and faintly triumphant smile. "I know it for a fact. As I mentioned before, I researched this thoroughly, read every single account I could get my hands on—reports filed by railroad officials, the Pinkerton detective on the case, and the sheriff, as well as the transcript from the trial. I have copies with me, if you'd like to read them yourself." The impish gleam in her eyes all but dared him to ask for them.

Rather than give her the satisfaction of dumping them in his lap, Luke dismissed the suggestion. "I'll take your word for it."

"Good, because it would have taken you most of the night to read through them. It's quite an impressive stack I've amassed."

"Why?" he wondered.

"Why what?"

"Why would you bother to do all that research when you claim the letter gives you directions to the gold?"

"For a variety of reasons, I suppose," Angie replied after giving his question some thought. "Partly to verify different things that had been told to me, partly to satisfy my own curiosity about the sequence of events, and partly to see what documents I could find about the entire episode. Do you know I actually have copies of the interview notes from a newspaper reporter who talked to some of the participants nearly thirty years after the robbery took place?"

"Interesting," Luke murmured, and he meant it.

"It was very interesting," she agreed. "A few were hazy about the details; a couple distorted the facts; but most told the same story from different viewpoints and managed to draw a clearer picture of not only what happened, but when and how." When she at last met his gaze, her eyes started to twinkle. "So you can see, I really am an expert on this subject."

"All right." For the time being, Luke accepted her claim. "What happened after the outlaws swung north?"

Again Angie directed his attention to the topo map. "The posse trailed them until they hit this rough country over here." She shifted to the first map, then aligned the two maps together. "Then the rain washed out their tracks. Some of the posse members wanted to give up and go home, but by then, the sheriff and one of his deputies were convinced the outlaws were heading for Hole in the Wall."

Luke nodded. "A logical assumption, especially in those days."

"Definitely. In fact, initially the train robbery was thought to be the work of Butch Cassidy and his gang. Anyway, the posse continued on, taking a route they thought the outlaws would choose, and hoping to cut their tracks."

"Instead, they ran into the outlaws."

"Right here." She pointed to the location he had identified as the canyon, then marked it with a red felt-tip pen. "So, we have the trail lost here and the outlaws caught here."

"And a lot of country in between," Luke reminded her. "For that matter, what makes you so sure they still had the gold when they entered that first patch of rough country?"

"Because the tracker with the posse commented on the deep imprints the horses left. Imprints that indicated they were carrying something heavier than single riders. And gold is very heavy. One ingot can weigh ninety pounds, and that's dead weight, the kind that can tire a horse quickly. Not only that, but the imprints in the canyon, where the outlaws were captured, weren't nearly as deep. Which means, they hid the gold somewhere between these two places."

"That brings us to the letter, right?" Luke guessed.

"Right." Abandoning the maps, Angie pulled a photocopy of the letter from her jeans pocket and passed it to him. "I'll pour some coffee while you read that. You'd like a cup, wouldn't you?"

"That's fine." He nodded absently, his attention already absorbed by the contents of the letter.

Her own was divided between sneaking peaks at Luke and retrieving ceramic mugs from the cupboard to fill them with coffee.

All the while, her blood hummed with excitement, sending little tingles of anticipation dancing through her.

She placed one of the mugs on the table before him, but Luke took no notice of it or the aromatic steam that rose from the coffee's surface. A furrow of concentration creased his forehead when he read the letter through once, twice, then a third time. Angie sipped at her coffee and waited, half holding her breath.

At last he lowered it and raised the narrowed study of his gaze to her. "You say there's a coded message in this letter?"

"Yes." Eager to show him, Angie sat on the bench seat next to him, shoved her coffee aside, and leaned closer. "See this date of 12 July in the corner?"

"That's the date the letter was written, isn't it?"

"I'm sure it is. But what makes it significant is that it's underlined," she explained.

"And why is that significant?" Luke was unconvinced of its importance.

"Because it tells his wife the cipher method he used."

"Which is?"

"Every twelfth word is part of the message."

"How do you know that?"

"Because it works. And, because if he had underlined only the day of the month, it would have meant every twelfth letter made up the message. It's a very rudimentary code, really," Angie informed him. "There are many more sophisticated ones he could have used, but fortunately he didn't. To a trained cipher, this would be a kindergarten exercise."

"You researched that, too, did you?" he murmured, the first glimmer of belief visible in his side glance.

"I did," she confirmed, beaming a little at the subtle approval in his glance.

For a moment, Luke was distracted by the radiant sparkle in her eyes. He shook it off and dragged his attention back to the letter. "So, the message is every twelfth word."

"Starting with the letter itself, not the salutation," Angie clarified quickly, then rose from the seat. "Let me get you a paper and pencil. It's easier to write it down as you go."

She was back with a pen and notebook. Hurriedly she flipped the book open to a blank sheet, then handed both to him. Luke began with the opening sentence, counting the words as he went. It read:

> *It grieves my soul to write this to you, my love. Gold (the twelfth word) is a curse. I regret that my crime cannot remain forever hidden (twelfth word) from you . . .*

Luke stopped, jolted by the sight of the two words he'd written on the lined sheet: gold hidden. He felt his doubt disintegrating with a rush and struggled to hold on to some fragment of it.

In barely restrained haste, he transcribed the rest of the letter, then stared at the resulting message.

> *Gold hidden bell hole pillar evening shadow points canyon entrance right eagle rock bury under shelf reward for return.*

"Well? What do you think?" Angie prodded when he remained silent.

It was more than sheer coincidence that every twelfth word seemed to provide directions, and Luke knew it. But he couldn't bring himself to admit it yet.

He avoided her question for now by asking one of his own. "This postscript he wrote: 'Remember. Always remember God's way is not man's way.' He underlined that as well. Is that significant?"

"In this case, I think he did it for emphasis."

"Probably," he agreed thoughtfully. "It definitely doesn't have a twelfth word in it."

Angie gave him a couple more seconds to study both the letter and its coded message, then offered her own interpretation of it.

"This is the way I think the message reads," she began. "The gold is hidden, and Bell's hole—which is a western term for a mountain valley—is the starting point. Somewhere in that valley there is a pillar, probably of rock. The pillar's evening shadow will point to the entrance to a canyon that opens from the valley. After you enter the canyon, you go along the right side until you get to Eagle Rock. The gold is buried below a shelf. He wants his wife to return it and get the reward that was offered. Is that the way you read it?"

"That's the most logical." Luke switched his attention to the topo map, pulling it back in front of him. "There is no Bell's Valley in this area, but there is Buell's Basin. Several canyons empty into it."

"*And*," Angie inserted, stressing the word to give importance to what followed, "it lines up with the place where their tracks were lost and the place where the posse found them again."

"That's what you meant earlier," Luke said as he remembered what she had showed him on the maps.

"Exactly."

Pulling in a deep breath, Luke straightened from the table and leaned against the cushioned backrest, frowning thoughtfully. "There's one thing that bothers me in all this."

"What's that?"

"His wife. Why would Ike Wilson think she would recognize the code he used? How would she even know about it?"

"I'm sorry," Angie declared, then released a rueful laugh. "I forgot to mention that her father was a spy for the Union army during the Civil War. She grew up listening to tales of his various escapades. In fact, it was her father who showed Ike Wilson some of the simpler ciphers that he used."

"Then, why didn't his wife ever come for the gold and claim the reward?"

"According to family stories that have been handed down, there was a variety of reasons," Angie replied, then began ticking them off. "She didn't have the money to make the trip. Their son was barely two, too young for such a journey, and she would never have considered leaving him behind. But mainly, it was the shame she felt over her husband being hanged as a thief and murderer, and she knew it was a stigma their son would carry with him the rest of his life. Plus, she was a devout Christian. I suspect that, to her, finding the gold and returning it for the reward would be the same as condoning the crime he committed. And two wrongs never make a right."

"I suppose . . ." Luke frowned at the realization that Angie's explanation raised another issue. "But if she felt that strongly about it, why didn't she do the right thing and notify the authorities, explain about the letter, and tell them where the gold was hidden?"

"Caroline tortured herself over that very thing. But turning the letter over to the authorities meant branding her husband as a liar because he had sworn he didn't know where the gold was. And you have to understand that she loved him very much. She knew as well that, however misguided his attempt, his intention had been to provide his family with the financial security in death that he hadn't been able to give them in life. The more days that passed without turning over the letter, the harder it became for her to come forward." Pausing, Angie took a sip of coffee, then lifted one shoulder in a vague shrug. "At some point, she must have decided it was too late to do anything."

"I'm surprised she kept the letter at all." Luke reached for his own mug.

"So am I," Angie admitted. "I guess we'll never know why she did. Maybe it represented a last link with the man she loved. Maybe it was the temptation of the gold. Whatever the reason, it survived."

"And your grandfather was the only family member who ever came looking for the gold," Luke mused.

"Until now," she corrected softly.

He smiled crookedly, noting with a sidelong glance the determination and thrill of adventure in her eyes. "You're right. Not until now."

"So? Have I convinced you?" Angie challenged with that old confidence. "Will you take me to Buell's Basin and help me find the rock pillar and, ultimately, the gold?"

"You honestly believe it's still there?" he countered.

"How long can it possibly take to find out for sure?" she retorted lightly.

"If you'd ask Saddlebags that question, he'd tell you a lifetime."

"But he doesn't have the directions that we have." She nodded to the message Luke had written in the notebook.

"Unless Ima Jane was right, and he somehow got his hands on your grandfather's effects."

"Having the letter doesn't mean that he knows where to look. We do."

"True," Luke admitted, doubting that he would have broken the code if Angie hadn't shown him the key.

He studied the message again, the first niggling seeds of curiosity beginning to sprout. Was it a written road map to the stolen gold or not? Like Angie, he knew he had to find out.

"Two weeks," he said. "If we haven't found it within two weeks, you're on your own."

With an exultant laugh, Angie tossed a silent prayer of thanks heavenward, then sank onto the bench seat opposite Luke and clasped a hand over his. "You won't be sorry. I promise."

With the radiance of her face before him, the dark-shining glitter of her eyes locked with his, he was already sorry. No man could spend two solid weeks in this woman's company and expect to come away from the experience unscathed. He thought of days to be spent riding side by side with her, and the nights beneath the intimacy of star-dusted skies.

He felt the pressure of her hand change and soften from a friendly firmness to something else. At the same moment, a note of wonder crept into her eyes. And Luke knew she must have seen some of what he'd been imagining. With the first trace of self-consciousness he'd observed in her, she withdrew her hand, her fingertips feathering over his skin, sensitizing its tanned and work-roughened surface.

But there wasn't a hint of it in her voice when she leaned forward, resting both forearms on the tabletop, hands clasped together. "How soon can we leave?"

"That depends."

"On what?"

"On whether you want to camp out, or come back here every night."

"Less time will be wasted if we camp out. That's why I brought along my sleeping bag. It's stowed right under here." She pointed to the bench she was sitting on.

Slumped on the trailer's living room couch, his long, skinny legs stretched in front of him, Tobe pointed the remote control at the television. As he surfed through the channels, Dulcie scampered across the living room on tiptoes.

"Hey? Where are you goin'?" he called when she headed for the front door.

"I gotta ask Angie something," she answered without pausing and slipped out the door.

"Never known her to venture outside after dark before." Fargo picked up the can next to his recliner and spit into it.

Tobe shrugged his indifference. "Must be something important."

"Luke's been out there long enough, ain't he?" Fargo murmured thoughtfully. "Wonder what they're talkin' about?"

A sly and knowing grin spread over Tobe's face. "You can bet they aren't discussin' the price of cattle."

Outside the trailer, Dulcie ventured beyond the light that spilled from its windows. Inky black shadows quickly closed around her. She fastened her gaze on the camper's white sides, gleaming like a beacon in a sea of darkness. Something scurried in the weeds, and she broke into a run, anxious to reach her destination.

When she reached the circle of light that enveloped the pickup camper, she slowed to a walk. The sound of Angie's voice drifted to her. Eager to talk to her, Dulcie quickened her steps as she rounded the back of the camper.

A moth, drawn to the lights, fluttered around her face. She paused to slap it away, then heard Luke's voice and hesitated, unsure whether she should interrupt.

"...tomorrow to get everything organized and gather the necessary provisions together," he was saying. "We can set out the day after to hunt for your gold."

Gold. That single word shattered any lingering hesitation. Agog with the thought, Dulcie dashed to the camper door, mindless of the insects buzzing at its screen. She spotted Angie through the dark mesh, sitting at the table. She didn't bother to look for Luke.

"Are you really going to look for the gold?" she asked with a kind of breathless awe.

"Dulcie!" Angie's startled glance flew to her. Luke poked his head around the corner as Angie rose from the bench and approached the door. "What are you doing out there?"

"I came to see you." Without waiting for an invitation, she opened the screen door and clambered inside the camper. "Is it true? Are you really going to look for the gold?"

Angie darted a quick glance at Luke, then nodded calmly. "Yes, it's true. Now, what did you want to see me about?"

With her head spinning with thoughts of the gold, Dulcie had to stop and think. "My hair," she remembered. "If you're still here on Sunday, I wondered if you'd fix it like this again so everybody could see me."

"I'd be glad to do it." Her smile gave the answer all the earmarks of a promise.

Luke rose from the bench seat to stand behind Angie in the

camper's narrow passageway. "Isn't it past your bedtime?" he challenged.

Guiltily Dulcie ducked her chin. "Only a little."

"That's what I thought." He leveled a look at Dulcie that all but pushed her out the door.

"We'll talk some more tomorrow," Angie assured her. "In the meantime, you'd better get ready for bed before you get in trouble."

"Okay," she mumbled in grudging agreement, her shoulders slumping in defeat. At a foot-dragging pace, she turned and headed out of the camper.

Moved by Dulcie's air of dejection, Angie watched until the towheaded girl disappeared into the shadows outside the camper.

"The cat's out of the bag now," Luke murmured somewhat grimly.

Angie guessed that he was referring to their plan to search for the outlaw gold. "It isn't something we could have kept secret for long, anyway."

"True."

Turning from the screen door, Angie unexpectedly found herself standing nose to chin with Luke. But it was the compelling male shape of his mouth that riveted her attention. The air was suddenly heavy with undercurrents rippling between them. She looked up and saw the darkening of similar awareness in his blue-gray eyes.

For a moment she was tempted to tilt her head and invite his kiss. But she knew it would forever change their relationship, taking it to a new level at a time that wouldn't be wise.

Breaking the contact, she stepped back and turned, then went through the motions of making sure the screen door was tightly latched behind Dulcie.

When she swung back around, she adopted a friendly but businesslike air. "What will I need to take with me?" she asked, then held up a hand before he could answer. "Wait. I might as well start a list." She slipped by him and resumed her seat on the bench, then retrieved the notebook and pen from his side of the table.

Roused by the sound of the front door opening, Tobe peered curiously at Dulcie. "You weren't gone very long. Couldn't you find Angie?"

"I found her," she replied a bit glumly. "She was in the camper talking with Luke."

"Talkin'. Is that all they were doin'?" He was oddly disappointed by her answer.

"Yeah." She wandered into the living room. "They're going to go look for the gold."

Her offhand announcement hung for a moment before the words actually registered. Fargo sat bolt upright in the armchair, nearly swallowing the wad of tobacco in his mouth.

"What'd you just say?" he demanded, doubting his hearing.

"They're gonna go look for the gold." Dulcie repeated her previous statement.

"How do you know that?" Tobe challenged. "Who told you?"

"I heard 'em talking about it, and when I asked if they were really gonna go, Angie said they were." She paused by the couch and drew little circles on the armrest. "Do you think they'd let me go with them, Tobe?"

"Don't be silly. You're only a kid." He dismissed that possibility without a thought, concentrating his attention on more important matters. "I could have sworn she said she didn't know where the gold was."

"She was feedin' us lies, that's what she was doin'." Fargo scooped his tobacco cup off the floor and spat into it.

"Angie doesn't lie," Dulcie declared indignantly.

"When money's involved, everybody lies, kid," Fargo told her, then waved her toward the bedroom. "It's time you were puttin' on your p'jamas and crawlin' into bed. Run along, now."

But Tobe was still anxious to get information from her. "They didn't happen to say where they'd be lookin' for that gold, did they?"

She shook her head. "But I heard Luke say something about needing visions. I got good eyes."

"Visions?" Tobe stared at her in utter bewilderment.

Fargo snorted in disgust. "Not visions. *Provisions*. Luke was talkin' about food and supplies." Then he added thoughtfully, "Sounds like they plan on campin' out. Wherever they're goin', it must be a long ride from here. Someplace a pickup can't get to." He sank back in the armchair, pondering the possibilities.

Doing some thinking of his own, Tobe gave Dulcie an absent push toward her room. "Get along to bed. I'll come in later to tuck you in," he promised from habit, but he didn't bother to notice when Dulcie trudged into the hallway leading to the rear bedrooms. "I'd sure like to know where they're goin'," he murmured wistfully and sat forward, drawing his feet up under him and resting his elbows on his knees.

"Humphh. We'll know that soon enough." Fargo pushed out of the worn, overstuffed armchair.

"How?" Tobe looked at him in amazement.

"Luke'll tell us." He observed the blank look of disbelief Tobe gave him. "You know as well as I do that Luke never takes off without sayin' where he can be found."

"Yeah, but he's goin' after the gold. This time he might keep it from us."

Fargo disagreed. "Nope. He knows the ways of this country, and he knows that wouldn't be smart. Gold's worthless if you're dead. And accidents happen, even to a careful man. He'll tell us when he comes in, mark my words," he declared, with a decisive nod.

"I hope you're right," Tobe murmured, then tried to figure out what good it would do him to know the vicinity of the search if he didn't know the location of the gold. He started to say something to Fargo but realized he had disappeared into the kitchen. Springing off the couch, Tobe hurried to join him, then frowned when he found him going through the cupboards.

"What are you doin'?"

"Checkin' to see what all we'll need. Looks like you'll be goin' to town tomorrow for supplies."

"How come I have to go?" he protested.

"Because I'll be helpin' Luke get all the rest of the gear together." Fargo pried off the lid to the ten-pound flour tin and peered inside, then muttered to himself, "Wonder how long he's figurin' to be gone."

The front door opened and Luke walked in. After throwing a verifying glance over his shoulder, Fargo pounded the lid back on the can.

"Good timing," he said when Luke joined them in the kitchen. "I was just wonderin' how long you planned on bein' out."

"Dulcie told you, did she?" Luke looked vaguely disgruntled.

"She said you were going after the gold. Is it true?" Tobe asked, half expecting to be told otherwise.

Luke's glance raked both of them before he answered, "It's true." He went to the cupboard and got down a glass and the fifth of Wild Turkey.

"Where?"

"Where what?" he said, acting deliberately obtuse.

"Where will you look?" Tobe said, impatient and half irritated.

"We'll start in Buell's Basin." Luke poured a double shot of whiskey into the glass, then crossed to the refrigerator for ice.

Fargo nodded in satisfaction. "I figured it had to be a remote section of the ranch you couldn't get to with a four-by-four."

"You did, did you?" He threw back a swallow of liquor.

"Where will you look after that?" Tobe waited for the answer with undisguised eagerness.

"I'm not sure. Angie has some ideas."

"Where'd she get them? Not from that letter, that's for sure," Tobe declared. "I read it, and so did Fargo. There wasn't anything in it," he stated, then hesitated. "Was there?"

"That's Angie's business. I'm just serving as a guide and outfitter."

"How long you plannin' on bein' out?" Fargo repeated his initial question.

"We'll only pack enough supplies for a week and come back in when we need more."

"Tobe'll have to go to town tomorrow to fill out what we'll need. What about the tents? Will we be packin' them along, too?"

"*We?*" Luke challenged.

"Of course, we," Fargo retorted huffily. "You're gonna need somebody to do the cookin' an' camp work." He paused, his eyes narrowing in accusation. "You weren't plannin' on her roughin' it the way you do, were you?"

Luke stared into his drink, then sighed. "No, you're right. I can't very well do that."

"You sure can't." With a smug smile, Fargo went back to checking through the supplies on hand.

"Fargo's goin' with you?" Tobe looked at the old man with a mixture of envy and dismay.

"That's what I just said, isn't it?"

"But . . . you can't leave me here to do all this work by myself," Tobe protested.

"You've always wanted a ranch of your own," Luke reminded him. "Now you'll have the responsibility of one."

"But you two are gonna be out lookin' for the gold." The chagrin he felt was written all over his face.

Chapter Eighteen

"It isn't fair," Tobe mumbled to himself for the hundredth time as he hoisted the mug of foam-topped beer, then downed another big swallow from it.

"What's unfair?" Griff lifted the rack of clean glasses onto the back bar counter and curiously eyed the young cowboy's reflection in the mirror.

With the back of his hand, Tobe wiped the beer suds from his upper lip and remained slumped against the bar, staring morosely into his drink.

"It's unfair that I'm stuck with doin' all the cooking and the ranch work with only Dulcie for help. Some help she'll be," he grumbled. "I'll never get anything done if I have to drag her along everywhere I go. Good grief, she doesn't even know how to ride. Course, Luke says that's my fault. He says I shoulda taught her a long time ago, and now's the time to rectify it. You know what I say?"

"What?" Indifferent to Tobe's complaints, Griff went about placing the clean drink glasses on their respective shelves.

"I say if he's all fired hot about Dulcie learnin' to ride, he can take her along with him, throw her up on old Jackpot, and teach her himself," Tobe declared, then rethought the statement. "Or, better yet, he can take both of us with him and leave Fargo behind. I'll be a dang sight more useful to him than that one-armed old cowboy. I can cook as good as he does, and I've set up tents before, and as many times as I've scoured that area at roundup time, I know it every bit as well as Fargo does. Probably better. But does Luke listen to me? No." Tobe snorted in disgust and took another swig of beer, then wondered aloud, "Maybe I should try talkin' Angie into lettin' me come along."

Alerted by the name, Griff turned a sharpened glance on Tobe. "What's the Sommers gal got to do with it?"

"She's hired Luke to help her look for the gold. Why do you think I'm so upset about bein' left out of the hunt? It's the most excitin' thing that'll probably ever happen, and I'm supposed to stay at the ranch, milk the cow, and do all the chores and wet-nurse my sister like I was some snot-nosed kid too dumb to do anything else."

After the first sentence, Griff didn't hear a word of Tobe's tirade. "She knows where the gold is, then." It was exactly what he'd suspected all along.

"I don't know. Luke just said she had some ideas." Tobe was too wrapped up in his own misery to notice Griff's sudden interest in the conversation.

Seeking to disguise it, Griff took the last of the glasses from the rack and placed them one by one on the glass shelves. "Luke didn't happen to mention where their search was goin' to start, did he?"

"Buell's Basin."

"Never heard of it. Is that on Ten Bar land?" he asked and listened attentively when Tobe described the valley's location, then nodded in comprehension.

"I think I did some huntin' there about ten years back. That's the area where the gold's supposed to be, is it?"

"I guess," Tobe replied, with a despondent shrug. "Nobody tells me anything anymore."

Sifting through Tobe's various comments, Griff gleaned from them a pertinent fact. "I take it they haven't started out yet."

"Not 'til tomorrow morning. They sent me into town to get the supplies they'll need." He then grumbled, "A glorified errand boy, that's all I am. It's not fair, I tell you. It's just not fair."

As Griff recalled, Buell's Basin was long and broad, riddled with side canyons—which didn't exactly narrow the search a great deal.

Midafternoon on Wednesday, the trio of Angie, Luke, and Fargo rode into Buell's Basin, two packhorses in tow. Far from being flat, the valley floor was a jumble of craggy hills studded with trees and boulders. A wide gulch looped its way around them, carved by a shallow stream that, in spring, carried the runoff of mountain snowmelt and the occasional torrential rains.

Single file, the horses splashed across the clear-running stream and lunged up the steep slope of its opposite bank. Leading the way, Luke pointed his mount at the nearest hill and let the bay gelding pick its own route to the top.

Halting at the crest, Luke waited for Angie to join him. She reined in alongside him and silently studied the rugged valley before them, seeking the pillar formation mentioned in the letter's coded message.

Slowed by the packhorses, Fargo topped the crest and pulled up on the opposite side of Luke. He cast a glance at the pair, noting their scrutiny of the valley's terrain; dallied the rope to the packhorses around his saddlehorn; and then took a can of Copenhagen from his shirt pocket, wedged it against the pommel, and pried back the lid to it.

"Ya know"—he dipped his fingers into the can and took out a fat pinch of tobacco—"if'n I knew what you was lookin' for, I could be of some help in findin' it." He poked the tobacco in his mouth, tucking it between his cheek and gum.

"The legendary rock pillar." With a wry smile, Luke reached back and pulled a battered pair of binoculars from the pouch of his saddlebags, then began glassing the valley.

"Like that one." Angie pointed to a formation roughly a half mile distant.

"There's another one farther up the valley." After checking it out himself, Luke passed the field glasses to Angie.

"I see it." She lowered the binoculars, satisfaction running smooth and strong through her at this early success. Soon, she would be taking that first, actual step to solve the letter's riddle and locate the gold's hiding place. A new eagerness gleamed in her eyes when she handed the binoculars back to Luke. "We might as well check out the closest one first."

"What's there to check?" Fargo wondered, then guessed. "It's the shadow business, ain't it? I figured that was nothin' but a story."

"We'll soon find out whether it is or not," Luke stated as he stowed the binoculars back in the saddle pouch, then collected the reins, gathering up the horse to move out.

"The shadow—is it supposed to be mornin' or afternoon?" Fargo unwound the dallied rope, the tied reins hooked over the stub of his left arm.

"Afternoon." Luke touched a spur to his horse, sending it down the hill in the direction of the first rock formation.

It was two in the afternoon before Griff Evans managed to get away from the cafe-bar. Within the last twenty-four hours, he had come up with, and discarded, a half dozen plans to gain knowledge of the gold's location. Short of holding the Sommers woman hostage until she revealed all she knew, he had only one hope of beating her to the gold.

Driving like a madman, he raced up the Ten Bar's rutted lane, wrestling with the steering wheel to keep the vehicle under control. Short of the ranch yard, he slowed down and pulled off the lane into a draw. Leaving his truck parked, he proceeded the rest of the way on foot.

The place looked deserted, nothing and no one stirring. Griff had counted on Tobe being gone, checking cattle or fences, his sister with him. For once it seemed he had guessed correctly.

Smack-dab in the middle of the ranch yard stood the pickup camper. He made a beeline for it. At its rear door, he paused; cast furtive glances around; then reached in his pocket, hesitated, and decided to try the door first.

It wasn't locked. He could hardly believe his luck.

Hurriedly Griff climbed into the stuffy camper and closed the door behind him. A glance around the neat and orderly interior gave him little reason to hope he would achieve his goal. But it was sheer desperation that had brought him here, and it was sheer desperation that drove him to rummage through the place.

All along, he had assumed that the Sommers woman had taken the outlaw's letter with her. But it was also possible that she had brought along an extra copy of it as insurance of sorts, in the event something unforeseen happened to the first. And it was that second copy Griff hoped to find.

He went through the contents of every cupboard and drawer, meticulously checking to make sure no paper was tucked inside cereal boxes or taped under a drawer or shelf.

Nothing.

Little mewling sounds of frustration and near panic came from his throat. He glanced wildly around, his eyes stinging with the sweat that rolled from him in the camper's hot, stale air. A second later, he spotted the small, compact refrigerator, an obvious but still ideal hiding place. More than once he had stashed the Rimrock's weekend receipts in the kitchen freezer himself.

He opened the door, barely noticing the cooled air that washed over him. Fumbling with frantic haste, he searched through its meager contents. When he lifted a half-full carton of milk from its shelf, it slipped from his hand and fell to the floor. He snatched it up, but not before milk glugged out, leaving a small, white puddle on the vinyl flooring.

Out of habit, Griff tore off some paper towels and mopped up the spill, then opened a lower cupboard to throw the sodden towels in the plastic wastebasket. By pure chance, he noticed a wadded-up sheet of paper torn from a spiral notebook. Something was written on it, but only one word was visible. And that word was *Gold*.

For a split second, he froze. Half afraid to believe it was significant, Griff scooped up the balled sheet and tossed the sodden towels in the basket. With painstaking care, he smoothed out the crumpled sheet and read the words written on it.

His heart tripped over itself as a gurgle of triumphant laughter rose in his throat. A pulse beat later, he erupted with it, tears of joy and relief running down his sweaty cheeks. Clutching the paper to his chest, he did a graceless pirouette and bumped into the table, hard enough to jar him to his senses. Swallowing back the hysterical laughter, he gazed at the paper again, then carefully tucked it in his pants pocket and glanced around the trailer to make certain that everything was in its proper place.

A visual check of the ranch yard confirmed that no one was about. Confident that Tobe hadn't returned yet, Griff slipped out of the camper and trotted across the empty yard and down the lane to the draw where he'd left his truck.

In all, his search of the camper had used up almost two hours. Mentally he calculated the time it would take to gather the things he would need, and he knew there'd still be some daylight left. The Sommers woman already had a head start on him and he wasn't about to let it get any larger.

The paper crackled in his pocket when he slid behind the wheel. Griff chuckled again at his good fortune, then shook his head in amazement that the Sommers woman hadn't burned it. Too trusting, that's what she was.

*   *   *

The sun hung low in the western sky when Tobe walked out of the barn, toting the pail of warm, fresh milk. Abandoning the kittens, Dulcie ran to catch up with him, then had to trot to stay even with him.

"I'm hungry," she began.

"You should've eaten that other bologna sandwich I fixed for you," he grumbled in ill temper.

Dulcie stole a quick glance at him, noting his irritable scowl, and refrained from reminding him that she didn't like bologna. "What are we gonna have for supper?" she asked instead.

"How should I know?"

Wisely, Dulcie didn't respond to that. Tobe had been in a sour mood all day, ever since Fargo had rode out with Luke and Angie that morning.

Her stomach rumbled a reminder of its emptiness. Deciding that if she was hungry Tobe had to be as well, she ventured hesitantly, "Maybe if you had something to eat, you'd feel better."

Tobe shot her a look of exasperation. "Food isn't going to make me feel better."

Certain that *she* would, she was puzzled that he wouldn't. "Why?"

"Because I'd have to cook it, that's why," he snapped in answer, then followed through with the thought, "Just like I've had to do everything else by myself—the work, the chores, everything—while they're off lookin' for the gold." He got madder about being left behind every time he thought about it, and he'd thought of little else all day long. Rebelling, Tobe declared, "I'll tell you one thing for sure—I'm not doin' any cookin'."

Halting in her tracks, Dulcie stared at him, horror-struck and ravenous. "You're not?!"

"No, I am not," he asserted, with a determined jut of his chin. "We're goin' into town to eat. And Luke's gonna pay for it, too. Room and board, that's what he's supposed to furnish. There was nothing in the agreement about me having to cook the food and wash the dishes."

Relieved to hear they weren't going to starve, Dulcie ran after her brother. "But how can Luke pay for it? He isn't here."

"We'll just tell Ima Jane to charge our dinner to him."

Dulcie's stomach growled noisily all the way into town. When they arrived at the Rimrock Bar & Grill, only one other vehicle was parked in the lot. It was almost as empty inside.

"Hey, Ima Jane, bring me a beer and a Coke for Dulcie, will ya?" Tobe called to the woman behind the bar and slid into a vacant booth. Dulcie climbed in on the other side. "You'd better be deciding what you're gonna have," he told her.

"I already know. A hamburger with fries."

He relayed the order to Ima Jane when she arrived at the booth with his frosted mug of beer and Dulcie's Coke, then asked for himself, "What's the special tonight?"

"We don't have one."

"What do you mean? Griff always fixes one," Tobe frowned.

In agitation, Ima Jane rubbed a hand over her apron. "Griff isn't here tonight."

He scowled at her in disbelief. "Not here? Griff is always here."

"Not tonight," she murmured, distraught over her husband's absence and no longer able to conceal it.

"Where'd he go?"

"I'm not sure."

"Didn't he tell you where he was going?" Tobe asked, growing more and more confused.

"No." Ima Jane pressed her lips tightly together, fighting back the tears.

Incredulous, Tobe stared. "Well, when's he coming back?"

"I don't know." Ima Jane broke down and wailed, burying her face in the folds of her raised apron and weeping in earnest.

Momentarily at a loss for something to say or do, Tobe sat there with his mouth open. Worried that she was going to collapse right there at his feet, Tobe got up and helped her to a chair, awkwardly trying to comfort her.

"Don't cry, Ima Jane." He patted her shoulder. "He'll be back."

"No, he won't," she declared, with a wild and weeping shake of her head.

"You don't know that for sure." He tried to sound confident, a difficult task when he was feeling far from confident about anything, including the right way to console her.

"Yes . . . I . . . do," she said between hiccoughing sobs.

"How?" The word was out before Tobe could question the wisdom of asking.

"Because he sa . . . said so," Ima Jane replied and was afresh.

"Why? What did you two argue about, anyway?"

"We di . . . we didn't argue."

"You must have fought about something," Tobe insisted. It was the only thing that made sense.

"But we didn't. That's what's so awful." Sniffling back tears, she lifted her head, the sobs subsiding as she scrubbed at the salty wetness on her face with the heel of her hand. "He said . . . he hated this place . . . that he'd always hated it. As soon as he . . . gets the gold, he's leaving here and never coming back."

"Gold? What gold?" Even as he asked, Tobe knew what the answer had to be.

"The outlaw gold." Her lower lip began trembling again.

Dumbfounded, Tobe forgot all about comforting Ima Jane and sat down in the nearest chair. "He's going after the gold, too," he murmured in amazement, then frowned. "But he doesn't know where it is." He looked at her again. "Does he?"

Ima Jane stared back at him for a long, blank second before concluding rather lamely, "He must."

But how? That's what Tobe wondered. Then the unfairness of it hit him all over again. Here he was stuck being chore boy while everybody else was out looking for the gold. He envied Griff for walking off and saying the devil with the restaurant. He had half a mind to do the exact same thing.

"Who's gonna cook my hamburger then?" Dulcie asked in a small, worried voice.

For Ima Jane, the question was a prodding reminder of her new responsibility. "I will, sweetheart." Her quick smile was a bit strained, but back in its usual place, as she rose from the chair. "And what would you like me to fix for you, Tobe?"

"Same as her, I guess." With visions of shiny gold bars dancing in his head, food was the furthest thing from his mind at the moment.

The rock formation stood like a giant stone finger, rising some fifteen feet from the top of the hillock. The afternoon shadow it cast angled in an easterly direction toward the far side of the valley.

On a level stretch near the foot of the knoll, Angie kicked free of the stirrups and slid to the ground. She felt the betraying quiver of leg muscles that weren't used to so many hours in the saddle yet. Giving them a chance to recover their strength, she idly stroked the sweaty neck of the bald-faced roan and ran an admiring glance over the rough and rugged country.

The vastness of it dwarfed her, yet it invigorated her, too. It was wild and untameable, which Angie suspected was its greatest lure. She lifted her gaze to the incredible blue of the sky arcing from horizon to horizon. A scattering of clouds floated across it, plump and white as the distant snow-capped peaks.

"What's the verdict?" Slouching in the saddle, Fargo leaned a forearm on the saddlehorn. "Is this the pillar?"

Luke glanced toward the lengthening shadow, then flipped a stirrup across the saddle seat and began loosening the cinch a notch. "It's a little early to tell, but it doesn't look promising. I'd say the shadow will end up pointing to that far slope, but it'll be a while before we can tell for sure."

"So, what's the plan?" Fargo dismounted to stretch cramping

muscles. "Are we givin' the horses a breather and ridin' on to the next, or what?"

Luke threw an assessing look over the area. "This is a good place to camp: level ground, the creek nearby, and plenty of deadfall for firewood. It's your call." He directed the statement to Angie. "We can stay or move on."

She didn't hesitate. "We'll stay."

Within an hour, Fargo had a kettle of water boiling over an open fire. Stripped of saddles and gear, the horses grazed on some nearby grass, their legs hobbled to prevent them from straying far. As Angie returned to the campsite with an armload of wood, Luke pounded a ground stake, securing the last pup tent in place.

She dumped the load onto a pile of previously gathered branches. "Do you think we'll need more?" she asked Fargo and paused to dust off bits of bark and dirt from her hands and arms.

"That should do it." He began ladling the boiling water into an enamel coffeepot. "Coffee'll be ready in a short snort."

"Sounds good." Tired, Angie sank onto a flat boulder a few yards from the stone-encircled campfire.

"Was a time when a body could drink the water straight from the stream without needin' to boil it first," Fargo recalled, then smiled at another memory. "Last time I tried that, everybody got such a bad case of the trots, we had genuine traffic jams around every bush. That was one miserable camp, I'll tell you."

"I believe you." She swept off her ball cap and shook her hair free.

"You'd better," Luke told her, joining them. "It's true. As one of the victims, I ought to know."

Angie clucked her tongue in mock sympathy. "Poor guy."

"Got the tents up, have you?" Fargo surmised and took the kettle off the fire, then hung the coffeepot in its place.

"All done."

"It seems a shame to sleep in a tent when it looks like it will be a perfect night for sleeping under the stars," Angie murmured with a touch of wistfulness.

Fargo snorted in disagreement. "You won't think so when the bugs start flying and the snakes come slithering out of the rocks."

Angie shuddered expressively. "Let's don't talk about snakes."

"All right." Luke grinned. "Instead of snakes, how about shadows? Want to see if we can tell where this one's pointing while we're waiting for the coffee to get done?"

Before Angie could respond, she was distracted by a rattling in the brush to her right. Thinking it was one of the horses, she turned and found herself staring into the bearded face of Saddlebags Smith.

With dark eyes glowering beneath the floppy brim of his hat, he challenged, "What're you doin' here?"

Calm once again after that first skitter of surprise, Angie rose to face the scarecrow-like man in baggy clothes. "The same thing you are," she replied, with a smile. "Looking for the gold."

"You think the shadow from that rock'll guide ya to it?" He aimed a skinny finger at the tall boulder atop the knoll. "If ya do, you're wastin' your time. It ain't gonna point you to nothin' but heartbreak. Ya think I ain't followed it? Ya think I ain't looked in every direction? I scoured every canyon, an' it ain't here. An' if I can't find it, you won't either!"

But Angie wasn't about to admit defeat before the search had begun. "We'll see."

Pain and anger twisted through his expression. "You won't see nothin', I'm tellin' ya!" His ill-fitting dentures clicked and clattered, creating an odd background cadence to his near shout. "Open up them ears o' yours an' listen!"

Recognizing the futility of arguing, Angie tried another tactic. "I'm willing to listen," she told him. "We were about to have some coffee. Why don't you join us?"

"The coffee ain't ready yet or I'da smelt it," Saddlebags retorted, back to glowering with narrowed, accusing eyes. "You weren't about t' drink it. You was goin' to see where that shadow pointed. I heard ya talkin'."

"The sun's still too high. I was about to tell Luke that when you showed up," Angie replied.

He grunted his doubt. "But you was plannin' on checkin' it out."

"Later." She sat back down on the rock and patted the broad space next to her. "Come have a seat. The coffee will be ready soon."

Saddlebags shot a wary look at Luke, questioning his welcome. "Like she said, have a seat." Luke motioned to the rock. "I'll rustle another cup out of the pack."

Still chary, Saddlebags sidled closer to the fire but steered clear of the flat boulder and rested his haunches on a rotted log instead. "You shoulda done like I told ya an' gone back home. What was your folks thinkin' anyway, lettin' you come out here by yourself? You do got folks, ain'tcha?"

"My mother's still living. I lost my father a few years back," Angie replied.

"How come she didn't come with you?" His gaze darted about, alert to every move Luke and Fargo made.

"She's busy on the farm." A smile tugged at a corner of her mouth. "And, to be perfectly honest, she thinks it's sheer foolishness to look for the gold."

He nodded, his glance falling to the ground near his feet. "You shoulda listened to her. You really shoulda," he said with a kind of ache in his voice.

"What about your family?" Angie wondered, certain the old man was thinking of them.

"I ain't got no family. Not no more," he said, without looking up.

"Where was your home?"

His head came up, his gaze slicing to her. "This is the only home I got. An' it's the onliest one you'll have, if you don't get outta here quick."

"Why?" In her side vision, she saw Fargo when he wrapped a towel around the handle of the enameled pot and lifted it off the fire.

Steam rolled from the spout, aromatic with the scent of fresh-brewed coffee. One by one, he filled the tin cups that Luke had set out.

"Because lookin' for that gold'll make you crazy." The wildness of it was in his eyes—and in his dirty, unkempt appearance. "It'll get to where you can't think o' nothin' else. You'll forgit t' eat, t' sleep"—Saddlebags noticed his grimy fingers and nails as he reached for the cup Luke held out to him—"and t' wash."

She watched when he took the cup from Luke and drew it quickly close to his chest in an attempt to hide his dirty hands from her sight. "I don't think you're crazy, Mr. Smith."

Fargo breathed out a scoffing snort and muttered, "Not much, he ain't."

"A crazy person wouldn't notice how dirty he was," Angie pointed out, as much for Fargo's benefit as the old man's.

"She's right, Saddlebags," Luke inserted. "A bath, a shave, a haircut, and a clean set of clothes that fit, and nobody would recognize you."

"Just a bath would be an improvement," Fargo stated and spat into the fire. There was an instant sizzle and hiss.

Glaring at him, Saddlebags raised his tin cup. "This coffee'd taste a sight better if'n ya put an egg in it t' settle the grounds."

"You're danged right it would," Fargo agreed, bristling with offense. "But the only eggs them packhorses can tote are the powdered kind. And they don't taste too good in coffee."

Without another word, Saddlebags threw a contemptuous look at Fargo, set his cup on the ground, and stood up. Fargo started to rise as if to meet the old man's challenge. But Saddlebags turned and left the campsite at a trot that more closely resembled a fast, side-to-side waddle.

Angie was instantly on her feet. "Saddlebags, wait," she called after him. "Come back. You haven't finished your coffee."

When she took a step after him, Luke laid a detaining hand on her arm. "Let him go," he advised.

"But"— she frowned in confusion—"why did he take off like that?"

"Don't be lookin' at me," Fargo declared. "It couldn't a been nothin' I said. He was the one makin' insultin' remarks about my coffee."

"I know, but . . ." She looked in the direction Saddlebags had taken, but he'd disappeared into the brush. Sighing in regret, Angie turned back toward the fire. "There were so many questions I wanted to ask him." Questions like, What did he know about the rock pillar and the significance of the shadow? and Had he found her grandfather's effects, including a copy of the letter? "I wish he'd stayed longer."

"It looks like your wish is about to be granted." Luke looked beyond her at the spindly-legged old man hurriedly waddling back to the campsite.

He walked right past Angie, straight to Fargo; grabbed his hand; and placed a small, speckled egg in his palm. "Put that in the coffee."

Fargo stared at it. "It's a bird egg."

"A chicken's a bird, ain't it?" Saddlebags challenged, then waved at the egg. "That'll work the same as a chicken's."

After a moment's hesitation, Fargo cracked the egg open, checked the yolk, then tossed the egg in the coffeepot, shell and all. Saddlebags nodded in approval.

"The next cup'll taste a lot better." He picked up his cup and slurped at the hot coffee, then wiped his mouth on the sleeve of his coat and shot a quick look at the sun, measuring its distance from the horizon. "I'd best be goin'." When he turned to leave again, he leveled a hard glance at Angie. "Mind what I said. That rock ain't gonna point ya to nothin' but heartbreak. Go home."

Angie shook her head. "I can't."

A look of pure rage blazed in his eyes. "By God, I'll make you go!" he roared and took a threatening step toward her.

Luke moved into his path. "Careful, old man," he warned quietly.

"You have a care," Saddlebags snarled right back. "An' get her outta here!" He flung a hand in Angie's direction, then took off, vanishing into the brush only yards from camp.

Although she was reluctant to admit it, the fury in his expression had left Angie a bit shaken. She tried to cover it with a show of casual indifference as she sipped at her coffee.

"I wouldn't discount him as being totally harmless. There was some truth in what Saddlebags said," Luke told her. "I hope you realize that. For years, he's lived out here like an animal. And animals are very territorial."

"Yes, but his bark strikes me as being too loud and too ferocious," she remarked, thinking back over the encounter. "He wanted to scare me, I think—and he almost succeeded," she acknowledged with a wry smile.

"Maybe it's too bad he didn't," Luke mused.

Determination lifted her chin. "I am not about to give up before I've even begun to look."

Luke made no comment and glanced instead at the rock formation. "Saddlebags certainly didn't give any credence to the shadow thing."

"He mighta been tryin' to throw us off the scent, too," Fargo suggested.

"Maybe." Luke nodded slowly and swung back toward the fire. "We'll know for ourselves in a couple more hours."

With the sun sitting atop the rim of the western horizon, Luke and Angie climbed to the base of the stone pillar and halted in its shade. The long shadow it cast stretched far across the valley, its black finger pointing toward a treed slope on the far side. Through the binoculars, Luke scanned the area.

Lowering the glasses, he informed Angie, "There's no entrance to any canyon over there. Which means this isn't the right pillar."

"Not necessarily."

"Look for yourself." He offered the binoculars.

"Oh, I believe you," she assured him.

"Then what are you talking about?" His eyes narrowed in puzzled confusion.

Angie hesitated, then smiled ruefully. "I have a confession to make, Luke. I wasn't entirely honest with you the other evening."

"About what?"

"When I let you believe there wasn't anything particularly significant about the postscript that was underlined in the letter," she replied. "You see, I'm ninety-eight percent certain that it's really the key to the entire message."

"What? How?"

Chapter Nineteen

Ignoring his questions for the time being, Angie asked, "Do you remember what the postscript said?"

"Not exactly, no."

She dug the folded copy of the letter from her jeans pocket and handed it to him. With the sinking of the sun, a breeze had sprung up. It tugged at the edges of the letter when Luke unfolded it.

He turned, using his body to shield it from the playful wind, and reread the postscript aloud.

" 'Remember. Always remember God's way is not man's way.' " He arched a questioning glance at Angie. "Which means what?"

"Which means . . . God's way is usually the exact opposite of man's way—or woman's, for that matter." But Angie could tell that Luke didn't follow this line of thought. "For example, the three things most people want are money, power, and position. But the three things that God values are generosity, service, and humility. In other words, a person with a giving heart, someone who puts the needs of others before his or her own, and someone who doesn't think he or she is better than anyone else."

"I see." Frowning thoughtfully, he examined the letter again.

"So you think this postscript was deliberately underlined to indicate that—"

Angie jumped in with the answer, "All the instructions in the coded message need to be reversed. Instead of an evening shadow, it's a morning one; instead of following the right wall of the canyon, you go left."

"It sounds reasonable." But there was a note of reservation in his voice.

"It has to be that way. It's the only thing that makes sense."

"Why?"

"Because my grandfather knew about the twelfth-word code. He had deciphered the message before he came out here, yet in his last letter he wrote that it was all confusing—nothing made sense. Which can only mean the instructions in the message didn't lead him to the gold." Eager, excited, energized—she was all those things. The animation in her face and eyes fascinated Luke. "When I realized that, I knew there had to be something more in the letter. Something more than that kindergarten-level code."

"And you're convinced it's the underlined postscript," Luke stated.

"Why else did he underline it?" Angie reasoned. "Something tells me there isn't a single thing in the letter that's there by accident. Ike Wilson carefully thought through every word and every stroke in it. I've often wondered how many drafts he made. I know he must have been worried that someone other than his wife would read the letter and stumble onto his simple, twelfth-word code. Somewhere along the way, he came up with the idea of flip-flopping the direction. After that, it was probably an easy step for a minister's son to make the connection with God." She paused for a breath, her eyes sparkling. "So, in a way, I was truthful when I told you that I thought the postscript was underlined for emphasis. But what I didn't tell you was that it's the second—and vital—key to the message. Without it, we could look for years, just like Saddlebags, and never find the gold."

"If you're right," Luke tacked on the qualification.

"Like I said, I'm ninety-eight percent sure I'm right. Let's find out if I am." Her smile radiated confidence when she reached for his hand and led him around to the other side of the towering boulder. "Look."

With the sun's red blaze directly in his eyes, it was a moment before Luke could block off enough of its glare to see where she was pointing. There, half hidden by the long shadows of sundown, was the entrance to a canyon.

"I'd bet anything," Angie said, "that the rock's morning shadow will be aimed directly at the mouth to that canyon. What do you think?"

He checked the stone pillar behind him, gauged the placement of the sun, and nodded agreement. "I think that's a safe bet."

"So do I." The certainty of it smoothed her expression and brought a glow to her eyes. "Plus, the pillar is close enough to the entrance that Ike Wilson would have noticed the reach of its shadow when he and the gang rode out of the canyon in the morning."

"It sounds like you think they camped there the night before."

"It would have been logical." She turned from the canyon entrance and the setting sun's blinding glare. "After all, they'd ridden long and hard to elude the pursuing posse. Their horses had to be exhausted from carrying the double burden of the gold. And, it had to take them some time to stash the gold where it couldn't easily be found. I don't think they just dumped it somewhere and tumbled a bunch of rocks over it."

From somewhere off in the distance came the putt-putting rumble of an idling engine. Luke turned an ear to it, trying to discern the direction of it, but it had bounced and rolled off too many rocks and hills to make any accurate determination.

"What's that?" Angie wondered.

"It sounds like the neighbor's ATV. He must have been out fixing his fence this afternoon," Luke guessed.

"On an ATV?" Angie considered the choice of transportation curious, to say the least.

"Bob claims he can haul more with an all-terrain vehicle," Luke replied, then added with a grin, "But the real truth is, he can't stand horses."

"A rancher who hates horses?" Angie repeated incredulously. "Isn't he in the wrong line of work?"

"He probably was until they came out with ATVs." A faint smile continued to crease his cheeks. "Now, he does just about everything but rope off of one."

"It might be a bit difficult to dally a rope around the handlebars," she remarked, amusement dancing in her expression.

"More than a bit, I'd say," Luke agreed with a smile, then glanced toward the west. Only the top half of the sun remained above the rim, staining the sky around it with its crimson hue. "We'd better head back to camp while there's still some light."

Without conscious thought, Luke placed a hand on the back of her waist and guided her toward the campfire's flickering light. Far off, an engine revved. The breeze stiffened, carrying the noise of it to them and making it seem much closer.

Astride the ATV, Griff Evans roared along the bed of the coulee, steering well clear of the camp Luke and the Sommers woman had set up near the base of the valley's first stone pillar. The wrong pillar, he thought and smugly smiled to himself.

Perfect timing, that's what it had been, reaching the valley while there was still enough daylight to see that the shadow from the first pillar pointed to a solid slope; there wasn't a canyon within fifty yards of it. Now the Sommers woman was stuck in camp for the night while he checked out the other formation. Luck was still running with him.

The coulee bed roughened before him, forcing Griff to ease back on the throttle, reducing the engine's roar to a steady rumble. Sunset's shadows thickened around him, the gathering darkness warning him there wasn't much light left. He pulled down his protective goggles, letting them hang about his neck, and increased the speed a notch, ignoring the jolting bumps it caused.

He spotted the second rock tower just ahead and slowed the vehicle again. This time the long shadow stretching from it wasn't as distinct in the dimming light. The edges of it blended with the surrounding darkness. But there was a canyon on his left. As close as he could tell, the shadow fell about five feet to the right of the opening to it.

Deciding that was close enough, Griff drove out of the coulee and swung toward the canyon. Camping there tonight would put him a jump ahead of the others. If his luck held, tomorrow he'd locate the eagle rock and the gold before the Sommers woman reached the canyon.

Suddenly everything smelled sweet to him.

After making a final check on the horses, Luke headed back to the camp, the boot scuff of his steps sounding loud in the evening stillness. Behind him there was the companionable chomp and rip of a horse tearing off another mouthful of grass, while from the campsite came the muted clank of the coffeepot as Fargo puttered about, readying things for the morning.

The fire burned low, throwing off a dim and wavering glow that deepened the shadows surrounding it and cast a flickering highlight over the nearest tent canvas. Automatically Luke scanned the outer ring of the fire circle as he drew near camp. He identified Fargo's bulky shape right away, but there was no sign of Angie.

He glanced toward the tents, thinking she might have turned in for the night, but all three appeared empty. He checked the path to the latrine area next, then caught a glimpse of her silhouette, outlined by the star-studded night sky. She faced the canyon, but her head was tilted toward the heavens.

Altering his course, Luke crossed to her. "Star gazing, or thinking about the gold?" he asked, a whisper of amusement in the question.

Her lips curved in a warm and easy smile. "Actually, I was thinking about my grandfather, trying to imagine how he felt the first night he spent in this valley." She spoke in soft tones. The evening quiet seemed to dictate it. "Was he nervous, excited, eager? Was he thinking about the gold, or had his thoughts turned to home?"

"Assuming he was ever here," Luke inserted, his mouth quirking.

"Oh, he was here." Angie was positive of that. She could almost feel his presence. "It's funny," she mused idly. "Even though I never knew my grandfather, my grandmother talked about him so much that it feels like I did. I guess it's true that memories can keep people alive long after they're gone." Her glance strayed to him, soft with understanding. "But you know that better than I do."

"Yes." Luke was jarred by the unexpected reference to the loss of his wife and son. He hadn't wanted to be reminded of them, not at this particular time.

But Angie didn't appear to notice. "One thing I'm certain about, though—my grandfather was as awed by this sky as I am." Once again she lifted her gaze to the multitude of stars strewn across the night's velvet-black curtain like one-carat diamonds across a jeweler's cloth. The sight drew another sigh of admiration from her. "I keep telling myself these are the same stars that shine every night over Iowa, but they seem more beautiful, more magical here."

"There's no competition. No streetlights, no houselights, no headlights, no yard lights."

"You're right, I know," Angie agreed grudgingly. "But logic somehow takes away the wonder of it—the mystery. I don't want to know why. I just want to look and marvel. That probably sounds silly to you. No doubt you've seen so many night skies like this, you take them for granted."

"Probably," he agreed, but it was her profile he was studying, the pale radiance of her face in the starlight, and the dark, almost black, shine of her auburn hair. Her nearness livened his senses, making Luke aware of the stirrings inside. "I was dead to a lot of things for a long time."

She threw him a side glance, her dark eyes alight with approval and amusement. "That's encouraging."

He drew his head back in genuine puzzlement. "What is?"

"You used the past tense," Angie replied, making a quarter pivot to face him, all confident and vibrant.

His glance drifted to her lips, lying together in a faintly curved line, their rounded contours soft and inviting. He felt the pull of them—of her—but resisted.

"I'm not sure that's a good thing," Luke stated a bit more harshly than he intended.

That hint of a smile vanished from her face, her expression taking on a sad and somber tone. "No, I don't imagine you would think it is, would you?" she said, then murmured, "Poor Luke. Being careful not to care too much about anyone or anything probably seems the best way to protect yourself from being hurt again." Angie cupped a consoling hand to his face. "I'm sorry."

Startled by the contact, Luke went motionless, but Angie didn't seem to notice. Leaning closer, she lightly kissed him. It was an innocent gesture of sympathy and affection. But for him, it was like a bread crumb to a starving man. Before she could draw away, he pulled her back to take a larger sample.

Alive. He felt alive for the first time in years, stimulated by the feel of her in his arms and the giving warmth of her lips. Shaken by the feeling, the strength of it, he abruptly set her away from him, suddenly furious with himself—and with her.

"Luke, I . . ." She looked a bit dazed and dazzled, but her expression faded at the sight of his. Wisely she suggested, "Maybe we should just blame this on the starlight."

"Why not," he agreed, then made an abrupt switch of subject. "It's getting late."

Too late, Angie suspected, for both of them, but this didn't strike her as the appropriate moment to say so. "You're right. It is late. I think I'll turn in. Good night."

Luke was slow to echo the sentiment. She had already taken three steps toward the tents when he finally responded, sounding vaguely troubled and distracted. Angie understood the feeling. Something had happened between them that wouldn't be easy to ignore. The difference was, she didn't want to.

Morning sunlight poured through the dust-coated window on the barn's east side. Particles of hay and motes danced in its slanting rays. Dulcie ran through its path on her way to the closed stall, drawn by her brother's muttered curses coming from it. She climbed onto the partition and looked inside.

There was Tobe, crouching behind the milk cow, doing something to its hind feet while the orphaned calf butted its head against the cow's swollen udder and rapidly swished its black tail back and forth.

"What're you doing, Tobe?" Dulcie leaned over the top of the stall, trying to see.

"Taking off these hobbles, what does it look like?" he grumbled irritably.

"Why're you doing that?"

"To see if old Susie'll let this calf suckle without raising a fuss, that's why." He freed the last strap and stood up, slinging the hobbles over his shoulder.

"Aren't you going to milk her?" Dulcie looked but there was no sign of either the pail or the milk stool.

"Nope." Tobe moved to the cow's head and untied the rope he'd used to snub the cow to the manger, then stepped back to watch.

Dulcie pondered that for all of two seconds. "Why?"

"Because," he began as the cow buried her broad nose in the

grain mounded in the feed box and paid no attention to the greedily suckling calf, "if she'll let this calf suck, then I won't have to milk her and we can go look for the gold."

When the full meaning of his words sunk in, Dulcie gasped in delight. "I get to go, too?!"

"What other choice do I have?" he mumbled, then lifted his head, catching the sound of a vehicle pulling into the ranch yard. "I think we've got company. Go see who it is."

With alacrity, Dulcie jumped off the partition and ran to the open barn door. One glimpse of the patrol car with a light bar fastened to its roof, and she raced back to the stall.

"It's the police, Tobe."

"The police?" He frowned in surprise. "What do they want?"

Puzzled and curious, he vaulted over the side of the stall and headed outside, with Dulcie following as closely as his shadow. Tobe spied a uniformed officer climbing the steps to the trailer door.

"It looks like Beauchamp," he said absently, then cupped his hands to his mouth and yelled, "Hey, Sheriff!"

The man turned, looked, then raised a hand in acknowledgment and headed back down the steps. Tobe struck out from the barn to meet him.

"Mornin', Sheriff. What brings you out our way this morning?"

"I wanted to speak with Miss Sommers." Beauchamp's gaze strayed to the camper, parked under the yard light. "I called several times yesterday and this morning, but no one answered."

"I keep tellin' Luke he needs to get one of those telephone answering machines, but he doesn't think it's necessary since Fargo is usually home to take a message."

Beauchamp nodded indifferently. "I understand Miss Sommers is staying here. Is that her camper?" He flicked a finger in its direction.

"Yeah, but she's not here."

"Do you know where I can find her?"

Tobe hesitated over how he should answer that. "Luke took her camping out in Buell's Basin. It shouldn't be too hard to track 'em down, if you think it's important," he said, then added, "In fact, Dulcie and me were just about to saddle up and head that way ourselves."

"Buell's Basin," Beauchamp repeated thoughtfully. "How far's that from here?"

"A good half day's ride." Tobe saw the refusal forming and hurriedly inserted, "Course, we can always trailer the horses and cut the time to an hour or so." Then he thought of another angle that would still provide him with an ideal excuse. "Or I can take a message to her."

Beauchamp considered that option, then shook his head. "I think it would be better if I spoke to her."

"Whatever you say." Tobe shrugged. Either way worked for him. "Just give me a couple minutes to get the trailer hitched and the horses loaded, and then you can follow me."

"I'll give you a hand."

After hauling water from the stream, Angie poured it onto the still-hot embers of the morning's campfire, then gave the collapsible canvas bucket to Fargo to stow in one of the packs. As an added precaution, she shoveled a layer of dirt over the coals. Then she tucked the compact shovel under the ropes securing the other pack to its saddle.

With her ball cap pulled low on her forehead, Angie turned back and surveyed the area. "I think that does it."

"I think so," Luke agreed, then glanced at Fargo. "All set?"

"All set," he confirmed and stepped to his horse.

Taking his action as a signal, Angie gathered up the roan's trailing reins, hopped a foot into the stirrup, and swung onto the saddle, eager to be off now that everything was ready.

Luke tossed a glance at the sun when he mounted. "We're getting a later start than I had expected."

"That's because you had a novice helping break camp." Angie was quick to shoulder the blame for that. "But it's not all that late. For a lot of people, this would be the shank of the morning; not everybody gets up at dawn, you know."

"They're missing the best part of the day then." Luke reined his horse away from the camp and aimed it west, placing the sun at his back. He touched a heel to the horse's side, sending it forward at a shuffling trot.

"Some might argue that point," Angie chided lightly, her glance running to the canyon when she drew alongside him.

"How come we're goin' this way?" Fargo brought up the rear, leading the two packhorses. "I thought we were gonna check out the other pillar."

"There's been a change in plans," Luke replied over his shoulder. "Angie's decided it's supposed to be the morning shadow instead of the afternoon."

Fargo grumbled something and fell silent.

Within minutes their shadows merged with the one cast by the pillar. It stretched before them like an arrow on the ground, its tip pointing toward the mouth of the canyon. Its length receded with the slow rising of the sun. They rode out of its path before they reached the entrance itself.

Angie experienced a tingle of excitement when she saw the nearly sheer rock that formed much of the canyon's left wall— and most particularly the ledge that ran almost the entire length of it, creating a kind of giant stair step about halfway up its side.

"I wonder if that's the shelf," she said, drawing Luke's attention to it.

He studied it a moment, then nodded. "Could be."

"Could be what?" Fargo urged his horse alongside theirs, drawing the packhorses with him. "What are we lookin' for now?"

"A campsite with water close by, and a rock in the shape of an eagle," Luke replied.

"You're sure it's an eagle, now?" Fargo mocked dryly. "You ain't gonna change your mind later on and say it's supposed to look like a swan or a stork or somethin'?"

The challenging skepticism in his voice drew a smile from Angie. "It's definitely an eagle," she assured him.

"Long as you're sure." With a wad of tobacco bulging out his left cheek, Fargo talked out of the other side of his mouth. "I don't wanna be wastin' my time lookin' for somethin' that ain't there."

"Why don't you scout out a campsite while we do the looking?" Luke suggested.

As Fargo formed a reply, the boom of a rifle shot shattered the midmorning stillness. Luke immediately reined in and swung his horse around, an alertness gripping him. Before the echo of the first shot faded, there was a second one, followed by a third after a similar interval.

"That's no hunter," Luke concluded and reached for the rifle he carried in the leather saddle scabbard. "That's a signal."

"Tobe, you think?" Fargo speculated, cocking a bushy eyebrow.

"It's either him or someone in trouble. No one else knows we're here." He shoved a bullet in the chamber, pointed the muzzle skyward, and fired an answering signal, then pushed the rifle back in its scabbard and fastened the flap. "Let's go."

A dozen possibilities raced through Angie's mind, but she didn't waste time suggesting any of them. Like Luke, she understood they wouldn't know the answer until they found the person who fired the shots.

At a canter, they rode back to the mouth of the canyon. Luke's searching gaze quickly spotted the two riders coming off the slope into the valley. He pulled up, the bay horse shifting restively beneath him, stimulated by the fast canter. Standing in the stirrups,

Luke waved his hat over his head and whistled shrilly, drawing the riders' attention.

"That's Tobe, all right," Fargo stated, certain of the identity even at this distance. "But who's that with him?"

Unable to tell, Luke dismissed the question. "We'll know soon enough." At the touch of a spur, the eager bay jumped forward as Luke rode to meet the pair.

Chapter Twenty

A ngie was relieved to see a pair of small, slender arms wrapped tightly around Tobe's middle. No longer worried that Dulcie had been left alone at the ranch, she switched her attention to the second rider astride the sturdy gray gelding Jackpot. A snow-white Stetson shaded his face, but the gleam of a badge on the chest pocket of his uniform left her in little doubt as to the man's identity.

Yet the sheriff's presence lent a whole new air of gravity to the moment. He had come in some official capacity, but exactly what that was, Angie refused to guess. It seemed too much like borrowing trouble. After all, it might have nothing to do with her at all.

But her mouth was dry with tension when they finally met up, not far from their original campsite. The bald-faced roan picked up her edginess and sidestepped nervously tossing its head.

"What's the problem?" Luke's probing glance flicked from Tobe to the sheriff.

"It's no problem, exactly," Tobe answered and gestured toward Beauchamp. "The sheriff came by the ranch this morning to see Angie. I explained that you'd taken her camping. I offered to bring her a message, but—"

Beauchamp cut in, "I decided it would be better if I spoke to you personally, Miss Sommers." Saddle leather creaked as he eased his weight forward and rested both hands on the horn. "I knew you'd have questions."

"What's wrong?" Mentally she braced herself to receive bad news, thinking there had been an accident back home.

"Wrong? I can't say that anything is wrong, exactly. Just puzzling," he drawled. "All the results on the lab tests came in yesterday."

The lab tests—that's why he had ridden all the way out here? She was both amazed and relieved that it was nothing more important than that.

"Good." Angie released the breath she had unconsciously been holding. "That means I can complete the burial arrangements."

"I'm afraid not," Beauchamp replied.

"Why?" She stared at him in astonishment.

"According to the results of the DNA tests, the body we found is not that of your grandfather."

"What?" Her mouth dropped open, denial following on the heels of disbelief. "There must be a mistake."

"That's what I thought." He nodded in agreement. "So I called the lab. They told me they checked their findings forward and backward. There isn't any mistake. The samples don't even come close to matching."

"I don't understand," Angie protested. "What about the class ring? The dentures?"

"That puzzles me, too," Beauchamp acknowledged and studied the ground as if the answer were written somewhere near his horse's feet. "The dentures definitely belonged to your grandfather. So did the class ring. There's no doubt about either of those. If I had to guess, I'd say they were probably stolen off your grandfather, though people don't generally steal someone else's false teeth."

"I don't understand," Angie repeated again, this time in total confusion. "If it wasn't my grandfather, who could it have been?"

"I don't know," he admitted. "We're right back where we started from when it comes to an answer to that question. And this time we haven't got a single clue to go on."

Angie thought of her grandmother and her long-held wish that someday she and her husband would be buried side by side. "What about my grandfather?" she wondered. "Where is he?"

"Still among the missing, I'm afraid," Beauchamp said to her, offering a downturned smile of regret. "Dead, most likely. Maybe somebody'll stumble across his remains one of these days, but I wouldn't hold out much hope for that. I'm sorry you traveled all this way for nothing."

For a brief moment, her journey did seem pointless. Then she remembered the gold. "It won't be for nothing, Sheriff," Angie assured him and straightened with a different kind of resolve. "And thank you for making a special trip to tell me yourself."

"I'm sorry I didn't come with the news you expected."

"So am I, but you can't change the truth."

"No, you can't," he replied, with an agreeing shake of his head, then exchanged a few words with Luke and gathered up the loose reins. "It's time I headed back. Good day to you, Miss Sommers." He touched his hat to her.

Lost in thought, she automatically echoed his phrase, "Good day."

"Luke. Fargo." After nodding to the two men, the sheriff reined the gray horse in a quarter turn and glanced at the motionless Tobe. "Are you riding back with me?"

But the question didn't register with Tobe. He was too busy gawking at the tall stone boulder that towered atop the knoll off to his left.

Conscious of everybody staring at them, Dulcie tugged at her brother's shirt and urgently whispered, "Tobe, the sheriff wants to go now."

She succeeded in partially diverting him. He turned back toward the others, a feverish excitement in his expression. "That's it, isn't it?" He jerked a thumb toward the pillar.

"What's *it*?" The sheriff frowned.

Luke ignored both questions. "The sheriff's ready to head back, Tobe. You go with him."

Hot with rebellion, Tobe glared at Luke; hesitated; then jerked his horse around, pointing it back the way they had come. "If you're going, let's go," he half snarled the words at Beauchamp and jammed his heels in the horse.

It leaped forward, and Dulcie hung on for dear life. His curiosity aroused by Tobe's unusual behavior, Beauchamp followed, but at a more sedate pace.

Amber juice arced to the ground, adding a punctuation mark to the departure of the other riders. "If you plan on lookin' for that eagle rock yet this mornin', we'd best be headin' back to the canyon." Fargo gave a tug on the rope to the packhorses before he reined his mount toward the canyon.

Nodding, Luke gathered his horse, then checked the movement when his glance fell on Angie. "Are you all right?"

The news had left her feeling oddly bereft, but it wasn't something she either understood or could explain. "Still a little stunned, I guess, but otherwise okay."

The drive and determination to search for the outlaw gold was still there, Luke noted, but the old sparkle was gone from her eyes. He discovered he missed it. Somehow the innocent eagerness of it, untainted by avarice, had lent a spice to the search.

But he made no mention of any of it; like Angie, he kept his thoughts and feelings to himself. In silence they rode back to the canyon.

A dozen yards inside the entrance, Fargo split away to locate a campsite. He crossed a dry wash that in early spring carried the runoff from mountain rains and snowmelt. Except for pockets of mud, it was mostly dry. He didn't bother to look for any lingering pools of water; he had another place in mind: a spring-fed seep half hidden in a hollowed-out section of ground some distance from the coulee and closer to the canyon's left wall.

It had been several years since he'd been to the seep—in fact, not since he'd traded the open range for the kitchen range. Still, he had a fair idea where to find it. A moment later, he spied the rushes that grew along the edges of the natural pool.

Automatically he corrected his course and his glance strayed to the canyon's high wall, skimming the rim on the off chance he'd spot the eagle-shaped rock. No such luck.

In a level clearing near the seep, Fargo dismounted and stripped the packs and saddles from the horses, then strung a picket line between two trees and tied the horses to it for the time being.

Getting a fire going and coffee started was always the first order of business for any range cook, and Fargo wasted little time gathering wood and lighting a fire, with pine needles for kindling. Using the collapsible canvas bucket, he hauled water from the seep and poured it into the kettle, then hooked it from the tripod, suspending it over the crackling flames.

The first boiling bubble broke the water's surface when he caught the rapid pounding of fast-cantering hooves. He straightened from the supply pack, a bag of coffee in his hand and the enameled pot at his feet.

At almost the same instant that Fargo saw Tobe charging into the canyon, leading the riderless gray gelding, empty stirrups flopping, Tobe saw him and rode straight toward the clearing. He pulled up well short of the fire, both horses snorting and blowing.

"What are you doin' here?" Fargo scowled in surprise.

"The same thing you are," Tobe shot back with defiance. "Looking for the gold."

"You're supposed to be takin' care of things back at the ranch," Fargo reminded him.

"What do I care? It ain't my ranch." Grabbing Dulcie by the arm, he swung her off the back of his saddle and lowered her to the ground, then piled off after her. "If you care so much about it, you can go back and do the chores yourself."

"Luke told you to do 'em."

"That's too bad, ain't it?" Tobe acted tough, but Fargo had been around too long not to recognize nervous bravado when he saw it.

But the problem was between Tobe and Luke. It was none of his never mind. Just the same, he watched as Tobe turned to scan the canyon, as much to avoid Fargo's disapproving stare as any other reason.

"Where're Angie and Luke, anyway?"

"They're out lookin' for a rock shaped like an eagle," Fargo answered.

Surprised, Tobe wheeled around, all ears and big eyes. "Where?" he asked, suddenly breathless.

"If I knew that, I wouldn't be standin' here, now, would I?" Fargo scoffed in derision.

Irritated with Fargo's deliberate obtuseness, Tobe shifted impatiently. "You know darn well what I meant. *Where* are they lookin' for it?"

Fargo briefly toyed with the idea of playing with Tobe a little longer just to get his goat, but it was too easy. "They're expectin' to find it somewhere along that wall." He gestured to the left side of the canyon.

"When they find it, then what?"

"Beats me," Fargo admitted. "That Sommers gal's playin' it close to the vest. Hands out the information piecemeal."

Frustrated, Tobe swore under his breath, anger tightening his features. Without another word, he swung to his horse, slung the rein around its lathered neck, and grabbed the saddlehorn.

"Where're you goin'?" Fargo eyed him askance.

"To look for that eagle rock." He stuck a toe in the stirrup and launched himself into the saddle.

"What good's that gonna do ya?"

"If I find it first, she'll have to cut me in for a share of that gold," Tobe insisted, with a fierceness that had his chin quivering. "I'm not gonna stand around makin' coffee, like you."

"I'll get my share of it." That was a promise Fargo had made himself.

Meanwhile he was content to bide his time until the gold was actually found. Then, if she didn't cut him in, he'd do it himself. After all, in the confusion and excitement of finding the gold, it wasn't likely anybody would notice if one little bar ended up missing.

"You hope," Tobe jeered and kicked the sweaty sorrel forward.

"Tobe, wait!" Dulcie grabbed at the stirrup, forcing him to pull up. "I want to come with you."

"No, you stay here with Fargo."

"But I wanna look for the gold, too," she protested.

"Well, you can't. Now stay here like I told you!" Without a backward glance, he rode off and left Dulcie standing there with tears swimming in her eyes.

No tantrum followed his departure. No jutting pout of the lower lip. Just silence, and the wretching sight of a lost and broken child. It tugged at Fargo, and he used gruffness to cover the fact.

"Jackpot needs some water. Take him down to that little pond there and let him get a drink."

In glum silence, Dulcie walked to the gray gelding, gathered up the trailing reins, and led him toward the seep. Fargo watched for a moment, then went back to measuring out the coffee and dumping it in the pot.

When she returned with the gray, the water in the kettle had yet to boil the requisite length of time to purify it. Setting the coffee aside, Fargo took the reins from her, unsaddled the horse, and tied it to the picket line with the other horses.

She didn't utter a single word the whole time. Fargo pretended not to notice as he lifted the kettle off the fire and ladled scalding hot water into the enameled pot. But it was too much. Her silence finally got to him.

"You hungry?" He set the coffeepot on the grate to brew.

"No."

Fargo almost sighed in defeat, convinced the one-word answer would be the end of her reply. He was wrong.

"What's an eagle rock look like, Fargo?" She was hunkered beside him, balancing on the balls of her shoes.

He wasn't sure which startled him more—that she had asked a question, or the question itself. He searched for an answer, but there was only one.

"Like an eagle, o' course."

"Oh." Dulcie stared at the ground in front of her and poked at some of the larger stones as the silence stretched again. Stifling a sigh, Fargo turned and dug a couple of cans of beef stew out of the sack. "Can I go look for the eagle rock?"

Fargo rolled his eyes in despair, realizing he should have known she'd ask something like that. "No, you'd end up gettin' lost and I got the noon meal to start. I ain't got time to go lookin' for you."

"I wouldn't get lost. Honest." It was as close to a plea as Dulcie had ever made.

"You wouldn't mean to, but you would," he insisted gruffly.

"But . . . couldn't I just look right around here?"

He started to refuse, but he made the mistake of looking at her and then hesitated. "You'd have to stay right around here," he warned.

"I promise." Her fingers made a hasty X mark across her heart.

"I tell you what"—Fargo reached back in the pack and pulled out a blue towel—"you go tie this towel on that tree limb over there. Then you can go look wherever you want as long as you can still see that towel." Pausing, he drew the towel back, holding it out of reach of her outstretched hands, and looked her hard in the eyes. "You understand?"

"Uh-huh." She bobbed her head in eagerness, eyes shining. "I'll make sure I can see the towel all the time. Honest, I will, Fargo."

Relenting a little from his firm stand, he let a ghost of a smile soften the line of his mouth. "See that you do," he said and passed her the towel.

But his smile blossomed into a full-blown grin as Dulcie raced to the tree, the towel whipping behind her like a banner in the wind. At the tree, hardly more than a sapling, she halted and struggled to knot the towel around a low branch. Succeeding at last, she waved to Fargo and moved off to begin her search, shooting glances over her shoulder every now and then to verify the towel was in sight.

Satisfied that she would heed his instructions, Fargo returned to the business of preparing the noon meal. He knew, by nature, Dulcie wasn't the type of child given to exploring. She tended to be timid and cautious rather than bold and adventurous. If anything, the towel would give her the security to wander farther afield than she might have. Which meant she wouldn't be underfoot, and that suited him just fine.

Deeper into the canyon, the rock cliff disintegrated into a steep slope strewn with trees and jutting boulders. Reining in, Angie slowly scanned the new terrain. Few of the trees looked old enough to have been standing when Ike Wilson and his fellow outlaws had ridden through the canyon.

"How far back does the canyon go from here?" Her glance bounced to Luke, then back to the rugged slope.

"About three quarters of a mile, I'd say. Then it climbs to a plateau."

His answer confirmed what the topo map had indicated; this was not a so-called box canyon, with only one way in or out. Rather, it was accessible from several directions.

"Is the rest of it like this?" She nodded to the terrain before them.

"The slope gentles out, but otherwise it's about the same." The bay horse took advantage of the halt and stretched its nose to the grass and tore off a chunk. The rattle of bit and bridle chain as it chewed drowned out the whir of insects and the gentle sigh of the morning breeze. Only the exuberant trill of a nearby bird competed with it for dominance.

Silently Angie debated whether to continue on. But all her instincts said the eagle-shaped rock had to be somewhere along the nearly sheer cliff face.

"Let's make another pass along the wall," she decided. "Maybe coming at it from another direction, things will look different."

"They generally do," Luke agreed. "That's how people become disoriented and lost in the wild."

In this case, Angie hoped the change in their angle of approach would cause the eagle-shaped formation to leap out. There were easily dozens of oddly configured boulders, either in combinations with others or alone. Some protruded from the wall face; others stood along its rim. But none had reminded her of an eagle.

It was too early in the hunt for her to feel the heaviness of disappointment. But Angie was conscious of it pulling at her. She told herself that she'd been spoiled by the early success with the pillar. But she suspected much of it was a carryover from the sheriff's stunning news.

Try as she might, she hadn't been able to put it from her mind. It was definitely a large part of the reason she didn't feel like talking.

It was also the reason she failed to respond to Luke's comment. She'd heard what he said, even inwardly acknowledged the truth of it, then became distracted by other thoughts when she reined her horse around to retrace their route. Her gaze once again lifted to examine the cliff's changing face.

"You do realize," Luke's voice intruded again, "that it's been nearly a hundred years since Wilson was in this canyon." Then, always the skeptic, he added, "*If* he was."

"I know." Angie concentrated on the varied shapes before her, trying to overlay the outline of an eagle on them.

"That means a hundred winters with all their freezes and

thaws. Freezes and thaws that act like Mother Nature's chisel and change the sculpture of a rock that once resembled an eagle. You could be looking for something that no longer exists," Luke warned.

"It's possible." Her chin came up. "But it's much too soon to say that's the case this time."

Farther ahead, the smooth nose of a boulder jutted from the cliff like the gnarled stub of a broken tree limb. But the rounded contour of the tall rock above it was unbroken. By no stretch of the imagination could Angie alter its outline to fit the majestic silhouette of an eagle.

Her glance skipped to the next section of face, scanning first above the narrow ledge that traversed the cliff, then below it. Intent on her search, she didn't notice the rider walking his horse toward them.

"Tobe, what are you doing here?" Luke challenged in surprise.

Tobe pulled up looking startled and guilty, then made a valiant attempt to throw it off. "I'm lookin' for that eagle rock, same as you are." But the telltale reddening of his ears belied the assertive tone of his voice.

"How did you know about that?" Angie questioned in amazement.

"Fargo told me." Tobe welcomed the excuse to avoid facing Luke.

"I thought you were taking the sheriff back to the ranch." Luke's remark bordered on an accusation.

Tobe had trouble meeting his eyes. "I rode with him as far as his patrol car, then high-tailed it back here."

"Where's Dulcie?" Angie asked in instant concern. "You didn't send her back to the ranch with the sheriff, did you?"

"No. I left her at camp with Fargo."

"What about the work you're supposed to be doing back at the ranch?" The level of Luke's voice didn't change, but the reproach was inherent.

Tobe struggled to convey a careless indifference. "It'll wait, won't it?" But he was quickly unnerved by Luke's lack of response. "None of it was really important anyway. It won't hurt if it doesn't get done for a week or two. And there's plenty of grass in the pasture for the horses, enough that they can get by without bein' grained for a while. I put the orphaned calf with the milk cow, so it's not gonna be a problem if she don't get milked. And I left the truck and stock trailer parked on the ridge. I figured I could drive back every night just to check on things. That should be good enough. And if it isn't . . ." He faltered, searching for the words he had so carefully rehearsed in his mind. "And if it isn't, then . . . I quit." As if expecting an argument, Tobe rushed to add, "And you aren't gonna talk me out of it, Luke. There's no way I'm gonna stay at the ranch while everybody else is out here hunting that gold. Why should I, when I could be the one who finds it?"

"You don't even know where to look," Luke began, with a mildly exasperated shake of his head.

"Neither does Griff, but that didn't stop him," Tobe declared. "And it's not gonna stop me."

"Griff. You mean Griff Evans?" A disbelieving frown narrowed Luke's eyes.

"Of course I mean Griff Evans." Just saying Griff's name seemed to strengthen Tobe's resolve and confidence. "He walked out of the Rimrock yesterday afternoon to come look for the gold. Haven't you seen him?"

"No. Not a sign."

"That's funny." Tobe frowned over Luke's answer. "You'd think if you hadn't seen him, you'd at least have heard him. He borrowed the Daniels's ATV, paid 'em two hundred dollars for the use of it."

"We heard the ATV last night," Luke acknowledged. "But I didn't know Griff was at the wheel."

"I'm surprised he's not here," Tobe remarked, then grinned. "I guess he's still trying to find the pillar, huh? That means we're a step ahead of him, doesn't it?"

"*We?*" Luke drawled, all cool and lazy. "Taking it upon your shoulders to count yourself in, are you?"

Tobe split a worried and anxious look between Luke and Angie. "But if I help find the gold, I'm entitled to a share."

"Don't look at me. That's Angie's call to make." Luke smoothly passed the problem to her. "I was hired on strictly as an outfitter and guide. So if you expect a share of the gold, it's just as well you don't work for me."

Tobe looked a bit crestfallen that Luke was so ready to accept his resignation. In a way, he'd expected Luke to overlook it. Now, if they didn't find the gold, he'd be out of a job and a place to live. The possibility made it all the more imperative that the gold be found—and all the more imperative that Angie include him. Jaws clenched, he looked at her.

She studied him for a long second, then said, "Twenty percent of whatever I receive; does that sound fair?"

The breath he'd been holding whooshed from him, the tension evaporating. "Fair enough." Tobe tried not to sound too over-joyed with her acceptance—or the percentage.

"You understand that I have no idea how much that might be, if anything at all?" she added.

"Sure. No problem." Tobe did his best to ignore the feeling of desperation clawing in his throat.

Chapter Twenty-One

⌒⌒⌒

With her head craned back, Dulcie gazed in fascination at the towering rock bluff while she worked her way, step by slow step, along the outer edge of a small clump of trees. At first, she had seen nothing but the solidness of the cliff's long face. Now, patterns and shapes were beginning to emerge.

It was like cloud watching. Over there was a turtle; to the right of it, a hump-backed camel. Then, high along the rim, it kind of looked like the head of an old woman with no teeth sleeping with her mouth open. The image made Dulcie giggle into her hand.

She went a step farther, then stopped and darted a quick look over her shoulder. Between the trees, she saw a scrap of blue fluttering in the breeze and breathed easier.

A couple more steps and her attention was caught by the protruding roundness of a huge boulder. Her mouth opened in a round and silent O.

"An angel." Dulcie breathed in wonder.

As she took a step toward it, she tripped over a tree root and went sprawling to the ground. Embarrassed, she scrambled to her knees and examined the palms of her hands, then carefully picked off the tiny pebbles pressed into her skin. She brushed more off her elbows but found no cuts or abrasions.

Rising to her feet, she dusted off the knees of her jeans, then gave a little toss of her head, flipping the long, pale ponytail onto her back. She glared briefly at the protruding root that had tripped her, then ventured closer to the canyon's towering wall, this time watching where she walked.

Next to the massive trunk of an old cottonwood, Dulcie paused to search out her angel rock again. From farther down the canyon came the creak of saddle leather and the plodding clop of slow-walking horses.

Thinking it might be Tobe, or even Angie, Dulcie stepped from the tree to look. At almost the same moment that she caught a glimpse of two riders, she heard a faint, barely audible snort from somewhere very close by. She glanced around to locate the source and instantly froze, unable to speak or move.

There, on the other side of the tree, stood that scrawny and withered old man, his woolly beard all dirty and matted looking. The floppy brim of his hat hung low on his face, further shadowing eyes hooded by his tufted brows.

As if sensing her presence, he turned fractionally and fixed the black glare of his eyes on her. "What're you starin' at?"

The low growl of his voice broke the grip of silence.

"Y-you scared me," she whispered.

His eyes narrowed, appearing smaller and meaner. "You should be scared." Abruptly his glance shot to the two riders, only partially visible beyond some low brush. "*She* should be scared," he muttered to himself. Then his expression crumbled into something bitter and forlorn. "Guess I got too old to frighten anyone fer long."

Slightly reassured by his comment, Dulcie studied the cracked and splintering age lines that crossed and recrossed his weathered skin.

"You're really, really old, aren't you?" she marveled.

Saddlebags snorted. "Think you're a smart one to figure that

267

out, do ya?" Again his attention was distracted by the slowly approaching riders. "She's a clever one, too. But not clever enough, I'll wager. She'll come t' a stop here, jus' like I did."

Puzzled by his statement, Dulcie cocked her head, sending her ponytail swinging across the back of her shoulder. "Why?"

But she was denied an answer by Angie's questioning call. "Dulcie? Is that you?"

Turning, she saw Angie standing in the stirrups, a good forty yards from her yet.

"Hey, Angie!" Dulcie stretched an arm over her head and waved eagerly to her.

Immediately both Angie and Luke cantered their horses toward her location. Excited, Dulcie started to share the news with Saddlebags.

"Angie's com—" The word died on her lips when she discovered the old man had vanished.

Before she could even think about looking for him, Luke and Angie rode up. "What are you doing out here, Dulcie?" Angie questioned in concern.

"Looking for the eagle rock and—"

Luke interrupted before she could tell them about talking to Saddlebags. "Where's Fargo? Tobe said you were with him."

"He's back at camp." When she went to point toward it, Dulcie gasped in alarm and glanced frantically about. "The towel. I can't see it!"

"What towel?" Luke wondered.

"The one Fargo had me hang on a tree," Dulcie explained anxiously. "He said I wasn't supposed to go where I couldn't see it. I didn't mean to, honest."

"We know you didn't," Angie assured her.

Luke walked his horse to her. "Come on. We'll take you back to camp." Leaning low to the side, he scooped Dulcie off the ground, and as he straightened he set her across the front of the saddle. Her shoulders slumped in dejection. "Fargo's probably gonna be mad, isn't he?" Dulcie mumbled.

"A little maybe," Luke agreed. "But not as mad as he would have been if you had actually become lost."

They hadn't traveled more than a horse's length when Dulcie spotted the blue cloth. "Look!" She pointed to it, her whole face lighting up. "There's the towel right there. It was just hidden for a minute, huh?"

"It looks that way," Luke agreed, battling back a smile.

"I just couldn't see it for a little bit. That's not the same as not being able to see it at all, is it?" she declared, with growing confidence.

"It isn't exactly the same, but you were lucky this time," Angie told her. "Next time you might wander too far and really be lost."

"I won't. I promise." But Dulcie was sobered by her previous promise to Fargo before she set out to look for the eagle rock. The memory of that triggered another thought. "Did you find the eagle rock?"

"Not yet," Angie admitted.

"Me neither," Dulcie sighed in disappointment. "Tobe says we got to find it before we can find the gold."

"That's right." Angie's glance fell on the crudely tied towel hanging from the low branch of a young tree.

The roan's sides swelled a fraction of a second before the gelding nickered to the horses tied along the picket line. In the wide clearing to the right, wispy smoke curled from a campfire. Fargo was down on one knee beside it, stirring something in a large pot. Observing their approach, he pushed to his feet, the movement a bit jerky and awkward, indicating a stiffening of his joints.

"No luck, I take it," he guessed from their expressions, then waved the spoon toward the campfire. "There's coffee made and the stew'll be hot in a minute. Might as well get down and have something to eat before you go look some more."

Although Angie wasn't all that hungry, taking a break seemed like a good idea. So far she had seen nothing that remotely resembled an eagle. Already the tension and frustration had begun to mount. The lunch break would give her a chance to relax, re-group, and return to the search with fresh eyes.

Without a word, she dismounted and handed the reins to Luke when he reached for them. She accepted the cup of coffee Fargo poured for her, then wandered to the edge of the clearing to gaze at the canyon wall.

Several minutes later Luke joined her, cup in hand. She ac-knowledged his presence with a brief, smiling glance, then took a sip of her nearly cold coffee.

"You're unusually quiet," Luke observed, then changed his mind. Subdued was a more apt description. It was a word he never thought would apply to Angie.

"Thinking, I guess," she murmured absently.

"You've been doing a lot of that this morning. In fact, I don't think you've said more than a dozen words since you spoke to the sheriff."

She started to deny that, then realized the meeting with Beauchamp was the source of the heaviness she felt.

"I suppose that's true," Angie admitted, with a faint sigh. "I'm not sure I understand why, either. I guess I never realized it mat-tered so much that my grandfather's remains be found." She added hastily, "Don't get me wrong. I was glad they were—mostly for my grandmother's sake. But I . . . I had fantasized about look-ing for the gold for so long that . . . coming out here to claim his body seemed like the perfect excuse—one others would accept without thinking I was being foolish."

"And now?" Luke prompted.

She hesitated, still thinking it through. "Now I realize that finding the gold won't give me that sense of closure I expected. It will only end that particular chapter in our family's history. The story won't be finished until my grandfather is found." There was a glimmer of the old twinkling look in the side glance she sent him, a touch of wry humor curving her lips. "I don't know about you, but I'm irritated when a book leaves me dangling at the end."

"You prefer happy endings, do you?" he murmured dryly. "That's not very realistic."

"It's very realistic," she stated. "That's all life is."

"What?"

"A series of happy endings, one after another."

Intrigued by her statement, he cocked his head. "How do you figure that?"

"It's easy. Everyone has lean times, hard times, rocky times—either financially, emotionally, or physically. But they get through them. And each time they do, it's a happy ending. Pain is always balanced by pleasure, sadness by joy, bad times by good, sickness by health, et cetera, et cetera. Most of the time people don't recognize it as a happy ending because nobody types those two magic words *the end* on that particular page in their life."

"That's a bit simplistic, don't you think?" Luke countered, his mouth twisting wryly.

"Do you really believe it's more complex than that?" she parried with amusement.

"You yourself said that finding the gold wasn't going to give you the sense of closure you expected," Luke reminded her. "Shouldn't that be one of your happy endings?"

"Definitely. That's also why we don't usually recognize them—because we go by our feelings rather than facts." All this talk about finding the gold had her thoughts circling back to the problem at hand. "But it's also a fact that I won't find the gold until I locate that eagle rock."

There was a determined set to her chin. Luke knew that she wasn't about to let the morning's lack of success discourage her from the search. Truthfully, he would have been surprised if it had.

* * *

Immediately after lunch, Angie was back in the saddle. Trip after trip she made up and down the canyon wall, visually combing every inch of its face. She rode close to it, then drew back to view the shapes from a distance. Each time she met up with Luke or Tobe, making their separate searches, they shook their heads. They weren't having any more luck than she was.

With his breath coming in whiny little sounds of panic, Griff threw an anxious glance at the canyon entrance. Any minute now, Luke and the Sommers gal would come riding in, and he still hadn't found that rock shaped like an eagle. He'd been up with the first gray light of dawn—and searched nonstop ever since. Squeezing the throttle, he finished his sweep along the canyon's right wall, then halted in the thick shadows well short of the entrance. He scanned the area beyond it, but there was no sign of any horses and riders.

Where were they? Griff was worried now, worried that maybe this was the wrong canyon. Those shots he'd heard this morning, they'd been a signal of some sort, he knew, but what kind? Had it been to alert the others to the location of the eagle rock?

Another horrible thought hit him: what if they'd found the gold? An animal-like moan was ripped from his throat.

It couldn't be. The gold was his. He had to have it! He had to!

He roared out of the canyon, the ATV traveling at full throttle.

"I don't understand. It has to be here." Confusion etched a troubled frown on her face as Angie studied the rock bluff. "We must have missed something."

"If you say so." Luke tiredly pushed his hat to the back of his head and laid both arms across the saddlehorn. "But I don't know what it would be."

"Neither do I." She almost sighed the answer.

"I know one thing—these horses could use a drink. What do you say we ride back to camp, get them some water, grab a cup of coffee for ourselves, and stretch our legs a bit?"

Like it or not, the suggestion was a sensible one. "Might as well," Angie agreed. "We're not that far from camp."

"I know." Straightening in the saddle, Luke lifted his hat and set it back square on his head. "With any luck, Fargo will have supper started. We can eat and come back out when the light on the wall is different."

"Yes, that could make a difference." She warmed to the thought. "If the outlaws left the canyon early in the morning, then it's logical to assume they reached it very late in the afternoon or early in the evening."

"We'll find out," Luke started his horse toward camp.

Angie was quick to follow him on the roan. Before they reached it, Tobe joined up with them, looking tired and disgruntled.

"You struck out, too, didn't you?" he guessed and shot an accusing look at Angie. "Are you sure this is the right canyon?"

"I'm positive."

"Well, I'm not," he grumbled. "I'll bet it's one of the other ones."

"Maybe, but I'm not ready to give up on this one," Angie said to him.

Tobe muttered something under his breath and fell silent.

At the camp, Dulcie saw them coming and ran to meet them. Automatically Luke halted his mount short of the circle. Range etiquette frowned on anyone actually riding his horse into camp where it might foul the ground.

"Did you find it?" Dulcie fastened her hopeful gaze on Angie, watching as she dismounted.

"Not yet." Angie followed Luke's lead and loosened the saddle cinch.

"Oh." It didn't occur to Dulcie to hide her disappointment. "I thought you would have found it by now, for sure."

"So did I," Angie admitted. "But it didn't turn out that way."

"Tobe"—Luke gathered up the reins to both horses and passed them to him—"take the horses and get them a drink."

"I wish I could go look for it." Dulcie trotted alongside Angie when she crossed to the campfire. "I'll bet I could find it."

"If you didn't get yourself lost first, you mean," Fargo chided as he poured coffee into a metal cup for Angie.

"I wouldn't get lost if I went with Angie," Dulcie reasoned.

"She's got you there." Angie sent a teasing glance at Fargo over the cup rim.

Dulcie leaped on that hint of an agreement. "Could I go with you? I saw lots and lots of stuff when I looked before."

"You did, huh?" Angie murmured, her thoughts already beginning to stray from the conversation.

"Uh-huh. I saw a turtle and an old woman with no teeth and an angel and a camel—"

The list Dulcie rattled off started Angie thinking in another direction. She abruptly turned to Luke, shocked by a whole new possibility. "I just realized that I've been assuming all along that by an eagle he meant a bird. But what if he meant something else?"

"Like what?" He took a sip of his coffee, eyeing her skeptically.

"I don't know," she admitted. "But there are other definitions for the word. It can be a golfing score . . . or a gold coin—"

"Wait a minute," Luke broke in, his gaze suddenly slicing to the girl. "What did you just say, Dulcie?"

She shrank from the sharpness of his eyes. "Nothing," she mumbled.

"Yes, you did. You were telling us all the things you'd seen," he reminded her, while Angie looked on, thoroughly mystified. "What were they again?"

Deciding that maybe she wasn't in trouble after all, Dulcie began reciting her list: "I saw a camel, an angel—"

"How could you tell it was an angel?" Luke interrupted again.

"Because it had wings."

"Wings," he repeated in satisfaction and looked at Angie.

She knew exactly what he was thinking. She had just been struck by the same thought. Her pulse quickened with the rising excitement she felt.

"Do you think you could find that angel again, Dulcie?" Luke asked.

"Uh-huh. It's really big. You can't miss it," she assured him, then frowned. "Didn't you see it?"

"I'm afraid not," Angie told her. "Would you show us where it is?"

"Sure."

"Hey, Tobe," Luke called. "Cinch up those saddles and bring the horses back."

When Tobe returned with the horses, Luke lifted Dulcie onto his saddle, then swung up behind her. After checking to verify the others were mounted and ready, he asked the girl, "Which way do we go?"

"That way." Dulcie pointed to an area toward the right, then tipped her head sideways to look up at him. "It's over where I talked to that scary old man."

"Saddlebags?" Angie said in surprise. "You saw him?"

"Uh-huh." Dulcie bobbed her head affirmatively, her ponytail brushing the front of Luke's shirt. "Right after I saw the angel. He was beside a big tree."

"An angel?" Tobe stared at his sister as if she'd taken leave of her senses.

"Yeah, in the rock," she replied as Luke set out for the spot, flanked by Tobe and Angie.

"I hope it didn't talk to you."

"Not a real angel, Tobe," Angie explained when she realized he had taken Dulcie literally. "She saw the shape of one in the rocks." Feeling foolish, he fell silent. "You said you talked to Saddlebags. What did he say to you?"

After an initial shrug of blankness, Dulcie recalled, "He said he was getting too old for people to be scared of him. But I was . . . kinda." Then, pleased that she had remembered the compliment, she quickly added, "And he said you were clever. That was nice, huh?"

"It was. Did he say anything else?" Angie wondered.

Frowning, Dulcie thought hard over that. "He did say something about you being stopped," she recalled, then brightened. "He was wrong, though. You aren't stopped, are you?"

"Definitely not." Angie scanned the high canyon wall before them, searching for the rock formation that, to Dulcie, resembled a winged angel.

"Did you show Saddlebags your angel rock?" Luke asked.

"No, I—There it is!" she burst excitedly and stretched a finger toward the wall's upper section. As one, all three riders pulled up to look. "See it?!"

Angie made a rapid scan of the bulging cliff face but saw no formation jutting from it shaped like an angel—or an eagle, for that matter. "Where? I don't see it."

"It's right there!" Dulcie continued to point to the same area. "Don't you see it?"

"There's nothing there but solid rock," Tobe declared in disgust.

"That's an angel," Dulcie insisted. "A giant one."

Luke bent to the side to better follow the angle of her finger. "Show me where its wings are."

"One's right there. See its feathers going up and down." She made nearly vertical strokes in the air with her finger.

He searched for a similar pattern in the rock face—and found it. "Well, I'll be," he murmured in amazement and slowly straightened erect to stare.

"You found it? Where? I still don't see it," Angie said with growing frustration.

"Don't look for a rock shaped *like* an eagle. Look for the shape of an eagle etched into that tall boulder," Luke instructed.

"It's not an eagle. It's an angel," Dulcie corrected.

"Angel or eagle, it all depends on which one you want it to

be," he replied, then said to Angie, "See those long, natural folds in the boulder?"

"Yes," she breathed in answer, suddenly seeing the crude, winged form nature had carved into the stone. "That's it," Angie murmured and kept her gaze fixed on it as she stepped out of the saddle. Holding on to the horse's rein, she moved closer to the wall to stare up at it. "That is definitely it." This time there was a ring of conviction in her voice.

Hearing it, Tobe gave up trying to see it himself and decided to simply take her word for it. "We've found the eagle rock. Now what?"

From memory, Angie quoted the next phrase in the letter's coded message. " 'Bury under shelf.' " Her glance cut to Luke, certainty glowing in her eyes. "And the antonym for 'bury' is 'dig.' "

Tobe's eyes rounded in astonishment. "You mean it's here? The gold's right here?"

"Right here." Angie nodded emphatically, confident the search was over. "All we have to do is dig it up."

"Ride back to camp and get the shovels, Tobe." Luke dismounted to swing Dulcie off the saddle and onto the ground.

With a sawing of the reins, Tobe turned his horse toward camp and whipped it into a gallop, shouting the news to Fargo. "We found it! We found it!"

Dulcie ran to Angie's side. "I helped find it, didn't I?"

"You certainly did."

"Where's it buried? I could start digging," she offered eagerly.

"It should be buried directly below the eagle." Angie glanced at Luke. "Wouldn't you say?"

"Somewhere in that area, yes."

While they waited for Tobe to bring the shovels, they drew an imaginary line down the cliff face from the eagle rock to the ground. With their hands, they began scraping aside the layer of loose stone at the base of the wall.

When Tobe galloped back with the shovels, Fargo was with

him. Sliding his horse to a stop, Tobe piled out of the saddle and ran to join them, hastily tossing a shovel to Luke. Fargo didn't lag far behind him.

"This is the spot, huh." With avid eyes, Fargo examined the section of ground partially cleared of gravel, then belatedly handed Luke a pair of heavy work gloves. "I grabbed these out of the pack. I figured you'd need 'em if you had to do a lot of diggin'."

"Thanks." He paused to pull them on, then picked up the shovel.

By then Tobe had already made his first jab with the other one, but had barely made a scratch on the ground's hard surface. "Man, this is like concrete," he muttered. "We're gonna need jackhammers to get through it."

Over and over again, they pounded the area with the points of their shovels and gradually chipped away the top crust. Standing to one side, Angie watched their slow progress. At last, the first big bite of dirt was taken out of the firmly packed soil. The real digging had begun.

"You're wastin' your time," a voice declared, scratchy with age.

Startled by it, Angie spun around as all work stopped behind her. She stared at the scarecrow figure of Saddlebags Smith standing not ten feet away, baggy clothes hanging off his bone-thin frame, dirty white hair poking from beneath his floppy hat.

"It's our time to waste. And who asked you anyway?" Tobe shot back.

"Nobody. Jus' thought I'd volunteer it." He paused, a slyness invading his expression. "Ya think ya found the gold, don't ya? But you ain't."

"You don't think we're gonna take your word for that, do you?" Fargo sneered. "That'd be real smart of us to quit diggin' on your say-so. Why, the minute we walked away, you'd step in and claim the gold for yourself, and we'd be out."

"You're out anyways. All your work's gonna be fer nothin'. When you're done, you'll only have sweat an' blisters to show for it. The gold ain't there."

"How do you know?" Angie studied him closely, trying to judge whether he was telling the truth.

"'Cause I a'ready looked. Sweat an' blisters, that's what you'll get," he repeated. "Sweat an' blisters."

Cackling to himself, he turned and disappeared into the trees at a waddling trot. Angie stared after him, struggling to ignore the niggling doubt he'd planted.

Tobe was the first to throw off the seed the old man had cast, muttering, "The crazy old coot, what does he know?" He stepped a foot on the shovel and pushed the blade deep in the firm soil.

When Angie turned back to the site, her gaze briefly locked with Luke's. She read the unspoken question in it and thought back over the message's phrase. Her conclusion was still the same.

"It should be buried somewhere right around here," she stated.

Luke nodded an acceptance and went back to digging.

A few inches deeper, the dirt became less compact, and the work went more quickly. Soon, they had a good-sized hole, but it wasn't large enough for two men to continue digging at the same time. They started taking turns, with Tobe leading off.

Angie wasn't sure when she first noticed the humming sound. It had been a background noise for so long that it had almost ceased to register. As it grew steadily louder and louder, she became aware of it again. She tipped her head, listening to it, certain she'd heard the sound before.

"The ATV," she remembered and glanced at Luke.

"Must be Griff." He gazed thoughtfully toward the canyon entrance.

"Man, is he gonna be mad when he finds out that we know where the gold is." Grinning tiredly, Tobe tossed another shovelful of dirt out of the hole.

A moment later, the roar of the ATV echoed through the canyon as the vehicle barreled into view. It seemed to be headed toward the campsite. Then the driver obviously noticed the saddled horses grazing near the canyon wall and whipped the ATV toward them.

When it braked to a stop a few feet from the site, Angie saw the frantic wildness in Griff's eyes. The day-old beard growth that shadowed his cheeks gave his face a gaunt and haggard look. His sweat-stained clothes were dirty and rumpled.

The instant he saw the hole they were digging, he sprang off the ATV. "You found it. You found the gold." He looked and sounded stunned. In the background, the engine continued to putt-putt at an idling speed. "But . . . how? It isn't supposed to be here."

He turned a confused glance on Angie. In a flash, his whole demeanor changed, his expression wavering between fury and frustration.

"*You* did this." He ground out the accusation through clenched jaws. "You planned this whole thing."

Angie frowned in bewilderment. "I don't know what you're talking about."

Immediately he was in her face, making no attempt to control his rage. "Don't play dumb, lady. You aren't foolin' me one bit." His whole body vibrated with anger as he shook a crumpled sheet of paper in front of her. Somewhere behind her a shovel clunked to the ground. "You deliberately left this just to throw me off track."

"Left what?" She tried to focus on the moving paper. "Griff, you aren't making any sense."

"I'm makin' plenty of sense, and you know it!" he shouted, neck muscles bulging, hot tears filling his eyes. "You knew I'd find this in the wastebasket! You did it to trick me, and I fell for it! I oughta—"

"Back off, Griff." Luke grabbed his arm and spun him away from Angie. "Back off now!" For a tension-charged second, the two men glared at each other. Breaking it, Luke muttered, "What kind of loco weed have you been eating anyway?"

Reaching out, he snatched the crumpled paper from Griff's grasp, looked at it, shot an accusing look at Griff, then passed it over to Angie. It was the decoded message from the letter, the one Luke had written on the notebook paper. "You found that in the wastebasket, did you? What did you do—break into her camper?" Luke demanded.

Chin quivering, Griff snarled, "You can't call it breakin' in when a place isn't locked."

"Maybe this time it wasn't," Luke conceded, "but what about the first time?"

Griff struggled to maintain his air of bellicosity, but he had trouble meeting Luke's eyes. "All right, so it was me who picked the lock and went through her camper the first time. So what? I didn't take anything. No harm was done." He shot a sudden glance at Fargo, his expression turning sly with malice. "At least I didn't hit her over the head like he did."

Luke swung around to stare at the one-armed cowboy in disbelief. "You?"

The redness of shame and embarrassment flooded Fargo's face, his mouth working soundlessly for a moment. "Luke, I didn't—I was careful not to hurt her, honest. I only meant to—" Fargo began lamely, then broke it off to point an accusing finger back at Griff. "It was all his doin'!" His voice went shrill with a kind of defensive anger. "He was the one who said the letter she showed us was phony, that she still had the real one in her purse. I just wanted to stun her long enough to grab the purse and skedaddle. That's all." He hesitated guiltily. "With that letter, I figured I could find the gold. Dammit, Luke, I need it."

"Why?" Luke stared at him with a growing sense of having been betrayed.

"Why?" Fargo laughed out the word in disbelief, then spoke with a catch in his voice, "That's a fool question to ask a sixty-eight-year-old man with one arm and no money and no family. One of these days I ain't gonna be able to do your cookin' and cleanin', ya know. Then what's gonna happen to me? Where am I gonna live? How am I gonna survive with jus' a measly pension check from the government? Why, that piddly amount wouldn't be enough to keep me in beans for a month. But with that gold . . ." He choked up, leaving the sentence unfinished.

"Gold," Luke repeated in a voice that was grim and hard. "It was all for the gold. Look what it's done to you." His gaze sliced from Fargo to Griff, then bounced to Tobe, including him in its censure. "It's turned you into a bunch of muggers, thieves, and slackers, out for what you can get regardless of who suffers along the way."

"You're a fine one to be preachin'," Griff challenged. "You want that gold as much as we do."

"You're wrong," Luke told him. "That gold can't buy me what I want. It can't bring back my wife and son." Pivoting on his heel, he swung away from them and flashed an angry look at Angie. "I warned you that gold changes people, turns them into complete strangers."

Perhaps she should have felt as hurt and outraged as Luke, but she only felt sad and sorry. "It wasn't the gold, Luke. It's the greed for it," she reminded him.

"The two seem inseparable, don't they?" he taunted without humor.

Ignoring that, Angie glanced at the crumpled notebook paper, then up to Griff. "I want you to know, Griff, that I threw this away because I didn't need it anymore. It never occurred to me someone would go through my trash." On impulse, she handed it back to him.

"Well, I did." He kept his head down to conceal the bitter tears still swimming in his eyes. "I thought this paper was gonna be my ticket out of that fleabag bar. But it turned out to be worthless." He balled the sheet in his fist. "Now you've found the gold, and I'm gonna be stuck in that dump the rest of my life, never havin' a real restaurant of my own."

"We're still looking for the gold, Griff. We haven't found it yet." She watched him, pulled by the intense longing in his voice.

"Lot of good that does me." Turning, he heaved the wadded ball into the air. But the lightness of it carried it only a few feet.

Angie hesitated, then went with her instincts. "If you'd like to help us, I'll offer you the same deal I made with Tobe: twenty percent of whatever I receive for the gold. There are no guarantees it will be enough to buy you a real restaurant, but . . . something is better than nothing."

He was instantly leery. "You'd cut me in? Why?"

"Why not? It's only money," she reasoned, then smiled. "Why be greedy about it? There're five of us here. As long as we each do our share, why not split it five ways? It seems to me that's the only fair thing to do. What do you say? Shall we count you in?"

His glance darted to the others as if he still believed there was a catch to it. Finally he gave a fierce nod. "You're darn right you can count me in." Immediately Griff went into action, crossing to the hole and taking the shovel from Tobe's hand. "Here. Let me do the diggin' for a while."

Luke tugged off his gloves, eyeing her askance as he murmured for her ears alone, "I hope you know what you're doing."

"So do I." But she'd already searched and found no regrets, no doubts.

Moving away, Luke walked to the idling ATV and killed the engine, then glanced at the fading light overhead. Already the lavender-gray of twilight tinted the eastern sky.

"It'll be dark soon," he stated. "You'd better get supper started, Fargo, while there's still enough light to see by. Tobe, take the horses back to camp, unsaddle them, and hobble them for the night. You might as well go with them, Angie. I'll stay here and give Griff a hand. We'll give a shout if we hit anything before nightfall."

"I guess there's not much point standing around here, is there?" She curved a hand over Dulcie's shoulder. "Come on. We'll walk back together."

"We aren't going to quit digging when it gets dark, are we?" Tobe protested. "Can't we rig up some sort of light, start a fire or something?"

"If we uncover any of the gold yet tonight, we will," Luke stated. "Otherwise, we'll start work again in the morning."

Chapter Twenty-Two

The sun had climbed above the eastern horizon over an hour ago, but its rays had yet to shine on the canyon's high wall. Within its shadows, the air retained an invigorating crispness that sharpened all the senses.

The smell of freshly turned earth rose from the dirt pile next to the hole and mixed with the fainter scents of coffee and pine resin in the air. Using the extra shovel, Angie pushed more of the dirt away from the side of the ever-deepening hole, then stood back.

For a moment, the rhythmic chunk, scrape, and thud of the shovel, as it bit into the ground, scooped up dirt, and dumped it onto the pile, dominated the morning stillness. Then Tobe paused and wiped the sweat from his upper lip on his shirtsleeve.

"How much deeper do you think we need to go?" he asked when Luke stepped into the hole to relieve him.

"Another foot probably," Luke replied, then glanced at Angie, seeking her opinion.

"I can't imagine they would have buried it any deeper than four feet," she agreed. "I think it would have taken too much time. Time that would have been better spent covering up the fact the area had been disturbed at all."

Stepping on the shovel, Luke drove it into the ground. The instant Angie heard the distinctive clink of the blade striking something hard, her heart skipped a beat. But it turned out to be another large rock, one of a score they'd encountered.

Minutes later Griff drove up on the ATV, hauling a thermos of coffee and a big jug of drinking water from camp. He set them both on a flat rock that had broken off from the cliff long ago.

"How's it goin'?" He hurried to the hole.

"Nothing yet." Luke tossed another shovelful of dirt onto the pile.

The digging continued.

At a depth of four feet, there was still no sign of the gold. Keenly disappointed, Tobe turned searching eyes on Angie. "I thought you said it would be here."

"I thought it would be." Clearly she'd been wrong. "Maybe it's buried farther out from the base."

The excavation was expanded to cover another three feet in length. The sun rose higher as they worked. Still nothing. Next they chopped away at the right side, widening the hole.

The sun was at its zenith when they broke for lunch, still with nothing to show for their labor. For the most part they ate in silence, communicating in grunts and grumbles, the underlying mood turning cranky and irritable.

When work resumed, they attacked the left side, and the sun crossed to the western half of the sky. Muscles began to feel the strain from all the digging.

More underlayers were exposed, still without revealing any glint of gold. Weariness and frustration worked on nerves that were already taut, fraying tempers and dashing hopes.

Less than a foot from the desired depth, they hit a layer of large rock chunks. Straightening, Luke stepped back to survey the area yet to be excavated.

"We're wasting our time digging out this section," he concluded. "The gold's not going to be here."

"You don't know that," Griff snapped angrily and scrambled

into the rectangular hole that now measured six feet by nine. "Those outlaws coulda dumped those rocks on top of the gold just to make some fool like you think that way. Now, gimme that shovel and get out of the way."

"Have at it." Luke held out the shovel.

Griff jerked it from his grasp, then began an assault on the rock layer, channeling his anger and frustration into furious action. Tobe jumped in to help, using his hands to pry out the rock chunks near the surface.

Luke climbed out of the shallow pit and paused next to Angie. She stood near the edge, watching Griff's feverish efforts, a small worry line running across her forehead. Luke tugged off his dirty gloves and absently pressed a hand to the small of his back, arching spine and shoulders to stretch cramping muscles.

"It doesn't look good," he told her quietly.

"I know," she murmured, the line deepening with confusion. "I don't understand, either. It has to be buried somewhere in this area. Maybe we have to dig deeper."

"Maybe." But he still doubted they would find anything.

Moving away, he headed for the water jug on the rock, then hesitated, as he spotted Saddlebags sitting in the shade of some brush, watching the diggers with interest, bony arms resting on upraised knees.

His bright-black eyes encountered Luke's gaze, and he cackled with a kind of malicious glee. "Didn't I tell ya? It ain't there. It surely ain't," he declared and cackled again.

Incensed by the taunting sound, Griff reacted with a snarling one of his own. "Why? Because some tottering old coot couldn't find it when he looked?"

Stung by the insult, Saddlebags scrambled to his feet. "I wasn't old when I first looked!" he shouted, gesturing wildly. "Ya can dig all the way t' China an' ya still ain't gonna find it anywheres along here."

"That's a lie." Griff renewed his attack with the shovel, muttering under his breath, "It's here. It has to be here."

"Lyin', am I?" Outraged, Saddlebags scuttled closer to the hole. "You ain't dug up a ounce of soil that ain't been touched by my sweat or the water from my blisters." He bent in a crouch, hands on his knees, legs bowed. "Ya hear? Sweat an' blisters, that's what you'll find with all your diggin'."

"Shut up," Griff growled out of a corner of his mouth.

"Sweat an' blisters. Sweat an' blisters." Saddlebags broke into an awkward jig and chanted the taunting phrase over and over. "Sweat an' blisters. Sweat an' blisters."

Griff spun around, gripping the shovel like a weapon. "I ain't gonna tell you again—shut up!!"

Breaking off the jig, Saddlebags bent again, propping hands on bowed knees and giving him a mean-eyed glare. "Why should I? I already dug up the ground under this eagle rock three times. I even dug deeper'n you are. An' I dug all the way back to where he's a-standin' too," he declared, thrusting a skeletal finger in Luke's direction. "Afore I was through, I dug from one end o' this wall t' the other. An' there weren't no gold bars nowhere!"

Angie stared at him with a mixture of shock and dismay, her heart sinking. As much as she didn't want to, she believed him. She believed every word he said. The gold wasn't here.

She turned away, trying to understand how that could be. The letter, the coded message, the second key . . .

Behind her, Griff exploded out of the pit with a roar of rage. There was a whack of the shovel and a yelp of pain. By the time she swung back around, the old man was on the ground with Griff on top of him, the shovel abandoned in favor of his fists as he screamed at Saddlebags to shut up.

"Griff, no!" Angie moved to stop him.

But Luke had already sprang toward them, dropping his water cup and grabbing for Griff. He dragged him off Saddlebags and shoved him to the ground, then momentarily stood over him. "Have you gone crazy?" he demanded in a half-savage mutter.

Ignoring them, Angie dropped to her knees beside the motionless old man. His arms were crossed over his eyes and head as if shielding them from more blows, leaving only his nose, mouth, and bearded jaws exposed to view. The floppy hat was still on his head. But he wore it pulled so low that Angie doubted it could easily be knocked off.

Bright red blood flowed from a corner of his mouth, spreading into his beard. Belatedly she noticed the set of upper and lower dentures, yellowed with tartar, lying on the loose dirt near his head, bits of soil clinging to them.

"Saddlebags, can you hear me?" She gently laid a hand on his thin arm while she ran her gaze over him, looking for other obvious signs of injury.

There was a slight movement of his head, then a low moan and a faint grimace of pain. One bony hand moved weakly toward his mouth; the other shifted toward the back of his head.

"How bad is he hurt?" Luke knelt on the other side of him.

"I don't know. He has a cut inside his mouth for sure, and some pain at the back of his head. He could have a concussion."

"Tobe, take the ATV and go get the first-aid kit," Luke ordered crisply.

When Tobe scrambled out of the hole and ran to the vehicle, Angie carefully lifted aside a thin arm, stunned by the weightlessness of it, the lack of substance, as if his bones were made of air. Automatically she checked his pulse. It was rapid, but not alarmingly so.

The ATV sputtered to life and roared off toward camp.

She noticed a redness and a hint of swelling near the point of his left cheekbone where a blow from Griff's fist had obviously landed, but the skin was unbroken. Gently she lifted an eyelid to check the pupil and watched its attempt to focus on her as he stirred again and moaned.

"I don't think he's concussed, just dazed," she told Luke, who was busy running exploring hands over the old man, checking for broken bones.

"There're no obvious breaks," he concluded.

"He's bleeding." Hovering close, Dulcie peered over Angie's shoulder, her eyes big with worry.

"I know. We'll need some water. Would you bring that jug over?" Angie gestured to the insulated jug on the rock. Dulcie rushed to get it.

"Let's lift him up and take a look at that cut in his mouth." Luke slid an arm under the old man's shoulders to prop him up, careful to cradle his head.

But when Angie attempted to see inside his mouth, Saddlebags roused and pawed at her hand. "Lea' me alone," he protested in a toothless mumble. "Le' me go."

"Your mouth's bleeding," Angie explained.

"I can take care o' it." More blood seeped from his mouth corner when he tried to twist free from them. "Le' me up."

Luke glanced at Angie and nodded. "We'll sit you up. Just take it easy. You might have some cracked ribs."

"I'd feel 'em if'n I did," Saddlebags grumbled but didn't resist their efforts to sit him upright.

Dulcie trotted back, her knees knocking against the heavy jug she held in front of her with both hands. "Here's the water, Angie."

"Thanks. Do you have a handkerchief, Luke?"

"Right here." He dragged it out of his hip pocket. "It's clean."

Angie took it from him and held it under the jug's spout to moisten it. Griff still sat on the ground just beyond Luke, watching their ministrations in sullen silence, his shoulders hunched over his raised knees. When the rumble of the ATV signaled its return to the area, he rolled to his feet and stalked back to the shallow pit, jumped into it, and started digging again.

With the wet cloth, Angie started to wipe some of the blood from the old man's mouth. Saddlebags turned his face and pushed her hand back with a surprising strength for all his frailty.

"Le' me be," he complained, gumming the words as a bubble

of blood dribbled from between his shriveled lips. "Don' need no woman fussin' ober me."

"I need to see how bad your mouth is cut." But the roar of the ATV drowned out her words as Tobe drove up. Fargo rode behind him, a large kit marked with a red cross clamped under his left arm.

Again Saddlebags rebuffed Angie's attempt to blot the blood seeping from his mouth. "Don' need tha'. Go' my own." Scowling, he fumbled in his coat pocket and pulled out a rag for a handkerchief.

Tobe braked to a stop and cut the engine as Saddlebags started to jam the rag in his mouth.

Angie grabbed at it. "Don't you put that in your mouth. It's filthy."

"Gimme tha'."

A brief tug-of-war ensued before Angie managed to wrest it away from him. But she gave up the rest of the battle. "Here. If you insist on doing it yourself, use this." She handed him Luke's clean handkerchief.

He glowered at her for a moment, then took the cloth, turned his head to the side, and spat out the blood in his mouth, then poked around inside with the handkerchief, several times wincing visibly.

Tobe brought the kit to Luke. "Is he okay?"

"Seems to be." Luke snapped open the box.

"Not surprised." Fargo lumbered over. "He's a tough ole bird."

"Would you like to rinse your mouth out with some water?" Angie suggested.

Saddlebags glared at her warily, then nodded. When Angie signaled to Dulcie to fetch one of the metal cups used for drinking, he began looking around him. "Where's m' teeth?"

"Right here." The minute Angie picked them up, he grabbed for them, but she held them out of reach. "They have to be washed before you can put them back in your mouth. They're covered with dirt."

A sound of disgust came from his throat, but he watched in silence while she rinsed them off under the jug's spigot. Luke handed her a bottle of disinfectant. She squirted a liberal amount on both dentures before handing them to Saddlebags. He slipped first one, then the other in his mouth and clacked them together, wincing and pressing a hand to the side of his mouth where the inner cut was.

Angie sat back on her heels, satisfied that other than still being a little shaken and sore Saddlebags was all right. With the near-crisis over, she felt free to consider all the nagging questions he always seemed to arouse.

"Saddlebags," she began thoughtfully, "how did you know about the eagle rock?"

"How do ya think?" he retorted, with a narrow-eyed glare. "I got it from the letter, o' course."

The admission came so readily, Angie was momentarily taken aback by it. A second later the floodgates opened, unleashing all the stored-up questions. "How did you get it? Did you find it? Where? When? My grandfather—do you know what happened to him?"

He eyed her warily, and she sensed he was on the verge of clamming up. He jerked a dirty-nailed thumb toward Luke. Both Tobe and Fargo were grouped behind him.

"Why'nt ya ask them?" Saddlebags challenged. "It was them what found his bones."

"That wasn't my grandfather," she told him.

He released a dismissive snort. "It ain't nothin' t' do with me."

"But it does," Angie persisted. "At least, indirectly. You admit you have a copy of Ike Wilson's letter. How did you get it? . . . Did you find it? . . . Where?"

She paused a beat after each question, giving him a chance to answer, but he acted like he didn't hear a single one. Trying another tactic, Angie began making guesses of her own.

"I know my grandfather wouldn't have given you that letter,

which means you must have found it among his things. What else did you find, I wonder," she said thoughtfully. "His clothes would have worn out years ago. But he had a pocketknife and a gold watch. You had to have found them when you discovered the letter. You wouldn't happen to still have them, would you?"

"That ain't none o' your blamed business," Saddlebags declared.

"He has a pocket watch pinned inside his vest," Luke told her. "I felt it when I was checking to see if he had any broken ribs."

"I'd like to see that watch, Saddlebags." Angie held out her hand, palm up, every inch the teacher calmly but firmly ordering a student to turn over an item.

"It's mine." With that angry cry, he made an attempt to scramble to his feet only to be hit with a sharp pain and a wave of dizziness. He sank back with a groan, cupping a hand to the back of his head. Both Angie and Luke reached for him.

"We'd better see what you've done to your head." Before Saddlebags could reject the offer or even guess his intentions, Luke removed the floppy hat.

The pallor of his forehead and the crown of his head showed thinning, yellowed-gray hair that the hat had plastered to his head. It gave the illusion of a skullcap with the longer, darker, and dirtier strands poking from beneath it.

"Gimme m' hat," Saddlebags complained when Luke parted the thicker layers of straggly hair to examine the bump his searching fingers had located.

"In a minute. He has a good-sized knot back here," he told Angie. "Probably he hit his head on something when Griff knocked him down." Glancing behind him, Luke spotted a likely looking rock chunk. But the cause was immaterial. It was the injury itself that needed to be dealt with. "The skin's broken, but I can't tell how deep the cut is. Give me one of those antiseptic wipes from the first-aid kit."

Angie retrieved one from the kit, tore open the packet, and handed it to Luke.

"It ain't nothin'. Le' me be. Aah." He grimaced and sucked in a hissing breath when Luke got past the worst of the blood to probe the wound itself.

"You're hurting him, Luke," Dulcie murmured in concern, her own face contorting with sympathy pains.

"I'm almost done," he said, then glanced at Angie. "He'll need a bandage but no stitches." She supplied him one from the kit over Saddlebags's continued objections.

"I don't need none o' that stuff, I tell ya." But it was only a halfhearted protest, with no attempt to back it up with action.

When Luke finished, Saddlebags gingerly felt the bandaged area. Distracted by the soreness of it, he didn't immediately notice when Luke opened his vest and began unpinning the watch fastened to it.

"Hey! What're ya doin'?!" He clawed at Luke's hands to stop him, but he hadn't the strength to match Luke.

"Taking a look at this watch." Freeing it, he passed the gold pocket watch to Angie.

She'd only caught glimpses of its scratched and grimy surface while Luke was removing it from the vest. Now she held it, with only a meager description from her grandmother to identify it: gold with a scrolly leaflike design around the outer edge and the initials JW inscribed—but Angie couldn't remember where she was supposed to find them.

"You gimme that watch! It's mine, I tell ya. Mine!" In a frantic rage, Saddlebags hurled himself at her, hands grasping to seize it from her. Angie turned, using her body to shield it from his reach while she checked first the front, then the back for the initials. "Give it t' me, ya hear! It's mine by rights."

Deaf to his shouts, she located the clasp and opened to look inside the face cover. There, wedged in the circle was an old black-and-white photograph, taken in the late teens or early twenties, of a young woman, her fashionably short hair styled in finger waves. Angie stared at it in shocked recognition.

"This is a picture of my grandmother." She swung to confront the old man. "How did you get it? Did you take it from his wallet?"

She jerked her hands back when he tried to snatch the watch from them. Luke pulled him away.

"No, no, no," Saddlebags raged helplessly. "Thieves! That's what ya are! Thieves! Stealin' from an ol' man."

"Where did you find this?" Angie fixed her determined gaze on him, refusing to let up until she received some answers. "Tell me where—"

She broke off the question, her attention drawn to the small dark patch on his forehead centimeters from his receding hairline. Staring at it, she leaned closer.

"What's . . . blue boy," she whispered in disbelief.

But there was no mistaking the small, bluish birthmark, high on the right, almost hidden in the hairline—exactly as her grandmother had described. Her lips parted in amazement.

"It is you." With her fingertip, she went to touch it, but Saddlebags pulled away, an angry pain darkening his eyes.

"Blue boy?" Tobe frowned. "What's she talking about?"

"That was my grandmother's pet name for him," Angie explained, a softness in her eyes as she gazed at the old man. "The watch does belong to him. This is my grandfather."

She pressed the watch back into his palm, then covered her hands over his. He tried to pull away from them, eyes closed, his head jerking in mute denial. A faint, surprised laugh slid from her throat.

"I came looking for the gold, and instead, I found you," she realized.

"I ain't your grandpa," he growled. "Never was an' never will be."

"Why don't we talk about that over coffee?" Angie suggested, unwilling to have this moment spoiled by discord. She directed a smiling glance at Fargo. "There's still some left from lunch, isn't there?"

He drew his head back, mildly offended by the question. "I never let a pot stay empty."

"In that case, let's all go have some coffee." Luke rose, giving Angie a hand as she helped a silent and listless Saddlebags—nee Henry James "Hank" Wilson—to his feet. "You, too, Griff." Luke glanced toward the hole where Griff still labored with the shovel.

"Nope." He jammed his foot onto the shovel, driving the point of the blade deep into the soil. "I'm not leavin' here without that gold."

"Give it up, Griff," Luke stated, a grimness in his voice. "You heard Saddlebags. There is no gold here, or he would have found it years ago."

For an instant, Griff was motionless, sweat rolling off his forehead. Then he bent to scoop up the next load of dirt and throw it from the hole.

"You can believe that if you want to." He glared at Luke. "But not me."

There was no reasoning with him. They all saw it, but none said anything as they turned and walked from the canyon wall and the crude shape of an eagle etched on its face.

Chapter Twenty-Three

At the camp, Angie's grandfather's story came out in bits and pieces. In the beginning, Angie did most of the talking, catching him up on information about the family and telling him about his wife, the life she'd made for herself, the home she'd made, the love she'd given and the love she'd never lost for her absent husband.

The thrust of Angie's words was always positive, never with a hint of reproach for his absence, because she knew that was the way her grandmother would have wanted it.

When she finished, Saddlebags sat for a long time staring into his nearly empty cup. "I al'ays figgered she'd marry again," he said at last, indirectly confirming his identity for the first time.

"I don't think the thought ever crossed her mind," Angie told him. "You were her husband. She never wanted any other."

He nodded without looking up or making a comment.

"One thing puzzles me," Fargo spoke when the silence began to stretch. "Who was that guy we found with your teeth?"

Angie had a feeling she knew the answer to that, but she waited to see if her grandfather would tell them. In a grassy area under the trees, a horse snorted and stamped at a deerfly. There was a scuttle of leaves as a squirrel leaped to another tree branch. Then all was quiet again.

"Amos Aloysius Smith is who he was," Saddlebags confirmed her suspicion. "Met up with him in the yard at Laramie. I'd decided I wasn't never gonna find that gold, an' I knew our first baby was gonna be born soon. I wanted t' be home for it. By then, I didn't have a dime t' my name. I figgered I'd ride the rails back t' Iowa. Everybody was doin' it then, not jus' no-good tramps."

"That doesn't make any sense," Tobe protested. "If you met up with him in Laramie, how'd his body end up on the Ten Bar?"

"When I got t' the yard an' found out I'd missed the eastbound by an hour, I was feelin' purty down—knowin' there wouldn't be another one through 'til the next day. Amos, he had a bottle an' he offered me a drink. Afore I knew it, I'd told him about the gold, showed him the letter, explained about the code an' all—an' how it hadn't led me nowhere. Turned out he was a preacher's boy, jus' like my grandpa Ike. He got all excited, said he knew where the gold was an' for half of it, he'd show me. I wanted that gold. Givin' up half didn't sound like so much. So, back we come. Once I showed him the rock pillars in the valley, he figgered he didn't need me no more."

"There was a fight," Luke guessed.

Saddlebags came off the log, eyes blazing with pain and the leftover fury. "He tried t' bash m' head in. I had t' fight back. We went at it purty good, too. Then he had me on the ground tryin' t' choke me. I hit him. It didn't seem no harder than other times, but he went down an' didn't get up."

He paused, remembering, all the anger dissolving. "I let 'im lay there a while whilst I saw t' myself. My nose was broke, an' my jaw, pro'ly some ribs, too. My face was swoll up so bad I couldn't hardly see."

Unconsciously he ran his fingers lightly over his nose and cheekbone, as if feeling the old injuries.

"It got t' botherin' me the way he jus' lay there, not movin'. Somethin' tol' me he was gonna die if he didn't get help." Lifting his head, Saddlebags looked straight at Luke, but his thoughts were still in the past. "The Ten Bar was the closest place I knew t' get help for 'im. I got 'im as far as I could, but all the jostlin' of totin' 'im . . ." He sank back onto the log, head bowing in guilt. "He was dead, an' I as good as killed him."

"But he tried to kill you first," Tobe protested, voicing Angie's own thought.

Fargo snorted in agreement. "Sounds like a plain ole case of self-defense to me."

"But there weren't no way for me t' prove it." His brows knitted together in a way that told Angie her grandfather was still haunted by the choices he'd made all those years ago. Injured and scared himself, he'd obviously panicked.

"What if some judge sent me t' prison? I couldn't have the shame o' that fallin' on Hannah, not with a baby comin'." Saddlebags hung his head again.

"So you decided to bury the body and conceal Smith's death." Rising, Luke crossed to the fire and refilled his cup.

"It wasn't hard. Good thing 'cause I wasn't in no shape t' do much diggin'. It'd rained a couple days afore an' softened the ground up. I saw the big hollow under that cut bank an' dragged 'im there, then caved in the bank t' cover 'im up."

"Wait a minute. What about the ring and your teeth?" Angie remembered. "Why did you want people to think you were buried there?"

He shot her a startled look. To him the answer was obvious. " 'Cause I figgered if the body was found, it was better for Hannah t' think I was dead than t' know I'd killed a man. Course, I got worried some about his teeth. I knew Hannah would figger out quick it weren't me when she found out about 'em. Pullin' his weren't hard. He didn't have no chewin' teeth an' most o' the rest of 'em got knocked loose in the fight. My own mouth was cut up so bad inside I couldn't stand havin' m' teeth in it anyways. Afterwards"—he dragged in a long breath and let it out in a heavy sigh—"I hightailed it outta there. I didn't want anybody aroun' here seein' me, beat up like I was. They'da known right off I was in a fight an' start wonderin' about the other guy. I went t' Caspar. Nobody knowed me there." With a scornful, snorting breath, he recalled, "Right off I got throwed in jail for bein' a vagrant."

"Told 'em I was Amos Aloysius Smith an' showed 'em his wallet to prove it. Later they got a doctor in t' patch me up some. But nothin' healed right." He rubbed a finger over his crooked nose. "Didn't look like m'self no more. An' with a beard, not even Hannah woulda guessed it was me."

Privately Angie disagreed, convinced her grandmother would have recognized him, even with a beard and badly broken nose. But second-guessing his decisions was pointless.

"What happened after you were released from jail?" she asked.

His thin shoulders lifted in a vague shrug. "Bummed around for a while, got work when I could, an' watched the papers for any mention of a body bein' found here. Kept thinkin' about that gold, though, an' finally figgered out what Smith'd seen in the letter. But I was leery a comin' back t' look for it. People mighta got suspicious—two people comin' to look for that outlaw gold, one right behind the other—specially if that body'd been found. I waited better 'n two years afore I figgered it was safe. Then I was careful to fight shy of any that'd knowed me afore. Figgered it was safest t' keep t' m' self." He stared into the middle distance, seeing into the past. "Found this canyon straight off. An' the eagle on the rock, too. But no gold. Dug down six feet without findin' it."

"But you kept looking for it—all this time. Why?" That was what Angie didn't understand.

"'Cause I knew it was out there somewhere laughin' at me, that's why," he flared with sudden impatience, but it quickly subsided into a vague grumble. "'Sides, I kept thinkin' that if'n I had that gold, somehow I could make things right. So I kept on lookin'. Then it got too late t' make things right," he acknowledged. "An' I was too old. What else was I gonna do? Where else was I gonna go?"

Angie wondered if he saw the irony. All those years ago he'd feared being convicted of killing Amos Smith and sent to prison. In the end, he had sentenced himself; this canyon land had become his prison and the gold, his warden. It was sad. Too sad to discuss.

Crossing to the fire, she picked up the speckled enamel pot and walked over to him. "Would you like some more coffee, Grandpa?"

His glance darted to her face, wary and uncertain. "Makes me feel funny t' hear you call me that," he admitted, then studied the deep red color of her hair, his expression losing some of its stony hardness. "Ya got her hair. An' her freckles, too."

"The sun brings them out," she acknowledged and poured coffee into his cup, keeping a finger on the lid to the pot.

"Did with Hannah, too," he recalled, falling silent with the memory.

After refilling her own cup and setting the pot near the fire again, Angie returned to her own seat on the log. Dulcie stole up behind her and whispered close to her ear, "Is he really your grandpa?"

"He really is." Angie nodded.

Dulcie snuck another look at the bearded and grimy old man, then whispered, "Are you glad about that?"

"Very glad. I've missed not having a grandfather. Now I have one." Automatically she reached over and laid an affectionate hand on his arm.

Through the cloth of his coat sleeve, Angie felt the tensing of his wiry muscles in instinctive resistance and withdrew her hand, realizing it would take some time for him to become comfortable with physical contact. He'd lived too much of his life without it.

"I wish I had a grandpa." Dulcie slid onto the end of the log, careful to keep Angie between her and the old man.

"I'm sure you do." Smiling gently, Angie smoothed the flyaway wisps of Dulcie's pale hair, tucking them into her ponytail band. "But you do have Fargo. That's almost the same as having a grandfather."

"I guess." With a big sigh, Dulcie dug a toe into the dirt, then turned questioning eyes on Angie. "Aren't we gonna look for the gold anymore?"

Before Angie could answer, her grandfather growled, "You forget 'bout that gold, little girl. Won't bring ya nothin' but grief. Grief and loneliness."

"I thought it was sweat and blisters," Tobe declared, making an attempt at a joke.

But Hank Wilson's sense of humor had deteriorated from lack of use. "Ya'll get them, too," he stated, with a serious and emphatic nod.

"It looks like Griff found that out," Fargo observed, studying the weary figure walking toward them.

Griff's shirt was drenched with sweat, his head and shoulders slumped in soul-sick dejection. There was a leadenness to his step and a dullness in his expression when he approached the camp. His glance slid over them without ever making eye contact.

"The gold wasn't there." His head moved from side to side in a kind of dazed shake, a bleakness in his eyes. "I dug out every bit of dirt, and it wasn't there." He stared at Angie. "You said it would be there."

There was no anger, no accusation in his voice, just a kind of hopelessness.

"I thought it would be—" she began.

"Where is it, then?" Griff looked around, bewildered and empty.

"I don't know." Angie realized she didn't really care either. Somewhere between the time she had discovered Saddlebags was her grandfather and this moment, she had lost the desire to search for the outlaw gold.

"All these years you've looked for it and never found it," Griff said to Saddlebags, then punctuated it with a soft, bitter laugh. "Maybe there never was any gold. Maybe it was all one big joke."

"Wouldn't surprise me a bit," Fargo declared. "The posse probably found it shortly after they caught the outlaws and never told nobody."

As if too weary to stand another minute, Griff sat on the ground, jaws clenched against the pain of disillusionment. "It isn't fair," he muttered in frustration. "That gold was my one chance. My one chance. And now it's gone."

Fargo cleared his throat but said nothing, silenced by the finality of Griff's statement. Head down, he directed a sightless stare at the ground and absently reached across his body to cup a hand over his left arm where the sleeve was pinned back. There was something about his flat expression that conveyed a deadness of spirit, of hopes lost and dreams broken.

"I should have known there wasn't any gold," Tobe mumbled, a shine of tears in his eyes. He pivoted away to hide them, his young shoulders drooping.

A stillness settled over the campsite, depressing in its heaviness as each withdrew into the privacy of his or her own dark thoughts. The moment threatened to stretch and bury them in a silent gloom.

Luke broke it, drawling, "If you aren't a fine bunch." With a downward fling of his cup, he emptied out the coffee dregs. "Here you are all down in the mouth over that gold and what it could have got you—without ever realizing you already had it."

Confusion, denial, and indignation flashed through the group, but Luke gave them no chance to voice it. "Fargo, you wanted the gold because you were worried about where and how you were going to live when you're too old to be useful. The Ten Bar's always been your home and it always will be. As for you, Tobe"—Luke turned to him—"you wanted a ranch of your own mainly because you think it would make you a full-fledged cowboy in other people's eyes. But folks around here don't think of you as anything else. Then, there's you, Griff. You want a restaurant when you already have one."

"That place?" Griff curled his lip in derision.

"Yes, that place," Luke countered smoothly. "I know you,

Griff. You wouldn't be happy with a fancy steak house in the city for long. You wouldn't have time to butcher your own meat, grow your own produce, or any of the hundred other things you take such pride in."

Griff struggled to deny the logic of that. "Maybe . . . but—"

"There're no maybes about it. It's a fact," Luke drawled, then gestured toward Saddlebags with his empty cup. "It's no different with Saddlebags, there. To him, the gold was a way of redeeming himself with his family. There he is, grieving over not finding it, and his granddaughter is sitting right beside him." His glance rested on Angie, something gentle and wry about the look in his eyes. "Angie's about the only one in this whole group who hasn't been wearing blinders, and that includes me."

"You?" Tobe frowned in disbelief, protesting, "But you didn't even want the gold."

"No, I didn't," Luke agreed. "But like you, I couldn't see what I had. I've been too blinded by what I'd lost. I guess it took watching all of you to finally open my eyes to that."

Hearing him, Angie experienced a surge of elation. She was glad for him, and proud, too. But there was something deeply poignant about the moment that kept her silent, some nameless emotion clogging her throat with happy tears. The others clearly sensed it, too. A kind of awkwardness seemed to grip them, averting their gazes as they searched for something to say.

Luke solved the problem. As he set his metal cup on one of the stones that formed the fire circle, he declared, "It's going to take some time to fill that hole back in. We might as well get started."

"Good idea." Quick to agree, Angie rose from her log seat, then glanced back at her grandfather. "Are you coming, Grandpa?"

Distracted by her use of the unfamiliar term, he paused as if rolling it over in his mind, then gathered his spindly legs under him and pushed off the log. "Might as well. I'm dang near an expert at fillin' in holes." His dark eyes gleamed with something very close to humor.

She laughed softly. "I'll bet you are."

Automatically Angie shortened her stride to match his scuffling gait, but her attention was on Luke, walking ahead of her with a long and deceptively lazy stride. Maybe it was her imagination but she thought she saw a new peace in his face, an acceptance of the deaths of his wife and young son, one that didn't diminish the loss or their memory in any way. Yet it was one that allowed him to look forward to tomorrow. Knowing that lightened her own step.

When Tobe jogged past her to catch up with Luke, Dulcie split away to join Angie. "How come we got to fill in that hole?"

"Because some animal could fall into it and get hurt."

"What kind of animal? You mean, like a cow?"

"Or a horse or a deer or a rabbit, just any kind of animal."

Dulcie mulled over that possibility. "Do you think something coulda fallen in while we were gone?"

"It's possible, I suppose," Angie agreed.

"I'd better go see." Off she went at a dead run, long ponytail whipping behind her.

When Dulcie raced by Luke, he slowed his steps and cast a questioning glance at Angie. "What's her hurry?"

"She's checking to see if any animals have fallen in the hole," she explained, with a faint smile.

"I don't think that's likely." Luke waited to walk with her while Tobe continued on.

Luke's glance slid from Saddlebags to linger on her, a new level of interest in his eyes. It ignited a warm pleasure somewhere deep inside. All too soon, he directed his glance to the front.

"I guess you'll be heading back to Iowa with your grandfather in a few days," Luke remarked.

"Probably." Actually Angie hadn't thought that far ahead.

She discovered she had very ambivalent feelings about it. The desire to stay was as strong as the desire to take her grandfather home. She swept her gaze over the rugged landscape, a wistfulness creeping into her expression.

"I'll definitely miss this country, though," she realized.

"Maybe you can come back sometime and hunt for the gold again," Luke suggested.

Before Angie could respond, Saddlebags broke into the conversation, his voice sharp with warning. "Don't you let the spell o' that gold lure ya into huntin' for it. Grief, that's all ya'll find for your trouble."

"I know, Grandpa." But it wasn't the lure of the outlaw gold that would bring her back to Wyoming. It was the warm look of interest Luke directed at her.

The ATV rumbled up from the rear, then swung in a wide arc around them, Griff at the controls and Fargo perched behind him, one hand propping the water jug on his thigh.

When they reached the section of canyon wall below the eagle rock, Tobe and Griff were already at work, shoveling the loose dirt back into the shallow pit. Luke pulled on his work gloves and picked up the other shovel to join them.

Dulcie left Fargo's side to run to Angie. "There weren't any animals in the hole when I got here."

"That's good."

"Yeah." Her glance strayed back to the three men and the loads of dirt flying into the hole. "I wanted to help, but Tobe said I was too little."

"You're big enough to help me throw some of the bigger rocks in," Angie assured her, then cautioned, "Just be careful that you don't get in the way of those shovels. We don't want you getting hurt."

"I'll be careful," Dulcie promised and dashed to pick up the nearest stone, eager to have a role to fill.

They worked in silence, the stillness dominated by the thud of dirt and the clatter of rolling stones. After about twenty minutes, Tobe paused to wipe the sweat from his upper lip and swiped his mouth across his shirtsleeve. He waited while Angie gathered up an armful of rock chunks from the dwindling dirt pile near his feet.

"You know," he began thoughtfully, "it's probably just as well we didn't find that gold. If I'd bought a ranch with my share of it, I probably would have ended up goin' broke."

Startled by his pessimism, Angie asked, "Why?"

"'Cause I don't know enough about the business side of ranchin' yet."

She eyed him with approval. "It's very wise of you to realize that, Tobe."

"Yeah, well . . ." He ducked his head, suddenly self-conscious and secretly pleased by her comment. "It's the truth."

"Luke would probably teach you about it, if you asked him."

"Probably." Nodding, he poked the point of his shovel around in the dirt pile in testing jabs, then scooped up a pile and tossed it into the hole. As he bent to shovel up another load, Tobe remarked, "I can't shake the feelin' that we're buryin' something. I mean, this is like fillin' in a grave."

"It sure ain't the gold we're buryin'," Griff grumbled.

"Maybe it's the idea of it," Tobe suggested, still pondering the feeling.

"If it is, you can be sure it will rise again," Luke declared, amusement riddling his voice. "Sometime, somewhere, there'll be someone who'll get the urge to search for it and it'll happen all over."

Rise again, rise again, rise again. The phrase echoed in Angie's mind with a persistence that couldn't be ignored. She struggled to grasp the significance of it, but the reason kept eluding her.

"Rise again," she murmured softly, her gaze unconsciously traveling up the wall's steep face to the boulder's crude carving of an eagle several feet above the ledge. She breathed in sharply, dropping the rocks cradled on her arm. "Luke! Grandpa!" She spun from the wall to locate her grandfather, then spotted him crouched in the shade of some brush. "We were wrong!"

"Wrong? What are you talking about?" Luke frowned, letting the point of his shovel dip toward the ground.

"What's the Biblical opposite of burial?" But she didn't wait for them to answer. "It's resurrection. Ascension. The gold isn't below the ledge. It's above it!"

All eyes turned toward the ledge high above their heads, too high for anything on it to be visible from below.

"It makes sense." The longer Angie thought about it, the more convinced she became. "No one would think to climb up there and look for it. And it can't be seen from below. Anyone backtracking them would have been looking for indications of freshly turned earth or a place where the ground had been disturbed. She stepped back to study the canyon rim. "It probably can't even be seen from above."

"How the heck are we gonna get up there to find out?" Tobe stared at the sheer drop below the ledge. "It must be twenty feet or more."

"A better question would be, how did they?" Luke countered, visually inspecting the rock face.

Saddlebags scurried to Angie's side, his avid gaze fixed on the distant ledge. He laid a bony hand on her arm, fingers curling into it. "Do you really think it's there, girl?" he asked, a thin thread of hope in his voice.

"It has to be, Grandpa." Angie knew she had said the same thing before, but this time she was positive she wasn't wrong. "Once you're up there, it would be easy enough with a rope to haul the gold up. But Luke's right—how did the outlaws reach the ledge? It would take an experienced climber to scale that wall."

"Or someone handy with a rope," Luke corrected. "See that?"

He pointed to a toothlike rock embedded in the lip of the ledge about six feet to the right.

"That's it." Angie smiled with the certainty of it.

"Tobe, go bring me a rope," Luke ordered.

Little was said while they waited for Tobe to return with the rope. They had already had their hopes severely dashed once— and in Saddlebags's case, more times than he could count. They weren't about to let their expectations get too high again. But the tension was palpable, thickening throats and tightening muscles.

Within minutes Tobe roared back, hopped off the ATV, and tossed the coiled rope to Luke. Shaking out the loop, he moved into position and made the first cast. But he misjudged the height, and the loop fell short of the rock by two feet, producing a collective breath of disappointment from all but Saddlebags.

Silently Luke recoiled the rope to make the second try, shook out the loop, and threw it again. This time it snagged the point of the rock tooth and hung there, without sliding over the rock itself. With a practiced flip of the rope, Luke settled the noose over it, then pulled it tight, testing it with his weight to make sure it would hold.

"I'm going up," he said needlessly and began the hand-over-hand walk up the wall.

Angie watched along with everyone else, listening to the scrape of boot leather on the rock face, feeling the strain and pull of muscles. Her whole body was tense with anticipation. As he neared the ledge, Saddlebags tightened his grip, increasing the pressure on her arm, something frantic yet hopeful about the way his gaze clung to Luke.

When he got within reach, Luke grabbed onto the jutting rock, hooked a foot onto the ledge, and hauled himself onto it, momentarily disappearing from view. The tension on the ground below went up another notch.

"Do you see anything, Luke?" Tobe waited by the rope, a hand clutching it. "Is the gold there?"

On his feet now, Luke came back into view, his head turned, his gaze scouring the ledge on either side. "There's something here." His voice drifted down to them.

"It's the gold. It's got to be the gold." Griff's fervent murmur willed it to be so, while a kind of fear filled Saddlebags's dark eyes. Seeing it, Angie smoothed a hand over the bony fingers digging into her arm.

Luke moved along the narrow rock shelf and knelt down about three feet from the rope. "It looks like old saddlebags," he called the news to them. "The leather's all dry and rotted."

"What's inside? Have you looked?" Barely suppressed excitement gave a high pitch to Tobe's voice.

In answer, Luke straightened, his gloved hands wrapped around something small and very heavy. He stepped to the edge of the shelf, his gaze going straight to Angie. "It's the gold."

His announcement was greeted with an eruption of shouts, hoots of laughter, and squeals of joy. Tobe threw his hat in the air while Fargo and Griff pounded each other's shoulders. Only Angie's grandfather remained silent and motionless.

Angie turned to him, an exuberant smile lighting her entire face. "Did you hear that, Grandpa? We found the gold. Together."

He had a dazed, disbelieving look on his face that tugged at her heart. She gave him a quick, warm hug, then swung around to look up at Luke.

"Will you throw that bar down?" she called. "I want Grandpa to see it."

"Yeah, toss it down!" A chorus of voices echoed variations of her request. "We wanta see it!"

"Better back away, then," Luke warned. "It's heavy."

When the area directly below him was clear, he rocked his hands forward and let go of the bar. Sunlight glinted off its rich yellow color as it fell to the ground, straight as an arrow. It landed with a solid thud, sending up puffs of dust on all sides.

As one, they all moved toward it, with Angie drawing Saddlebags along with her. Tobe went to pick it up and almost failed.

"Man, this thing's heavier than I thought." He stared in amazement at the gold ingot that required the support of both hands.

"It weighs right around ninety pounds," Angie told him and gazed at the bar, satisfaction running strongly through her.

"Can I hold it, Tobe?" Dulcie touched the bar with her finger.

"Are you kidding?" Tobe scoffed. "It weighs more than you do."

"Really?" She looked skeptical.

"Really," Angie confirmed.

"How many more bars you got, Luke?" Griff shouted up to him.

"About eight or nine, I'd say."

"Throw 'em down," Fargo urged, with a motioning wave of his arm.

"All right. Move back," Luke repeated his earlier warning and went to fetch the next one.

One by one, he tossed them to the ground. After each bar landed, it was retrieved and added to the stack. With the addition of the last ingot, the total came to ten gold bars.

In a kind of awed silence, they gathered around them, Luke joining them after making his descent down the rope. Saddlebags had tears in his eyes as he gazed at the pile of cross-stacked bullion. He wavered unsteadily for a moment, then his legs crumpled and he sank to the ground beside it, still staring at the ingots' muted-gold gleam.

Knowing this was an emotional moment for him, Angie knelt down next to him and curved an arm affectionately around his shoulders. "Happy?" she guessed, thinking of the long years he'd spent looking for the outlaw gold.

His head bobbed in mute admission. After a slight pause, he said, "Not as happy as I spected, though. I figgered I'd be a-jumpin' in the air, hootin' an' a-hollerin' . . . It don't make sense."

"Yes, it does," Angie said softly, understanding at last. "It's just gold. It can only buy you things that will make you laugh or keep you warm. It can't love you or hold you or make you feel good inside."

"Guess I threw all that away," he murmured and glanced around, looking lost. "What do I do now?"

"I'd like it if you went home to Iowa with me," she told him. "Wouldn't you like to finally meet your daughter?"

He shook his head. "She ain't gonna care about a father she never saw afore."

"Maybe not at first," Angie agreed, knowing her mother. "But she'll come around in time. You'll see."

"Maybe." Doubt lingered in his voice.

"Believe me," Angie promised gently, "she may not welcome her prodigal father with open arms the way she should. But you will hurt her much more if you don't come back."

Saddlebags mulled that over, then nodded. "Not goin' would be wrong, I 'spect. Sure ain't nothin' to hold me here no more."

"One thing's sure, Saddlebags," Fargo declared. "All this gold means you can get yourself some fancy duds and go home in style. Do any of you know how much money's sittin' there?" he challenged. "Why, it must total up to three or four million."

A low whistle of surprise came from Tobe. "That much?" he murmured in awe.

"Easy," Fargo stated emphatically.

Griff shook his head in amazement. "Out of my share, I'd have enough to buy three or four restaurants . . . if I wanted them."

"I don't think so, Griff," Angie said.

"Are you kidding? Twenty percent of four million—"

She cut in, "It won't be four million. Or even three."

"What are you talkin' about?" Fargo demanded, with a frown. "Why not?"

"Because it isn't ours. This bullion is the property of the United States government," she explained. "It has to be returned."

Luke's soft chuckle was wry with amusement. "I should have known," he murmured, smiling at her with admiration and approval.

"Known what?" Tobe looked at him in confusion.

"Angie told me she had plans for the gold when she found it," Luke replied. "I should have guessed she intended to make restitution."

"It's what my great-great-grandfather ultimately wanted—for it to be returned to its rightful owner. It's taken longer than he thought," she admitted. "But it's finally being accomplished."

"You mean, we aren't gonna get anything?" Tobe stared at her, stunned and deflated.

Angie shrugged and smiled. "With any luck, the offer of a reward still stands. It probably won't be enough to buy you a ranch, but you might be able to lease land and buy a few cows to at least get you started."

"What about my house?" Dulcie asked, all sad eyed. "Won't I get it?"

"I—" Angie began hesitantly.

Luke broke in, "You'll get your house, Dulcie. Just as soon as I get my own place built, you and Tobe can have the trailer to yourselves."

Fargo's mouth dropped open. When he closed it, he nearly choked on the wad of tobacco. "You're gonna build?"

"It's high time, don't you think?" Luke countered easily, but each was careful to avoid any direct reference to the fire-charred rubble of the Ten Bar's former ranch house or the deaths of Luke's wife and son.

"High time," Fargo agreed, masking his astonishment with matter-of-factness.

"What are you gonna do with your share, Angie?" Now that she was assured of a home of her own, Dulcie was eager to know that Angie would realize her dream as well.

"Probably save it," Angie replied.

"Save it. Why?" That didn't sound at all exciting to Dulcie.

"So I can come visit sometime."

"More than once, I hope," Luke stated.

Angie hoped the very same thing.